Weeping Underwater

Looks a Lot Like Laughter

Michael J. White

Weeping Underwater

Looks a Lot Like Laughter

G. P. Putnam's Sons

New York

PUTNAM

G. P. PUTNAM'S SONS
Publishers Since 1838
Published by the Penguin Group
Penguin Group (USA) Inc., 375 Hudson Street, New York, New York 10014, USA •
Penguin Group (Canada), 90 Eglinton Avenue East, Suite 700, Toronto, Ontario M4P 2Y3,
Canada (a division of Pearson Penguin Canada Inc.) • Penguin Books Ltd, 80 Strand,
London WC2R 0RL, England • Penguin Ireland, 25 St Stephen's Green, Dublin 2, Ireland
(a division of Penguin Books Ltd) • Penguin Group (Australia), 250 Camberwell Road,
Camberwell, Victoria 3124, Australia (a division of Pearson Australia Group Pty Ltd) •
Penguin Books India Pvt Ltd, 11 Community Centre, Panchsheel Park,
New Delhi–110 017, India • Penguin Group (NZ), 67 Apollo Drive, Rosedale,
North Shore 0632, New Zealand (a division of Pearson New Zealand Ltd) •
Penguin Books (South Africa) (Pty) Ltd, 24 Sturdee Avenue, Rosebank,
Johannesburg 2196, South Africa

Penguin Books Ltd, Registered Offices: 80 Strand, London WC2R 0RL, England

Library of Congress Cataloging-in-Publication Data

White, Michael J., date.
Weeping underwater looks a lot like laughter / Michael J. White.
p.   cm.
ISBN 978-0-399-15590-1
1. Teenage boys—Fiction.   2. Friendship—Fiction.   3. Iowa—Fiction.   I. Title.
PS3623.H5787W44   2010   2009023789
813'.6—dc22

Printed in the United States of America
1   3   5   7   9   10   8   6   4   2

BOOK DESIGN BY MICHELLE McMILLIAN

FOR NATE GEORGE,

MY BROTHER AND YOURS, TOO

Acknowledgments

All my thanks to Denise Shannon, Kate Davis, Nanci McCloskey, and Koren Russell, for their faith; Jaime Manrique, Nicholas Christopher, Ben Marcus, Victoria Redel, Ben Taylor, and Jonathan Dee, for their kind wisdom and encouragement; Frank Tarsitano, for offering me incredible employment as I wrote; all my students, for their inspiration; all my family, for their love.

Messy, isn't it?

—RICHARD BRAUTIGAN

Part

One

On our debut night in Des Moines, Nicholas Parsons murdered a high school senior in the hotel room directly beneath us. The following morning we received a call from the front desk receptionist announcing a cancellation of the complimentary breakfast buffet, due to the conversion of the hotel restaurant into a provisional police headquarters. All guests were to remain in their rooms until they were cleared for checkout by one of the FBI agents who were at that moment conducting brief inquiries room by room. Our inquiry came by phone three hours later, long after my dad had missed his first meeting as the new branch manager at Faith Harvest Insurance, around the time my mom began snapping bird's-eye photos of the parking lot in the hopes of capturing killers disguised as crime-scene loiterers, and minutes after Zach leapt off the windowsill and yelled, "FUCK!" in response to injuriously pinching his hindquarters in the shifting vents of the air conditioner. My dad let the phone ring six or seven times. I'll describe him as a kind man, but also a Vietnam War veteran built of two hundred fifty pounds of flexible girth with a voice that sounds as if it originated from an even bigger man who lived in harsh conditions among harsh women.

"This is Leon Flynn, room five-seventeen. We were supposed to check out at seven-thirty this morning, after breakfast. May I ask what this is all about, locking folks in a hotel where someone may or may not have been murdered?" He sighed and thrust his neck out (the way all men in my family do when feeling self-righteous or threatened), clearly reacting to a scripted line of questioning. "We didn't hear a peep. My wife and I were in the double. My eldest son was in the single by the window. His younger brother was in a sleeping bag by the door."

At the next question his eyes and head rotated machine-like toward me—first the eyes, then the head. "He's right here," he said, passing me the receiver despite my mom's punitive eyeballing that suggested he might as well hand me a loaded pistol for my turn at our family rendition of Russian roulette.

Let me explain that back in the nineties the West Des Moines Holiday Inn was a mid-level business accommodation with upper-end ambitions and a hollow atrium center where you could lean over the railing to observe guest activity on any of the floors above or below. If the girl screamed, I should've heard it. But I didn't hear it, even though I'd been awake a good part of the night, planning to flee Des Moines for some sun-drenched archipelago where I'd grow a beard and live off the land. (Davenport was our home, and we were still finding our feet after the Great Flood, which brought losses comparable to those in Des Moines, though in all honesty *their* losses were not *our* losses. I remain convinced that if we'd had even one living grandparent left in Davenport, including our drinking grandfather who caused his family so much grief, we never would've left.) I put the receiver to my ear, immediately surmising by the special agent's captious tone that he was not a happy person, that over the course of his life he had known many disappointments.

"You're the guy in the bag by the door?"

"That's correct," I said.

"When did you get into town?"

"Yesterday."

"Yesterday morning? Last night? Crack of dawn? I asked when you got into town."

"Yesterday afternoon. Around four p.m."

"Fine," he said. "So did you hear anything?"

"No, sir. I wish I would've, but I didn't."

At that, Zach made a grand motion of unzipping his suitcase, mumbling something to the effect that my pretty-boy responses would probably result in an invitation to a full interrogation. My mom halted his unzipping with a reared set of claw-nails perfectly manicured during the course of our pay-per-view detention. The special agent yawned, unconvincingly, which made me sense he was preparing a trick question.

"Says here you're from Davenport?"

"We're *from* Davenport, but we're in the middle of moving *here*. It's supposed to be our first day in the new house."

"Your first night in Des Moines?" he asked, as though finally stumbling on something interesting. "And a seventeen-year-old girl gets corded one floor below you?"

"She got what?"

"I'm sure you'll read *all about it*," he said, implying that the public's increasing access to crime specifics was a slight on his profession. "Do you have any more information?"

"No, sir."

"No strange noises? Nothing to report?"

"I don't think so—"

"You don't *think*?"

"I'm sure."

"Fine," he said, just before the line cut out. I held the receiver to my ear at least another five seconds, thinking it best to leave my family with the impression that the call ended more graciously than it did. "Have a nice day," I said, then hung up. Everyone was still but for their eyebrows shifting through poses of anxiety, disbelief, accusation, etc. I considered that until I opened my mouth again it might've all been construed as a mishap, an overblown robbery, maybe even a joke orchestrated by one of the pranksters from the old neighborhood. My dad drew a finger along the inside of his collar, again thrusting his neck out.

"You're sure of what, George?"

"It sounds like she was strangled. With a telephone cord."

My mom turned to my dad. My dad turned to the ceiling. Zach turned to the parking lot six stories below. I remember feeling that all the furniture in the hotel was clenching each one of its screws, that the sun shining on the carpet and bed had suddenly sucked back its ultraviolet rays. But the moment hardly lasted five seconds before my dad was barking at Zach to drag the suitcases to the car, then disappearing downstairs, probably to visit the front desk and argue over the bill. I ended up checking for personal items under the beds and in the bathroom while my mom paced from one side of the window to the other, moving at half speed and stroking her upper left arm as though consoling it. On the drive from West Des Moines to Urbandale my dad tried to lighten the mood with a deadpan anecdote about the convoluted transportation of a Japanese lighthouse—or bell house, he wasn't sure which—granted to an Iowan judge by the mayor of Kofu, Japan, one of Des Moines's sister cities. We passed newly built shopping villages, megastores, labyrinthine parking lots, at least a dozen restaurants with cutesy misspelled names. Whereas in Davenport we were all content to restore our neighborhoods just as clean and cozy as they were before the flood, it appeared the goal in Des Moines was to take the opportunity to recast the city as a trendy metropolis on the move. I started feeling nauseous, suspecting we were traveling the same mysteriously looping streets and that any minute we'd be pulled over by the FBI.

The first thing I noticed in the new neighborhood was the lineup of wimpy cedars with bobby socks and braces to keep them growing healthy and right. Our house sat on high ground halfway up the block, a red ribbon on the mailbox gaily proclaiming it SOLD BY GUNTHER REALTY! Most of the moving team was sprawled out and smoking on the lawn, looking even more hungover now that the time had come to hump our furniture uphill. My parents lined up at the sidewalk to take a full breath of their two-story home, likely comforting themselves with thoughts of the next flood, the shingled roof-islands of every house on the block but ours. Zach reminded them of the track star from Bettendorf who'd severely disabled himself while pushing a lawn mower up a schoolyard slope—a comment that only backfired. "They saved his legs," my mom said, perking up. "There was even an article in *Reader's Digest*. He's back to hurdling again and he's even faster than before. He broke a record at the Quad City Regionals." My dad was already halfway up the driveway, scoping out every cigarette butt and Coke can tossed slovenly about his lawn. The movers staggered to their feet, knowing as well as we did that there was no point in pouting or putting up a fight.

I spent most of that first night in my new bedroom above the garage, arranging my furniture and unpacking my boxes, for the first time fully appreciating all those plain familiar faces in the hallways of St. Boniface High, the outlandish sermons of my philosophical wrestling coach who went a full six minutes against the Great Dan Gable, even our next-door neighbor Randy Baker, who'd been teasing me with the same worn-out redhead jokes since I was six years old. I ended up trashing half the knickknacks I'd collected over the years, including a monkey carved out of a coconut and several Pine Derby race cars I'd whittled during my time in the Cub Scouts. While I had been unwilling to part with these juvenile treasures the week before, that night I hardly noticed giving them up, even faced with a set of bare bookshelves. My best explanation for this was a sudden preoccupation with the notion that the FBI agent I'd spoken to was actually the perpetrator of the crime he'd alleged to investigate. I was also overcome by jealous imaginings about my best friend Kevin Ralston's pornographic future with Eva Davis, the girl I'd had a crush on for five years and never even kissed. Around midnight I called Kevin as though he were still living just down the road. I could see him pacing a horseshoe path around his garage-sale water bed when he promised to steal his dad's car for a joint Mardi Gras getaway. (In the coming weeks, additional calls to my wider group of friends suggested a theory that in the absence of extreme boredom or abandonment, nine times out of ten the egocentric adolescent mind will flippantly shun the continued building of the sorts of connective memory bridges that long-distance loyalties so critically demand.) The trip never happened, probably because Mardi Gras was still five months off, and Kevin's dad was a firefighter and Eucharistic minister whom Kevin admired too much.

Two

St. Pius High School was only ten minutes down Seventy-third Street on a hodgepodge campus occupied largely by a series of sexless concrete structures with the low stances of elementary schools committed to cold war. Never before had I witnessed such institutional pride in pint-sized statues on man-made knolls, obviously part of an attempt to project a multilayered landscape of saintly scholarship. The sports complex was located half a mile down the road, a honeycombed monstrosity of hallways leading to small workout rooms crammed with fetishistic, wire-based weight machines. On one of its many surrounding playing fields, during the first day of training camp, Zach drilled a running back so hard and rendered him senseless for so long that the kid arrived at his locker the next morning to discover all his football equipment replaced by a single cross-country jersey hanging on a hook. By the time school began Zach had already been noted in a *Des Moines Register* football preview as the Central Iowa Metro League's "defensive secret weapon," which, combined with his claim to be an integral assistant to the FBI's search for the strangler Nicholas Parsons (he built a mysterious sympathy for himself by bowing his head and wandering off anytime someone asked what he'd heard in the middle of the night at the Holiday Inn), was enough for a virtual petal parade of acceptance into the St. Pius inner sanctum. I, on the other hand, after two weeks of classes, hadn't formed a single promising alliance. I even found myself victim to several note-passing offenses of the following nature:

"Your socks and sandals are sooooooo hot."

"Please extinguish the fire in your crotch."

"Maggie Whitcraft . . . third row, buckteeth . . . is looking for a lover/orthodontist."

It didn't help matters that somewhere in the move I lost my sense of humor and couldn't remember anyone's names. I also couldn't overcome the sensation that my fellow classmates were all strangely disproportional with oddly shaped craniums packed with perversions. I didn't know any Germans, but Des Moines's teenagers all seemed a little German to me. Even the homecoming play, a simple tale about a group of blind children lost in the forest, was written by someone named Eckhard von Wolf. Which brings us to the scene where this story should have begun: my entrance into a makeshift and acoustically ramshackle theater cramped with student nitwits pegging one another with pennies, the air glinting coppery for my initial sighting of the lion-haired heroine Emily Schell. After finding an open seat at the far side of the front row, I embarked on an immediate voyeuristic operation to pinpoint the exact location of her beauty. This effort concluded on the joint effect of her heart-shaped cheeks and the curve at the tip of her nose. Based on her athletic confidence and ease, I had no doubts about the impressive figure roaming beneath her amorphous black frock. She searched the proscenium (if there was no actress named Emily Schell, then there was no proscenium, either; it was a rectangular stage with pleated skirting and a knee-high guardrail), swatting imaginary mosquitoes and poking branches. She crumbled to her knees. "Boys!" she cried out. "Where are you, boys!"

Two waifs pawed their way from the peripheral darkness to the halo of light at center stage, cowering in their suspenders. The actress swung around and—her theatrical contacts rendering her as blind as her character—reached for the sound of their footsteps while accidentally leg-swiping a plastic tree. Despite the blunder she remained astoundingly in character, addressing the noise of the wobbling stand as though reacting to a roiling thunder deep in the heart of the forest. Laughter broke throughout the auditorium, beginning at the front row and rolling backward. I cackled urgently along, attempting to rein in the distraction so that I could quickly end it and we could return our collective focus to the simple movements of the blind actress whose bare legs were now shimmering long and white in the direct gaze of hot canned lights. She pulled her tawny hair taut over her forehead. When she squeezed herself for warmth, I put myself in that squeeze. I turned to a ferret-eyed classmate next to me, craving the actress's name more than anything else, but too meek with loneliness to ask even that.

"What year is that girl?"

"Junior. Future class of nineteen hundred and ninety-five," he answered, in a professorial whine, which I supposed was his way of suggesting that he'd only shown up for the extra credit, and that this theater crap had dragged on long enough. "What year are *you*?"

"Junior," I said. "When does this thing end anyway?"

"Quarter to titty," he replied, suddenly smitten by the performance and therefore upset by my interruption.

A recording of wailing winds and flashing thunder screeched through the auditorium. The actress's fear was so real I was tempted to storm the stage, grasp her by the shoulders, and inform her that there was no place in this pubescent world for such honest and precise emotion. I swore I detected Zach's voice among the band of idiots hooting and hollering a few rows back, but even they couldn't break the performance. (While I can't claim to have initially recognized how to interpret this play, after having seen it performed several times since in various theaters throughout the Midwest, I now judge it as either a dramatization of the fallacy of theocratic faith, or, conversely, the potential of atheistic hope. Either way, I considered the St. Pius production of *Into the Night* a brave and ambitious undertaking, especially in consideration of the venue.) In the final scene, as the heroine led the singing schoolboys to the safety of a convent, I experienced the dizzying notion that if I traced my personal history I'd find Emily Schell back in Davenport, crowding the memories of my childhood.

In less time than it took for the auditorium lights to warm up, most of the audience had already shoved their way out the rear exit. While the cast gathered at the front of the stage to receive the congratulations of their teachers and friends, I wandered the penny-and-gum-wrapper perimeter. My lackadaisical floor perusal soon drew the attention of a beady little priest and part-time administrator I'd met during my admissions interview (which was conducted as if St. Pius were a competitive institution that chose its students based on criteria above their ability to reduce the burden of its perennial financial crises). After pressing me to admit to whatever contraband I was obviously searching for, he asked my opinion of the performance, then skipped over my response in order to relate anecdotes of his own lovely acting days. He was midway through an animated description of an autistic prop master when I noticed Emily Schell emerging from backstage in jeans and a form-friendly T-shirt that claimed ELVIS *GIVES*. She shared a fast laugh with a few fellow actors but kept moving along, all the while rubbing her glazed eyes with the butt of her palms, appearing much more worldly-wise than her persona onstage. Whatever compliments she was offered over the next few minutes were received while she folded and stacked chairs alongside the stagehands, a few of whom shot me glances suggesting that if I enjoyed the performance enough to attempt mingling with the cast, I might at least lend a helping hand. The priest, obviously exempt from such labors, was soon pacing alongside the actress, offering her a long-winded criticism of the auditorium's poor acoustics. She took his comments in stride, inserting a polite affirmation here and there, but hardly saying a thing. Despite having just watched her perform for two hours, I was already desperate to hear her speak again, to gather as many clues as I could about the girl behind the mask. To this end, I decided to encounter her at the chair racks near the storage room, where we'd inevitably end up stacking two chairs at once, and they'd bang together, at which point one of us would say, "Excuse me," and the other would say, "No, really, excuse *me*," and soon we would be conversing. But after more than a dozen ill-timed trips, I lost my patience and saddled up next to the priest—interrupting prattle about his favorite playwrights—and improvised.

"Who was your muse?" I blurted out, much louder than I intended.

"Are you asking him or me?" she asked, glancing over to the priest, giving little hint of an initial impression beyond confusion. I was certain she didn't realize that I was a new student, which is to say a foreigner and a person she'd never laid eyes on until that very moment. But I was getting used to this sort of treatment and proceeded more or less undeterred.

"*Muuuuse?*" the priest groaned, loud enough to share his doubt with the entire cast and crew. "A muse is a Greek goddess. A muse is a myth."

"So if it's not a myth, it can't be a muse?"

"Of course not."

"Did Homer have a muse when he wrote myths?"

"What could you possibly be talking about?"

"The theater," I said, as though reaching a grand philosophical conclusion. "It really is a whole other world. A magical one."

At that, I thanked him and made a beeline for the farthest row of unfolded chairs, realizing along the way that I hadn't given the actress even the slightest glimpse of attention beyond my initial approach. For the next fifteen minutes I folded and stacked chairs at twice the speed of the stagehands, several of whom went missing and later resurfaced reeking of menthol. Then Emily left and I realized that I was basically the only person still working and I quit. But on my way out of the building I discovered her plopped down on an old church pew next to a willowy guy with long gesticulating fingers, likely waiting for her ride. (I guessed Zach had driven home without me, an action he'd likely excuse by the fact that I'd befriended the theater crowd, which signified it was time for me to fly on my own.) By then the lobby had mostly thinned out, though there were still patches of students huddled in circles, mostly arguing over where to waste the rest of the evening. Without breaking my stride, I looped around in the direction of the actress, picking up the odd scrap of paper or pen cap, unsure if it was even me cleaning up or some obsessive new personage developed instantly for the task of industrious loitering. I continued for the trash bin just past the pew. By the lull in their conversation I sensed that one of them was nearly on his or her way. I stalled at the water fountain across from them, drinking and waiting.

"Are you new or something?" the gesticulator asked. I took my time turning around and wiping the water from my mouth, feigning a pleasant aloofness when I finally nodded in affirmation. "We've got janitors here," he said, chuckling to himself, clearly aiming to co-opt the actress. But she was squinting at the clock down the hallway, appearing less in the process of checking the time than decoding it.

Soon enough the gesticulator dragged his way back into the auditorium. The actress turned to me, still squinting, rubbing her eyes, and waiting.

"Where did you transfer from?" she asked.

"St. Boniface. It's in Davenport."

"What's Davenport like?"

"You don't have to lock your doors," I said, wishing I'd mentioned the nighttime riverboat tours, but feeling it was too late and I ought to balance the comment with something more critical. "Everyone says we need a flood wall. Apparently we're the biggest city on the Mississippi without one."

"The floods only get serious every fifty years. What's the point of living on the Mississippi when you can't even see it?"

"I'm glad to hear that," I said, taking a seat next to her, just as casually as if we were both waiting for the bus downtown. "Actually, I'm really sick of people giving us so much trouble about it. I was just saying that because . . . well, you know."

"To beat me to the punch?"

"I guess," I said, shrugging, perhaps even blushing. "I'm George."

"I'm Emily," she said, pushing herself against the seatback and out of her slump. Her gaze wandered to the pink paper-thin scar over my right eyebrow. Her eyes were no longer white and blind but soft hazel palettes—eager, intelligent eyes with big volcano centers. "You don't meet too many teenagers named George."

"It was my grandpa's name. He drank a lot of whiskey and crashed a lot of tractors. He died of liver failure a few years back."

The actress nodded along, rubbing her eyes again and taking my queer confession in stride. I had the feeling that she sensed my estrangement in the most exact way, understanding in a few words that I was a generally confident teenager suddenly friendless and questioning the purpose of his existence. Perhaps she sensed these things because I wanted her to sense them. But then I realized that she was only rubbing her eyes because she was smirking and didn't know what to say. She was still smirking to herself when her mother arrived, nearly as frantic as the schoolboys in the first act of *Into the Night*. Mrs. Schell apologized for getting caught up at the hospital, then backtracked by explaining that she wasn't *that* sorry because she really had no choice in the matter. While her dainty black purse and matching pumps lent the impression of a cutthroat businesswoman much more than a doctor or nurse, she clearly acted like a nurse, wasting no time pressing her thumbs to Emily's cheeks to better check the whites of her eyes.

"Did you use the dropper?" she asked, her tone suggesting grave doubt.

"They're fine," Emily said, struggling to her feet in spite of her mother's pressing thumbs.

"They're not fine. They're bloodred. I still don't see why you can't *act* blind like everyone else."

"I'm not the only one. Woody wore the contacts, too."

"Woody doesn't even show up until the third act. Woody doesn't even have a line."

"This is George from Davenport."

Mrs. Schell turned to me, forgoing the customary smile or handshake in exchange for a brazen visual survey that started at my scuffed boots and ended on the red curls bunched up over my ears. "Hello," she finally said. "Hello," I said back, then returned her visual survey, though with much greater tact. My first impression was that Mrs. Schell was untrustworthy, despite being matronly attractive, particularly in terms of her high cheekbones and a long swan neck. She was digging in her purse for a dropper when two dapper junior girls—I slightly recognized them from various B-track classes—turned the lobby corner and circled in, congratulating Emily and greeting her mother. I was almost out the door when Emily broke from them and caught up to me. She handed me the plastic container for her blinding contacts.

"If you feel like it, you can try them for yourself. I've got a couple of sets. Those ones have never been worn, so you don't have to worry about conjunctivitis or whatever."

"Your performance was really exciting. I won't forget it for a long time."

"You didn't show up just to see if I'd march off the front of the stage?"

"I don't know why I showed up," I said, feeling that I was finally starting to make sense. Emily looked over her shoulder to where Mrs. Schell was listing options for dinner restaurants, getting the girlfriends riled up. She turned back to me and sighed.

"I've got to go. Be careful with those, okay? I got pretty banged up during rehearsals."

"See you at school?"

Emily smiled, and might've even bowed slightly before walking away.

I rolled out of bed early the next morning to test the contacts while the house was still quiet. Almost immediately I felled a standing lamp that woke everyone up banging against the fireplace brick. But I didn't quit and next thing I was on all fours, bumbling my way into chairs and walls, petting empty patches of air, feeling more vulnerable than ever.

Three

My next sighting of Emily Schell came the following Monday morning through a smudged attendance office window imbued with spidery shatterproof wire. She was standing in the middle of a long line, fanning herself with a stationery note. The time after that she was leaning out of her idling matchbox Volvo, sizing up one of the last remaining parallel parking spaces along the main entrance. It was a hot, muggy morning, the pavement afloat in its own blacktop reflection. I was taking a shortcut over the grass, having just reached the peak when I stopped to watch from my bird's-eye perch as she made her sharp, minimalist maneuvers. It must have taken her five minutes to cut the rear end against the curb. At that point she began systematically nudging the Chevy Blazer behind her, then the Ford Escort in front of her, rolling forward and backward inch by inch, confidently, as though this method was in perfect accordance with the parking diagrams in the driver's manual. By the time she cut the engine there was hardly enough space to slide a ruler between the bumpers at each end. I continued down the far side of the hill as she stepped out to survey her work, soon shrugging and nodding to herself as if engaged in an inconclusive debate. Just about the time I caught up to her, she turned around and headed for the main entrance, where she ended up holding the door for several seconds longer than common courtesy demanded. When I thanked her she smiled congenially, though with no sense of recognition. A month later she would deny this exchange ever occurred, which was somehow sweet considering her visit to my chemistry class that Friday, when she poked her head through the door at such a peculiar downward angle that the unseen portion of her body must have been balanced on her left leg while her right leg stretched waist-high across the hallway. After twice referencing her clipboard, she informed my teacher of an urgent message for George Flynn. I stepped outside to find her looking stern, with her lips pursed and a pencil behind her ear. Our second conversation was a beautiful, seamless act that couldn't exist twice.

"Need your address, Flynn," she said, pushing a pair of invisible glasses up the bridge of her nose. I noticed an Irish Claddagh ring on her right hand, but given our close quarters and her quick hand movements, it was nearly impossible to determine whether the crowned heart was facing inward or away.

"It's near the hockey arena," I said. "One hundred thirty Arlington Street."

"And your phone number? Just in case."

"I'm not sure," I said, digging for my wallet where I'd placed a ripped-off matchbook cover with my new number. Emily let her clipboard fall to her hip. As soon as I start reading it to her, she snatched the matchbook cover, clucked her tongue, and wrote the number down herself.

"Tino Gomez will be picking you up for a party tonight at eight. Hadley will likely be riding shotgun and his car will likely be low on gas and I wouldn't be surprised if he asks you to chip in. You might want earplugs. Tino is very proud of his stereo."

"Who's Tino Gomez?"

"The guy picking you up."

"Are you going to be there?" I asked, getting ahead of myself, my giddy adoration echoing in each word. She dismissed the question with a no-nonsense flick of the wrist.

"I was informed that you were never contacted by your student ambassador. Is that correct?"

"I don't know anything about a student ambassador."

"There's supposed to be someone to make sure you know your way around. *Your* ambassador is a lazy little guy named Marcus Panozzo. He'll be in the car tonight, even though he normally wouldn't."

"Marcus Panozzo? Maybe I did meet him, on the first day. He told me there was a secret sauna for the wrestlers."

"Shhhh. Whadareyoutryintado? Getusdisqualified?"

"Sorry."

"Eight o'clock."

"Yes, ma'am," I said, as she raised the clipboard to her mouth to cover a delicate yawn. I'm pretty sure the yawn was only a gesture of the secretary character she was playing, who was much less tolerant of my missteps than the girl I met in the lobby outside the auditorium.

"A final suggestion," she said. "You don't have to like everyone. But you have to like Tino and Hadley, and Lauren and Ashley, and of course Smitty, whose real name I won't bother telling you because he never goes by it. Marcus and everyone else are up to you."

"Thank you," I said, feeling I'd just received what would prove the most intimate tidbit of the exchange. "I meant to ask, were you really crying during the scene where that schoolboy wandered off on his own? Usually when actors cry it seems so fake, but for a while I thought, she's *really* crying."

Emily tucked the pencil behind her ear. I don't think the way she pushed onto her toes and then down again was part of the act.

(It could be argued that this movement was a precursor to her imminent and total break of character.) "The last time I cried was probably
1959, back when JFK got shot."

"I thought he got shot later on. I thought it was in the mid-
sixties."

"I'm pretty sure it was 'fifty-nine," she said, repeating the up-and-
down motion. "And I would know because I'm an actress. It's our job
to know pretty much everything about everything."

"Were you a child actress or something?" I said, as Emily stroked
her chin and sharpened her gaze, as if on the verge of deciding that
there was something very off about me. "I mean, it's obvious that
you've found your calling, but it must take a long time to get to the
point where you look like *even you* forgot that this is all a play, and
these lines aren't real, and you're really just pretending."

I still don't know why I followed this statement by offering her both
hands as though pleading for a Middle East peace accord, but in all
likelihood it was only a reaction to the great pride I felt in having won
Emily's startling, and completely denuding, disbelief. She eventually
shook my hands, during which time her expression changed from that
of a frightened first-time small business loan recipient to that of the
banker who's just issued the loan, whose day was finally yielding the
results she'd expected of it. I smiled but Emily did not. Apparently
there were still a number of compatibility issues to assess, unknown
chemical elements to add and subtract, human factors that deserved a
firm and honest attention.

Four

That first night I met Tino and Hadley, they showed up almost two hours late, dragging a trail of muddy tire tracks that stretched from an Urbandale kiddy park through my neighborhood and up my driveway. On the way to the party Tino's fuzzy mop flopped side to side as he bobbed his head and waved his arms as he expounded the legality of claiming a doe left dead on the road. Hadley was ruddy and mostly silent, with feline eyes that didn't miss a thing. He spent most of the ride knocking back a mixture of Everclear and Kool-Aid, more or less ignoring my presence except to glance into the side-view mirror whenever Marcus, my backseat companion, made some grand claim I was probably better off not believing.

As soon as we crossed the plane of Pat Downing's backyard, Tino and Hadley grabbed their beer cups and disappeared, leaving me subject to Marcus's urgent task of pointing out all the girls he'd supposedly laid. Almost everyone was smoking. Whenever Marcus left to refill his cup, I'd lurk the perimeter of seemingly affable conversations involving classmates with the least asymmetric craniums. (I'd turn slow circles with one hand stuffed coolly in my pocket, the other scratching athletically at the rear of my neck, often checking my watch, alternating hand positions, attempting to appear pleasantly bored while focusing my sight line on safe targets like slow-leaking garden hoses and empty bags of birdfeed balled up in wire fences.) But as soon as I'd build the courage to invite my way into a conversation, inevitably Marcus would dance forth just in time to scare off my prospective new friends. It started raining. I started drinking. Eventually everyone crowded under the back porch and into the garage, where our loudmouthed host (a fine example of the heavily browed Germanic element so prevalent in Des Moines) was pumping death metal on a boom box splattered with dried paint. This is where I finally found Emily Schell, who'd just been deserted by two dissatisfied girlfriends resolved to change the music and who was now humming to herself while propped up on a stack of drywall, looking bored. While I attempted to approach her with only a minor affect of rebelliousness, I ended up cocking my head in a brash, jerky way that I somehow felt entitled to blame on my brother.

"Hey there," she said, perking up only long enough to realize I was half drunk and flying solo. "Where're your friends?"

"Probably in Kevin's basement, back in Davenport."

"Your *new* friends. Tino and Hads."

"Somewhere out back," I said, like I hadn't thought about those guys in a while. Emily shrugged, acting like she'd done her part and it was my life to live in complete friendlessness if that's what I wanted. She leaned forward to read my T-shirt that depicted a muscle-bound oaf urging students to get BACK TO THE BASICS: READING, WRITING, WRESTLING!

"If you're planning to wrestle at St. Pius, Coach Grady will expect you've been keeping in shape over the summer at freestyle tournaments, Greco-Roman tournaments, all that stuff. Practice for you guys starts in a couple of weeks."

"Isn't that illegal?" I asked, taking a few nonchalant gulps of beer. Emily shook her head, like I needed more help than she originally thought.

"That sort of talk won't get you very far around here. Maybe you should consider joining the newspaper instead. You could start off by writing an article about yourself. You know, clear up all the rumors and give us the straight scoop."

I hopped onto the drywall stack. "For starters, it would be nice if everyone stopped asking me if I'm a hemophiliac. I wasn't home-schooled, either."

"That could be the headline," she said, taking a swig of beer that made her cheeks puff out and her lips tighten. She glanced up at a network of spiderwebs that sucked in each time the back door opened. "At first I was joking, but maybe it would be a great idea to just lay it all on the table. I work for the paper, so I could probably make it happen."

"I'd rather be the photographer."

"I used to be the photographer, but my photos had a bad habit of never turning out. They were always cloudy, or underlit, or something. Now I'm the editor, which is basically my punishment for wasting so much film."

"So if I wrote this article, I guess I'd be working for you."

"Not exactly. You'd be working for the paper. But I *would* have the power to fire you, if that's what you're asking."

"Then I'll do it," I said, thinking the whole scenario sounded pretty sexy, and now honestly considering writing a sensational backstory for myself, if only as a personal dare. The next few minutes were passed relatively quietly as we eyed over clusters of chatty classmates reeking of sweet alcohol and perfumed sweat. While Emily was no longer wearing the Claddagh ring I'd spotted in the hallway, I still guessed it was only a matter of time before her boyfriend came kissing around. (And if he didn't, I was sure I could count on one of the macho attendees already attuned to our conversation to prove an adequate replacement.) Soon Zach showed up hefting a fresh keg on his shoulder. I didn't have to say a word before Emily was squinting and panning from him to me, despite the fact that Zach was two inches taller and practically blond when juxtaposed to my radiant redness. Immediately after showing off his expert tapping skills, he marched over to place a firm fatherly hand on Emily's shoulder and warn her that I'd only been drunk twice, and turned Mr. Hyde–violent both times. (In truth I was a wary drinker and borderline teetotaler, dually anxious and flattered by regular comparisons between myself and my alcoholic grandpa George previously mentioned.)

"Has he seen a doctor?" Emily asked.

"Oh, there've been plenty of doctors," Zach chuckled. "Only problem is that none of the pills they give him are compatible with the booze."

"I appreciate the warning," she said, glancing askance to inspect the level of my beer. Zach was grinning big and brave as he sauntered off next to Pat, whom we both identified as a pathetic replacement for his best friend, Jeremy.

"He had his own psychiatrist in grade school," I said. "He used to brag about it."

"How would you like to meet Ashley and Lauren?" Emily said, dismissing the remark and nodding at the two girls who'd joined her after the play. "Lauren's single and supposedly she's a very good kisser. I don't know exactly what she does, but apparently it's very good. This is not gossip, by the way. It's common knowledge, she's my friend, and I'm just proud to be the first to tell you. What's not common knowledge is that she and Hads hook up every once in a while. But no one's supposed to know about that."

"What do people say about you that no one's supposed to know?"

Emily set her beer down and crossed her arms. "So now you're Don Juan of Davenport?"

"Sorry. I'm just trying to figure out how you fit into the whole scene."

Emily pushed herself off the stack and pulled her hair back. "If you really want the scoop, you'd better ask one of these other people. Anyway, I think I've had enough smoke and B.O. It's not even raining anymore." She tossed her cup into an industrial bin, then turned to face me. "Never mind what I told you about Lauren and Hads. It's none of my business really. I don't know what I'm doing talking about it."

"I'm still planning to ask about you," I said, shoving onto my feet.

Emily shrugged off the comment and headed for the back door, gathering her girlfriends along the way. Despite marching me from one group of classmates to the next, she was much harder to talk to after that and I was sure that our personal-revelation part of the night had officially concluded. Emily's introductions began with Ashley, a high-browed brunette in a push-up bra, and Lauren, a tall platinum blonde with amicably poor posture. (While both of these girls were categorically cute, I couldn't help feeling that their faces belonged to generalized type groupings with ubiquitous representatives that covered every state in the union. As for my own face type, I'm certainly not a member of any larger type grouping, nor even a redheaded subgrouping. My face displays a Celtic fullmouthed symmetry suggestive of a jovial inattention, capped by naturally upstanding curls in a shade of auburn that is especially striking in reflection.) After asking where I lived, Ashley informed me that I was lucky I hadn't enrolled at "*Scurv*andale," where I'd surely have ended up a motorhead addicted to methamphetamine. Lauren offered me a piece of watermelon gum and offered me up to Smitty, an evident straight shooter with a steady handshake and a 1950s-combed cut. Smitty taught me all about the wrestling team's challenge match system, then related a long account of his short career as a Cutpro scissors salesman, including the day he cut his first showroom penny in half only to watch in suspended time as a fraction of that penny whirled its way into the eye of a would-be customer. And this is when I discovered that when Emily starts laughing, when something really tickles her in the right place, there's no way she'll stop. She shook madly, bursting forth in a seizing and unexpectedly high-flung hoot that overwhelmed and eventually embarrassed her.

Near the end of the night the backyard was overtaken by a muddy tennis ball war that began as a slopping game of catch with a buzzed golden retriever. Eventually Tino came stumbling up alongside me, ragingly affectionate and roaring about all the fish we'd be catching and deer we'd be shooting. Hadley apologized about the mud tracks up my driveway. When the kegs emptied and everyone cleared out, Emily offered us all rides in her Volvo, which she touted as having achieved a perfect safety rating. This news proved comforting when I discovered that she was an oblivious driver who showed little concern for any roadway actions that didn't involve the twenty yards of pavement directly in front of her. But despite the symphony of car horns that made me feel we'd just left a winning basketball game, she never panicked and seemed only to interpret the castigations as neighborly noise that was none of our business. While her highway abilities appeared utterly opposite her abilities onstage, she was similarly at ease in both roles, going so far as to lend the impression that if we found ourselves head-on with a brick wall, she'd only end up snoozing on her airbag, and wake up fresh as a daisy to face the following day.

At some point during the drive home, when I was the only passenger left, I was struck by a second—or third, or fourth—wave of infatuation. This occurred at the moment of Emily's wrong turn onto Hawthorne Drive, when I realized that in her presence I felt on the verge of artistic greatness, like a magician at the precise moment of his maturation when he steps out into the spotlight perfectly assured of his heroic and earth-shattering new trick. Soon enough I was breaking a promise to myself and telling her the story of my family's first night in Des Moines. (By then everyone knew that the Patterson girl had lied to her parents about an overnight babysitting job in order to spend the intermediate hours with her first official boyfriend. Nicholas Parsons turned out to be a jealous neighbor who did his strangling while the boyfriend was out in the parking lot digging in the backseat for music, for the mood.)

"Her name's Missy," Emily said, after the second time I'd referred to her as "the victim."

"Did you know her?"

"Vaguely," she said, as a sudden sadness weighed in that seemed to catch her off guard. But she controlled it and it passed quickly. "We had some junior sports together, and a dance team camp. I only remember a couple of conversations. My friend Mandy lives in her neighborhood. Mandy knew her pretty well."

"I thought Des Moines was supposed to be a safe place."

"Yeah, well, so did I. My mom is completely freaked out. She probably thinks I'm being strangled right now. I just try to stay calm and think about it logically. Are there even CD players in hotel rooms? How was Josh planning to play whatever music he was getting from the car?"

"Who's Josh?"

"Missy's boyfriend."

"Right," I said, noticing a new strictness in my voice. I was mostly sober again. "Maybe he had a portable boom box. Or else he was planning that they'd end up lying in bed together sharing headphones."

"Something's fishy. If it was their first big night, and he was so concerned about the music, I'm pretty sure he would've prepared something beforehand."

"Don't forget that they went to a movie earlier that night. If he wanted to have everything ready and waiting, he would've had to check in in the middle of the day."

"Which would've been impossible because he was working at the hardware store."

"Exactly," I said.

"I heard something on the radio the other day that someone might have seen him out in the parking lot talking with Josh. That's the strange part, *if* it's true. Personally, I don't think the cops are even sure it wasn't Josh who killed her. They could be pretending it's Nicholas, while the whole time they're secretly building their case against Josh. Maybe Nicholas was the first to find Missy's dead body, and he was so destroyed by it that he fled for the woods, or some crowded city, or wherever he went."

"They'll catch him," I told her, trying to build the conversation back up. "You can't get away with murder these days."

"Or maybe Nicholas disappeared because Nicholas is dead," she said, smirking and throwing her hands up at all of our various conjectures. "The main question for me is how do I know *you're* not the strangler?"

"You don't," I said.

"You really didn't hear anything?"

"No. But I haven't eliminated my brother as a suspect. He got up at least once to go to the bathroom."

"That's some luck for your first night in Des Moines."

"That's what the detective said. He kept asking me all these questions about what I heard. All I kept thinking was, Jesus, what did everyone *else* hear? Was she screaming for help? While I was up there, snoring? Actually, I don't snore, but my brother and father, they can really snore."

"I'll tell you what I would've done. I would've hopped into the family wagon and hauled ass back to Davenport."

"That would've been the smart thing to do."

"But not the fighting Flynns," she said, raising a proud finger in the air.

"Nope. We're gonna to stick it out, see what happens to us down here in Des Moines."

"I wouldn't call it *DEE-moyn*," she said, hitting the brakes. "But I guess I'm glad you're sticking it out. This is your house here, right?"

I thanked her and said good night, not realizing until then that we'd already passed my house, that Emily had employed the cul-de-sac at the end of my block in order to more perfectly time our arrival with the lighthearted conclusion to our conversation.

"See you Monday," she said.

"See you," I said, stepping out and trudging my way up the driveway, wondering for the hundredth time why they hadn't flattened our lot like the rest of the lots on the block.

Five

While this account contains no shortage of scandals that for plot purposes I would be mistaken to withhold, I choose this moment to reveal one peripheral disgrace for the simple reason of its psychological effect on our heroine, Emily Schell. But first a scrap of context concerning the weeks following my introduction to Smitty, Tino, Hadley, Ashley, and Lauren.* Even today I can hardly flick a cigarette out the window without recalling that first string of weekend nights driving circles around the city, the girls in one car, the guys in another, our fiery cigarette cherries streaming in the wind (occasionally revisiting us via the back window as a result of Hadley's routinely poor release), all of us hoping to stumble upon an adventure that nine times out of ten shaped up as "cosmic billiards" under the dark lights at

---

*I haven't seen any of these people in seven or eight years. I heard at one point that Tino was happily married to his second wife, despite splitting his paychecks with his crazed first wife who once set fire to his carport and the fire spread to the neighbor's trees and living room. Hadley works at the Chicago Board of Trade, which I assume means he's a trader, though I really don't know. Ashley is an employment headhunter and cancer survivor, Lauren the owner of a less-than-solvent fitness club. We'll get to Smitty later, but it should be known that I consider him a patriot in the best sense of this oft-misconstrued term.

Merle Hay Mall, midnight pancakes at Perkins, or guzzling beer in the basements of houses under construction in West Des Moines. It was during this time that I discovered Tino's knack for not-standing and not-sitting in awkward pseudo-yogic positions that lent every conversation with him a sense of uncertainty. I also learned that Hadley was exactly the same person when he was sober or drunk, and that when Smitty went silent and then hypercritical, urging us to think twice about whatever inane, illegal act we were about to commit, there was probably a cop car about to round the corner. Our gang never missed a Friday-night football game, and more than once I woke on Saturday morning to find Emily Schell in one of the sports-page photos, cheering from the stands with a red bandanna and painted cheeks.

Of course over time I received all sorts of reports about Emily, including her periodic tendency to retreat underground, her frequent travels to flea markets without ever buying anything, and most of all, the fact of her famed virginity. Apparently she'd never had a boyfriend, despite a relationship near miss with a fellow junior named Peyton Chambeau who thought his future was set because he made the varsity basketball squad his freshman year and his dad owned a shoe outlet. (The two of them were always on cheap commercials, flying around on magic carpets, barking about sale items direct from the warehouse.) Though I never asked, I was certain that Peyton had attempted to close the deal by his purchase of the aforementioned Claddagh ring, a sneaky and arm-wringing maneuver if ever there was one. The last major piece of news, and certainly the most shocking, was that Emily's thirteen-year-old sister suffered from an extremely rare incident of pubescent multiple sclerosis. According to Smitty, Katie Schell's assorted symptoms were dominated by the fluctuation of pain and deadness in her legs, which at times were rendered useless.

I draw closer to the scandal in question. Despite my desire to ask

Emily to the homecoming dance, I didn't, mostly because our budding relationship seemed dependent on her unspoken trust that, unlike
a number of my classmates, I wouldn't suddenly profess my undy-
ing love, then describe all the lovely nasty miracles we'd discover on
the fifty-yard line at Valley Stadium, or under the Thirty-fifth Street
Bridge, or for that matter on the roof of our only skyscraper at 801
Grand. My hesitation came back to haunt me when Emily reversed her
vow of unrestrained freedom by accepting an invitation from Peyton
Chambeau, who even Ashley and Lauren thought she'd erased from
her field of hypothetical dates. (I ended up accepting an offer from
Jeannie Gammet, who had swim team practice at six o'clock every
morning and always slept during homeroom and woke up one day to
ask me to be her date. Even on the night of the dance she suffered from
chlorine-lashed skin and crimped hair tinted algal green. I have grave
doubts whether this date deserves description, though I should probably mention a notable "Lady in Red" slow dance when, while pressed
against happy-go-lucky Jeannie, I succumbed to an unmanageable
erection at the sight of Emily's peach-firm buttocks bursting with little
sparkles that lit up in sequence as Peyton spun her in his jazzy, selfish
sort of way, adding unnecessary little flares precluding any possibility of a shared rhythm.) The point is that Peyton and Emily attended
an after party hosted by Heidi Sneed, a senior who'd shown up to the
dance with a pack of female roamers, downed a bottle of Southern
Comfort, then embarked on an impromptu mission to poach as many
of her rivals' dates as possible. This goal reached fruition around four
in the morning when she invited five juniors with passed-out dates to
her backyard gazebo. By all accounts she gave each of them blow jobs,
including Peyton Chambeau, who reportedly engaged in further dis-
course after the others had left.

Of course by the following Monday this episode was widely spread,
often in combination with the news that earlier that evening, Peyton

and Emily had locked themselves in the master bedroom for over an hour. With this final fact in mind, over the next two weeks the St. Pius community divided itself into camps based on their beliefs concerning Emily's habitually referenced purity. Meanwhile, Peyton spent most of that time chasing her from classroom to classroom arguing his integrity. His pleas were met with oblivious silence and an eventual suspension when he finally quit begging and stomped across the school lawn shouting, "You're sick! You're really sick!" before dive tackling a young birch tree dedicated to a sophomore who'd rolled his Jeep on a ski trip to Fun Valley. Emily pretended not to care about the situation, and perhaps she didn't care. While she neither confirmed nor denied the rumors of her lost innocence, she did surprise everyone by resigning as editor of the school newspaper, a rash decision that in the fallacious mind of the St. Pius community closed the debate. As for my own estimation, while I may have arrived at the same conclusion as my classmates, my opinion was based less on Emily quitting the newspaper than on the fact that in all the time we spent together, she never once mentioned Peyton's name.

first met Katie Schell in mid-October at the Whitfield Preparatory Academy, the most expensive school in Des Moines and the only nondenominational private school in the city. The academy was brand-new (as was everything else in Clive, at that time the westernmost suburb of the city), but built in the old tradition with a long, snaking driveway that arrived at a gardened roundabout designed for mothers of the nouveaux riches to vie for prime idling spots, encouraging them to arrive earlier and earlier in order to prove to teachers and fellow parents their superior nurturing intellect. But on the day in question Mrs. Schell had a USTA doubles match with a rival team from Ankeny who Emily explained were known to feign minor third-set injuries (1) as a technique of rhythm-breaking, (2) to exploit their opponents' sympathy, and (3) as a preemptive justification for losing. Emily and I arrived at around four in the afternoon when only a few students remained, wandering in circular self-reflection, practicing card tricks, kicking at their backpacks, etc. Katie was sprawled out on the squared sod next to a glimmering metallic crutch, sulking in the sun, staring daggers into Emily's tires as we curved into view.

"Looks like her engine's running a little hot," Emily said. "Left *all alone* with the future drug addicts and whores."

In an attempt to prove myself conscientious and gentlemanly (everything that Peyton Chambeau and his doggish cohorts were not), I stepped out of the car to give Katie the front seat. At this point she paused in reaching for her crutch, a combination of curiosity and accusation crossing her brow when she realized that Emily wasn't alone. I had the feeling Katie was counting to herself a moment later as she made the transition from two knees to one knee and one crutch, then one knee, one crutch, and one foot, and so on as she pushed herself awkwardly upright. She made a slow and deliberate path across the lawn with her school bag swinging from her shoulder, her back erect and head high, now and then sidestepping to protect her bright white tennis shoes from the occasional pool of week-old rainwater or thicket of fallen leaves.

While I would likely never have marked the Schell girls as siblings, whatever resemblance there was between them was clearly evidenced in their nobly heightened foreheads and the grave angle of their eyebrows when they squinted. Katie was at least Emily's height with feathery brown hair, bright boyish cheeks, and a prominent adult nose she had yet to make her own. As she neared the sidewalk she brusquely tucked her crutch under her armpit, lending the impression of an athlete making the showy case for her full recovery. Becoming aware of my ornithologist-like attention, I turned to the schoolyard fence and beyond it to the Clive water tower and the harvested cornfield littered with shredded stalks. I was just glancing back to the sidewalk when Katie's right leg quit, buckling at the knee and tipping her upper frame sideways. I shouted and threw my hands out like a crossing guard, unable to jump forward quickly enough to catch her. She crumpled hard to the pavement. By the time Emily ran around the front of the car, Katie was rocking and gripping her elbow. Two hive splotches blossomed on each side of her neck. A thin strip of blood began its course from her knee down along her shin.

"You *moron*," Katie mumbled, tossing her crutch into the grass like it hadn't done its job. There was something unintentionally funny about the comment that added an extra uneasiness to the situation. Emily took no more time than necessary checking the damage. "I *don't* like blood," she said, rolling her eyes and grimacing in the face of her rising nausea. I felt foolish just staring at Katie and almost made the mistake of treating her like a child by bending her elbows and knees as a way of assuring her that nothing was broken. She was embarrassed and wouldn't face me. I ended up retrieving her school bag from the curb. Katie grunted with all the lassitude of an overworked field hand as Emily helped her to her feet.

"That crutch has been trouble since day one," Katie said. "The little bitch."

"Oh lovely," Emily said. "You kiss your mom with that mouth?"

Katie flicked her head in my direction in a way that seemed to relate her impression that I was the reason Emily was late, and that Emily being late deserved even more blame for her fall than the crutch. "Profanity's good for your circulation," she said. "Who's *he*?"

"*He* is the new guy from Davenport, and his name is George Flynn. You can stop pretending you don't know all about him."

"*George Flynn?*" Katie repeated, still wincing but also trying to appear quite certain that she'd never heard of any new guy from Davenport named George Flynn. When she finally faced me, she jutted her chin out and threw me a fast nod, which I took as an instruction to hand over her school bag and get hopping into the backseat. During our ride through West Des Moines she communicated her remaining frustrations by incessantly fidgeting with the armrest power buttons. For ten minutes it was all groaning windows and changing winds, the electronic clap of doors locking and unlocking. Despite that, Katie's stubbornness reminded me of Emily in her dealings with Peyton the week after the dance; I was sure she'd tapped into a much deeper and more hostile source.

"Katie's working on a comic book," Emily said, half-shouting into the wind in an attempt at congeniality that, however unintentionally, came off as akin to the third-person praise often showered on shy toddlers. "It's all about a dysfunctional high school. Recently Katie's been dropping a lot of pianos on people, but when Katie drops a piano on someone, it's usually a player piano that kills them and then plays the most perfect farewell song." Emily turned to Katie, thinking for some reason that she might take over from there. But Katie only opened the glove compartment and started rifling through it, like she wasn't hearing a word. "Anyway, she's got this mean math teacher character, and in one scene he yells at his students about how math is the most important subject, and how mathematicians have to be more responsible than regular people because mathematicians who make mistakes can accidentally blow up the world. Then all of a sudden a piano comes flying down and kills him and starts playing 'One Is the Loneliest Number.'"

"It's not funny if you don't know the song," Katie protested, barely loud enough for me to hear.

"I know the song," I said, sliding to the center of the seat. "It's Three Dog Night. My dad used to play their albums all the time, especially on the drive to my uncle's place in Cedar Falls."

"You don't keep any Band-Aids in your car?" Katie said, slapping the glove compartment shut. I noticed that the splotch marks on her neck had almost cleared.

"*Saa-haar-reee,*" Emily said, heading south down 128th Street, obviously deciding it best to drop her sister off before me. But as soon as we reached University Avenue Katie started explaining what little homework she had, and how she thought she remembered running out of skin repair lotion, "the stuff that works like a miracle and that you'll never find on your own because it comes in a small tube they usually hide in those big Walmart bins filled with a bunch of non— skin care products [*deep peasant sigh*], and the bottom line is that you might as well keep driving, I'm sure there's a Walmart nearby wherever *George Flynn* lives." Emily didn't argue, even if she wasn't exactly with us anymore when Katie started flipping through radio stations at a pace just slow enough to leave me believing that each turn of the dial was her last. After scanning the entire FM selection she turned it off, opening the glove compartment and dedicating the following minutes to tender compact disc massage, invoking a frozen quietness that she commanded like a general's silence for his mutilated soldiers. After adjusting the bass, treble, and volume controls, she chose her track and was already lounging and perfectly relaxed when we heard the first twinkling notes of "Riders on the Storm," in my opinion the greatest road tune of all time. Emily changed lanes, looking over her shoulder and meeting my eyes just long enough to let me know everything was all right. She reached over and pinched her sister's thigh.

"You sure *aloe* is the best thing for a cut like that?"

Katie didn't answer. She was busy feeling it with her eyes closed and the wind in her hair, playing Ray Manzarek on the keyboards, the bony fingers of her right hand dancing over the dashboard where I could see them perfectly timed, tapping the notes just right. I caught her checking my reaction in the side mirror, peering out behind thinned eyes and draped lashes. I had the feeling if I proved myself to Katie Schell, I'd never have to prove myself to anyone ever again.

Seven

In the face of such an authorial tag team of feminine artists, armed with respective Old Soul wisdom and modern savagery, my first reaction was to eschew all sentimentalities in order to reinvent myself as an avant-garde realist, or at least a scientific-minded critic, both of which assumed a departure from my past as a quixotic bush leaguer always swinging for the fences. But I already sensed Emily's faith in me—a gift uncommonly bestowed, especially in light of her recently battered sense of male trust—and yearning to bring me into the fold of her privacy, which at this point I imagined was real estate well lorded over by her younger sister. While I had little intention of according Katie more power than she already possessed, I admit a brief attempt to prove myself the sort of radical, older friend who'd never pull a punch for the sake of courtesy, the kind of guy who understood that people who described themselves as "physically challenged" were just gimps surrounded by obtuse, run-of-the-mill optimists. I spent a good deal of the following month attempting to arrange three-way dates for such edgy entertainments as underground thrash concerts, irate poetry readings, or midnight cult films at Billy Joe's Picture Show where you could smoke, eat, and drink, and where half the nights ended with waitresses posting themselves at the emergency exits to prevent underage drunks from ditching their bills. But every time I informed Emily of these plans Katie was always resting, or catching up on homework, or "booked today from dawn to dusk." While I took these excuses as my hint that Katie had no intention of playing the romantic middleman, the real story was that she was much sicker than I knew, and Emily more worried than she ever admitted. She finally told me the truth one Saturday morning after spotting me along Sixtieth Street on the way back from a roller hockey game. I was hobbling along with my blades slung over my shoulder, looking like a hobo jock who didn't realize that anyone with skating skills would take to the ice like a real man. Emily was puttering along at about ten miles an hour in a no-passing zone, characteristically unconcerned by the delay she was causing the three or four cars lined up behind her. She suddenly hit the brakes and leaned over the passenger seat, mildly hydroplaning as the car following her swerved over the yellow lines.

"Hey, Big Red," she shouted. "You trying out for a Gatorade commercial?"

I bent down into the window, exaggerating the pain of my bruised hip, already detecting a note of self-perceived failure in Emily's attempt to lighten her own mood. My first impression was that her patience had stretched beyond its limit, that in reaction to the dwindling gossip related to her big night with Peyton Chambeau, the reality of his betrayal had now rushed forth to lean on her with its full weight. She waved me into the car. The rain was warmer now, so light that if I didn't see it bouncing off the windows I might've thought it quit. We were hardly up to speed before there were tears dripping from her jawline and it all came pouring out.

"It's not like I want to talk about it all the time, because at home, it's practically the *only* thing we talk about. But Ashley and Lauren, sometimes I think they don't even care. I mean, they were *sooo concerned* for those first few weeks after Katie got diagnosed. We were taking her out for ice cream, bringing her movies, playing board games. Then all of a sudden it was old news. Like when they realized there wasn't a cure, they decided all their efforts to cheer her up were just a waste of time. I'm not saying this to make you feel bad. You at least make an effort, even if you always come up with events at places that would probably never admit us, let alone my sister. Anyway, you weren't here when it first happened, and you don't know my family the way Ashley and Lauren do. I've got photos with them every first day of school all the way back to kindergarten. They've known Katie forever, but it's like they don't have enough time just to ask, *Hey, what's up with your little sister? How's she doing these days?* Ever since Katie got this stupid disease, it's like she's a fucking ghost to them. And it's really starting to piss me off."

The tears had mostly stopped by now. They were replaced by anger and frustration, not only at Ashley and Lauren, but at her parents and the doctors and nurses and everyone else who promised Katie would beat this disease that was in fact having its fickle way.

"She was in a *wheelchair* last week," she said. "Katie's missed so much school, there's no way she'll catch up. She doesn't know it yet, but she's gonna be doing seventh grade again next year. Jesus, I can't wait for her to get the news about that."

Emily's breath signaled its last stutter of self-pity. She must've known how beautiful she was to me, but I don't know if that made things easier or more difficult. She drove past the hockey arena and my house, gripping the wheel at ten and two, checking all mirrors, trying her best to control her emotions. I swore I could hear every drop of rain and palpitation of the engine, even the hum of the seams in the concrete.

"Let's pick Katie up," I said. "We can head over to Gordo's Mexican and eat for half price. Zach's working until four."

Emily was already shaking her head and reaching for the radio, tuning it to the AM sports channel. It was only the first quarter and the Hawkeyes were already down by ten.

"Did you see Zach made the Sports Extra?" she asked.

"Was it in color or black and white? If it was in color, he's probably already found a frame for it."

"It was more like a *reference*. Some Valley players were complaining about a St. Pius linebacker singing Johnny Cash before the snaps and in the pileups."

"We don't have to hang out with him. We can just order burritos and a bunch of virgin Margaritas and ignore him. I'll make sure we get the discount."

"He's not *that* bad," she said. "He might be strange, but so what? He finds his own way to win, and it works. If he's more creative than the other guys, why should he have to play the game the same way as them?"

"I've heard complaints that he bites people in the pileups."

Emily laughed and slapped the steering wheel. She must've thought I was joking. A minute later she was murmuring inaudibly, tilting her head and biting her fingertips (a perfect example of a vacillating aside, when everything about her body language made me swear she was a closet smoker).

"Katie's stuck at Mercy Frederick for a bunch of tests. But if you really want to see her, I guess we could work it out. It's been a while since anyone good dropped in. You really want to go?"

"Of course. She won't mind me showing up unannounced?"

"You never know," she said, making a sudden turn onto Hickman. A long, whining honk sounded from a truck still cruising down Merle

Hay. Somehow this seemed to relax Emily, and soon she was steering again with one loose hand flopped over the top of the wheel.

"I don't want to piss her off," I said.

"Oh come on, George. She might pretend to be pissed off, but if you think that means she doesn't like you, then you've got a lot to learn about Katie Schell."

"Why don't we pick some B-Bop's?" I said, pointing at the sign, at which time she made another seat-belt-locking stop, flipped her turn signal, and proceeded for the drive-through.

Just for kicks we strolled into the hospital through the emergency entrance, which proved even more exciting than we expected. At the triage counter a half-crocked fisherman was barking at the nursing staff, waving a right hand dangling with a treble-hooked bass lure. "Ya want me to lose ma thumb!" he shouted. "Gimme some attention! This boiy here with the busted nose, you ain't gonna fix that. Boiy needs a plastic surgeon!" "Dang straight," Emily said, cocking her head back and motioning to spit. "Boiy needs a dang boxing coach, too." After receiving our visitor wristbands we took the elevator to the eighth floor, where the walls were lined with bubble-lettered quotes like "If I'd known I was going to live so long, I'd have taken better care of myself." A diminutive nurse in a cubicle waved to Emily, then sneered in mock jealousy at my B-Bop's sacks. We found Katie in bed propped up on two pillows, static haired and pale but contentedly absorbed in Willa Cather's *My Ántonia*. Before troubling to acknowledge our interruption she continued reading to the end of the page, then replaced her bookmark and tenderly pivoted and looked up. Then she whipped the bedsheet over her face and shrieked.

"Em-Ma-Lee!"

Without the slightest pause Emily plopped herself onto the edge of the mattress and tugged the bedsheet from her sister's hands. While Katie might've taken charge on the ride home from school, it was now clear that Emily held the reins and wasn't looking to give them up.

"What are you doing! You could've at least warned me. Like there aren't enough people around here already invading my privacy."

"Sue me," Emily said, straightening her shoulders, sexier than ever as she laid down the law. "George wanted to hang out with you last week and the week before and the week before that. Today he insisted and I was too tired to fight him."

"*You're* too tired. That's a good one. I about had a hernia lifting the fork to eat a bunch of mushy green beans." She made a nasty green bean face, then shaded half her face as she pretended to barf over the side of the bed. Next she shook a clenched fist in my direction. "So it's *you* stinking up the whole hallway."

"Sorry," I said. "Emily caught me just after a hockey game."

Katie burst into laughter. She laughed almost as convulsively as Emily, only it came out in two high-flung hoots instead of one, and didn't embarrass her at all. "I'm talking about the *B-Bop's*. I smelled it a mile away and wanted to kill whichever little piggie was so selfish that he didn't care about torturing the whole eighth floor. But if it's for me, well, that's a different story."

She threw a nod at the dinner tray and its mechanical arm that was stretched out against the wall. Emily cleared her throat, subserviently bowing as she swung it over Katie's lap, then passed the burgers around, setting each of them up with drinks and napkins. After eating half of her fries, Katie started telling us about *My Ántonia*, which she claimed as the fortieth book on her fifty-book reading list for a citywide competition called the "Literary Olympics."

"My favorite scene so far is when Jim and Ántonia go on a picnic where they run around playing 'Pussy Wants a Corner' and eating pickles and getting real worn out. *Weeeeell,* according to Mr. Manrique, a boy narrator is not always a boy narrator, and a simple country picnic isn't always so simple *because* a pickle's not always a pickle. So the question is, do you, George Flynn, eat pickles?"

"She's gunning for your sliced pickles," Emily said, cutting her burger into neat halves, then quarters. I lifted the top bun and handed them over. Emily pushed the slices to the outer edges of the wrapper, then emptied three ketchup packets in the open space in the middle. (My last girlfriend, on our second date, cut her burger in exactly the same way. Perhaps it's the reason I was initially drawn to her. Over the following two years I only witnessed her repeat the gesture once, which I find extremely odd.)

"Where's Mom?" Emily asked, cupping her ear toward the sound of high heels clicking down the hallway.

"Don't worry. She called an hour ago telling me if I'd ever seen how nasty Mrs. Amato's kitchen was, I'd know why she had to retrieve her casserole dish this very minute. She's not coming till the afternoon."

"It's technically the afternoon right now," Emily said, picking up one of her burger quarters. "Okay, George, time to chomp down."

Katie kept steadily at her fries. Already her cheeks seemed to have brightened and she tossed her pillows aside to sit upright with her legs crossed, soon giving me the scoop on Mrs. Amato's neighbor, who she introduced as a "formerly esteemed mother of six" married to a "sacrosanct back surgeon" named Roland Hathaway.

"About a week ago," she continued, half whispering to invoke an element of suspense, "a vagabond named Pike showed up at the Hathaways' doorstep, claiming to be Mrs. Hathaway's first husband. Apparently he was all bearded and sunburned, with homemade boots cut out of tire treads. I don't need to say it was a little shocking, especially for the kids, who all sung in the church choir at one time or another. But the strange thing is that, according to Mrs. Amato, Mrs. Hathaway took it all in stride. She called a family meeting and pretty much told her family the whole story from the beginning. She didn't apologize even, but just told them what happened, like it was no big deal. Maybe she didn't *call* it a hippie phase, but you know, that's basically what it was. When she was eighteen she moved to a commune near a big Indian reservation in South Dakota. Long story short, she married this Pike guy, who was like the founding father of the group. I think they called themselves the Strike Out commune."

"Strike *Three*," Emily said, unable to hold her tongue, despite appearing to have heard the story enough times to want to see it hurried along. "And the marriage wasn't official."

"Yeah, okay," Katie admitted. "You want to finish the story?"

"Go ahead. You've got George on the edge of his seat."

"What's the holdup?" I said, perhaps pouring it on a little heavy considering that I was already leaning on my forearms against the railing at the edge of the bed.

Katie went on to describe Jonathan Pike's three-week stay at the Hathaway house, which, despite his passivity, resulted in a host of domestic disentanglements. (Mrs. Hathaway must have convinced her husband to let Pike stay with them, at least initially, though this was never clearly stated.) But as soon as Katie started describing Dr. Hathaway's increasingly erratic behavior, which she'd witnessed firsthand in the hallways of Mercy Frederick, she not only lost the thread of the story, but appeared suddenly oblivious to the topic altogether. There was nothing casual about it. While in one second she was relating details down to units of obsessive hedge-trimming and deliberately off-key renditions of "Gentile or Jew," in the next she was panning back and forth between Emily and me as though straining for the answer to a question that neither of us had asked. I was positive I would soon witness a second outbreak of hives, even in the face of Emily playing off the lapse as minor and mundane.

"What I want to know," she said, poking Katie in the thigh, "is where you got all these specifics about this Pike character's big night camping in the backyard with the twins. Did you say that happened *last* night?"

"He's been eating them out of house and home for two weeks. Ask Mrs. Amato. Ask anyone."

Emily balled up her fry container and swiped a napkin across her mouth, appearing to transition from acting agitated to being agitated. "It makes me sick. The whole parish is eating it right up. They love it that Dr. Hathaway's become some kind of depressive jerk, and they love it even more that Jonathan's a drifter who can't even afford a room at the Days Inn. If anyone deserves to be judged, it's *Roland* Hathaway."

"His friends call him *Rollie*," Katie said, smirking slightly, but shoving her tray away and reaching for her pillows again like a cynical soldier sick of his own war stories. "He's telling nurses and patients and everyone else he meets about how his whole life is a sham."

"And that he can never trust his wife again!" Emily said, slapping the mattress. "He's acting like she's a complete stranger, as if all that Christian volunteer work she does is so different from what she was doing back in the day on the reservation."

I thought about it, not wanting to align myself with Dr. Hathaway, but knowing that a certain amount of jealousy would be impossible to avoid. "Maybe Rollie just wishes he was the one sleeping on a buffalo mattress with sweet young Sharon."

"Obviously," Katie said. But Emily was already shaking a raised index finger like a master debater about to prove that we were all missing the main point.

"Isn't it possible to love someone and not tell them everything about your life before you met them? Is that what marriage is, an agreement to confess every mistake we ever made, every thought or memory that passes through our heads? I don't think it's fair to call Sharon a liar because she never told Roland about her time at the reservation. She's always been a dedicated mother and wife, and I don't see any reason to complain."

"How long did the marriage last?" I asked, turning to Katie.

She yawned and mentioned something about how Sharon and Rollie first met. In the middle of the comment her voice trailed off and she closed her eyes. I repeated the question, but Katie only rolled to her side and tucked her hands under her head. I'd never seen fatigue happen so fast. Emily walked over to the fuchsia plant on the windowsill and pruned a few dead leaves. A minute later she removed one of the pillows from under Katie's head. I gathered the fast-food trash and pushed my chair back. It was strange just leaving without saying goodbye.

"Is she really sleeping?" I asked on the way to the elevator.

"Maybe. Sometimes she loses it pretty fast."

Emily shrugged and left it at that. I wasn't sure whether our visit had ultimately succeeded or not, but took it as a sign that it hadn't a few minutes later when Mrs. Schell marched into the first-floor elevators as we were about to march out. (She was, however, wearing a silky yellow skirt and thin-strapped sandals that offered a perfect display of her waxy tennis legs and rose-painted toes.) She pressed the button for the eighth floor, failing to notice us as she reproached her husband for dillydallying when he was only waiting for an elderly patient to get a grip on his oxygen tank before his nurse wheeled him out. Mr. Schell was a thin guy with an intelligent oval face, looking tidy and somewhat childish in a pair of suave dock shoes and a powder blue Polo. He'd obviously seen Emily and me, but respectfully avoided any gestures that would give us up.

"*Hell-oooo?*" Emily said, surprising me by quitting the game so quickly.

"Oh, Emily. Good. Is your gown in the car? I don't know how we'll shop for heels with you in nothing but jeans and a T-shirt."

Mrs. Schell flashed me a smile that dropped off as fast as it came up. Her cheap politeness reminded me of the bitter insurance customers who occasionally showed up at my dad's office thinking it the perfect venue to unleash the frustrations of their less-than-inspired lives. In noticing the grease streaks across my shin, she scrunched her nose as though she'd just become stuck in an elevator next to a patient with a rare, infectious rash. This made it all the more pleasurable when I stepped forward for a handshake, not even for a second acknowledging my dried-sweat presentation. Since Mrs. Schell was pressing the HOLD elevator button with her right hand, she ended up giving me her left, all the while smirking uncomfortably, as though under such circumstances this formality was not only silly, but dangerous. The buzzer went off just as Mr. Schell stepped inside, grinning as he reached and rattled my hand.

"Richard Schell. You're George from Davenport, right?"

"Yes, sir. Nice to meet you."

"Who won the game?" he asked, also noticing the grease mark.

"The other guys," I lied. "Barely got us by one goal."

"Roller hockey," Emily said, helping him out.

"Sure, sure. I'm more of a quad skate kind of guy, but those Roller-blades are pretty slick."

The elevator lurched into action. Mrs. Schell remained face forward, anxiously awaiting the blinking floor numbers on the digital display. "I didn't know you and Katie were acquainted," she said.

"We've only met once," I told her, a moment too late to notice Emily's attempt to sway my answer. "But we were going to B-Bop's and thought it would be nice—"

"I'm sure she enjoyed the visit, even if you've only met once," she said, giving me the feeling that she was sure Katie *wouldn't* enjoy a visit from someone she'd only met once. Mr. Schell reached into his front pocket, soon producing a leather business-card holder.

"Oh, my God," Emily said, burying her face in the corner.

"Hey, you never know. This guy's an athlete." He chuckled and handed me the card, acting as if he was only doing it to tease his first daughter. "Did Emily tell you that I had an uncle from Davenport? One time he took us to the Wharton Field House to see Red Auerbach's Blackhawks during their first season in the NBA. Of course, the Blackhawks didn't stay in *Moline* very long."

Mr. Schell slapped me on the back. Apparently he thought the mention of such a place as Moline was a joke in itself. I smiled, but made a point of not laughing.

"Now we've got the Quad City Thunder," I said.

Mr. Schell pretended to be impressed, but was still chuckling to himself as the elevator doors opened. Mrs. Schell started in long strides down the hallway, allowing an inadvertently generous view of her flexing calves (which, combined with the sight of her painted toes that I imagined stretched out under a cloth-covered banquet table, nudging at my crotch, made it well worth the ride back up).

"There's no *rush*," Emily complained, hurrying alongside her. "She's sleeping."

"What does your father do?" Mr. Schell asked, hinting that we ought to hang back and chat for a minute.

"He works at Faith Harvest Insurance."

"Terrific. I'm sure we know some of the same people." Mr. Schell paused and tapped his right temple, taking longer than he would've liked to come up with his next line, but giving me a little wink when he finally got it. "Together everyone achieves *s'more*."

"Excuse me?"

"I made the T-shirts for their team-building weekend last spring. It's a variation on the T.E.A.M. acronym, but with s'mores. I believe there was a big bonfire for the finale. That's where the s'mores came in."

"Oh, yeah. I remember something about that." (I didn't remember anything about that. Every once in a while my dad had driven to Des Moines for team-training excursions, but he didn't feel the need to give us the details. I'm positive he'd never wear a T-shirt that said TOGETHER EVERYONE ACHIEVES S'MORE.) "I heard you make shirts for all the high schools."

"Most of them," he said, clearly wishing he had enough time to explain the reasons why he'd been unable to land the business of the remaining few. But we'd already reached Katie's door and Mrs. Schell was waiting. "Well, welcome to Des Moines, George. Don't get discouraged by our big-city ways. Des Moines folks just take a little time to warm up to outsiders. Ask Maureen, she's from Bolivar, Tennessee."

Mrs. Schell shined a final squinty smirk, like wouldn't she love to tell me all about it, and perhaps even invite me to Bolivar for a bicycle tour around town. I gave Mr. Schell a farewell handshake, then stopped halfway through repeating the gesture with Mrs. Schell, choosing instead to nod and meet her eyes in a way that let her know how obvious it was that she didn't enjoy shaking my hand the first time, and I didn't plan to put her through it again. (I couldn't help it, and for a long time afterward I was convinced that this was her official excuse for disapproving of me.) When we stepped back into the elevator, Emily was already apologizing without actually apologizing.

"*Heels heels heels!*" she said, covering her ears. "Here's an idea, maybe I'll just go to the wedding on *quad* skates."

I burst into laughter, then reenacted Mr. Schell's "s'mores" commentary, which was thoughtless and eventually put Emily in an even worse mood. By the time she dropped me off I felt like a complete jerk, especially now that I was considering the parental dialogue that likely followed our exit from the hospital. I knew that Mrs. Schell would accuse me of bald-faced classlessness and I could only hope that

Mr. Schell would prove himself magnanimous enough to defend me. Whether this ever happened remains in question, but for the moment it turned out that good fortune was on my side. The next afternoon I received a phone call reporting that Katie had been issued a series of encouraging test scores and an unexpected release from the hospital. According to Emily, her superstitious father, whom I somehow managed to like, despite his Des Moines snobbery and goofball self-promotion, was convinced that this stroke of luck was substantially affected by my surprise visit. What's more was the jolt I received a few hours later in the form of an express delivery containing a five-page original comic book with cover art centered on a yellowed string of flypaper hung inside a dank sports closet, only the flies glued to the paper were actually prep school students in uniforms. *Jackknife Janitor*, it was titled, in gooey blood lettering, and signed by none other than Katie Schell.

I spent at least an hour huddled on the basement steps, paging through what read as the illustrated diary of a misanthropic janitor's injurious pranks. While none of the drawings met the standard of detail set by the cover, the dialogue was hilariously grotesque, the student characters one-dimensional yet somehow convincingly real. What impressed me most about Katie's work was the impending doom implied by the angle of the drawings, the point of view often through a missing ceiling tile or a telescope aimed from a duck blind in the woods. It even concluded with a promo for a follow-up series, doubly titled *The After-School Incidents, or Wipeout at Whitfield Prep*.

I called the Schell house immediately afterward to thank and congratulate Katie, but only reached the answering machine, which always made me feel like a phony performing for Mr. and Mrs. Schell. I hung up a few moments after the beep, suddenly struck by an undeniable guilt in having co-opted Katie for the purpose of winning her sister. I confronted this guilt over the following weeks of idle afternoons with the Schell girls—Emily was now Katie's and my official after-school chauffeur—when I challenged myself to militant avoidance of less than sincere questioning, or laughing, or any variation on those themes. Even as the autumn leaves reached the stride of their sleepy downfall, when Katie relapsed and was rendered more or less bedridden, I never resorted to platitudes or false tenderness or pity. When I visited Katie in the hospital I visited her because I was inspired by her truculence in the face of her pockmarked doctor and his know-it-all assistants. I visited her because I didn't feel the need to make a fraud of myself in order to win her ease and affection. I visited her because most of the time I managed to distract her enough to make her laugh, and my response to this laughter was one of the cleanest sentiments I'd ever known.

So now can I admit the pride I felt in winning Katie Schell's approval and implicit support in pursuing her sister? The hope I gleaned from the knowledge that I'd passed a checkpoint where even Emily's closest girlfriends were stopped short? I won Katie's favor to a degree that Emily was soon asking my advice on how to better encourage her sister to comply with her doctor's instructions and stop threatening to replace him with a bee venom therapist. She even started loosening the reins on her infamous self-discretion (which I somehow related to her walking and talking much faster than before), giving me hope that we'd soon engage in a less ambivalent course of romance. Of course Mrs. Schell still remained an obstacle, but whatever efforts she made to discourage our friendship probably only pushed Emily even closer. At least it added an element of danger to things, which in my mind made our courtship even more bittersweet.

Eight

That first winter in Des Moines I grew a final inch and a half, cut fifteen pounds, and by some feat of smitten bravado outwrestled my four main competitors for a slot on the varsity squad. I credit much of this success to Emily's techniques of thespian vicariousness that allowed me to wrestle as a man more muscular than myself. *"Who are you?"* she would ask me. "The Great Dan Gable," I'd answer. "The greatest there ever was. The lightweight from Waterloo who won state three years in a row." But most of my free time was dedicated to Gable-esque training routines and even my lazy afternoons with the Schell girls were forced to the fringes. Weeknights were occupied by three-hour practices that left us so drained we could barely make the steps up to bed, while weekends were dedicated to tournaments and Saturday-night celebrations relegated to team movies and celery sticks, the "negative food" that supposedly took more calories to digest than it contained. I wrestled at one hundred forty pounds, despite a natural weight of one hundred fifty-five. Half my mornings before school were spent in a rubber workout suit riding a stationary bike. On match days I transferred the same routine to the sauna in order to lose as much water weight as possible before the afternoon weigh-in. Occasionally I'd receive a note from Coach Grady excusing me from French, which in view of the emphasis on crepe-making and Gérard Depardieu screenings, was considered a faux pas subject for wrestlers. When Grady noticed too many of us appearing fatty-jowled and energetic, he'd shut off the water fountain at some secret underground source, then post an OUT OF ORDER sign so no one could accuse him of mistreating us. The wrestling room thermostat was often OUT OF ORDER as well, cranking itself up to ninety degrees in synch with his fantastical temper. Grady even taught a geography class for wrestlers that he split between rote statistical memorization (capital populations, square footage of city centers, percentage of religious minorities, etc.) and film review of the previous week's matches.

We were a tightly glued unit, if not by our hunger, then by the chorus of our coach's cries for a return to the furious days of national champions and Olympic contenders that our team had known under his own tutelage in the seventies and eighties. But unlike Smitty—my undaunted comrade, bound to the sport by filial duty—my reasons for sticking with the program had greatly changed since the early Davenport days when it was enough just to view myself as a scrapper and socially esteemed brute who didn't turn his back to anyone. Given the new dedication required of me, my expectations of the sport swelled in proportion with its demands. I now required answers from my opponents, considering each of them an unwitting host to a particular question related to my quest for futuristic certainty. "Will I ever hump that older Perkins hostess and reputed emotionally detached cherry-popper who'll teach me all the tricks for expert sex with Emily Schell?" I'd puffed my chest out and throw my chin in the air as I marched onto the mat. "You tell me, Anthony Turner. You Mason City son of a bitch."

But I lost more matches than I won and by Christmas break I was hungry, depressed, and at great risk of losing the faith that I would ever know Emily Schell as more than a friend. Our entire socialization was now taking place in the confines of a religious arts course that met once a week and was only subsidized by lesser, more random encounters reigned upon by nagging teachers and student show-offs. (The effect of these installments could be compared to the sexual teasing of a circus elephant in an overcrowded tent moments before his juggling act.) I can't count the number of times that, in grave hunger and frustration, I nearly succumbed to a midnight spaghetti binge and subsequent trip to West Des Moines for a tree-climbing, love-pronouncing, second-story proposition. In Emily's absence music was just racket, the brightest and most fantastical clouds no more than loitering vapor. I'm now reminded of a night I spent slumped over my bedroom desk listing the health hazards of wrestling and the benefits of quitting when she called to report the news that Katie's MS symptoms had officially remitted. (While *My Ántonia* contains no shortage of pickle references, I've since scoured its pages only to find, time and time again, in differing editions, that there exists not a single pickle in the pastoral picnic scene Katie related during my first hospital visit.) The pain in her legs had fallen to a minimum, which implied a return to what the Schell family called her "big time" mood or, in its most extreme form, her "great balls of fire" mood. Feeling an immediate remission of my own, I learned that Katie's initial resurgence manifested itself over a hardworking Saturday spent choreographing a front-yard Christmas display, which included a life-sized Santa Claus gleefully whipping his reindeer. By noon she'd already hung enough strings of light to safely reach her goal of doubling the electric bill. Then she wrapped the mailbox in a garland and lined the driveway with illuminant candy canes, all the while arguing the case for her father's purchase of an artificial snowmaker in case Mother Nature refused to comply with the Christmas spirit. Apparently Mrs. Schell was in a big-time mood as well, as Emily explained:

"Yesterday, out of nowhere, she bought eggnog and rum and called all the girls from her tennis team over. It started off pretty tame, with holiday music, a bunch of middle-aged girls making pine wreaths for their front doors—"

"She didn't call *me* over. I like eggnog and rum. Your mom and I have more in common than I thought. I have a pretty good backhand, too. It's two-handed."

"My mom will be *thrilled* to know," she said. "The point is that by about five o'clock she was feeling pretty good. I can't say she was drunk, but she was pretty good and tipsy. That's when my dad showed up from the basement with an old guitar. There was *no way* she could say no with her friends all buzzed up, hooting and cheering her name. Well, let's just say I learned a little something about Maureen Schell. Not only can she *play*, but the woman can friggin' *sing*."

"Where did this guitar come from? What other secrets is she keeping? Do you even know this woman?"

"I thought I did. Have you ever heard a song called 'Edelweiss'?"

"My mom's got a music box that plays 'Edelweiss.' *The Sound of Music* is her favorite movie."

"Well, we practically grew up watching that movie. Every time we had a babysitter we watched it, and Katie knows all the lines by heart. I'm talking verbatim."

"Did you know your mom even had a guitar?"

"Hang on," she said, the sound of her voice immediately reverberating. "Someone wants to talk to you."

"Merry Christmas, George Flynn," Katie said, after a long pause. "Can you believe it? It's unreal, isn't it? Did you know my mom used to be Southern Baptist? She converted after she met my grandma Schell, who when you meet her someday you'll see that she wears rosaries like costume jewelry."

"Merry Christmas," I said. "It sounds like there's some kind of revolution happening over there."

"It's *huuuuge*. So when are you coming over to view the most fantastic holiday display in greater Des Moines? I can assure you it's not over-the-top, either. It's very tasteful, as opposed to the display put on by those fanatics from Ankeny who made the front page of the communities section with a shining blood-and-guts Jesus on a cross. Our Jesus is sleeping peacefully in a crib, well protected by two wings of nutcracker soldiers. Have you heard that I'm requesting a dog for Christmas?"

"No one ever gets a dog for Christmas. That only happens in commercials for long-distance phone companies."

"Listen here, pal, I've been tolerant all year long. I'm not planning to beg, but this is all I'm asking for. Nothing else, just a dog who only answers to me."

"Miniature poodle?" I asked, relieved to hear Katie admit such a wish and finally act like a seventh grader with a normal IQ. This sentiment fizzled as soon as she began paging through a canine encyclopedia, giving what seemed a planned presentation on the pros and cons of half a dozen breeds.

"*The bulldog suggests stability, vigor, and strength. His disposition is equable and kind, resolute and courageous, not vicious or aggressive.* Of course I'm smarter than to ask for a bulldog for Christmas, despite the Yale connection, which would score big with my dad. Anyway, near the end of their lives, they drool a lot and breathe super heavy. Not gonna go over very well with Maureen."

"What about a retriever or a Weimaraner?"

"Too big and too hairy. They'll shed all over the carpet. Besides, I don't want a dog whose name I can't even pronounce. *Weimaraiemer?* That's not going to work at all. Listen to this. *The beagle is gregarious, outgoing, and playful. He is happiest around people, especially children, and makes a great family dog."*

"Sounds perfect for you."

"Perfect for everyone! Of course they shed a tiny bit, but that can be reduced by buying high-quality food, like Nutro. And don't be fooled by their size—they make very good guard dogs. I'll probably have to take it to college with me anyway, so I might as well have a dog that can give me some protection. Anyway, what are *you* asking for? A new Speedo for your spring break trip to Cancún?"

(More than once I fell victim to an overwhelming suspicion that Katie Schell was reading my mind. While I would likely never have saved enough money for a spring break in Cancún or Lake Okoboji or anywhere else, the mere mention of the word alerted me to the details of my previous night's dream, which was highlighted by a diving excursion where I scared off a barracuda on the verge of attacking a yellow-bikinied and scuba-uncertified Emily Schell. This confrontation involved a series of matador-like taunts with Emily's bikini top, and ended with Emily throwing her mask off and wrapping her arms around my neck the moment I met her at the surface. Then she kissed me as though expecting this kiss to keep us afloat and motor us back to shore, which it did.)

"The only thing I'll be getting this year is a case of cauliflower ear."

Katie sighed and repeated my answer to Emily. "You're making yourself sick. Even my mom said so. Coach Grady shouldn't be able to just tell you what weight you're going to wrestle."

"Your mom's worried about me?"

"Well, not exactly. She made it sound like it was your own damn fault for letting him push you around. If you don't start eating right, there's a good chance your hair will fall out and nobody will recognize you anymore, and one day when you show up to school the security guy will be like, *Hurry it along, you old pedophile! You kiddie porn-monger! Scram!*"

"Gimme that phone," Emily shouted, laughing, but also attempting in all seriousness to pull rank. By the sudden giggling and rustling through the receiver I understood that Katie wasn't ready to give the phone up, and they were now grappling over it. (I figured that Katie would eventually lose, likely surrendering in the midst of being tickle tortured. But I also assumed that as soon as she could take no more, she'd probably hang up.)

"WE MISS YOU, GEORGE!" she shouted, then loosed a series of atomic yelps. By the sound of Katie's and her sister's spastic breaths, it seemed the match was livening up to more than a casual scrapple. I could only guess the following thumping, crashing, and screeching noises to be the natural sound effects of a chase sequence involving multiple flights of chairs, two slammed doors, and at least one kitchen chair (close-combat barrier?) knocked over onto a hardwood floor. While sitting idly on the other end of the line I could've confessed all sorts of truths about my desire to join the pursuit and furthermore direct the battle to what I imagined was a spacious master bedroom bed. I could've stated my crude thoughts loud and clear, casually, without any embarrassment, and in fact I did. The question is if either of the Schell girls ever heard them.

Nine

Over the following two months the St. Pius Dragoons suffered a series of rivalry-intensive dual match losses that more or less devastated the season, despite our last-minute comeback to place fourth at the state tournament. In standing with previous seasons, I finished with a dual match record of 10–10 and a healthy collection of tournament medals for third place, which in Coach Grady's opinion weren't worth mentioning because they only highlighted my unrealized potential. But the disappointment of proving myself a varsity-level failure was almost immediately nullified by the news that the triptych Emily and I produced as a main requirement of our arts course (picture Emily's three winged warriors in broad strokes, goggle-eyed and fat as senatorial gluts, resting by their spears and breastplates of gold-leaf gilt, my Masonite panels and leather-bound framework) won the art department's award for best collaborative work. What was most significant about this achievement was that our triptych was displayed in the main hallway with our names rendered below it in roman calligraphy on goatskin parchment, courtesy of an unnamed parish house artisan.

This final detail, in combination with a glossy photo of Emily half blushing with her head against my shoulder, gave several of her devotees the notion that I'd finally consummated our relationship. This meant that for the time being they were better off gunning for Christina Walters, St. Pius's own Cinderella, who in the last year sprouted forth from horsey-faced obscurity to local goddess. (While I admit to attending more than my fair share of volleyball games and even allowing Christina the occasional minor role in the burlesque striptease of my bedtime self-abuse, I never considered her horny little strut any match for Emily's talent, which inspired a much greater volume of jealousy than any of us would have wished.) In addition to the suggestion of our publicized art, the student body's assumptions could also be attributed to a few of my nonverbal, but undoubtedly coy, responses to their prurient queries concerning the depth of our communion. After one such response, in a rare moment of religious self-criticism, I accused myself of chickenshit disloyalty and vowed never again to succumb to such weaknesses of my Davenport past when I'd exaggerated sexual encounters that in reality amounted to no more than fumblings with girls I didn't care much for—savage tongue attacks at the movies, a few dry humps behind the couch in Kevin's basement, a dizzying hand job in shouting distance of bare-legged teachers and hyperactive volunteer lifeguards at a school anniversary pool party.

I would like to think that the decision not to overplay my relationship with Emily reflected a budding sense of maturity and self-confidence. Unfortunately, this is not the case. In my heart I knew I was acting on base superstition, the feeling that even the most minor duplicity would sow a seed of bad luck that would grow and spread and consume everything around it. For the time being I took nothing for granted, knowing it was possible that Emily had greater plans for us, but equally possible that I would remain no more than her most devout supporter whom the impending business of college and real life would all but erase.

For better or worse, in the weeks after the state tournament Emily and I returned to our idle afternoons, wandering trails at Walnut Creek, catching matinees at Billy Joe's Picture Show, or simply people watching and eavesdropping at the coffee counter of the Flying J truck stop. Katie joined us for at least half of these outings, whenever she wasn't tied up with physical therapy, or debate team, or any number of tutoring sessions related to her vast array of academic ambitions. On these days I almost always voted to spend the afternoon at Lions Park, where, for one reason or another, while sprawled out on the lawn, Emily was prone to share her opinions on matters more personal than Greek tragedies and theatrical schools of thought. I remember perfectly the day we secreted ourselves to a small patch of lawn beyond the sight barrier of two tennis courts with ivy-cloaked fences, the soft purr of a riding lawn mower droning to and fro, the cries of an umpire calling balls and strikes, the high-pitched clinks of aluminum bats. Next come the scents of watermelon bubble gum, freshly cut grass, the musky perfume of Emily's leather backpack softening in the sun. Summer was making a gallant move and we were unusually quiet that day, careful not to scare it off. Emily was lying on her back with her knees up and her bare feet sliding back and forth over the grass, blowing small green bubbles, shading her eyes with one hand, scratching at the odd chigger bite with the other. Meanwhile I perused the sports pages, occasionally pinching the padding of weight I'd suddenly regained in my hips and torso, and torturing myself by a furtive attention to the squiggling adjustments of Emily's unsilenceable form.

"Want to hear my theory?" she finally asked, curling up under the light of my increasingly emboldened gaze.

"About what?"

"About that little scar on your eyebrow."

"I ran into a stop sign," I said.

"So you don't mind me guessing, right?"

"Go ahead."

"It was a knife attack," she said. "I guess it started out as a small scrapple, but then the kid got frustrated, probably because his dad was a liar, and he'd just been diagnosed with dyslexia, and next thing you knew he pulled a Swiss army knife out and started slashing. It's a good thing you were wearing a skateboard helmet. He might have cut your ear off."

"I ran into a stop sign," I said, tossing aside the sports section. "I was about eight or nine, running alongside a school bus and shouting to a friend of mine. The stop sign jumped in my way."

"That was my next guess," she said, rolling to her side and propping up on one elbow. "Did you used to get into fights as a kid?"

"Only once. With a couple of older kids. There was a dog kennel in my neighborhood and the people who owned it had two fat kids, the Berbee boys, who used to love to sneak into our part of the woods to destroy our forts. We used to build a lot of forts, tree houses, wigwams. All that stuff."

Emily shook her head in dismay, sprinkling a few blades of grass in the breeze. "Nothing like a team of brotherly terrorists."

"Eventually we got back at them, much better than they ever got us. Their dog kennel had a bunch of outdoor cages and one day we let all the dogs loose. I don't remember how Zach stole the keys, but I think he walked right into their house, which was also the kennel office, and just snatched them off the hook. There must have been thirty dogs running loose, barking and chasing each other, really going crazy."

I chuckled to myself, remembering the pure glee we'd felt in finally winning our revenge. Emily chuckled along with me, even if she didn't find the story quite as funny as I did. "So where does the fight come in?"

"The fight comes in a few weeks later when the Berbees and a few of their friends caught up with Zach. Four or five guys beat the crap out of him. I tried to help him and then I got beat up, too. But that was just the beginning of it. Over the next couple of years, I'm pretty sure Zach caught up with every one of those guys when they didn't have any friends to back them up. When you fuck with Zach, eventually you get fucked with. He's not really one to turn the other cheek, or however it goes."

"You mean like the bumper stickers: WHAT WOULD JESUS DO?"

"Jesus probably wouldn't have done what Zach did. He rang one kid's doorbell and kicked his ass on his front doorstep, right in front of his mom."

"That's bold."

"You could say that."

Emily sat up and tugged at another tuft of grass. "Come on, George, even if most people would be too scared to do what Zach did, wasn't he just doing what we've all been taught? Even the military has priests to make the soldiers feel that attacking their enemies is perfectly all right, that that's actually what God *wants* them to do. And when I say enemies, of course I'm talking about God's other children, the foreign ones. *Turn the other cheek.* Blah blah blah. Not even the priests take that stuff seriously."

"You know Smitty's applying to the Air Force Academy?"

"That's exactly what I'm talking about. How advanced of a country are we when a sensitive, intelligent guy like Smitty starts thinking his way of helping people in the world is by getting trained to fly a thirty-million-dollar killing machine? This girl from my workshop called me a radical the other day. I know it's stupid to say, but it sort of hurt my feelings. I mean, what could possibly be more radical than going to war after war after war, expecting peace to suddenly break out."

"But after a war, peace usually does break out. I don't see the Kuwaitis complaining. What's there to complain about getting your country back?"

"Because, George, peace that's accomplished like that can never last. If someone maims your brother, or rapes your mom, or kills your dad—" She cut herself short, shaking her head at her own rising volume and flailing arms. For the next few seconds both of us paused to watch a jogger popping in and out of the shade, struggling along the perimeter of the park. Emily flopped onto her back again. "Oh, whatever. I just need to stop expecting people to make sense. God bless the bomb."

I didn't say anything. Emily covered her eyes and started blowing bubbles again, obviously working through the rest of her argument on her own. I scooted over a few feet to catch a few at bats of the Little League ball game. But the game was almost over and soon the boys were lining up for high fives as their parents flushed out of the bleachers. I wasn't sure if Emily was right, but I knew she was trying to be right, that her only aim was to decide something practical about how to improve upon the old traditions. I also knew that if I didn't say right then what I'd meant to say when we first came to the park, that she'd somehow discover the news on her own. I reached for the section of the paper I'd tucked into the front pocket of my backpack, slowly unfolding it to build the drama.

"You gonna read me the front page or what?" she said, uncovering her eyes. "Any updates on Nicholas Parsons?"

"Even better."

"That'll be tough."

"Hollywood's coming to Iowa. They're filming *The Bridges of Madison County* on the real bridges of Madison County and you're gonna be the star."

Emily gave her stomach a little drum, then glanced in the direction of a group of ballplayers huddling into a minivan. "I really doubt that, George."

"You're gonna be an extra who's such a natural star that Meryl Streep looks like an extra."

"Meryl Streep?"

"All you have to do is go down to Winterset Elementary School next weekend and wait in line."

Emily crawled sideways and bent her neck to view the headline ("Madison County Gets Casting Call") that I'd deliberately hidden from her. "Gimme that," she said, grabbing the article and spreading it open on the lawn. She leaned on her elbows and began reading, her legs slowly scissoring behind her.

"Coming this summer," I said, in my best theatrical trailer baritone. *"A love story set in Iowa . . . that's Iowa . . . the state below Minnesota . . . above Missouri . . . three hours from Chicago . . . "*

Emily ignored me. She took her time reading and scanning the side box filled with additional details and directions. "Think the crew can make it here without getting lost?" She cracked a smile as she searched with her pointer finger, then read aloud: *"The Winterset city council was hesitant about inviting Hollywood to their quiet town, until Warner Bros. offered to gift them a new auditorium.* Ha! Like they'd really say no to Dirty Harry."

"Could be your big break."

"It says they'll give preference to Winterset residents."

"They'll see your qualifications."

"That's what I'm worried about," she said, already doubting how she'd measure up in the eyes of the casting folks from California, despite her success at the Public Playhouse and the fact that she was the only high school student accepted to the Shakespeare workshop at Drake University. (That said, I always felt her insecurity about her talent was her most valuable professional asset.)

"Maybe you should bring a few clips from your Burlington Coat Factory commercials. Or that hair style poster they've got hanging up over at Great Clips."

Emily folded the article and handed it back to me. "You're not supposed to know about those things. And anyway, I'd have to read the book before Saturday. I'm not much of a speed reader, you know."

"That's what Katie told me."

"I'm sure she did."

I folded the paper until it was thick enough to slap in my palm like a playbook. "I'm waiting for the movie. I know you'll get the part and

I don't want to want to stress myself out trying to guess which scene you're gonna show up in. I wouldn't be surprised if they hire you as an extra, then end up writing you into the main story. If I saw you on the set, I'd rewrite the whole thing. Probably send Meryl packing."

Emily smirked and briefly met my eyes. She spoke softly, in a tender and downcast whisper. "You really think I'm gonna be famous, huh?"

"I'm sure of it. So long as you steer clear of idiots like Peyton Chambeau. Last week in the locker room, he pissed on a freshman for missing a free throw."

"That's not a good place to piss."

"It was just a scrimmage," I said, chuckling as though it were a humorous anecdote unrelated to us. I had no idea what possessed me to mention his name, at this particular time or any other.

"Okay, George. I'll try to take your *completely obvious* advice, for what it's worth."

She shoved her chewed wad of gum in its wrapper and checked her watch. Then she threw her backpack over her shoulder and stood up.

"Sorry," I said, which I could never stop myself from saying and which always annoyed Emily even further. I blocked the sun and stared up at her. "But tell me honestly, do you think you'll get the part?"

"No."

"Care to bet?" I said, reaching into my backpack, soon holding out a mint first edition of *The Bridges of Madison County*. Emily stared at the cover for a while without reaching for it. She sat down next to me and took it and opened it to the first page. She read the first sentence. She thought about it. Then she read it again out loud.

Ten

The truth is that Des Moines was and continues to be one of the safest cities in the country, a well-earned achievement regularly noted on top ten lists of most desirable American cities, often adjunctive to the category of child rearing. But the systems by which these rankings are calculated often fail to account for the trauma inflected by certain rare but heinous crimes, such as that of one teenager tugging on a telephone cord that he forcefully wrapped around the neck of another at a business hotel in the suburbs. They also neglect the grave effects of legally permissible crimes, including the daily gossip-mongering and passive-aggressive nitpicking that in my experience thrive on such hosts as midsize Midwestern cities with inextricable ties to their state's agricultural economy. I turn to the example of Maureen Schell, a transplanted Des Moinian, dually progressive and small-town stubborn, whose priggish parenting style effected consequences that stretched far beyond the borders of her front lawn.

I received a harsh lesson in the extent of these consequences during the three days of excused absences that Emily spent on set with *The Bridges of Madison County*, which involved twelve-hour shifts largely confined to a corner booth at the Northside Café, mouthing silent small talk so as not to disturb the recording of Clint Eastwood's exchange with Lucy Redfield, the town harlot. Lauren begged me to meet her at the Civic Center downtown for one of Ashley's dance team competitions, despite the fact that we had almost nothing in common and struggled excruciatingly in the absence of the rest of our group. Perhaps this awkwardness (not to mention our confrontation with such a bizarre contest, primarily judged on components of turbo crotchwork and surgical smiles) deserves the most blame for that afternoon's backstabbing revelation. According to Lauren, Emily was systematically lying to her mother about the time she spent with me. If the two of us went for tacos at Valley West Mall, she explained, Emily would likely tell her mother she was watching *Aladdin* for the hundredth time with Ashley, who was stuck babysitting her nephew. If we went to a movie, she'd say it was a dull night at the bowling alley with a bunch of basketball players who were pitching balls from one lane to the next and obfuscating all the scores. In terms of explanations for Mrs. Schell's negative opinion of me, Lauren's best guess was that it had something to do with Marcus Panozzo getting caught stealing boat motors up at Gray's Lake, and the fact that his accomplice had escaped unnamed. The word on the street was that despite proving his loyalty at the police station, back on his mother's antique sofa (humped from Sicily by his poor plumbing grandfather), Marcus blamed his uncharacteristic thievery on the influence of the new kid from Davenport. Lauren hinted that this fabrication had probably spread from Mrs. Panozzo to a good number of St. Pius mothers, but she did so with great tenderness and consolation, going so far as to criticize Mrs. Schell for harboring prejudices that extended far beyond juvenile delinquents to include exotic pet owners, anyone over thirty in a miniskirt, people with BEWARE OF DOG signs (or yard signs that try to trick people into thinking there's a woman with a big fat ass and a polka-dot apron bent over in the garden), territorial Italians from the South Side, the fat blobs who needed electric wheelchairs to grocery shop, etc. As Lauren prattled on I considered that the mere mention of my name had Mrs. Schell summoning images of cheap motels with crack pipes and Betacams, fraternal redheads with country bumpkin boners, and other criminal threats that invoked acid nausea at the thought of my representing them.

I should mention that by this time Katie's crush had grown increasingly eye-battering and obvious, most fully present in her feigned, pirouetting healthfulness and the simpering lilt of my name off her lips. A few hours after Ashley's competition I exploited these feelings by way of a shamefully entrapping phone call that paved the path for a vile and secretive line of communication. Katie not only confirmed Emily's fictions related to our daily excursions, but also shared her opinion that the entire drama related to Peyton Chambeau was misconstrued. "She was *relieved*," Katie said. "She had the perfect excuse to walk away. You think she really wanted to date that guy? I'm sure she was curious about *something*, but as far as I can see, she's pretty occupied with her acting, and discovering the deep mystery of herself. I don't know, George. Maybe you'd better let this one go for a while."

While I wonder to this day exactly what Katie meant by *letting this one go*, I had every intention to probe for the reasons why Emily encouraged her mother's misconceptions about me by attempting to deceive her. The situation came to a head after her last day of shooting, on our way to a roller-skating event organized by Smitty and his fellow youth ministers. With an utter lack of artfulness, I informed her of all the technical information related to that evening's college fair at Lincoln High, suggesting the event would provide a convenient alibi.

"Why would I tell her I went to a college fair?" she asked. "I already know what colleges I'm applying to. What are you getting at?"

"I just don't see Tino or Hads showing up, and Smitty's said he'd be busy running the music. So it's basically just me and you tonight."

"So why would I need an *alibi*?"

"I don't know. I have no idea. Do you need an alibi when you hang out with Hads or Tino? What about your free golf lessons with Jordan Pratt, or your *meditation for actors* with that guy from Drake?"

"You mean Tony, my teacher?"

"How would you like it if every time we went to a movie, I told my parents I was studying for the national French exam with Christina Walters?"

"You really want to know the answer to that?" she said, hardly braking as she turned into the Skate South parking lot. We pounced over a speed bump, drawing a shout of censure from the male driver of a station wagon packed with a group of skating youngsters. "You don't understand anything, do you!"

Emily and I had never argued about anything that really mattered, and she'd certainly never yelled at me. But I found the inherent drama erotic enough that after we parked I decided to aggravate her even more. "If your mom knows as much as you say she does about all that's happening around town, then she should know that I'm not your boyfriend. We've never kissed or even come close to kissing, and this crap about high school couples lacking the social skills to form new friendships in college, well, that's nothing but Maureen Schell horseshit!"

"That's not even the point. The point is that she has to know everything. But you're *my* business and I'm not going to ruin it by sharing *you* with *her*!"

"Fine!" I shouted back, perfectly satisfied with her response, but feeling pressed to maintain my anger. Emily slammed the car door and stormed her way into the roller rink. After sulking for a few minutes, I bought a ticket and changed into my Rollerblades. I found Smitty in the snack bar, where we had a few laughs at a guy who'd shown up in flower-power bell-bottoms and couldn't skate. When it was his turn to play DJ, I skated to the rink and started looking for Emily. For the next fifteen minutes I searched the arcade, the locker area, the snack bar, every corner of the building. Emily was nowhere to be found. Eventually I ended up checking the raffle registration that everyone signed after purchasing their entrance ticket. Emily's name wasn't on the list. My only explanation for this was that she'd hidden herself in the lobby restrooms, then slipped out after I'd passed inside. I changed into my shoes and walked out to the parking lot, just to be sure, but already knowing her car wouldn't be there.

Eleven

n the following weeks of calculated noncommunication—I knew Emily's potential for hardheaded detachment and did my best to match it—I consoled myself with the notion that no couple has ever learned the skills of forgiveness and reconciliation without first experiencing the sting of an insult by the person to whom they've given the power of their greatest trust. Whether Emily and I ever benefited from our first fight is hard to say, but of course our troubles eventually blew over, as it turns out during the course of the Iowa State Fair, where we spent the better part of ten days bouncing from game booths to bumper car courses, mini track races, grandstand musical performances, and all the variations of cattle competition ever invented. It was hard to hold a grudge while stuffing ourselves with deep-fried Twinkies, turkey drumsticks, and every meal-on-a-stick the Iowegian mind could fathom, especially with Katie stealing the spotlight by berating every fairgoer who stepped in the way of her crutches. In the buildup to the greased-pig and hog-calling competitions, she even demanded we check out a wheelchair from the first-aid tent in order to claim prime seats next to the ring.

"It all started with Judas Iscariot," she announced, choosing a bout of downtime in the shade of the technology tent to slyly broach the dilemma behind the blowup just described. "He was a redhead. It's proven. That's why the older generations are so reluctant to accept them. There was a time when people were so ashamed of redheads they'd keep them locked up in the attic, tell their neighbors they only had two kids when they really had two kids and a redhead."

Emily twirled her ice cream cone, licking it contemplatively and looking pretty upset about the whole nasty phenomenon. A group of inventors lined up onstage, one by one announcing their discoveries and groundbreaking gadgets to the sparsely peopled stands.

"Yeah, redheaded men really don't make the grade in a lot of circles. Probably the reason why there's never been a redhead on the Hollywood A-list. Not a guy, at least."

"John Wayne was a redhead," I said. "Hard to tell with all those black-and-white films and cowboy hats, but it's true."

"John Wayne's real name was *Marion*," Emily joked.

Katie balled up in laughter. A feisty woman with oversized glasses pointed at the slide-show screen, listing the technical components of her biological food spoilage indicator. We watched a few more presentations, during which time I decided it best just to forget what Lauren had told me about Marcus Panozzo. There was no telling if the rumor was even true, or if there was any logic at all behind Mrs. Schell's negative opinion of me. Soon enough Katie was bored again and making her wobbling descent down the metallic steps, drawing the unabashed distraction and shameful stares of the inventors. Back on the midway Emily joined the serpentine line for the Bungee Rocket. In the meantime Katie requested I push her to the nearby Butter Cow, which she explained was sculpted every year by a lady named Elesia Ellington, an artist from Riceville who worked her way up from papier-mâché and epoxy clay to dairy butter. (Her masterwork was a butter interpretation of Leonardo da Vinci's *Last Supper*.) I leaned down over Katie's shoulder so she didn't have to yell. She asked about Zach's living arrangements in Iowa City, predicting that if he could keep himself in line, he'd provide the exact spark the Hawkeyes defense so desperately needed. I knew we'd end up discussing my troubles with Emily without discussing them directly.

"Talk about *macho*," Katie said, chuckling at two shirtless bodybuilders strutting down the midway. "What kind of girls actually end up with these guys?"

"No idea. Whenever I see guys like that, they're always walking around with *other guys*."

"Reminds me of my uncles in Bolivar. Not that they're big studs or anything, but my oldest uncle, he *walks* as big as a brick shit house. Speaking of which, did Emily ever tell you that when my mom used to visit her grandpa, and he had to take a crap in the middle of the night, he'd send her to the outhouse to plop her buns down to *warm the seat!*"

"You've got to be kidding me."

"Hey, what's the hurry? I'm here to soak in the atmosphere."

"And people tell me I'm from the sticks."

"You mean to say you didn't have an outhouse in *Davenport*?"

"Oh yeah, Zach used to warm it for me all the time."

"I have a feeling you'd be warming it for him," she said, chuckling and covering her mouth. "Would you slow down!"

A minute later she was ordering me to speed up toward a shaded set of railroad ties facing the Bungee Rocket, where Emily was only halfway to the front of the line. The bungee jumpers were being catapulted from two cords attached to tall metal beams, slinging at least sixty feet up. When they launched, their faces went gaunt and ghoulish. "Tell me more about Bolivar," I said, still considering Mrs. Schell's unlikely path to the Wakonda Country Club elite.

Katie pushed herself onto the railroad ties. I sat down next to her as she rested her feet on the side of the wheelchair. "My grandpa was the big-time judge in town," she said. "He was always talking about the importance of education . . . *for men*. The stupid thing is that everybody loved him, even though he covered the tuition for my uncles and didn't pay a penny for my mom. Her younger brother, my uncle Steve, he went to college before she did, and he probably never read a book in his life. My mom was the salu-da-dicatorian!"

"Salutatorian?"

"Yeah yeah yeah," she said. "So you know what my mom did then?"

"Picked up her *gee-tar* and went *a-wanderin'*?"

Katie pointed a strict finger at my face. "She got a job at the local café while she applied for scholarships to every college in the state. It took two years to get the hell out of Bolivar. And the only tip she got at that crappy café she worked at was, *Don't get too big for your britches*."

Katie slapped the railroad tie. She stared me in the eyes and scrunched her forehead and seethed. Despite myself, I was starting to like Mrs. Schell. "You're passionate women," I finally said, in a voice much more emotional than I'd intended. But I wasn't joking and Katie knew it. She nodded to the bungee platform, where Emily was now taking her turn. Her spotter was a middle-aged guy, bald and mustachioed. He led her to the catapulting position and attached the cord to her harnessed vest.

"Do you mind me saying something, George?"

"What's that?"

"You show your affection too easy."

"I know."

"But it puts you in a bad position."

"Maybe you're right," I said, just as Emily shot into the sky, her body floating in a zero-gravity standstill before making its flailing earthbound descent. They shot her up three times, the third of which she looked like she could've easily done without. After thinking it over, I decided to take Katie's criticism for what it was worth, a simple piece of advice on how to achieve a better balance of respect with her sister. (This turned out to be the last we ever spoke of such matters behind her sister's back.) By the time Emily came stumbling our way and pressed a hand to my knee as she hopped onto the railroad ties, whatever tension that remained between us was washed away.

Near the end of the afternoon we returned Katie's wheelchair and ambled happily to the parking lot, all three of us smirking to ourselves, knowing we'd be back the next day, rain or shine, for an afternoon fiddle fest and hoedown. At one point I threw my arms over the Schell girls' shoulders, promising them a fanciful summer of champagne dinners, country club banquets, and Caribbean cruises. I pulled them close and felt bigger than ever, proudly engaged in a three-way love affair, the biggest man at the Iowa State Fair.

But that wasn't the official end of our outing. Before we left, Katie directed us to the eastern end of the lot and the statue of historian James Wilson, where she recited his stone-etched quotation in such an instructional way as to confuse the exiting fairgoers into thinking she was performing a daily ceremonial duty. Her voice invoked singers of national anthems, fallen soldiers, the great unseen statesmen of Old Time Radio. Her solemn tribute concluded with the following proclamation:

"No one meets and mingles with twenty thousand Iowa men, women, and children on the fairgrounds—the only place they can be brought together—without growth of sympathy. This is the most valuable effect of the state fair. The fraternizing, humanizing consequences of *BRINGING OUR PEOPLE TOGETHER!*"

Twelve

t need not be explained that rising humidity can be cruel to a young man nearing the summit of his physical strength, in love for the first time and desperate for that love to coalesce into a perfectly brazen and impromptu carnal awakening. In Iowa's golden tassel summer Emily was a squinting cowgirl, deliciously cherry in the shoulders and the very tips of her nose and ears. From time to time she'd search me with her big brown eyes and such guileless affection that I felt on the verge of crumpling to my knees and giving up every aspiration I'd ever known. She'd just stare, sometimes smiling and sometimes not, but in a way that made me feel she could see our entire futures. Then she'd usually say something like, "You know, if I wasn't mooching all your time, you'd probably have a couple of girlfriends by now" or "You wouldn't run off to some other girl, would you, George? Even Christina Walters?" We still hadn't kissed or even held hands, but after logging hundreds of circuitous country road miles and exchanging enough bright-eyed glances on dead-end nights beneath the Thirty-fifth Street Bridge, I understood that Emily needed me, even if it wasn't in the same urgent and blistering way that I needed her. It was a romantic summer if only for the fact that we fell asleep so many times on the beach at Saylorville Lake that we thought nothing of waking to a sky hailing with every tinge of paint on the palette. In greedier moments I overstepped my boundaries. I slipped my arm around her waist in the mall, acting like her long-established lover in an attempt to trick her into making out with me as a mere matter of course. I picked things out of her hair that weren't there, just to get close, letting my lips hover in front of her face, hoping something might happen. Once I made an obvious assault on her right breast in the complete darkness of a Magic House exhibit where the challenge was to drop to all fours and feel your way through a maze of blind tunnels. It was the greatest goblet of garmented flesh I'd ever known, so warm and vivacious that my palm clung to what it sensed was an essential absorbent force. "*That's* not the way," she'd said, half sniggering and squirming as she delivered my hand back where it belonged.

While these misplays no doubt upset the balance Katie had warned me about, the scale tipped in the other direction at the last moment when the August sun had nearly winked its last and Emily purported her own desire with a series of conciliatory but inarguably amorous kisses on the neck. It happened at a freestyle tournament at Valley High, after I'd been instantly pinned by a five-point throw, my body generating such a resounding smack against the mat that the audiences of all the other matches looked over to mine, reacting with a guttural symphony of "Oooooooh!" and "Ouuuch!" if not merely laughing like cut-rate comedians at my wheezing, breathless embarrassment. While these kisses only piqued my desire and thus sharpened my suffering, in the moment of feeling her lips on my skin I moved from experiencing one of the most emasculating public humiliations to sensing that I'd just struck a debilitating blow to those disgraceful forces of nature that for one reason or another place love in the hearts of those who will never know it requited.

Thirteen

I recall almost nothing of my senior year. Perhaps I recall some things, but only in pieces. I remember Emily telling me she was applying to Yale and other elite institutions out of my academic and financial reach. I remember considering myself an environmental hero because I spent three weekends with my physics teacher in the nocturnal, catch-and-release pursuit of crawfish frogs. I recall a float trip on the upper Iowa, but not much beyond the fact that it rained one night and we all crowded into a domed tent where Ashley kept whining about the hole in her sleeping pad and Hads demanded his money back for Tino's cousin's bunk weed and Smitty botched the ending of a long-drawn-out ghost story and when we finally went to sleep the top of Emily's head was nearly touching the top of mine and her hair smelled like mixed fruit. I remember a reported sighting of Nicholas Parsons that amounted to naught. I remember Zach showing up in our front hallway as forlorn as a forced retiree, leaning against the coat closet while my dad waited at the edge of the kitchen and my mom paused halfway down the steps, admitting that he'd been kicked off the team for "drunkenness and other related infractions." I remember Emily playing the lead in the school's rendition of *Our Town*, a drama involving a marriage between characters named George and Emily. I remember the corporal vibrations of hunger and sexual aggravation rattling me in my sleep. I remember Tino bragging of his senior-year stamina after banging his girlfriend on the stairways and in the basements of half the houses still under construction out in Clive. I remember a stuttering twitch in my left eyelid that followed an unfulfilled evening with Emily Schell. I remember a sharp reduction in my powers of impersonation and concentration, the frightening realism of my dreams. I remember the torturous smell of steak smoke drifting through the back door and up the stairs and into my bedroom, which makes me feel I remember more than I thought.

One night I stole Zach's car and arrived unannounced at the Schell house on one of those pre-winter nights when it was only seven o'clock but dark and it seemed like ten.* By this time I'd made some headway with Mr. Schell, who, when we were able to avoid the topics of Yale or his T-shirt business, proved himself a pretty decent guy. He never treated me like a potential date rapist and always made a point of asking about my parents in a warm way that didn't strike me as superficial. But Mrs. Schell remained vigilant, even if she'd resorted to such petty insults as refusing to aim her glare at anything below my hairline. On the night in question she answered the door in a velour sweat suit that struck me as the only sweat suit in the world fancy enough to wear to a cocktail party at the Marriott's revolving restaurant overlooking the river.

"She's studying, George. She doesn't have time to fool around this semester."

---

*Is this episode necessary to share? While sitting at my kitchen table next to a *Beckett Sports Card Monthly* that has informed me of the relative worthlessness of my vast baseball card collection, all my memories seem vital. But my sense memory tells me that this episode is important, and my sense memory is much clearer than my factual memory, which makes me think the rule of this narration should be to let the senses lead the way. But first one fact: the Schell house has been on the market for years now and finally sold last week for the asking price of $700,000. I have reason to believe Mr. and Mrs. Schell have left the state, and possibly the country, though this is purely an instinctual reaction, hardly based on anything.

"It's mostly a business meeting," I said. "Emily and I have a pop quiz tomorrow in economics. Can you just give us a few minutes?"

"How can it be a pop quiz if you know it's tomorrow?"

"Mr. Dougal calls them pop quizzes, but he works on a kind of unconscious system that I've basically figured out. Third week Thursdays are almost a sure thing."

"Emily's really got to focus," she said, like I'd just been yammering on about my disappointment that Guns N' Roses had never made it to Des Moines. She checked her watch against the clock in the hallway, hinting that I was severely disrupting her night's entertainment. "This year's grades are even more important than last year's. A lot of kids don't realize that. Some of the colleges will ask for your grades right up to the end."

"Mornings are the best time to study," I said, as energetic as an excitable pony. "I read all about it. It's proven."

"Uh-huh. Where are *you* applying?" she asked, crossing her arms and treating herself to a long, histrionic blink.

"Iowa and Northern Iowa."

"Uh-huh," she repeated, relishing the thought of my humdrum ambitions.

"Can I just talk to her for a quick minute?"

Mrs. Schell responded by staring like she'd asked *me* a question and not the other way around. Then she told me to wait while she checked if Emily had a moment to spare. I sat down on the porch steps, watching a pile of leaves roll across the neighbor's lawn and into the street. A minute later Katie stepped outside in a leather jacket with woolen lapels. It was obviously her dad's jacket, probably the manliest thing he ever owned.

"What're you eating these days?" she asked, making a face at the sight of my waistline. She took her time lowering herself down.

"A lot of salads. I can eat real food on Saturday."

"Who do you wrestle next?"

"Valley."

"Snobs."

"They had a ringworm outbreak."

"Gross," she said, setting one crutch over her knees. "Every time I hear that word, I picture worms crawling under my skin."

"You coming?"

"I'll be there, but you'd better win this time."

"The last match you watched was against the guy who won the Cedar Falls tournament. His name is Shane Weiss and he's pretty tough."

"Shane *Wuss*. You could've beaten him. He just muscled you. Everyone could see that."

"Maybe. He kind of psyched me out, too. Before the match, he barked at me. He shook my hand and barked, real soft."

"What a creep."

"Yeah, but it worked," I said. Katie nodded along, but she didn't like it. "I'll wrestle him again in Ames."

"You'll beat him. If you weren't cutting so much weight, you'd be state champ for sure."

"A winning record would be a good start."

Katie leaned back to take in the view of the swaying branches, acting like she didn't hear me. "Yeah, you could be state champ."

"Thanks."

"How's your brother doing?"

"He's designing a new bachelor pad in my parents' basement. He's working up at Gordo's again."

"Ouch," she said. "Tough break for such a cute guy. I can't figure out why he never settled down. He could get any girl he wanted."

"You looking to be set up?"

"Maybe. Got any shower photos?"

"I don't even have a camera." Emily came out bundled up in her biggest woolen sweater. She plopped down, hugging herself and rubbing her temples. "Let's go for a drive," I said.

She laughed a series of short huffing hoots. (Emily's laughter had become highly communicative, and was now her most developed theatrical tool. "Wrong button!" it said. "But don't worry, because you've raised the exact issue I was hoping to discuss.") "Three nights in a row!" she complained. "All I want to do is rent a movie, and each night after dinner she gives me this big sad face and says, *Why don't you just stay home tonight? I don't like you driving at night.* Since when has anyone had a problem with driving at night?"

"Lots of deer accidents," I said.

"It's tragic," Katie said, "though they *are* overpopulated."

"She's getting worse."

"*Es la verdad. Estoy de acuerdo.*"

"*Sí,*" I said. "As long as you're not talking about me."

Katie leaned forward to face her sister. "I don't get why she's making you study so much. I'm *obviously* the brain in the family and you're *obviously* the little actor. You need to concentrate less on the books and more on your *bod.*"

"I swear the next time I leave the house I'm driving all the way to the real Broadway to see *Kiss of the Spider Woman*. I don't want to wait until I'm twenty-five, after all the best actors have won awards and moved on. Who's up for a drive to New York?"

"It's my senior year," I said. "No time for fooling around."

Katie slapped her thigh and clapped, more than displaying her appreciation. "Speaking of *fooling around*," she finally said, tugging at her leather jacket lapels, "do you think Dad had a lot of girlfriends back in the day? He used to be a lightweight boxer, you know."

"It's not exactly clear if he ever won a fight," Emily said.

"I'm going to dig around Grandma's attic and see. I bet I'll find a trophy or two."

I nodded optimistically, despite having a hard time picturing Mr. Schell hitting anything other than a telephone pole while backing up in his Beemer. Emily started pacing between the front porch and the driveway, stretching stiff-legged from one stepping-stone to the next.

"Did Katie tell you she's got an admirer?"

"Shut up. I do not."

"Let me guess," I said. "It's someone from your Spanish club."

"He's not an admirer. He's just some kid who only talks to me when my symptoms are out of whack. He's creepy."

"He just wants to help," Emily said. "That's his in."

"It's still creepy. Even if he's the only guy in the school who actually listens when someone else is talking."

"What's his name?" I asked, surprised by my own anxiousness.

Katie slumped and threw her hands at the sky. "It's Thomas Staniszewski. He's nobody. Just some weirdo with a perm and a name no one can pronounce."

"A *red* perm," Emily said, hopping toward us and raising her eyebrows. "He's got red hair."

"No he doesn't," Katie shot back. She grabbed her crutch and pushed herself up. "God. My shows are coming on. See you later, George."

"See you at the match."

"You seemed to pronounce his name just fine," Emily said, smirking and hopping to the next stone. Katie paused at the door and leaned back around. "You know, she can be really immature sometimes. It's kind of sad, especially knowing that she's my *older* sister and there's nothing I can do about it."

"You can buzz off," Emily said, "that is, if you have any interest in me taking you for a driving lesson when Mom and Dad head out to dinner tomorrow night."

"You coming, George?"

"I'll be too hungry to go driving while I'm thinking about what your parents are ordering for dinner."

"Poor George," she said, shaking her head as she stepped inside.

Emily hopped over and sat down again. It would be another month or so before the first snowfall, but it was a dry breezy night, already swirling with the crisp cologne of winter.

"Any word on *Bridges of Madison County*?"

"Not yet. It probably won't get released until the summer. Anyway, they cut out a lot more footage than they use. The camera only faced my direction a couple of times."

"Everything okay?" I asked, watching her heel at the cement, realizing she was more upset than I thought.

"I just wish things were different. My mom and I used to have a good time together. Let's face it, Katie got her sense of humor from someone, and it wasn't my dad. The only time he's funny is when he thinks he's being serious. But every time I feel like opening up to her, she says something rude that makes me want to punch her in the nose. And she always strikes when I'm in a good mood."

"Maybe she doesn't notice what she's doing? I mean, maybe if you two had more conversations about normal things, it wouldn't come off so badly when she gave you advice."

Emily was already shaking her head and kicking at the cement again. "She makes it impossible. The other day I was complaining about this guy in the play who didn't know anything about Shakespeare. I'm talking like, this guy probably thought *Macbeth* was the name of a new breakfast sandwich. We pay all this money to study with this bigwig writer, and my partner can't even remember his lines. So I start complaining, and then my mom turns beet red and calls me a snob. I mean, I know my dad makes a lot of money, but am I really spoiled? Do I act like a rich little snob?"

"You're not a snob. Jan Lewis is a snob. Even Ashley's a bit of a snob. Your mom is a total snob, and probably a *prude*, too."

I laughed a queer little laugh, like I was just giving her mom a hard time in order to make her feel better. A second later, when Emily searched my eyes, I swore she found every petty thought in my head. I might as well have punched her in the stomach.

"So am I, huh? A *prude*."

"You're Emily Schell," I said, like that was the best achievement anyone our age could expect, like she was perfect.

"Emily Schell is a tease."

"I don't care about that. My problem is that you're my best friend, and you spend more time with me than anyone else, and I'm still jealous. I don't even know *who* I'm jealous of. But you're the only actor I've ever known and the only actor I ever want to know."

"All right," she said, ending my little ode with a big wave to her neighbor who was pulling up into the driveway next door. The woman stepped out of the car, shining us a smile as she grabbed her briefcase from the backseat. For some reason this made Emily laugh ("Distract me," the laugh said). My stomach growled like the long woeful chirp of a paralyzed cat.

"You've got to eat, George. This one-forty business is ridiculous. You should be wrestling at one-fifty-two, at the least."

"If I wrestle at one-fifty-two I'll be the only senior on the junior varsity squad. Colin Franzen wrestles at one-fifty-two, and I've never come close to beating him."

"You could try. You don't know until you gain some weight and give it another shot."

I knew in that moment that Emily would rather have talked about anything other than the details of our sexless relationship that no one, including ourselves, knew how to interpret. We talked about her workshop for a while and then I drove home, recognizing that while our classmates were fretting over SAT scores and potential careers, my only real ambition in life was to love Emily in the same fierce and noble way I'd loved her from the beginning. I'd nearly told her how I felt.

Fourteen

W hile I'd never considered myself a competitor in any radical sense of the word, by midwinter of my senior year something changed, and I can't help but think the new intenseness I discovered in myself came as a direct retaliation against my established mode of circuitous and biddable wooing. At this point of the season we were all scrapping dogs wrestling on death metal and invented egos, tapping into any and all sources of energy that might stave off our hunger, distract our better instincts, and prove our warrior-like worth. I was cutting more weight than anyone and any lines of weight-loss methodology I'd previously vowed not to cross were summarily erased. I practiced in a rubber suit, chomped laxatives, binged and purged. The severe effects of such a regimen included mood swings, headaches, dizzy spells, and lapses of short-term memory that might've bested Katie at her recidivist worst.

But by then I'd become a core member of the team who'd impressed Coach Grady enough in the first half of the season that he'd begun to notice every detail of my technique and form. He attempted to fine-tune my skills in such a way that I occasionally felt my human potential being scientifically weighed, that I was no longer training for the state tournament but attempting to stretch the boundaries of my life's possibilities. My guess is that my new attitude also owed a great deal of credit to the surprise visit we received by the Great Dan Gable. In response to our waning team morale, Grady assembled a crew of former St. Pius state champs who began showing up before practice to narrate the episodes of their greatest, life-altering victories. But even Grady was caught speechless when Will Warner and a few of his University of Iowa teammates stepped into the room with Coach Gable, whose hyperintensive workout routines were the bastion of our daily education.

Given the theme of my resolve during this period, I'd like to take a moment to describe the presumed source of Coach Gable's determination, which could be traced to the Memorial Day weekend of his sophomore year, when he and his parents were away fishing and his sister was raped and murdered in their family home. After that day Gable never lost a high school match. He finished with a record of 64–0, then a collegiate record of 118–1, his only loss coming his senior year against Larry Owings in the final showdown of the NCAA tournament. (Afterward he cried so vehemently that I swore the camera operators and even their cameras and microphones were crying with him. Perhaps Dan Gable is a more complete man for having experienced such a moment of fallibility and public grief, but on each viewing of that match I feel my heart collapsing like I imagine a star dying, and I weep.) The legend went that every time Gable took the mat, he imagined his competitor as his sister's murderer.

Despite the fact that Will Warner and his teammates did most of the talking that day, I can hardly report a word of what they said. I only remember staring at Dan Gable and peering through the windows of his amber lenses in an attempt to absorb a small amount of the wisdom I detected in the pale tension of his cold brown eyes. He sat in a folding chair outside our huddle, leaning forward on the balls of his feet—his hands clamped, chin protruding, one shoulder slightly raised—practically in a standard starting position if he'd only lifted a few inches off his chair. There was no need for him to open his mouth. His presence in the room was enough, besides the fact that his wrestlers were regurgitating his own words anyway. "You make it tough on yourself," Will kept saying, "but even tougher on your opponent. You win the match by winning every second of the match, and the only way to do that is to attack." At some point I found myself reliving my first night in Des Moines, a memory easily triggered by the story of Gable's sister, whose murderer, like Nicholas Parsons, was also an obsessed neighbor. I had the feeling that while Coach Gable was sitting before us grinding his hands, he was actually reliving his senior bout with Larry Owings, still set on the perfection he'd sought all those years when he'd only had to look in the mirror to meet his most ferocious competitor.

While I never exchanged a word with Dan Gable, after that afternoon's visit I began training with a previously unknown severity. I quit complaining about the conditions of wrestling under Coach Grady, feeling the sudden need to purge myself of whatever weakness had prevented me from the romance that had always remained one painful step away. I decided I wanted to win, to push myself to the physical extreme and see what I was really made of. My new regimen allowed almost zero time for Emily or anyone else—I hardly owned an idle minute anyway—a sacrifice I justified by the possibility that something good might come of letting her miss me for a while. In the end, it wasn't the state trophy I was after, but the success that I associated with that trophy: winning Emily.

For the rest of the season I stepped onto the mat with the intention of looking *through* my opponents, to recognize their limitations as though recognizing my own, then set about exposing them. I started eating more, figuring out how to pack the most energy into the least amount of calories, and working off every bit of excess that I'd previously resorted to spitting, puking, and shitting away. I knew that in a couple of months it would all be over. I'd return to a regular diet and be able to look back in admiration of what I'd accomplished at eighteen years of age, after which time every man begins experiencing a gradual physical decline. Instead of attempting to impress my teammates by showing off on the bench press and squats, I worked the ropes and chin-up bar, developing my wrists and ankles, my forearms and grip, beginning and ending my days with a hundred push-ups, sit-ups, whatever challenges I could invent and find the strength to overcome.

Smitty did his best to keep up with me (though there was no denying which one of us cast the more beastly reflection in the weight-room mirror). He finished the season strong, despite getting pinned twice in Dubuque at the last tournament of the year, which meant he didn't qualify for state and disappointed his father and uncles, who were all die-hard supporters. While I had major difficulties making my final weigh-ins, I placed first in Dubuque and won twelve of my last fourteen dual matches. These wins were accomplished by every amount of aggression I could muster, many of them ending with pins in the first period. I qualified for state and spent the night before the tournament running stairs and jumping rope, then taking a warm bath filled with Epsom salt my mom bought to help release the lactic acid in my muscles. With a remaining two pounds to cut—an ordinary and somewhat manageable condition—I spent the early hours the next morning riding a stationary bike in the wrestling room. Minutes before our bus was set to leave for the Civic Center downtown, I weighed myself one last time. I was still six ounces over. I said nothing to Coach Grady. We were greeted by big banners, TV trucks, and as many teenage girls in heavy makeup as stooped old men with thick glasses and official programs.

First thing, the state qualifiers crowded into the locker room for weigh-in, where I wasn't the only one straining on the toilet for ten minutes. Starting with the lightweights, we all stripped naked and squatted cross-legged on the metal scale. When they called my name I sat down and closed my eyes and prayed for a miracle. I heard the scale tip. The judge asked me to get off and try again, but in the following ten minutes nothing changed; I was still five ounces over. "Sorry, son," he said, shaking his head as he scratched my name from his list.

Coach Grady didn't bother asking what I'd eaten the week before, or explain how I'd robbed myself of the chance to make the grade for all-time. He stepped right past me, mumbling a gruff and bitter *"Excuse me"* before he started coaching Colin Franzen, like I'd graduated fifteen years before and was no longer of any use. (I wasn't the only wrestler that year to lose to the scale; the other guy, a middleweight senior from Adel, bawled hysterically, then cut his forehead open banging it against a locker.) It was still a few hours before the first match. The other state qualifiers started loading up on orange juice and power bars. After drinking a few glasses of water I called my dad from a pay phone in the gym.

"If you don't feel like coming," I said, "you don't have to. I didn't make weight."

My dad let go a loud breath. The receiver filled with static, then the sound of a fist pounded on the countertop, rattling plates. "How much over?" he asked.

"Five ounces."

"Will they give you more time?"

"No. Everyone has to make weight before nine. It's already past."

A security guard unlocked the gym doors. The crowd piled in, each of them carrying enough blankets and drinks and snacks to last a week. I couldn't figure out why I hadn't shoved a finger down my throat behind some bush.

"Five ounces, huh?"

"Yep."

"All right, George. You want me to tell your mom?"

"That's fine."

"What did Grady have to say?"

"Nothing."

I could hear the porch door squeal open as my dad stepped out back to smoke. "Never liked him," he said. "But doesn't matter much I guess. Shit, you were overweight on day one. Dropping loads so big we could hardly keep the diapers on you." There was another deep breath. "Well, I'm sorry, son. I would've liked to seen you get another chance at that kid from Sioux Falls."

I didn't answer. The porch door squealed open again. My dad must've covered the mouthpiece. I could hear him whispering (which is to say shouting under his breath), but couldn't make out the words. "Wait a minute, here's your brother."

"You didn't make it!" he screamed, personally offended, like I'd been sabotaged and he was determined to find out who was responsible.

"No. I'm five ounces over."

"You should've been wrestling one-fifty-two in the first place. Grady should've put Smitty at one-forty-five and Franzen at one-sixty. Franzen would've made state no matter what. He would've made state at one-seventy!"

"There is no one-seventy. It's one-seventy-one."

"It's a miracle you made it through the season without passing out and cracking your fucking head open!"

"I'm coming home."

"You're really done?"

"Yeah. I'll see you soon. I'm coming home to eat."

By the time Smitty drove me back, my mom had already reheated a casserole dish filled with sausage lasagna she'd stored in our neighbor's refrigerator so I wouldn't have to think about it overnight. The recipe was usually enough for the whole family with a few pieces to spare. Smitty and I ate the entire casserole in fifteen minutes, then washed it down with a liter of cola. For the moment it was all I needed to pad the disappointment. I was already four pounds heavier by the time I showered and changed into jeans and we headed back to the arena. On the way Smitty told me all about the fast food he'd been wolfing down over the previous week, which somehow led into a story about his Air Force recruiter hassling him about how it was obvious that he didn't spend enough time in the gym and how Iowa wrestling wasn't what it used to be and how unfortunate it was to see so many young men raised in relative peace taking their freedoms for granted. In a surprising bout of pessimism Smitty suggested that the ill-fated conclusions of our wrestling careers was just one indication that we'd never look back on our high school years the way we wanted.

By the time we stepped back into the Civic Center my stomach hurt so bad I wasn't sure if I could sit. It didn't help matters that I'd forgotten to call Emily to warn her of what to expect when she arrived downtown. After walking a few languid laps around the circular hallway, Smitty and I took to the stands to join the rest of our teammates who didn't make state. Hadley's dad and a few others gave me big pats on the back and stern *Be strong* words of encouragement as they climbed up to their seats. A few friends bought me candy bars and nachos. I nodded to everyone, trying my best to smile and thank them but barely letting go a word, afraid of the emotions that might let loose if I did.

When the Schell girls finally found me, Katie drew all sorts of attention to the both of us by standing at the bottom of the bleachers waving her arms and pointing her crutch at the electronic tournament board that had mysteriously omitted my name. This did little to improve my mood, which grew worse when she kept up the charade during her excruciatingly protracted ascent that involved stopping every few steps to stare up in wait for an explanation—all this in front of a match tied at nine points in the third period. When I couldn't take it anymore, I marched down the steps and scooped her up like sack of potatoes, a gesture I suspected she wouldn't appreciate. It turns out I was wrong.

"Holy smokes, George! You could *stab* someone with these muscles. What did you do, spend the last month with the American Gladiators?"

"I didn't make weight," I said, heading back up the steps, clenching my jaw at the sensation of my face growing flush. Emily was still waiting below, watching the match, probably having figured out what happened and now trying to decide what to say.

"So you didn't even wrestle?"

"You didn't miss a thing, except the heavyweight whose coach slapped him when he started crying."

"You're not going to start crying, are you?"

"No," I said, as a slight shiver ran through me.

"All right. Set me down next to Smitty."

Smitty happily scooted over. As soon as I set her down he started updating her on the match in progress. I sat a few rows back and waited for Emily, knowing that as soon as I stepped away Katie would ask him for all the details. Emily sat next to me and shot me a quick smile and didn't say a thing. She probably guessed that if she kissed me again, like she did after the freestyle tournament over the summer, I wouldn't let her get away without kissing her back. Then she'd have a decision to make that she probably didn't feel like making. (The fact that I didn't receive another kiss only further encouraged my remembrance of every athletic letdown I'd ever experienced, not to mention every heroic Peyton Chambeau slam dunk I'd ever seen. Before long my thoughts sank so deep into the gutter that I found myself imagining the uncovered footage of Peyton and Emily frolicking under the sheets in the master bedroom at Heidi Sneed's.) The next hour of the tournament proceeded in grand style, the crowd roaring at the sight of hip tosses and last-second escapes. Colin Franzen pinned his first three opponents. I kept waiting for Emily to nod off, like she usually did at some point during all-day tournaments, no matter the noise level. After a long bout of waiting and watching, I let her know I was ready to talk with a snide remark about the Catholic school from Marshalltown whose team name was the Maroons, despite their school colors of navy and gold.

"A maroon is a slave warrior fighting for his freedom," she said. "They still exist today. Whenever regular people come around, they just keep moving deeper into the jungle."

"Did Katie tell you that?"

"She's not the only source of information around here. I *occasionally* read, I hope you know."

"I *occasionally* streak across stadiums during wrestling tournaments, I hope you know."

"This is an interesting change. I'm usually stuck in the stands with a bunch of boring old men talking business."

"I wish I was a Maroon."

"Some of the Maroons were cannibals, George."

"Great," I said, like we were making perfect sense. "Maybe we should try that sometime. Maybe we should find someone who can afford to give up a few fingers, or an arm—"

"Fine by me."

"Like a kid or something. Somebody who's not really contributing anything."

"Whatever you say. I came here thinking it was *your* day today, and I still haven't changed my mind. Let's just do whatever you say."

"That could be anything."

"I'm not in the mood to argue," she said, pointing at the names of the advancing winners just listed on the tournament board. She leaned back and looked around, pretending to soak in the various expressions of the surrounding fans. She didn't meet my eyes until her old friend from elementary school called her name and hiked up the bleachers toward us, fake panting along the way. Emily turned and touched my shoulder. She sighed and dropped her shoulders in a way that made me feel I wasn't harboring my loss alone. A few minutes later, after she and her friend went for snacks, Katie scooted down next to me, demanding play-by-play recaps of all the matches she'd missed while listening to Smitty describe biological-attack training procedures in the gas chambers at Fort Leonard Wood.

"Now tell me what the heck's happening with Saunders," she said. "Is he as tough this year as everyone says he is?"

"You don't even know Saunders."

"But he's tough, right? I heard he had a wrestling mat in his basement and a bunch of scouts from Arizona State following him around."

"Where did you hear that?"

"Pretzel line."

"Yeah, he won pretty quick. He'll probably win it all."

"Good ol' Saunders," she said, as she drew her focus on the beginning of the next match, which from the first whistle was dominated by a wrestler from Cedar Rapids I'd beaten two weeks before. He earned a solid lead and was soon dancing around, locking up for as long as possible, wasting time instead of going for the pin. I decided I was better off not giving the match my full attention. It was only making me more upset.

"So, you're not going to say *I told you so*?"

"About what?"

"Wrestling at one-forty instead of one-forty-five."

"You mean one-fifty-two?"

"Sure."

"What do I know," she said. "I guess you'll just have to leave your mark on the world in some other way. If you were state champ, you'd probably be talking about it for the next fifty years, and that's *all* you'd be doing for the next fifty years."

"You know Saunders isn't the only one who's gotten a few phone calls from recruiters."

"Whoop dee doo," she said, going for an unclaimed bag of peanuts on the bench in front of us. "You planning to starve again in college?"

"I didn't say I returned any calls. Anyway, how are you planning to make your mark on the world? Ever send your comics out?"

"I'm not sure I'll make any mark on the world, George. Maybe I'll leave it *unmarked*. But I'll tell you this, someday long after I'm gone, while a bunch of kids are building a sand castle, or digging up the forest for a new dirt bike path, they're going to discover something truly amazing, and that something is gonna be my *time capsule*. Have you ever heard of someone finding a time capsule? It happens every once in a while, and when I hear about it, I get so jealous I could scream."

There was only a minute left in the match. I was glad when Katie started shouting out for the underdog, even if the kid from Cedar Rapids was still looking to stall long enough to win. "What are you planning to hide in your time capsule?"

"Just a few mementos of the age. You know, for the historians and ethnographists. There'll be some predictions for the future of the Schell family, America, the human race. A few secrets revealed, a few questions posed. A map. Maybe none of those things. Maybe all of them. It wouldn't make much sense to be exact about what I'll put in there. The whole thrill of discovering what's inside is what it's all about."

"But I'll be long gone," I said, already thinking of where I might bury my own time capsule. (I can't reveal the location I eventually chose, knowing that one of you might be tempted to search along every train track beneath every arrow-shaped and dynamite-blasted boulder in Davenport.) During the next round of matches Katie and I started betting quarters on the outcomes. Of course I was familiar with most of the wrestlers and didn't think there was any way she'd take my money. But it turns out Katie had a knack for choosing the winners, apparently based on the way they walked onto the mat. By some strange luck she was able to separate the phony talents from the real fighters, judging instinctively the mere musclemen from the scrappers who'd rather see their arm snapped off before turning their back to the mat. By the time Emily returned, my teammates were huddled all around us, having a big laugh at Katie's spot-on guesses that made me wonder how serious she was about the predictions in her time capsule. The confluent thrill of gambling and wrestling reached a climax during Colin Franzen's final match, which took place on the mat closest to our section.

"Franzen's gonna chomp this Wilson guy up," Katie said. "See the way Wilson's rolling around that one shoulder? He didn't start doing that until a minute ago, when he first saw Franzen. I'll bet you an extra quarter that Wilson's first move is a step backward."

"I'll take that," Smitty said, tossing a quarter on her blanket cum bookie's stand, trying to talk the same game as Katie. "Guys with braces never take a step back. Braces in this sport make you look meaner."

More quarters started piling up on the blanket. Almost everyone on our team was in, as well as a few wrestlers from other schools.

"Okay, boys," Emily said. "I hope you've got rolls for all that change. We didn't bring our piggy banks."

"*We?*" Katie scoffed. "I'm the one doing all the work here. And if it's legal tender, it's good enough for me."

The gamblers cursed with amusement. Emily pinched my arm and whispered, "Think anyone's getting a little big for her britches?"

"It's a cocky sport," I said, just as the referee chopped his hand and Wilson took a step back. Katie clapped and collected her coins. It was a close match, but Colin scored two takedowns in the final round and won by three points. We stayed for the closing ceremonies when he climbed the pyramid to receive his trophy. Coach Grady called a brief team meeting to congratulate Colin and remind us of his unsated appetite for three or four individual titles and a team championship. Most of the seniors didn't give a shit—he'd used us and we'd used him and that was it. While exiting the arena, when it was clear I had a responsibility to get wasted with my teammates, Emily patted my chest and stomach (perhaps trying to sway me toward another plan, though this is hard to say), urging me not to drink too much or let my figure go too quickly. During this hypothetically decisive moment Smitty tossed me a set of stolen wrestling room keys and I stepped back to catch them and we all shouted and were soon jumping into cars and speeding across town like loosed devils toward the familiar stink of two wrestling mats that were less alive than the day before, already dusty and stale like an ancient armpit. We uncorked six jugs of team cider we'd been fermenting all winter. We tag-team wrestled. We bare-knuckle boxed. We climbed the ropes with jugs tied around our waists and cigarettes in our mouths and chugged at the top like possessed half-wits. I woke the next morning overcome by the sense of being trapped in a foul and long-neglected gerbil's nest, soon asking myself if Emily was serious about *whatever I wanted*. At this point at least thirty state champions glared down at me from their victory pyramids within their plastic frames, shaking their heads, some shielding their medals, others turning their backs, all of them pinching their noses.

Fifteen

shudder to admit it, but this past October I was arrested. Beyond the speeding tickets I inevitably fall prey to every three or four years, it's the only time I've ever found myself at odds with the law. I spent a night in jail and very nearly lost my job. The arrest came after a party hosted by a fellow teacher that ended in my keys being taken from me after I downed a near fifth of whiskey of a brand previously unfamiliar to me. I can't remember ever drinking so much, so fast, in all my life. But that night while making small talk about this fellow teacher's satellite, his dog's foul breath, his brother's new telescope, etc., I knocked back drink after drink with the ease of a lifelong drunkard who had no interest in humankind beyond their capacity for the production of white noise chatter as a pleasant backdrop during a binge. For the entire night I found myself incapable of focusing on anything other than my relationship with the Schell girls and the possibilities of the lives originally intended for us. These thoughts were obviously triggered by my pre-party viewing of the local six-o'clock news, when I'd caught Emily interviewing a relationship author for a human interest report on how to understand men through their dogs.

At some point in the night I blacked out, to say the least, and can only guess that after falling into a card table adorned with casserole dishes of artichoke and spinach dips, I was belligerent enough about the decision to walk home that no one insisted on stopping me.

But as it turns out, I didn't walk home right away. After hearing a metallic banging in her backyard, a housewife a few neighborhoods over stepped outside to find me severely hunched over and howling through the freshly broken window of her husband's toolshed. Then she grabbed her video camera and filmed me. I saw her footage for the first time in court. I was not only hunched over, but hooked sideways with my head somewhere near my right elbow, which explained why my back had been so mysteriously sore for such a long time. I still wonder how many copies of this video exist and into whose hands it has passed. I wonder what my students would think if they saw me looking like a mad trapper who'd finally ensnared a moose only to realize he'd lost the key to his room-sized trap. I ask myself what I was so hungrily seeking on the other side of that toolshed door that wouldn't give way and I can only guess it had something to do with the answer to the existential question of how Emily, Katie, and I would ever find our way back to our proverbial Garden.

But I'm getting ahead of myself and would be better to return to the spring of my senior year during a strange spell of heat waves, heavy downpours, and foul moods in reaction to speculations of a summer flood that would wipe out all the farmers who'd barely found their feet. Emily was wait-listed at Yale, which caused a new set of complications in her relationship with her mother, despite offering me a sinister hope that Emily would find herself rejected from all her prospective colleges, in which case I'd renounce my letter of intention to the University of Iowa, then rent a high-ceilinged apartment south of Grand with French doors and a freestanding bathtub—with brass legs ending in eagle's claws—where we'd comfortably conduct organic dialogue exercises and I'd discover my innate skills as a theatrical director. This fantasy only intensified during a two-week run of *Othello* at the Public Playhouse, where Emily's coquettish but chaste Desdemona was better publicized and reviewed than the entire cast combined. The storms continued through the first half of April, which I remember based on my dramatic curbside reading of a wet, semi-translucent letter, lacking a return address, but stained with a scent I can only describe as heart-shaped and unmistakably Emily's. It read simply, in breezy cursive:

> *Dear George, you are formally requested to accompany me at 7:00 on the evening of Friday, April 12th, to the Iowa Theatre Winterset for the nationwide premiere of* The Bridges of Madison County. *E*

In order to avoid hurting Katie's feelings, and out of respect for her father's longtime crush on Meryl Streep (a dear friend from Yale, he used to tease, I imagine whilst propping a patched elbow upon the hearth) and her mother's fanaticism for Robert James Waller, Emily told her family that the production company had allowed only one ticket per extra, just the same as for the locals whose shops and houses were featured in the film. While this disallowed the possibility of picking her up in my dad's double-waxed Taurus like a respectable theatergoer on an official date, there was little to complain of when the time arrived to meet her in the parking lot at Valley West Mall. It goes without saying that Emily was in rare form, light as a feather in a swaying skirt and low-cut blouse, legs and shoulders ashine as she strode in the waning twilight from her car to mine. I'd been waiting for twenty minutes listening to smooth jazz in a pair of thin corduroys and a yellow oxford cloth shirt, untucked, loosely buttoned at the top and bottom, sans T-shirt. (I've accepted that a good woman *should* arrive late. What sort of desire can a man possibly muster for a prompt date? A couple of months ago I signed up for an Internet matchmaking service, but can hardly remember a thing about my past few dates other than the fact of their apolitical postures and sugary small talk and their promptness.) We were late and Emily was perfectly unrushed. I stepped outside and walked around to open the door.

"Good evening," I said.

"Good evening," she said. She leaned inside to take a deep whiff of the freshly cinnamon-scented upholstery. "I was serious about probably being cut out."

"I know," I said, shrugging, like it wouldn't be the end of the world. She stepped inside and we set out for the interstate and Madison County.

"Did you read the book yet?"

"Are those new shoes," I asked, checking all my mirrors. "Don't think I've seen those before."

"You're pathetic, George. Did you know that *Bridges of Madison County* sold more copies than the Bible?"

"With that kind of money, you think they'd just rebuild Iowa out in Hollywood."

"You really didn't read it?"

"I didn't want to ruin the movie."

"Oprah's already seen it and she loved it. She filmed a TV show from one of the bridges, she loved it so much."

"Oprah's from Mississippi. What's a Mississippi girl doing shooting a TV show on our goddamn bridge?"

"You've got a point there. It isn't right. But it isn't right that you didn't read it, either. I told you about Meghan, right? She's the extra I sat next to the whole time. She said she was planning to show up to *Othello*, but I haven't seen her yet."

"You really think you got cut out?"

"It's very possible."

"If you're not in it, I'm going to storm out of the theater halfway through."

"What if I show up in the movie after that?"

"Touché."

"Please never say that word again. It's very un-George."

"All right."

"Nice shirt."

"Thank you."

"It's not ironed, I see."

"Thanks for noticing," I said, feeling very well attended to. For most of the rest of the ride we were content just to cruise along appreciating the night's possibilities. It was my first time to Winterset and its Main Street of brick two-story buildings with narrow alleyways between every fourth or fifth shop. When we arrived one block from the main square a police officer directed us to the side streets. "Hey you, Polk County," an elderly woman shouted from her lawn, just as I was reaching for the keys to cut the engine. "You get any farther from the curb and I'd think that car was parked on the other side of the street." That was just the beginning. Almost every older couple we passed on the way to the theater shot us a suspicious stare, or turned and whispered, apparently emboldened by their suddenly valuable small-town sense of right and wrong.

First thing after stepping into the main square, we passed the Northside Café, the location we'd likely see Emily if she ended up in the movie. Situated on a patch of prim lawn at the center of the square was a modest but graceful courthouse with a Victorian steeple and long gaunt stairways. The Iowa Theatre Winterset stood opposite the café with its old-fashioned triangular marquee and every bulb shining bright. Cameramen were already lined up beneath it, primed to provide a thick buffer between the commoners and the stars. At least half the town was milling around the square, the men mostly in clean work boots and collared shirts tucked into jeans, their wives painted thick with mascara, many of them with big frozen bangs and long menthol cigarettes, reminding me of the Veterans Day events at the American Legion back in Davenport. When the limousines arrived the teens all sprinted for the curb directly in front of the theater, where they were immediately ushered to the sides. Emily and I squeezed in near the entrance as close as we could get to the velvet ropes. Soon enough we were cheering a dark-haired Meryl Streep stepping out onto the red carpet. A frizzy-haired girl next to us explained the whole story behind the actress deciding to rent her house during the shooting. Meryl Streep waved at the girl and even paused at the ropes to tell her what a treat it had been living in a farmhouse. "Good luck, Miss Streep," Emily said, just as she was turning away. Among the various other shouts and salutations, Emily's words came off with a hint of Old World respect, like she'd found the simplest, classiest way of saying, *You're my hero*. For a brief moment, while everyone else was staring goggle-eyed at Meryl Streep, she was gazing at Emily, tilting her head, her pale cheeks rising as she smiled. A hundred lightning bolts flashed. I hardly noticed Clint Eastwood and the other actors passing by as Emily gushed and her warm hand found mine. We shuffled in behind the stars. Emily was still squeezing my hand as we wound our way up the steep stairway to the balcony.

The movie started without any special introduction, the only highlight being Clint Eastwood's little salute to the upper balcony on his way to his reserved row. The anticipation of the extras was overwhelming and seemed to harbor its own unique scent, something akin to the combination of overripe apples and dry ice. When the opening credits ended and the chatter died down you could feel their nervousness—men, women, and children impatiently searching for themselves on screen, eager for their big moment. In distinct patches the audience cheered minor glimpses of their historic houses and classic cars, signature storefronts, familiar pedestrians crossing the frame. Emily stiffened at first sight of her cinematic self swirling a glass of orange juice at the breakfast booth. As the philandering Lucy Redfield entered the café, Emily's character folded her arms and whispered something nasty to her on-screen sister. It was a small movement but specific and revelatory, her character instantly revealed as a snotty older sister who knew just exactly how to make life more difficult than it really was. Emily appeared a second time as Robert Kincaid (Clint Eastwood) was walking out, this time on the receiving end of a whisper, even if she was too busy eyeing the stranger to fully register the message.

I held my tongue, deciding it a greater compliment to regard the scene as a natural flowing element of a narrative that had my full attention. Emily remained tense for the entire movie, gripping the armrests like we were about to take a roller-coaster plunge. It seemed that half the audience had already cried and dried their eyes at least once, only to lose it again when Francesca and her husband pulled up behind Robert Kincaid on his way out of town. As the credits rolled we all stood and clapped for a good fifteen minutes. We waved at the exiting stars as though it was their final public appearance, marking pinnacle performances that they wouldn't dare attempt to outshine. For some the action of cheering was so emotional as to appear desperate, as though they believed that the moment they stopped clapping the crew would immediately board their plane, the spell would be broken, and they'd all be left to grind forward with lives that now seemed trivial and undaring and obscure. It was Emily's idea to take a walk around town, to stay in Winterset a little longer, which made me think that the locals weren't the only ones who would've preferred that the story had never ended.

We didn't talk much as we strolled along under streetlights in the shadows of trees whose roots, in places, had burst open the sidewalk. There were a lot of reasons to love Emily Schell, and while I was ashamed of my cowardly desire to see her detained in Des Moines, I couldn't understand why she didn't apply to at least one college I could afford, what she was waiting for, why I was a virgin, and what she expected me to do about it all. We passed Roland's Barber Shop and Shelly's Express Subs. We passed houses with front lawns lit by the trance blue light of TV screens through living room windows. Aside from the advertisements for the famous bridges or the John Wayne Museum, I discovered Winterset a town no different from all the small places I'd traveled for weekend wrestling tournaments.

Eventually the street we were following dead-ended. We continued through a grassy meadow and along the edge of a cornfield. I missed the eeriness of the country that I'd known so well on my grandfather's farm. Emily kept pacing ahead with her hands folded behind her back, avoiding my eyes, occasionally looking up or off into the distance. Corn tassels swayed in the breeze like a community of willowy worshippers bowing to the white moon. It wasn't until we'd fully separated ourselves from the neighborhood and its streetlights that Emily finally spoke up.

"I sort of hate Robert James Waller," she said. "How could he put Francesca in such an impossible situation? Why couldn't her husband at least have been a bit of a jerk, or having an affair of his own? It just kills me. Even the way it was raining in that last scene, so Robert and Francesca could hardly see each other through the window. I don't think I could do that to a character. It's too cruel."

I thought about it, wondering if the author ever viewed the situation in such terms, acknowledging himself as the cause of the tragedy. "So it would've been better if Robert never showed up?"

"Oh, God. It hurts too much to think about it. I wish someone would've just pulled the fire alarm ten minutes before the movie ended."

Emily stepped closer to the nearest row of stalks, brushing her hand over them as we passed. There was something heartbreaking about the gesture. Our walk wasn't the amorous saunter I'd imagined, but revealed itself as the bittersweet culmination of a hundred indefinably tender moments that might have ended in starry-eyed embraces and never did. Watching her tromp stubbornly over the clumped earth, a flexing siren in sandals, lifting her skirt as she bobbed along left and right—I braced myself for the decision to once and for all desist.

"It's even worse that her kids were so rotten," she said. "Those actors didn't even sound Iowan."

"Iowegian."

"Is that how you say Iowan in Davenport?"

"According to Katie, Iowegian is more correct than Iowan. She said some newspaperman from Missouri bought the *Daily Iowegian* and changed it to the *Daily Iowan* without consulting anyone."

"I wouldn't believe everything Katie says about people from Missouri. A couple of years ago she went there for a camp for sick kids and ended up coming home after three days. She kept complaining that the counselors were all speaking in double negatives. And just so you know, she doesn't bother asking me anymore why we're only friends. I'm pretty sure she's decided to keep you for herself."

Emily laughed ("Take five!"), but so nervy and unnaturally that I could have mistaken it for the laughter of one of the teen characters in the movie. Then she spun around as though suddenly sensing that we were being followed. Of course there was no one there, but she saw the action all the way through, holding a hand out to keep me quiet as she listened for the source of her alarm.

"Sorry," she finally said. "Thought it might've been ol' Bubba from *Dark Night of the Scarecrow*." She hopped over a muddy patch and continued along. I looked back a few times toward the road, like I might've heard something, too.

"What would you say when Katie used to ask you about that?"

"Ask about what?" she said, placing a hand on her forehead, feigning embarrassment at forgetting what we'd been talking about. She was acting now, further convincing me that our night would only end in a nerve-racked rejection. I walked faster, raising my knees higher, marching along as I begged myself just to get it out of the way.

"When she used to ask you why we're only friends, what did you say?"

Emily sped up for a few paces, then thought better of it and suddenly stopped. She searched the stars like a chess player trying to read a chessboard with many more pieces than she knew how to play. She finally sighed and faced me.

"Just promise not to marry my sister, okay? At least not until she's eighteen."

"You want me to marry your sister?"

"I was joking," she said. "Why are you looking at me like that?"

"I don't want to marry your sister."

"Relax."

"If you ever wanted to kiss me, but you didn't because you were afraid of what Katie would think . . . well, I don't know what I would think. Tell me this, if that was me driving out of town, and if you didn't do something fast, you'd never see me again, what would you do? Just tell me, so I won't have to spend the rest of my life wondering."

While Emily's hands were already hanging at her sides, at that moment they seemed to fall even further. Next she raised them to her hips and glared at me through the same stern secretary eyes that she'd employed in the St. Pius hallway the second time I met her. But this time she was genuinely speechless, and in the window of her perplexity I nearly jumped the gap between us and kissed her. Then a strange thing happened, which was that I was marching over to her and she wasn't backing away even as I combed my hands into her hair and pressed her mouth against mine to thieve a five-second kiss. When I stepped back Emily was already wide-eyed on her tiptoes, covering her cheeks and then her lips where my lips had finally tasted them.

"I love you," I said, perfectly timed to a tornado siren whaling off in the distance. "If you want to go, we can go, but you were the most beautiful girl in the movie, and I'm not saying that because you're my favorite actor and I love you. Now please stop covering your cheeks. I know you're blushing, so there's no point trying to hide it."

Emily stopped covering her cheeks, which is when I detected them pooling in hot crimson that spread to her forehead and neck, and even heated her eyes so that they were soon protecting themselves with a thin layer of watery reflection. With every word I knew I was pushing her closer to losing the control she was attempting to establish with her jaw locked, her brow flexed, her shoulders pulled back against the desperate urge to cower.

"I'm sorry," I said.

"Really?"

"No."

"Then why did you say that?"

"I love you."

"Shit," she shouted, throwing her hands into the sky. She turned a circle and slapped her side, then stepped forward to hit me open-handed in the chest. "That's *my* line," she said, placing her hands on my shoulders and raising on her tiptoes again to be kissed.

Sixteen

Like a prison guard on the scent of a detainee who's had enough, who can't take another prison meal or group shower, or lay awake for another long deafening night of profane shouts and makeshift drumsticks banging against metal beds, Maureen Schell knew that her elder daughter was about to fly the proverbial coop. I was convinced that bad luck had nothing to do with her announcement the morning following the premiere that Emily would be taking the SAT exam a third time in an effort to sway the Yale admissions board. For two weeks following our first kiss Emily had to attend a Princeton Review cram course that met every weeknight from eight to eleven. Given her extra-curricular activities, there was suddenly and literally no time for fooling around. Then, as a reward for Emily's efforts, the following weekend Mrs. Schell took Emily and Katie on a shopping trip to Chicago. Completely fed up, I called late one night, probably waking the whole house.

"This new schedule isn't working. What is this? Some new kind of Catholic torture?"

"Trust me, I don't like it, either, but keep it together, George. Meet me tomorrow morning at the park and we'll hook up before school."

"What about now? What I am supposed to do right now?"

"Write me a poem. Or a song."

"Write you a what? Or a what?"

"A poem or a song."

"WhaddayouthinkI'msomekindasicko? I want to kiss your lips. I'm not a singer and I'm sure as hell not interested in pervy poetry. I respect you a lot more than that."

"Thank you."

"And maybe I want to brush my hands against your breasts, with the outside of my hands. That way I won't really be able to feel anything, but you will. Let's not rush things. But I want to say that pretty soon these things won't be pervy at all, and you'll want me to use the front of my hands."

"I agree," she said, completely serious. "These things are not pervy, but it's a good idea to start with only the backs of our hands and the bottoms of our feet."

"Exactly."

"Good."

"Great."

"See you in the morning," she said, which turned out a bright quiet morning rocking gently on a swing set getting to know the lips I'd longed for from every angle. Emily didn't kiss at all like a prude. Her mouth fell open soft and supple as her neck heated up. She was graceful in her tender desire but urgent to be held, recognized, understood in every way. Her proud girlish body was a kettle quaking at a near boil. We raised up and tasted each other's tongues, biting the tips, slowly searching along the ridges of teeth, really tasting and feeling until our mouths were synchronized in pliability, wetness, temperature, and coiling movement, our pressing bodies bursting beneath corduroys and thick schoolgirl bras, the blossoming fire below her belt, my own sex seeking out that heat, reaching desperately to be smothered by it.

We drove to school together, then entered the building from opposite wings, enjoying the secret that we knew would only last for so long.

It came as no surprise that our stealthy new demeanor only drew more attention from Smitty and the rest of our friends, who kept bugging us for details about our big night in Winterset. Emily told them we got towed after double-parking and blocking in Clint Eastwood, who gave us the finger. I returned all Smitty's questions by whistling old Irish tunes taught to me by my sly grandpa George. I refused to say anything to jinx my sensuous new life that swelled as big as the Mississippi River, spilling muddy brown east and west to both seas. Emily and I made excuses to leave an hour earlier for school, then met up at the rear parking lots of strip malls, on covered dugout benches, and in any number of woodsy settings along the greenbelt bike trail between Urbandale and Clive. Each time we advanced our romantic cause and hardly marked the same territory twice. Several times that week she pulled me into the courtyard with its tall wrought-iron fence, rusty and grand, still preaching the days of clerics and caged puberty that we now felt destined to destroy. Her hair fell in front of her face like a nymphet veil and I brushed it back while we kissed, not caring at all about the grumpy hags judging us from the attendance office window. As we had been warned all along that it would, the last few weeks of high school blurred by trancelike, well flavored by expectations of newborn independence. With every touch and word passed between the inch of space from my lips to hers, Emily and I celebrated our own graduation into adulthood by way of a secret romance lorded over by larger events that had yet to articulate their imminence. I was never so restless or so sated by such little sleep. In the hours of her absence the Emily Schell of my imagination became braver, more charming, as wise as a black diva princess on dusty vinyl belting out the whole beautiful, decrepit truth.

Seventeen

The last weeks of school were marked by several dramatic episodes worth mentioning as a means of painting a more holistic portrait of our budding affair and the many emotions in its near periphery. Around this time Des Moines was introduced to its first group of resettled Sudanese who'd spent most of their lives in refugee camps in Kenya. There was talk of a major banking merger that would result in twenty thousand Wells Fargo workers' losing their jobs, though in the end the deal didn't go through. Mr. Schell was busy making arrangements on a second Schell's Shirtworks store in Iowa City. Emily committed to attending Northwestern in Chicago. Katie's symptoms were beginning to act up again, but she hadn't spent a night in the hospital in months and was now memorizing "Song of Myself" just for kicks. As far as school was concerned, in our final few days of secondary education my fellow classmates succumbed to hysterical farewells, overdue apologies, breakups, reunions, and raw attempts at last-minute hookups. Sam Traxler and Jacob Evans, who'd been rivals their whole lives, decided to finally duke it out in the cafeteria. It was an epic brawl featuring smashed tables, ancillary injuries, and nose blood splattered on potatoes and pork cutlets. (The lunch ladies who were being replaced by a cheaper food service company did nothing to stop it.) On the last day of high school, according to tradition, all the seniors skipped.

It seemed our entire student careers had led to that moment of careening down a wooded country road in the back of Hadley's truck with four kegs and a dozen classmates, laughing and shouting and holding on for dear life. Speakers blared and kegs tipped over and rolled and attacked. We gathered smoke and dust on our tongues as our eyes rattled and our faces blurred. Frightened bullfrogs leapt into a mangy stream, splashing in sequence as we blew past. The gravel road dead-ended somewhere out in Adel. Hadley slammed the brakes and Nat Fry fell out the side and landed in a bush with his beer can still upright in his hand. The ensuing caravan of seniors made the forest make room.

It was a long day of sport drinking and all the games that end in painful drunkenness. By noon Hadley found out that Tino went skinny-dipping with his younger sister, which Tino attempted to rationalize as "legitimate campsite bathing." This was followed by a shoving match and several Mexican insinuations, then a rollicking old-boy wrestling match that Smitty and I felt it our drunken duty to complicate. Around sunset I witnessed our valedictorian puke on her bare feet and wash them while dancing in the stream. The bonfire was burning out of control, its sparks a constant threat to forest and drunkard alike. Caught making out behind the picnic pavilion, Emily and I were outed, cheered, and finally designated the royal couple of the day.

"Can you do me a favor?" she asked, tugging at the purple string of Mardi Gras beads around her neck.

"Anything. You want my shoes? I got them on sale, direct from the warehouse."

"Shut up, George. I'm going to walk over to that bonfire and

I want you to shove me backward into the middle where it's good and hot."

"Are you drunk, finally? I'm a little drunk, but not nearly as bad as I was at noon."

"I'm bored. Is college going to be like this? All blood and puke?"

"Looks like it," I said, as Tino swerved his way over waving a lighter that he thought was still lit. When I clinked his cup it fell out of his hand and spilled. After staring at the confounding sight of foam melting into dirt, he sadly stumbled away.

"Let's go," Emily said, taking my hand. She led the way through the zigzag parking lot of cars and trucks, toward the bike path and the darkness on the other side of the road. A group of classmates with hoarse voices stumbled onto the path farther down, pissing and lighting cigarettes. We started the three or four miles back to West Des Moines as if answering the far-off call of traffic barreling down Interstate 80. A few times I fell a half step behind, just enough to view the back of Emily's legs, her neck, the sideways sway of her breasts. We hadn't exactly been taking things slow, but I'd yet to see her fully naked and still had a hard time believing this was all really happening. The increasing noise of motors and speeding cars against the wind sounded somehow pleasant and sparkling with life. Emily finally grabbed my hand and pulled me along.

"Katie says you're taking us fishing. Apparently you promised her."

"I was thinking Sunday at Saylorville."

"All right. I'll tell her."

"Think she knows?"

"There's very little Katie doesn't know," she said, like it wasn't as big a deal as I was making it out to be. "Excited about all the girls you're going to meet in Iowa City?"

"I don't think she knows," I said.

"That was evasive."

"I'm not sure about Iowa City girls. If I meet one with cute little feet just like yours, maybe I'll want to photograph those feet. But I wouldn't go any further than that."

Emily smirked and slightly swerved. At this pace it would've taken all night to get home. There were geographical dilemmas to overcome and pressing decisions to make, but we were content walking and putting them off for another night. Emily was my girlfriend and for the moment that's all that mattered. We were more or less sober by the time we hopped the fence into her neighborhood, setting off motion detectors that triggered security lights yard by yard as we strolled up her street. We plopped down in the driveway by the side of her garage and laughed off alcoholic classmates, bitter wrestling coaches, lazy French teachers, and unsolved stranglings. When the security lights had all clicked off we started kissing. For the last kiss Emily held my face and licked a slow line up my neck. We whispered our good nights and I watched her hurry across the lawn to the front door. She waved before covering her mouth and smelling her breath and slipping inside. Hiking the rest of the way home took almost two hours but she was with me and still there on my lips when I fell into bed, believing she was mine.

Eighteen

I overslept the Sunday morning of our fishing jaunt to Saylorville Lake, waking to the slow groan of the garage door as my parents returned from my mom's bell choir performance at the seven-o'clock Mass. This implied not only a partially broken promise to Katie Schell, who'd insisted we set out like professionals at the crack of dawn, but also a reduced probability of stealing away in Zach's car, which was already outfitted with rods and reels after his trip to Petoka the day before. But it turns out Zach had the day off at Gordo's and had therefore spent the previous night drinking himself authoritatively retarded among a group of bartenders and servers behind the locked doors of any number of closed-for-the-night restaurants or bars in the greater Urbandale–Windsor Heights areas. He didn't bat an eye when I entered his room to search every floor-strewn pair of pants for his keys. I returned upstairs to find my dad attending to a spitting slab of bacon whose prolific grease would soon be put to the task of frying eggs (this was five or six years before his first heart attack, which would prevent any such indulgences thereafter). "If you catch anything impressive," he advised, "throw it back. Shows respect. And keep your shirt on, all right? Girls don't like a show-off."

It was still only eight-fifteen when I set off for the Schells' house with the wind dragging my hair, grooving side to side on hot vinyl seats as I constructed the colors and smells of a summer love affair at an isolated cabin up north. Ours would be a laissez-faire love with speed options, each yearning squelched in a fleshy performance designed specifically to fit the need. I arrived at the Schells' doorstep bursting with a potency that felt like knowledge. This feeling was somewhat diminished when Mrs. Schell arrived covered in sweat with an unsheathed tennis racquet in her right hand, displaying the sort of disbelief of a national champ who'd just been cheated on a line call. I wouldn't have been surprised to find out she'd dashed off the court in the middle of league play, outsprinting the cars on the highway just to give me the third degree before I took her daughters out fishing.

"It's Sunday, George. Kind of early, don't you think?"

I mumbled an apology, even knowing this was all an act. Katie assured me she'd covered all the bases, leaving nothing to chance— her mom had been aware of our plan for at least a week. "Actually, I'm late. Katie wanted me here at seven. Today's our big day out at Saylorville Lake."

Mrs. Schell smirked, unhappily, offering nothing more than a prolonged gaze of disapproval, apparently expecting that under its influence I might confess whatever perverted scheme I'd expected to disguise by throwing a few fishing rods in the backseat. Our stare-down ended with a phone call that prompted Mrs. Schell to withdraw, but not before closing the door in order to remind me that her air-conditioning system wasn't designed for strays hanging out on the front porch. In her absence I entertained myself with the notion of swinging her onto the lawn for an impromptu tango, which would have ended with me dashing for the front door to lock her out of her own house.

A minute later Mr. Schell appeared in Hitchcockian distortion through the panels of his leaded-glass windows. A sip of coffee splashed onto his slipper as he stepped outside in a thick white robe with oversized pockets that made him look like some kind of Beverly Hills imp. Even the gray in his hair was babyish against the thick white cotton.

"Well, shoot," he said, casting me and the coffee stain equally inquisitive grins. He patted my shoulder, careful to avoid spilling any more coffee but clearly attempting a masculine exchange that would allow me to understand something he was feeling. "Sunday is THE DAY," he said. "The DAY of the week. So how goes it, George? Katie's been up since cock-a-doodle-doo. Where're the big dogs bitin' today?"

"Hopefully at Saylorville Lake."

"What are you going after?"

"Northern, mostly. Walleye, too, if we can find the right spot."

Mr. Schell nodded, centering the welcome mat with his foot. "Don't know if you've heard, but Emily's girlfriend Mel, from the volleyball team, she's moving into the ranch at the end of the block. She's a real sweet gal. Single, too."

"I heard that," I said. "But her freckles are pretty intense, and I think she's too tall for me."

"Tall is good. Isn't she one of the volleyball captains?"

"Yeah, but she always gets injured, and not during the games, either. Last year she tripped over a dishwasher door and broke her wrist. She's a serious hazard."

Mr. Schell chuckled as he stared absentmindedly around the yard. When he asked about our senior skip day, I told him I'd won some money playing horseshoes. (The last time I played horseshoes was probably in sixth grade, but horseshoes seemed the kind of subject a

Wakonda Country Club member out of the loop of manly entertainment might enjoy.) While I wasn't sure how to interpret his attempt to match me with Mel Gerbeck, I figured it was no more than small talk when he insisted I join him for juice and doughnuts instead of waiting on the porch like a Roto-Rooter salesman. As we passed through the front hallway I overheard Mrs. Schell drawing near the high point of an upstairs lecture related to our skip day and its effect on Emily's ultimate GPA. Mr. Schell led me to the kitchen, which was sparkling white with lavender napkins that matched the many curtains on its many windows. We sat at a big oak table where he slid me a box of sprinkled doughnuts. He was cutting his and eating it with a fork. The doughnuts turned out to be disappointingly dry.

"Pardon the mess," he said, nodding at the Schell's Shirtworks boxes stacked up beside the door to the garage. "I like to hand-deliver orders for my most important customers. Of course it drives Maureen batty, because I could just as easily leave them in the trunk. But when I bring them inside, at least I feel like I'm treating my product with respect."

"That makes sense," I said, trying my best to swallow my doughnut, the whole time thinking that this man needs a man. (I've since come to the conclusion that Mr. Schell was a regular guy once, before he was contained under the feminine authority of a barely legal actress, an anarchistic girl-woman eighth grader, and a castrating wife with tennis legs so sharp he was lucky to wake up with his feet still attached to his legs. Despite the fact that he'd run several T-shirt competitors into the ground, which implied some amount of backbone, I imagined that in private he mostly tiptoed around his wife, whose browbeating nature very likely extended to sex.) Within a minute or two we'd already run out of conversation and were both relieved at the sound of Katie trouncing down the steps. She was gripping the railing with one hand and two crutches with the other. I guessed her symptoms were now advancing from moderate to moderate-severe.

"You're late," she said, sighing in colossal disappointment. "The fish already ate breakfast without us."

"I've been down here since seven o'clock."

"*No te creo, amigo.* I've been up since six-forty."

When Katie hit the last step her neck twisted in a way that suggested her head was becoming an increasing heavy load. She swerved her way to her father and hugged him around the neck. I noticed a new charm in the way she surfed her stilted muscles, grooving like a karaoke singer who couldn't hear how off-key she really was. Maybe she'd learned something from our driving lessons over the winter at the icy Valley West parking lot, when I'd taught her to turn into the spins and ride them out. Her dad offered her the other half of his doughnut, but Katie just made a face. She swung her way over to the chair nearest the windows.

"What are you girls doing about church?" Mr. Schell asked.

"Mom said we can go to the short Mass at five o'clock at the hospital."

Mr. Schell scratched his chin, acting like he'd never heard of any short Mass at any hospital. "You were born in that hospital. Maybe you should go to the *long* Mass."

"There *is* no long Mass. They're all short 'cause there's no singing. Singing wakes up all the patients."

Mr. Schell threw me an amused look of suspicion. Katie started paging through the comics, washing her hands of the matter. Emily came down a minute later tugging on her right ear. The way she winced at the assaulting brightness said all there was to say about the argument she'd just had with her mother. *"Bonjour,"* she said, hard-heartedly, like we were all in trouble now that she was in trouble. "Katie. Dad. *George.*"

The way she said my name betrayed nothing but promised absolutely everything. While sitting next to Mr. Schell, I lost all sense of how much eye contact was considered normal. It was a rare pleasure to catch her just out of bed, still groggy, but I tried not to stare.

"Good morning," Mr. Schell and I said, in tandem.

"*Buenos días,*" Katie said.

"If there's no more doughnuts I'm going back to sleep."

"You can sleep once your line's in the water. Katie and I have big ambitions."

"By noon the fish will get too hot and hide way down deep," Katie said. "When they get hot, they won't eat a thing."

"Hope you're ready for a whole day of this sort of information. Last night Katie bought about five fishing magazines. I wouldn't be surprised if she read them cover to cover."

"Not true," Katie argued. "I read one article and it was in a *conservation* magazine, not a *fishing* magazine."

Emily picked at a few sprinkles at the bottom of the box. "I hope you've got weighters and floaties and all that stuff. We're not exactly outdoorspeople around here."

"We're set," I said, thinking Mr. Schell would be embarrassed by the comment, like he was just another coquette in their domestic rendition of *Little Women*. But he was entangled in a stare-down with the second half of his doughnut, seeming to have a talent for hearing only whatever pleased him, at least on Sunday mornings. Maybe he was devising a plan to calm his wife. Emily lowered her head to drink from the kitchen faucet. I loved watching her drink from the faucet and I wanted to kiss her and drink from the faucet at the same time.

Mr. Schell brought his plate to the sink and placed his hand on Emily's shoulder. He spoke softly. "I think Katie's right. You'd better be off."

"Isn't Katie always right?"

"She's hovering around ninety-nine percent."

Katie folded the comics and bowed. While she was standing up, her hand slipped from her crutch and she fell hard against the table, sending a mug with her name in big block letters banging to the floor. Orange juice spread across the surface, soaking napkins and place mats. A split second later, while hopping up to block a stream of orange juice from spilling onto the floor, I smacked a knee against the chair next to me. This offered a perfect opportunity to divert the attention from Katie's blossoming embarrassment. I started hopping around and hollering, "Oooh! Aaah! Oww!" doing my best to convince everyone I'd seriously damaged myself. Mr. Schell and Emily surged forward with mirrored expressions of uncertain worry. As they lowered me to the suspect chair their eyes darted back and forth between my squeezing grimace, the spilled orange juice, the broken cup, and my naked unmarked legs, trying to piece it all together.

I howled a few more times to work out the imagined pain. "Is there a funny bone in the knee?" I shouted. "Oooh! Ahhh! I think I nailed it!"

"Okay, okay," Emily said, attempting to appear calm. I'd clearly convinced her and Mr. Schell that I was the one who'd knocked over the orange juice. It was a much greater performance than I'd intended.

"Don't worry about the mess," Mr. Schell said, running a hand over his scalp as he headed for the sink.

"That was my favorite cup!" Katie shouted, trying to suppress the laughter that inevitably escaped in a burst of pandemic snorting glee. "What *was* that! Barn dance hip-hop? George! Oh my God! Did you take *lessons* for that!"

"He's hurt," Emily said, then grew suddenly unsure. She stepped in front of me and stared into my face to make up her mind.

"I think it's acute," I said.

"What are you talking about?" Emily asked, increasingly leery.

"You know, the sort of pain that hits hard at first, but then wears off a couple of minutes later?"

"Katie," Mr. Schell called out, in warning, looking fearful of an impending lawsuit. Katie couldn't help herself. She looked away, but kept huffing and puffing until her face was streaked with tears. Emily picked up the broken cup pieces as Mr. Schell wiped the floor, both of them acting as though a quick disposal of evidence was the best way to dismiss their own embarrassment and alleviate my pain.

A few minutes later everyone accepted that I was officially healed. Mr. Schell asked me to get his girls back in time for the five-o'clock Mass. I told him not to worry, that I had lawn-mowing and garage-hosing duties later that afternoon. I couldn't believe that after all that commotion Mrs. Schell hadn't made an appearance. But then, as we were heading out the front door, her voice came streaming through the intercom speakers in the kitchen, living room, and front hall.

"SUNSCREEN!" she shouted, as if it were her final deathbed directive.

Nineteen

Out at Saylorville we marched along a mushy trail swamped with mosquitoes and biting flies further roused by our footsteps and Katie's crutches. We stomped over broken reeds and decayed logs, wooden planks thrown over mud pits. Katie was cursing from the start, aiming most of her frustrations at the Eagle Scout and his miniature wooden hut where we'd signed our agreement for the canoe rental. She couldn't slap at the pests biting at her hardworking arms, which were still grassy and slender, not nearly as muscular as I would've imagined. We found our canoe next to the rack lying upside down in the mud.

"Hurry up," Katie said. "Flip it over. The big ones are waiting."

I tripped on an anchor half-buried in the muck and fell to my hands. "The boat," Emily said. "She wants you to flip *the boat*."

On first sighting the canoe, I imagined Nicholas Parsons resting peacefully beneath it, sinking slowly into the mush that would leave a perfect imprint of his body. As soon as I stepped near it he'd leap at me with bloody eyes and a parasite-patrolled scalp, beads of sweat running down his cheeks like crude oil tears. I turned it over. A thousand crickets dashed in all directions.

Emily took one look and decided to fish off the shore. It wasn't a bad idea anyway. I gave her one of the rods and a small plastic case with a few jigs and surface lures. She wished us luck and set off on her own. I dragged the canoe to the edge of the lake, waiting for Katie to find her seat before shoving us into the water. She snapped into her life jacket and got her paddle wet for three or four strokes before I told her to relax and enjoy the ride. The trail had obviously worn her out, and I knew she would've kept paddling if I didn't say anything.

"You ever flip one of these things?" she asked, gripping the sides.

"Only once. But Zach was standing on the bow practicing crane kicks like the Karate Kid."

"That Eagle Scout sure was something. Sitting in a hut with a fake chimney. What an idiot." She put her sunglasses on and searched from one side of the lake to the other. There were a few groups at the beach on the far side, but only one other canoe on the lake. "Where're all the other fishermen?"

"It's no motors for a month. They're probably all out at Gray's Lake."

"Perfect," she said. "Crank it up, why don't you?"

I dug my paddle in, swiftly pulling us around the bend. We dropped anchor at a cove where a set of willow trees stretched over the water and shaded the surface. I handed Katie a rod equipped with a push-button reel I thought she'd find easier to cast than the spinning reels Emily and I were using. She still had difficulties, though, exacerbated by the stiffness in her arms that often resulted in the lure helicoptering and entangling itself around the tip of the pole. Other times she'd hurl it so hard and release it so late that the lure splashed wildly a few feet from the canoe. After six or seven tries she calmed down and managed a clean cast. With Zach's new reel I found I could cast almost double the distance. I aimed parallel to the shoreline, knowing I was covering hot spots the entire way back.

After ten minutes of quiet casting, Katie issued orders to move where the big fish were swimming deep. I paddled us out to the middle, thinking it was a good idea to do a little jigging where Katie could simply drop her lure and wait for a bite. I'd forgotten seat pads and a net and considered I'd be better prepared when I returned next weekend alone with Emily. We'd lay a camping pad across the bottom of the canoe and then sleep on the lake, floating wherever the wind directed us, kissing for hours. She wasn't far away, plopped down on a long flat boulder, digging into the tackle box. From the few times we'd been fishing, I knew she liked to change lures often, which meant her line wasn't in the water very much.

"How many have you got so far?" she shouted, knowing Katie would've made a big ruckus if we'd landed one. Her voice carried lightly over the lake.

"How many have *you* caught?" Katie shouted back. "And dead floaters don't count!"

Emily waved us off and went back to tying her lure. I looked around for the other fisherman, but he'd apparently disappeared into one of the coves. While Katie was pulling some weeds off her lure, I told her she was the only cartoonist I knew. She'd promised I could read her graphic novella a few months before, but then reneged, insisting it was still under construction.

"A book at fourteen," I said. "It's a little ridiculous, even for you. You're making the rest of us look like deadbeats."

"Anyone stuck in a wheelchair can draw enough pictures to fill a book. Eventually I want to write screenplays. If Emily's going to make it big, she's gonna need a good script, something written just for her."

Katie tried to cast but the reel jammed when the line was only half-way out. This meant that her jig couldn't reach the bottom, the only depth at which it was probable to attract fish. But by this time Katie was more interested in conversation. Instead of annoying her with all the problems she wasn't even aware of, I pressed her for movie plots.

"I've got this one idea I think is pretty good, though I don't know all the ins and outs of screenwriting. Not yet. But anyway, the protagonist is an orthodontist named Mr. Horner who has seven kids. There's only one shower at home, so they all bathe in the neighborhood swimming pool. Mrs. Horner, who's like real young and skinny and dumb, she's afraid to tell Mr. Horner that she's pregnant again, so she gorges on fried chicken and watermelon ice cream in order to fatten up, to disguise the pregnancy. She also dresses the kids for school the night before, to save time in the morning. Oh yeah, and instead of preparing lunch boxes, she puts all the ingredients in a big blender. Bread, bologna, chips, apples, all blended up and poured into thermal mugs. It's mostly a drama about a marriage, but I want it to be really funny. That's the most important thing."

I wondered to what extent the family in her script was based on the Hathaways. "However it works out," I said, "I'll be first in line."

Katie gave me a pleased little nod. She unbuckled the top of her life jacket and turned in my direction to stretch her legs out and roll her neck around. The Schell women had the most aristocratic necks and long summery legs, perhaps Katie more than any of them. She must have noticed me staring because she stretched even further, crossing her legs several different ways and even reaching down to massage her ankle and run a hand over her thigh on the way back up. I cast again, roughly squinting in order to suggest that I'd only turned her direction after being hit by a blinding glare off the water. But my attention hadn't gone unnoticed.

"Good to know these legs aren't totally useless. Think they're good enough for cameos? Or even a starring role in a shaving cream ad?"

"They're good enough," I said.

"You're lying."

"The panty hose companies might pay more," I said, then abruptly retreated to the previous topic. "So if Emily plays the mom, I guess she'd have to put on some pounds, huh?"

"I guess so, but the Hollywood bigwigs would probably change that and make it so she ate all this ice cream but never gained any weight. I think it would be funnier if she got super fat and then there'd be this wild scene where Mr. Horner takes her to the hospital after she complained about a really bad stomachache. Then she comes out with a baby. Anyway, I've heard that screenwriters are like the dogs of the movie business, so I wouldn't expect the bigwigs to keep everything the same."

"I get it," I said, realizing by the dozy sound of my voice that I'd stopped giving Katie my full attention. I always had at least one eye on Emily, who was marching up and down the shore, rising to her tiptoes each time she cast. After a while I pulled the anchor up again, thinking I ought to get Katie's jig closer to the bottom if I expected her to actually catch something. I paddled in Emily's direction, convincing myself that if I hooked a big muskie, she'd have sex with me later that night, or even before the five-o'clock Mass at the hospital.* As our canoe drew closer, Emily's voice sounded out, groggy and grim.

"Have we caught enough yet for lunch?"

---

*My most convincing dream during this time involved a visit to a debutante ball at a stately mansion in the Deep South. Midway through the party Emily had dragged me into the butler's quarters where we crawled inside a peculiar cupboard stacked with silverware the size of tractor attachments, and shiny porcelain plates like round skating rinks. After crawling inside a tank-sized teacup we sat facing each other, disrobing and throwing each article of clothing over the rim of the cup. Emily clamped her feet behind my back and we rocked back and forth, soon enough finding a common groove, just like when we'd kissed on the swing set before school. The teacup rattled and rocked along with us, banging against the plates as Emily shuddered and I came and we both burst out laughing, swearing, praising the gods of every religion we ever heard of. I woke the next morning with semen drying on my thighs and knotting my pubic hairs, feeling duped, cheated, etc. This dream still returns to me from time to time, with the same results, and I'm convinced it always will.

"How's about a worm sandwich?" Katie shouted. She'd only been casting every few minutes, convincing me that, like her older sister, she preferred the idea of fishing to the reality of the routine. The humidity bulged and I hadn't gotten a single strike. About fifty yards off Emily set her pole down and pulled a small notebook from her pocket, occasionally looking up to read the trace clouds and the sky. Reminding myself that Katie had never caught a fish, I snapped out of my daydream, determined to get her one. I paddled closer to shore where spidery trees hung over the water, appearing to dip over for a drink. The wind had died down. Without bothering to drop the anchor, I exchanged Katie's jig for a floating lure with leopard spots and an underside painted to resemble the pale belly of a frog. This lure was sure not to get caught in the shallow underbrush, and I liked the stealthy quality of its big blind eyes. For a moment I drifted off again, reliving the night I discovered Emily, the actress.

It seemed we'd found a perfect spot, until Katie's second or third cast, when the frog went sailing into the trees. She jerked her pole, which only dug the treble hooks in deeper. I thought for sure she'd snap the line. I sort of hoped she would, knowing it would be easier to let it go and tie on another jig, even if the frog lure happened to be one of my favorites.

"You little crapper!" she yelled, yanking the pole every which way. "Get out of that tree or I'll—"

Emily started walking along the shore to untangle the frog. But there was no clear pathway and the climb up the side of the tree would probably prove too difficult. Either way, Katie was looking to curse the tree from its roots before Emily got there.

"You little bugger! Shithead! Whatever your name is!"

The line snapped. Katie's first reaction was to laugh, even though a moment later she was flashing me an expression of grave guilt, like she'd ruined the whole day with one irreparable cast. I decided to jump into the lake. This decision also had something to do with my expectations of having sex with Emily. I took off my shirt and sandals and stepped onto the bench. I was careful not to rock the canoe as I jumped. The surface of the water was lukewarm. Near my feet it was cold enough to send a cool shot up to my head. I sidestroked to the shore.

"You didn't have to do that," Katie said, setting the pole down.

"It's a five-dollar lure," I said, kicking and gliding on my back.

"And a million-dollar farmer's tan. *Dang.* You're scaring all the fish away."

I swam up to a set of boulders near the edge, grabbing one of the stronger-looking willow branches to pull myself onto shore. As I climbed along the trunk of the willow tree, I imagined I was walking a dinosaur's prickly tail onto its arched spine. For as long as I could I ascended heel over toe with my arms out like an acrobat, then crouched down and shinnied. At some point I looked up to find Katie slightly crooking her neck to better gaze at me, forcing a sudden consciousness of my erect nipples and the red hairs curling over the waist of my shorts. When I could safely advance no farther I squeezed my legs around the trunk and gripped one of the limbs and leaned out as far as I could, scratching my chest and stomach as I stretched for the frog. Two of the barbs were embedded as deep as they could go. As I was stripping away a few offshoots to improve my reach, I looked up at the sound of a metallic thud echoing from the canoe. Katie had knocked one of her crutches against the middle bench. She stood up and pointed to the water just below me.

"George! I see one. It's a monster!"

I saw it, too. At first I mistook it for a long dark rock, but then its tail fanned and it turned in place. I didn't expect to find trout at Saylorville Lake, but there it was, a big lazy brown at least the length of my forearm.

"Take the other pole," I whispered.

"We'll put it on the wall!" Katie shouted, gripping the sides and stepping carefully over the middle bench. The canoe was steady but slowly rotating. She grabbed my pole and sat down, then searched the shallow water for her fish.

"You've got to open that metal clip first. Open that gasket. Just like that."

I lost the trout for a moment, until it fanned its tail a second time. Its flank design was like black rain splattered over dusk, its eyes obsidian stones.

"Hold the line with your left hand and when you cast, let go just like you're throwing a baseball. Throw it soft."

I kept my sights on the fish and tried to judge its weight. Emily had disappeared in the reeds, but soon the reeds were parting and I saw her arms brushing them from side to side as she pushed through. I hoped by the time she showed up that Katie would be holding a big brown trout with both hands, doing everything she could to keep it from flopping out of her grip and back into the lake. Katie practiced her motion, carefully waving the pole back and forth while keeping a grip on the line. My lure was swinging around the rod tip, sure to get tangled. She sat tall and looked down into the water.

"It's gonna sink fast," I said. "Try to aim in front of his mouth."

"I know. Shut up."

"Start reeling in right away and keep the tip up."

"I'm gonna eat it," she said. "I'm going to eat it whole."

As soon as the lure hit the water Katie grabbed hold of the line and closed the gasket. I'd rigged a white jig with a red worm. It was only a foot deep when the trout went for it. He went for it all the way and I knew she had him because the white and red completely vanished. He took off, running along the shoreline, directly away from the canoe but curving against the drag. It curved out toward the middle. Katie's pole was deeply bent.

When Emily popped out of the reeds there were thin red cuts on her shins and hands. She licked the top of her right hand and after that didn't pay it any attention. I felt the tree shake as she crashed into it and wrapped her arms around the trunk so she could lean out toward the water and cheer. Katie was reeling hard, cursing again, too. Every time she pulled the fish closer to the canoe, he'd dive under it. Then she'd stop reeling, not knowing what happened or why she couldn't see him yet.

"Flip it in the boat!" Emily shouted. "Flip it in the boat!"

"He doesn't want to flip! Dang! What's this guy's problem! The little bitch!"

I could tell the trout was on the other side of the canoe now and dragging out more line. Katie's rod started straightening out. I thought she might've lost him. "Keep reeling," I said. "Tighten the slack! Keep the tip up!"

"I'm gonna eat him alive!" she shouted, starting to reel again. The rod tip immediately bent down, which made me think her fish had swallowed the lure whole. I figured she'd land him even if she let the line go loose again. The wind picked up. The canoe started drifting farther toward the middle. I realized I should've dropped the anchor before swimming ashore.

"Don't stop reeling!" I yelled.

"Can you see it?" Emily shouted.

For the most part Katie kept reeling in, but occasionally she'd grab onto the bench to steady herself, allowing her trout to run off with more line. After a while she realized what was happening and got fed up. She took to her feet.

"Sit down, Katie!"

"Keep the tip up!"

"He's a whale," Katie yelled. "A real mean bastard!"

Desperate not to lose her fish, soon enough Katie figured out how to steady herself with one hand while holding the fishing pole with the line squeezed against it with the other, thus enduring that the pole continued jerking down. The canoe swayed slightly side to side. Eventually her trout broke the surface, leaping half a foot out of the water, writhing to hurl the hook from his mouth. (It must've been a five-pounder, as big as the biggest I'd ever caught in the streams back in Davenport.) A second after it landed the line went taut. Katie sat down with her back turned to us and started reeling again. She steadied the pole between her knees and shined us a hungry grin. By Emily's frantic cheers I swore she might raise the whole lake and turn it inside out until Katie's trout came slapping down on the shore. I knew Katie was almost there. The pole was jerking straight down.

"Bring it home, Katie!" Emily shouted. "Bring it home to Mama!"

Katie leaned over the side, trying to pull her fish out by the line that I prayed wouldn't snap. She'd already raised him to the lip of the canoe when it slipped out of her hand (or let it go; she might've thought she'd be bitten) and her trout flipped back into the water, the shock of which had her kicking backward, then forward again to catch her balance. The canoe dipped toward us and then away from us, tilting so severely that the only sight of Katie for a split second was her ponytail swinging to the side. The canoe stalled on this angle. At the sound of a second metallic thud the canoe dipped even further and tipped back and Katie wasn't in it anymore. The slap of her body into the water was no louder than the trout's splash landing a minute before.

"Katie!" Emily shouted, her voice shaking with what I first interpreted as inordinate panic. But when Katie didn't shout back and the splashing sounds turned to silence I knew this was no longer a mere matter of wet tennis shoes and a runaway trout. Without a thought

Emily jumped into the lake and scrambled over the hardly submerged boulders. I fumbled down through the branches, soon finding myself underwater ten feet from the shore, my feet sinking into the spongy bottom. (In the benumbed seconds before reality reared its claws, I imagined that Katie had decided to jump in and swim her fish ashore, that she was now floating on her back, calmly clutching her pole as she kicked her way around the canoe. This was my first reaction, even though it didn't make any sense.) We likely both broke state swimming records as we hurled ourselves out to the middle. I begged that Katie was either playing a trick on us or was simply too wet and scared to scream back. I didn't care whether she was laughing or crying, only that we'd find her treading water on the other side of the canoe. But we didn't. Instead we found two life jackets drifting in opposite directions. Emily was already breathing heavy when she made her first dive under. I did the same. Time was painful and hard to judge while diving under and swimming in circles and coming back up only to tread water and catch our breath and dive under again. Emily held her breath much longer than I did, terrifying me each time I surfaced before her.

It was cooler down below. One time I touched the top of the weeds that stretched at least ten feet from the bottom, but I was breathless and couldn't see anything and had to kick-crawl back to the surface. There were Emily's underwater screams: Katie's name, in big bellowing reverberations. I swam closer to the noise until I bumped into her. She grabbed my arm and dragged me to the top and took one breath and discovered it was me and went back down. I continued diving as deep as I could, but with each attempt the bottom only grew more elusive. When Emily screamed again, her voice cracked underwater and the cracks echoed like sonar. I thought I saw a hand way down deep, something white, but I couldn't get there without taking another breath. I tried anyway, but the white was gone and I started to think it was just a piece of sunlight that got pinned deep down. I became so tired, I ended up keeping myself afloat hanging on the back of the canoe. When I looked inside it the only item left was my tackle box. I swam toward Emily, fearing each time she went down that she wouldn't return and I'd have to swim out alone. She wouldn't let me pull her to the canoe. I went back to diving until I'd swallowed too much water and couldn't hold my breath anymore. I started screaming for help, even though the beach was at least two hundred yards off, much too far to matter. We had to swim back to shore.

Emily crawled up the slimy rocks. She fell down against a willow tree. We were exhausted, shaking, breathing wrong. Out in the middle the canoe made slow circles. It might have been twenty minutes since Katie went under, but it might've been ten, too. Emily stared out at the canoe hugging herself with shaking lips and elbows and knees. When I helped her stand up her joints hardly bent. I forced her to run with me around the lake to the dock where we'd started. Every few minutes she'd stop and step out to the edge and check the middle of the lake. We eventually spotted both life jackets bumping against the rocks not far from the dock. Emily retched in the reeds. I grabbed Katie's jacket, holding it in the air like some idiotic prize. The buckles were all unclamped. I threw it to the ground and then kicked it into the bushes, already understanding that I would never see her again.

Some small birds flew up out of the reeds and over the lake. When Emily sprinted for the car I immediately chased her and could hardly keep up. She seemed to grow stronger the nearer we got to the parking lot, where we discovered the rental hut shut down and no sign of the Eagle Scout. Emily continued running to the car and banged on the hood and shouted my name to hurry me along. The road back to the highway was covered in white gravel that eventually gave way to glistening black asphalt, then concrete. *"We've got to get to a hospital!"* Emily kept screaming, as though we had Katie in the backseat and might save her if we delivered her fast enough to a doctor. After three or four miles we came upon a Casey's General Store.

"There's been a drowning!" I yelled as I ran inside, scaring the young Native American girl behind the counter. "Call the police!"

The girl did as I asked but never took her eyes off me. I was shoeless, shirtless, dripping wet. I could still hear Emily screaming at me to get us moving to the hospital. "She's not *at* the hospital," I explained, my voice trembling but relatively calm in the face of Emily's increasing delirium. I couldn't get her to change her mind. I wasn't sure if I should. She shrieked as I stepped back into the driver's seat. *"The hospital! Fucking shit, Katie! What the fucking shit!"* I put it in drive and sped for the highway.

Twenty

E mily dashed into the Mercy Frederick emergency room, demanding Katie's location and her condition and screaming, *"Did you save her or not!"* The other patients stiffened in bright-eyed alarm, backing away from the triage desk, pulling their kids into their arms, shifting seats to the corners of the room. Of course the attendant nurse tried to calm Emily down and get more basic information. Emily claimed her sister had been in a boating accident. We were assured that there was no such patient in the emergency room. A second nurse who just arrived on the scene asked if we were under the influence of any controlled substances like methamphetamine or LSD. Emily stormed from one side of the room to the other, erupting with profanity. The nurse behind the desk checked her computer and made a phone call and then apologized, telling me we must've come to the wrong hospital.

"She can't breathe!" Emily screeched. *"She can't fucking breathe!"*

The second nurse speed-walked down the same hallway she'd just come from. I stopped Emily and gripped her by the shoulders, forcing her to look at me. "We'll check her old room on the eighth floor," I said, realizing this plan would lead nowhere, but figuring there was no point arguing after having brought her this far. The attendant nurse shot me a dirty look, shaking her head and turning to the other patients like now they all had *two* lunatics on their hands. Emily made for the elevator just as the second nurse showed up with a doctor (himself maniacal-looking, with sickly yellow skin), both of them banding together with arms spread to block Emily's way. They ended up each grabbing a wrist and pulling in opposite directions as Emily raved and kicked and cursed, shivering now as she tried to shake herself free. As the nurse behind the desk grabbed her legs from behind and helped pin her to the floor, I shouted out that her sister had just drowned at Saylorville Lake. When they didn't let go of her I pulled the doctor's left arm behind his back, only to let go a few seconds later at his innocent and frustrated assertion that I was only causing more harm. I half turned as he removed a needle from his pocket and quickly plunged it into Emily's thigh. She went quiet and limp, her eyes almost immediately rolling back.

A minute later they propped her onto a gurney and tucked a blanket over her before wheeling her down the hallway. The doctor looked around at the blood marks on the floor, keeping his distance as he pointed at my bare feet. By the time security showed up he was handing me a blanket like the one they gave Emily, asking a nurse with red hoop earrings to bandage my foot. I sat down and waited for the police. There were two of them and they sat on each side of me, asking detailed questions about the drowning. I only answered the older guy. More than once my voice cracked and I felt like I was turning circles, floating in my chair. I imagined a brown trout dragging my fishing pole along the bottom of the lake. I pictured my shoes and tackle box sinking into the weeds. The younger cop kept prompting me for the color of Katie's life jacket. His ruined little frown gave me the feeling there was worse news to come, that perhaps while I was fishing, a gas explosion had decimated my house and family, or that Smitty had been sideswiped by a drunk. I kept waiting for the doctor to return and tell me that whatever drug he'd given Emily would blur her memory and she wouldn't have the slightest clue what went wrong out at Saylorville. I tried to guess how much she'd remember when she woke up, whether she'd have any idea who to blame. Before I realized what I was doing, I was already posing these questions to the cops.

Part

Two

Twenty-one

The funeral was held at a brick manor house with a wooden balcony and white banisters on a wooded square of land off Eighth Street I'd probably passed a thousand times and never noticed. Its sign was etched with a chubby Celtic script that hinted of Irish merriment and street parades and Katie Schell hopping out of her casket completely undead. The first thing I noticed as we pulled into the lot was the new bumper sticker on Mr. Schell's Beemer claiming him a PROUD PARENT OF AN HONOR ROLL STUDENT AT WHITFIELD PREP! My parents flanked me along the path and up the stairs, apparently as a gesture of protection. Zach was the first to step inside, or hobble, I should say, as he was wearing an old pair of penny loafers that barely fit. (I didn't know yet that the ceremony would be closed-casket and kept picturing Katie's bluish face on a white silk pillow, her painted lips and fingernails, a Snow White corpse with a mouth molded into a lollipop grin. I considered an illusionist act even more grotesque than her death, a Huckleberry Finn episode ending with Katie revealing herself as the pissed-off hag in the wheelchair at the back of the room.) I attempted a prayer as we walked along the main hallway. In the obituaries the Schells "politely requested that students attend the burial but not the wake services." Deep down I knew I was making a mistake, despite thinking that the easy choice of avoiding the Schells couldn't possibly be the right one.

There were two funerals that day at the Cohen Funeral Parlor, one Jewish and one Catholic, demarked by small rings of mourners in loose lines along the left and right side of the main entranceway. My family was gestured into the appropriate line by a gangly funeral director with moussed bangs perfectly straight across his forehead, his goody-goody altar boy appearance only increasing my fears about Katie's cosmetology. The hallway was filled with St. Pius parishioners in their best jewelry, teary-eyed teachers, men in yarmulkes, frail Jewish women in all black, Wakonda Country Clubbers with golf tans, the fat and stern, the saintly and sorrowful, even a pockmarked man weeping in bright rubber-ducky suspenders and pin-striped pants. I recognized a few of Emily's aunts and uncles, a cousin perhaps a year or two younger than Katie but hanging on her mother's arm like she was five years old. I guessed Mrs. Schell's Tennessee crew to be the group of loud ruddy men huddled near the bathrooms, spouting platitudes for the rest of us to overhear and benefit from. One of them kept glancing at me with a sour expression that gave me the feeling he was privy to every terrible, sick thing I'd ever done. (It's possible I only imagined this, that he hadn't noticed me, and he wasn't even Emily's uncle.) Those who knew me gave me sad little smiles. Others averted their view, not sure what to say or do.

Eventually I stepped out of line to search for Emily, hoping to find her somewhere other than front and center next to her parents. After a fast survey of Katie's funeral room and the two adjacent hallways, I hadn't spotted any of the immediate Schell family. I decided to wait outside the Jewish service, guessing they'd secluded themselves in the private grieving room around the corner. Peeping through the double doors, I saw a middle-aged woman with pigtails strumming a guitar and singing: "You watched me take the stage and fall . . . and cheered when I caught the fly ball." It was an awful song, but something about her discordant howls and the bad reception she was given made me love that stubborn-looking father of hers. I wanted a yarmulke of my own, and a long black coat. Most of the elderly folks in the front row were staring at the floor, one of them with a numerical tattoo on her arm. Soon the veins in my neck were swelling and pulsing and I didn't know if I was crying for Katie or myself or the six million Jews killed in the Holocaust. I escaped to the bathroom where I threw myself against the locked door of a corner stall and bawled. It took some time to recover. I waited to come out until I was sure the bathroom was empty, which made it all the more surprising to find one of the urinals occupied by a guy who looked big enough to play lineman for the Chicago Bears. He was a middle-aged guy in a flannel shirt, jeans, and cowboy boots. Thankful that I didn't know him, I took my time throwing water on my face and drying it, only to find that after washing his hands, the man continued to wait around, apparently in order to introduce himself.

"Excuse me, sir," he said, his accent calming and countrified, his expression neither hopeful nor pained in conciliation. It was an ordinary expression, recognizing an emotional bridge that needn't be crossed. "I was gassing my truck where you and yer friend called the *poh-leese*. Then I read about you all in the paper. Just wanted to say I'm real sorry how it all turned out."

In the first few seconds I hardly understood what he was talking about and thought he'd confused me with someone else. My instinct was to thank him and leave, until his gaze caught mine (not only were his eyes crystalline blue and abysmal, but his gaze, too; I'd never known such time-transcending depth) and remained caught until I more or less remembered a big bruiser of a guy hunkering his way around the Casey's General Store when I'd sprinted inside.

"You were there?" I asked, filling in the details, trying to decide whether he was comparing different brands of motor oil or perusing the bin of discount CDs. The man nodded, scratching at the hat-head ring in his hair before apparently deciding that I was a man and he ought to just come out and say it. He shoved his hands in his pockets and kept nodding to himself, his thumbs sticking out of his jeans in a way that seemed to express everything about his passivity and the unpredictability of life.

"It was like you'd both got shot, 'cept there wasn't any blood. I was reading the paper again out in the lot. Nothin' good about it. Nothin' good at all. So that's all I meant to say. I'll be on my way now."

The man back stepped toward the door, awkwardly pausing for a beat before doing as he'd said. I figured he'd wanted to shake my hand but, considering the venue, decided against it. When I turned to the mirror again I found myself not only checking my eyes for evidence of unrestrained emotions, but probing them for the explanation of my role in the unfolding events, the karmic logic of Katie's drowning, the subconscious reasons for my decision to attend a wake, knowing in my heart that the parents of the deceased, and perhaps others, would hardly welcome me.

By the time I returned to the main hallway, I'd set my mind on finding my family and leaving. But then Emily was suddenly at my side, pulling at my wrist and leading me around the corner. Everything about her stride and expression let me know she meant business, as though her superiors were currently out of commission and she'd been left in command. In only three days the scare of death had drastically thinned her, and even peeled the tan from her skin. (With her jaded porcelain cheeks and combed eyelashes, she looked the way I now imagine the real Anastasia Nikolaevna Romanova would have looked if she'd actually survived the Bolshevik bullets and reappeared—many years later, without a physical mark of injury or aging—to reclaim her identity.)

"What are you doing here?" she asked, hawking over me.

"I don't know. I thought you might want me to be here. I came to find out."

"You didn't read the obituary?"

"I'm sorry. We're leaving now. You want me to leave, right?"

"You can go to the burial," she said, straightening up, suddenly conscious of her posture. "Just promise me you won't stand right up front. Let's not make a scene or anything, okay?"

"Okay," I said, confused by what sort of *scene* she had in mind. She glanced over at the line and sighed as though this were all a big headache that would end soon enough if she could only keep those mourners moving. I tried to kiss her cheek but she was already thanking me and walking away, like I was a valet attendant to whom she'd handed her ticket.

Twenty-two

My dad took the long route to Tillis cemetery, then waited in the car until the majority of the funeral procession had gathered around the burial site near the top of the hill. We found our place in the shade of a big hickory tree at the edge of the circle, at least twenty yards away from Emily and her parents, the inner sanctum of family and priests surrounding the casket that was now propped open like the upper casing of a grand piano. The main celebrant was Katie's religion teacher from her elementary school days, but judging by his stale metaphors on the delicacy of human life, you wouldn't have guessed he'd ever known her. Throughout the service I was confounded by Emily's professional composure. Her killer keep-it-togetherness reminded me of Mrs. Schell during doctor's meetings at Mercy Frederick, especially with her hair pulled at a strict angle over her scalp, bobby-pinned behind her ear. Later on she appeared no more than cynically bored, as though she found it so ridiculous to drag someone up from under the weeds and muck only to dig them a hole in a fancy lawn. I imagined the sort of scene she requested we avoid—me parting my way through the crowd, taking her hand and squeezing it just before her knees gave out and I caught her and held her up as she cried and groaned.

It was a bright, hot day. I looked around for the big man from the funeral home but couldn't find him anywhere. Most of the students were banded together on the opposite side of the grave, including Katie's classmates and a few St. Pius seniors. Even Peyton Chambeau showed up, slouching in cargo khakis, a loosely knotted tie, and round retro Ray-Bans. Not only did he look like a viable new character on *Beverly Hills 90210*, but one we should all suspect of ulterior motives. I was certain he'd only attended the service to satisfy a melodramatic lark and last-ditch effort for Emily's attention. Mrs. Schell's yelping sobs never ceased. The whole time she gripped Mr. Schell by the sleeve of his blazer, appearing as if, were he to remove his arm from around her waist, she'd crumple to her knees. Emily kept facing forward, jaw locked, cheek muscles flexed.

At the moment the priest urged us to grieve as a community, I noticed Mr. Schell turning from the casket. I thought at first he'd grown dizzy or nauseated staring down at Katie's corpse, that he wasn't looking at anything in particular, just looking away. But then he took his sunglasses off and knuckled at his eyes and he was staring directly at me, quizzical and severe, appearing ready to halt the proceedings in order to drill me for more concrete information. This was the point when I fully grasped that for a five-dollar fishing lure I'd let the incomparable Katie Schell sink to her death twenty-eight feet deep. I could feel the harangue roiling inside him as he put his sunglasses on and turned back to the casket. I promised myself I'd one day show up at his doorstep with my hockey stick. I'd say nothing, just hand him the hockey stick and listen to the way he breathed as he pummeled me. I'd stand up every time, letting him wear himself down, even after he knocked my teeth out.

Emily never broke down. When Katie was finally lowered into

the lawn, she covered her lips with one hand and began to whisper. She was speaking to Katie and there was no stopping the derelict yowl that escaped when my slow tears advanced to heaving sobs. Smitty stepped up from somewhere behind me, wiping his face, placing a hand on my shoulder while his own shoulders cranked up and down in quick bursts. It had been years since I'd seen Zach cry, but even he was plagued by a shivering chin and splotchy red cheeks. Emily didn't drop a single tear.

When it was all over, my dad took my mom's hand and she took mine. Zach followed closely behind, trying to pull himself together. We'd almost reached the car when Hadley, Tino, and Ashley approached, trailed by a few others. They ended up patting my back and drifting away. Smitty stepped forward and hugged me and squeezed my shoulder and stared into my eyes like he'd never see me again. As we were driving I spotted Emily marching away amid her humbled clan. They were heading down the hill to the place where the sun was sneaking sideways around the arching cemetery gates. I imagined them walking forever, a meandering procession up and down every street in the city, all wailing Katie's name.

Twenty-three

These days I most often think of Katie Schell when saddled at the kitchen table next to a stack of ninth-grade essays and a finger or two of whiskey creaking in a cold glass. This is especially true when faced with a sentence like the following, which I encountered a few nights ago: "It would be fallacious to say that the novel is dead, especially when the people who are eager to make this argument are mostly critics and poets—and critics have no imagination and poets are prejudiced against sanity—and so I can only challenge YOUR imagination and YOUR prejudice when you grade this paper that is now being written at three in the morning when I should actually be studying for a history test that will require me to rote memorize over one hundred supercilious people and places that have nothing to do with real life."

When I picture Katie Schell now, I occasionally see her as a fourteen-year-old still chasing that brown trout like an underwater rodeo rider gripping the fishing pole with both hands, barely hanging on as she skis through the weeds and moss, cackling and climbing her way up the fishing line to snatch him by the tail. But in the days after her death my highly visual imaginings were horrifying. I have no idea how I passed the hours, though I recall spending a good amount of energy searching for random mementos such as Cub Scout merit badges, initialized pocketknives, miniature travel checkerboards, and wheat pennies, all of which I bitterly accused Zach of stealing. One raw morning when my sight seemed to have gone pixellated and night-vision green, I ended up in the basement digging through the boxes we'd never bothered unpacking since our move from Davenport. My most interesting find was a broken portable turntable and a box of records from my dad's college collection. After spending an afternoon dismantling the player and making a parts visit to a stereo shop on the South Side, I played the *Pet Sounds* album several times from start to finish, relating so deeply to Brian Wilson's lyrics that I felt he'd somehow tapped into the most simple and honest sentiments of my broken heart. (Perhaps "broken" is not as accurate as it should be; I felt my heart had simply departed my chest and floated into outer space, or some other black and weightless place where it pumped all its blood out, then continued sucking on whatever else it could find, stubbornly, for no reason at all.) I was so fearful of Emily's blame and vitriolic rejection that part of me hoped that when I eventually found the courage to call her, I'd find her number disconnected, soon discovering that Schell's Shirtworks had closed and her first college tuition check had been canceled and Mrs. Schell had convinced Mr. Schell to transplant their remaining family to Bolivar, Tennessee.

A week after the funeral, while scouring the garage for a hose nozzle—frantically, as though it were my most precious possession—I looked up from a box of garden tools to discover Emily standing at the sidewalk, staring into the grass with one hand pinching the back of her neck. She didn't notice me at first, and the longer I watched her, the more convinced I became that her pose perfectly encapsulated a feeling of self-help massage connected to an ancient feminine heartache. "Hey," I finally said, walking down the driveway to discover that she'd been staring at two spotted eggshells lying in the grass. She looked up and flashed a squirrely little smile. Her eyes were two foggy fishbowls so caught by surprise that I felt I'd just woken a somnambulist during a middle-of-the-night flight. Emily's gaze wandered up from the eggshells to a nest crooked in the branches of the cedar tree overlooking our mailbox.

"Where did you park?" I asked.

"Around the corner. I wasn't sure I was coming here. I wasn't sure if I'd make it to your front door."

"It's a steep driveway," I said, attempting to joke, but not sounding like I was joking.

"I know," she said.

"Do you want to walk around back? My parents are eating dinner. They won't bother us."

"Maybe we could walk somewhere."

"All right," I said, padding my pockets for keys or matches or something else I thought I needed. It was just past sunset when we started up the street and onto the Urbandale golf course. Emily was more herself than at the funeral, but still a stranger, someone I was hesitant to touch for fear I would startle her and scare her off. She walked along the fissures of the golf cart path, occasionally looking up to admire the view of lightning bugs flickering over the fairways like the lanterns of a thousand far-off soldiers. I would've waited all night to find the right words, but I had no idea what those words were and had a feeling they wouldn't suddenly come to me. We moved step by step. I knew Emily would cry somewhere along the way—it seemed she was only searching for the best location—and it eventually happened on the pedestrian bridge over the interstate. Halfway across Emily backed up to the railing, gripping the chain-link fence and leaning away to stretch her arms. Our hair swirled in the wind of moving traffic and the hot exhaust of freighters that swept by in caravans along the right lane. When Emily finally let go of the railing and looked me in the eyes, my heart and stomach were one swelling, pulsing wad.

"What have you been doing?" she said. "I thought you would've called by now."

I shrugged and smiled, I don't know why. "I wish we could've talked. I wanted to apologize for showing up at the funeral home."

"You can apologize now if you want."

"All right. I'm sorry."

"No problem," she said, smiling, possibly mocking my own smile from a few moments before.

"So what have you been doing?"

"Reading Mary Higgins Clark. I've read three books in three days. I skip pages here and there. It's fun to try to keep up when you don't have all the information."

"Is it working?"

"What do you mean?"

I stepped to the other side of the bridge. I didn't step any closer to her. "Have you been crying a lot?" I asked.

"Why does that matter?"

"I just want to know if you've been crying or if you've been swallowing it."

"Maybe I haven't been *crying*, George, but I wouldn't be reading Mary Higgins Clark if I wasn't getting sick. Really fucking sick."

"What kind of sick?"

"Forget it. I wouldn't trust anything I say right now."

"Try me."

"Forget it," she said, turning away. When she spoke again, her voice was lower and less concerned. "It's kind of amazing really. They hardly ever cry at the same time. One turns it off, and then, *bam*, the other turns it on. Anyway, I don't know why I'm telling you. You hate my parents."

"I don't *hate* them. They think I lied about Katie's life jacket. I know they do. Did you tell them I wasn't lying?"

Emily grabbed the fencing and shook it several times, seeming to enjoy the sound of the links rattling against the poles. "The cops thought you were lying, too. Besides, that Eagle Scout at the rental hut said that when he went to check the canoes, he saw a *bunch* of life jackets by the shore."

"A bunch? There was one. It was *your* life jacket. Why didn't you tell him what happened?"

"How do I know how many life jackets were on the shore?"

"She slipped out of it. She was wearing the blue life jacket, and when she fell into the lake she slipped out."

"I see," Emily said, sarcastically, like I was really having a good time with the truth. "I guess she just felt like seeing the bottom then, huh?"

I buried my face in my shirt. I wiped my eyes with the butt of my palms. I tried to stay calm. "She never buckled the top buckle, but there were two other buckles and I know the straps on those were pulled tight. I watched her pull them."

"So then how did she slip out of it? And even if she did slip out, why wasn't it still buckled when we found it by the shore?"

"I don't know. All I know is that she was wearing it when she was fighting that fish."

"It doesn't matter," Emily said, flinging her arms in the air. "The cops aren't interested in the details. Anyway, there's no point in making any claims when there's no evidence to back it up."

"It matters!" I shouted, grabbing the sides of my hair, feeling on the verge of pulling and twisting it in every direction. "You need to quit the Mary Higgins Clark and tell your parents *what happened*."

Emily covered her ears. She'd had enough of my voice, the highway, other sounds, too. It was as if in that moment she was declaring herself off-limits to the entire world. When she finally lowered her hands, I hardly recognized my girlfriend—or Emily Schell, even—in the cynic staring me down. (I pictured her character from *The Bridges of Madison County* leaping out of the screen, shaking her clamped right fist, pigheaded and proud.)

"I told my parents that she drowned, and I couldn't hold my breath long enough to pull her out. All things for good reasons. Not like we can complain that our lives have been so hard. It's just our turn for some tough luck. Probably just the beginning."

"You really believe that?"

"We've had it good for a while and now our luck's run out."

"That's bullshit. What was the good reason for Katie to drown?"

"Maybe she didn't care enough to stop herself from drowning. For a fourteen-year-old kid, shit, free ride to heaven. Katie's probably dancing on her head right now."

"That's hilarious," I said, taking my turn to look away in disgust, to take a deep breath of exhaust like it was my first taste of freedom.

"It's just the beginning of a bad string. I'm sure of it."

"Then what's next?"

"For who?"

"Us."

"Suffering," she said. "A good bout of pain to balance things out."

"You're not making any sense. Maybe you shouldn't think so much right now."

Emily laughed ("Cheers, doc!") as artificially as the silent, pearly-toothed laughter of a cigarette poster from the fifties, perfectly timed to a freighter's horn blowing long and low as it passed beneath us. I screamed into the noise. There were no words, just my voice pushed barbaric as far as it would go. I screamed until I felt a warm scrape in my throat, then plopped down on the bridge. A gray Jaguar switched to the fast lane, cruising along. The Emily I knew was full of logic and reason, even in her worst moments. While I expected a few surprises that night, I never guessed she was capable of such sabotage and spite. She wasn't making any sense.

"All right, George. If you really want to know what I'm thinking, then stand up and look at me. That's right," she said, as I made my reluctant way to my feet. "Did you know that only four percent of people with MS get diagnosed as kids? When you consider the number of people with MS, that's some serious fucking luck. And ever since Sunday, I feel it in me, too. I don't know if it's MS or cancer or what, but there's something nasty inside me and it's on its way up. I feel it, like a toothache where I don't have any teeth."

She placed her hand over the center of her chest, stepping to the middle of the bridge and starting to cry. When the first tear rolled down her cheek, she swiped it away.

"It's small now, but I can feel it right here, moving, growing stronger. I know you don't believe me, but you can touch it. You'll see that it's real. I swear it's changing and the temperature there is different. It's burning now like a firecracker, crawling around under my skin. I want you to touch it. If you don't feel it, then I'll forget the whole thing."

Emily stepped closer, moving at half speed but exact, like Katie when she was intent on infallible motion. I knew no suitable words of protest. They would have sounded sillier than her own request, which now felt as rational and urgent as anything. She untied the back of her blouse that hung loose from a thin strap around her neck. When she turned around the wind took it by the tails, exposing her lean shadowy back and pale blue bra. I unhooked it and slipped it off her shoulders. "Tell me if you can feel it," she said. "It's moving around now."

The wind whipped her hair against my face. I imagined the sickness she'd described—a misshapen bulb, black and feverish. I let my hand slide up from her stomach onto her breasts, one at a time. Her skin was warm. Emily wasn't especially endowed but her breasts were bold, surprisingly vast in their nakedness. I searched them first with my index and middle fingers, pressing the sides as though checking their pulse. Emily gazed at the streaming lights below, wanting dispassion, just the facts, which I knew was impossible. One of her tears fell onto my forearm and I lost the meaning of what I was doing, what I was searching for. It was embarrassing to examine her like a doctor. When she started to step away I pulled her against me and began to feel her the way I wanted to feel her, the way I did when I imagined us communicating solely through sex, spending days in bed without saying a word. I pushed my hands flat over her breasts and gripped them until I felt them in my possession. I rolled them to the sides of her chest and then pushed them back together. I tried to understand. Her breathing was heavy now, her rosy cheeks blazing. It was all soft, healthy flesh.

"Do you feel it?" she whispered.

I didn't answer. I stroked her nipples that grew stiff and eager until they were the ripe nipples of Emily Schell in her prime. I kissed her neck. I imagined that embryonic formation under her skin, spidery and destructive. Emily reached back to redo her bra. I wrapped my arms around her waist and held her whole body, kissing her shoulders before tying the back of her blouse like a shoelace. My eyes tilted down to the space between her knees, to the links in the fence and the zooming lights below.

When Emily faced me again her cheeks were still red, even though her expression had changed from sympathy to sadness and guilt, embarrassment and regret, every draining emotion wrapped into one. (Since we'd begun dating I'd done everything I could to deny Katie's crush, which in that moment proved itself as undeniable as a raging elephant. Perhaps it was always there, even during our first kiss, but after her death Katie's crush was full-blown and doubly perverse.) In the long stare that followed I understood that I was no longer Emily's boyfriend, that the most important reason for her visit was to say goodbye. We walked back the way we came. When we reached her car she stood there dangling the keys and staring down the street.

"You know, Katie never let you read her graphic novella because she never drew it. The last few months her hands were so shaky she couldn't draw a thing. She'd only gotten three or four pages into it."

I nodded, acting like I suspected as much. "I still have a copy of *Jackknife Janitor*. I can get it for you if you want."

"You can keep it. She gave it to you."

Emily unlocked the door, taking her time, clearly waiting for a final word. "I think you should keep her comic," I said. "It was her best one. Why don't we meet up tomorrow, maybe go for a drive out to the bridges of Madison County. I could bring it to you then."

"I don't know, George."

"Otherwise, when will I see you next?"

Emily shrugged. "I'll call when I can," she said, stepping into the front seat and driving off without another word.

"See you later," I answered, as her taillights disappeared around the bend. I went upstairs to my room. When I couldn't sleep that night I wandered the neighborhood and the next neighborhood over, for the first time regretting Katie's drowning in a way that had nothing to do with Katie. (The recognition of this selfishness was another blow of its own.) Eventually I found myself in some stranger's backyard. I woke an old mutt in his doghouse to pet him. Then I went home to smoke my dad's cigarettes and cry on the porch with the crickets.

Twenty-four

While I see little value in reporting the ordinary sorrow of the proceeding weeks, I feel it my duty to reveal a few idiosyncratic features of my process. As anyone who has experienced the death of a friend or distant family member knows, inevitably you must endure questions aimed at ferreting out the depth of your relationship to the deceased. For me these questions were complicated by my more dear relationship to Emily than Katie, and my own share of responsibility in her cause of death. I mostly blame my own guilt at having left Katie in the canoe for my queer reaction to those bold many who broached the subject of her drowning at such venues as Dunkin' Donuts, Ace Hardware, the Urbandale public library, or the flowery parking lots of any number of shopping villages in West Des Moines. Despite the population boom and the city borders sprawling out like floodwaters, these inquiring souls proved difficult to evade, inspiring me to such extremes as to dive behind walls of decorative hedges, or to turn the car stereo up so loud while waiting for the light to change that I couldn't hear the voice of the busybody shouting my name from the lane next to me. These unavoidables included fellow classmates, parishioners, neighbors, my parents' friends, their work associates, etc., most of whom knew of my relationship to Emily, but were hardly familiar with my connection to her younger sister. What shocked me most was that a good number of them, likely due to Katie's schooling outside the Catholic system, weren't aware Emily even had a sister until she died. Given the cloak of deceit memory tends to pass over such periods, it's astounding I can so precisely recount these dialogues, a few examples of which I have listed, anonymously, in no particular order:

Q: I'm so terribly sorry. Did you know her well?

A: Like she was my own sister. My older sister, really. She was a genius, you know. An incredible, patriotic genius.

Q: I heard she was kind of a loner. But she must've opened up to you, right?

A: She was just starting to open up. She asked me to be her confirmation sponsor, but then she mostly skipped the classes. I guess she was more spiritual, you know?

Q: You've only been in Des Moines, what, a year and a half? I know about you and Emily, but how well could you have known her sister?

A: I knew a lot *about* her, but she was healthy so rarely that whenever I saw her, it was like starting all over again. Not many people really *knew* her.

Q: I'm worried about you. Should I be worried about you?

A: The way it was written in the papers, you'd have thought we were three peas in a pod. No need to cry for me. I only met her a few times. We weren't even fishing together that day.

(After relating these details, I've now decided to completely bypass my initial bout of anguish when I was certain I'd lost *both* Schell girls and would have settled for just hearing Emily's voice and knowing she was still alive. But before doing so, I'd like to share a short anecdote—no doubt of dubious meaning—simply to provide a context for judging the depth of my low point, that relative place often referred to by alcoholics when they describe "hitting bottom.")

A few weeks after the funeral I answered an ad for "temporary full-time work" for a lighting fixture wholesaler. Iowa Lighting Solutions was only a twenty-minute walk through the woods and across the back nine of the Urbandale golf course, which was patronized by a number of golfers who harbored few qualms about teeing off the moment I sprinted across the sixteenth fairway. (It was once explained to me by such a golfer that he was perfectly entitled to kill me because I was trespassing and he had a summer pass.) The work was tedious and mostly involved replacing inventory tags on thousands of fixtures covering the ceiling space above ten aisles of decorative lampposts, track lighting, flood lighting, cutesy night-lights, sockets, bulbs, every accessory of luminescence imaginable. Only a few days into the job my boss, Mr. Jaffe, hired a volunteer assistant from the Catholic Charity House to help me replace the tags. Strangely enough, while this assistant was Chinese and mentally retarded, he looked like Mr. Jaffe's twin, particularly in concern to the odd-mannered fat stores around his waist. Both of them had the habit of constantly adjusting their glasses, which when they stood together made them appear like windmills in perpetual motion. Whenever Hu was around, Mr. Jaffe acted like the most kindly, upbeat boss you ever met, apparently to prove to all his employees that he had a soft spot for the mentally challenged and wasn't simply exploiting the situation for free labor. "Hu's got a good back," he was always saying. "He's just a regular guy who wants to put in a regular day's work."

Anyway, since Hu's medication caused symptoms of vertigo, Mr. Jaffe decided to have him prepare the tags, leaving me with the sole responsibility of climbing a thirty-foot ladder to attach them to the fixtures. I didn't complain. It was still better than a happy-go-lucky job at the mall where my increasing frustrations would be placed on broad display. For the most part things went smoothly with Hu, until late that first afternoon when I noticed from the top of the ladder that he'd prepped a whole row of stickers upside down. I had no intention of putting up tags with upside-down stickers, especially since Mr. Jaffe loved to embarrass employees by making repeated public announcements of their mistakes. The day was nearly over. After pointing out the problem, I asked Hu if he wanted me to print a new row of stickers or put off correcting the issue until the morning. In what felt like a complete personality swap, Hu not only denied that he'd done anything wrong, but kept staring at the upside-down tags as though I'd just switched them with the proper tags he'd produced. The conversation ended with Hu giving me a look like I'd stolen something from him. Then he stormed off, bumping into several customers on his way to the bathroom where he slammed the door, shat on the floor, then picked up the shit and threw it at the ceiling, mirror, and walls. Then he smeared the shit. When this surreptitious work was complete, he washed his hands and face, then marched out the back door—he forgot to clock out—and hopped the bus back to the Charity House. My day ended with Mr. Jaffe handing me a collection of sponges and disinfectants. He insisted I undo the accident as penance for my lack of sensitivity in dealing with the mentally challenged. I'll skip ahead by saying that cleaning the mess was an unpleasant experience, but that in the face of the moment's larger and less easily resolved problems, I found myself in the unique position of tolerating this unpleasantness. At the very least the story won a few laughs from Smitty, which, when I told it to him, made me feel like a normal guy for a few minutes.

The next morning I returned to work trying to pretend that nothing had happened, even if all the other employees found the situation hilarious, especially the warehouse workers. One of them kept putting on a Jackie Chan accent and asking me, *"Hu flung poo?"* I tried to ignore him and focus on the routine of hanging tags. Inevitably my thoughts turned to Emily and who she was talking with and what she was telling them and whether or not she still loved me. I imagined meeting her randomly in Lions Park, checking for cancer again and not finding it, kissing her ballerina lips, pressing against her fiery cheeks, mixing our tears and holding each other up. I thought about Katie, Mr. and Mrs. Schell, my parents, my friendships, life jackets, police, news reports, etc., and over time grew used to the sensation that instead of climbing up and down a ladder at Iowa Lighting Solutions I was actually at home in bed, hiding under the covers and functioning by remote control. Hu and I more or less got along over the next few weeks, even if I'd occasionally catch a dirty stare when I'd sigh too loud after noticing one of his stickers covering the string that I needed for hanging the tags on the fixtures. These hurtful looks reminded me of an abused son who, if he takes one more lick, might just go for the ax. I avoided criticizing Hu in any way, but knew it was only a matter of time before Mr. Jaffe brought me another mop and pail.

It finally happened on a Friday afternoon when Hu decided to print the stickers without asking how the program worked. In doing so he erased a block of about five hundred prenumbered tags, which meant that someone would have to go back and type in each inventory number, then look up the corresponding model number in one of the thousand-page manufacturing catalogs stacked in the office. I explained the predicament to Mr. Jaffe, who told me that I shouldn't have let Hu use the computer. "You're the computer expert," he said. "What's he doing doing your job?"

Knowing I couldn't completely skirt the issue, I bought two Cokes and invited Hu to join me in the break area out back. I tried to act more sad than angry, like I'd just been scolded by Mr. Jaffe and felt lousy about it. "What made you use the computer without asking my help?" I said. "I never use the computer," he said, crossing his arms and shaking his head from as far as it would stretch one way to as far as it would stretch the other. "*I* do the stickers," he went on. "*You* do the computer." When I pressed Hu a second time, he took to his feet and starting huffing his way inside. Of course I had a good idea where he was heading, but I kept a few paces behind him, waiting until I was sure of his intentions before blocking his way or wrestling him into submission, if that's what it came to. Hu surprised me by slamming the service door and turning the bolt. I didn't hesitate. I jumped off the loading dock and sprinted for the front entrance, knowing it was no quick jaunt around the warehouse, but figuring Hu had better be damned fast if he planned on beating me. (I won't deny an initial joy in the challenge, the feeling of sudden resuscitation—adrenaline surging into my heart, blood rushing to the extremities, a momentary reprieve from my stress and directionless pain.)

Hu turned out to be a pretty good athlete. When I turned the corner and dashed past a customer through the sliding doors, I saw him trucking for the bathroom with his head down and arms crossed over his odd-mannered gut that never moved, no matter the activity, the side effect of a mood-stabilizing drug that obviously didn't work. He bowled over a contractor and a housewife, losing his glasses on his path toward a stocking clerk whom he startled into crumbling against a shelf. I was close to cutting him off and might've saved the day by dive tackling him, but I didn't, thinking I'd only end up getting sued by the Charity House. He came to a slamming halt at the bathroom door, then locked himself inside.

It wasn't long before Hu embarked on his mission of enraged splatterings. Mr. Jaffe arrived on the scene at the sounds of the paper towel dispenser being torn from the wall and then stomped. "It's okay!" he kept yelling, knocking and pleading. "We've got your glasses! Good as new! Come on out, Hu!"

One of the warehouse workers helped the housewife to her feet. The Jackie Chan impersonator shook his head at all the other customers, pretending to be professionally disappointed as a way of holding back his laughter. The ruckus died down after about fifteen minutes, even if the cursing lasted much longer. When it became clear that Hu wouldn't come out on his own, Mr. Jaffe called a locksmith. I'll never forget the moment when the door finally swung open, the sight of Hu plopped down Indian style on a shit-streaked floor, looking like he'd been brooding in his self-made prison for thirty years. When he cried his whole body trembled. Some of the shit fell from his cheeks and neck.

I asked Mr. Jaffe for Hu's glasses, then walked into the bathroom and crouched down to his level. "It's not your fault," I told him, placing the glasses on his face. "I'm sorry." Hu didn't look up. He threw the glasses against the wall and yelled, "Fuck you, mister!"

There was nothing left to say. I walked out the front entrance, filled with the sort of rage that permitted me to stroll off the premises just as easily as if I'd stopped in for a lightbulb and couldn't find the one I needed. But this is not the end of the story. Consider everything I've just relayed as backstory for the incident I initially set out to share, which is this:

While heading across the golf course on my way home I tried to put myself in Hu's shoes. I considered what it would feel like being rejected from stepping onto a city bus. I considered what it would feel like to walk along Meredith Avenue covered in shit. I considered what it would feel like to face the laughter and repulsion of the other residents at the Charity House. And now I arrive at the moment when, in the midst of these thoughts, a lanky member of a Sigma Pi foursome decided to try his luck hitting me with his tee shot. While I'll never really know the truth, to this day I feel certain there was a bet involved in this decision. Either way, his ball bounced about five feet in front of me, taking a long hop and another short one before skittering to rest in the shallow rough. In truth I didn't know whether his group had already arrived at the tee box when I started across the fairway, but this detail didn't seem to matter. I picked up his ball and threw it into the woods, as casually as if I'd found a perfect rock to skip across the surf. Then I marched up the center of the fairway looking happily anxious for the brawl that one might have imagined I'd made a reservation for at the pro shop earlier that week. The golfers readied themselves by adjusting their visors, flicking their cigarettes, and spitting. One of them went as far as to tug his sleeves up over his shoulders. These fierce gestures fell somewhat slack as I drew nearer, likely in response to my disregard for their Big Bertha drivers, and the Cheshire cat grin that seemed imposed upon me by a ghostly counterpart with an ironic sense of the moral edge. "We didn't see you!" the lanky one shouted, cocking his club like a baseball bat. "Don't make me do it!"

Then he hesitated and his swing arrived too late. The head of the club didn't even hit me and I hardly noticed the shaft striking me in the ribs. The club rattled onto the cart path as I hooked his long pinkish arm that he'd practically handed to me. I locked his head under my right armpit and lifted him as high as I could, bending my knees and arching my back in the manner of a textbook five-point throw over my right shoulder. After traveling an upside-down arc, my opponent was slammed flat on his back onto the cart path pavement. Soon a bright red carnation blossomed on his cheek. He rolled onto his side and covered his face, sucking noisily for the wind knocked from his chest. His fellow threesome stared in disarmed disbelief as the hair on one side of his head darkened with blood. The bravest of them, baby-faced and mustard-stained, edged toward his friend with his hands up in the air, apparently proclaiming himself a pacifistic medical intermediary. I shoved my quivering hands into my pockets and stepped back, feeling suddenly engulfed in a clouded kiln. The last thing I remember was coughing in some weird sick way, and the shouts at my back as I dashed for the woods.

Twenty-five

If you've ever been a wrestler, or ever loved one, you will probably be familiar with a phenomenon referred to as "muscle memory." As Coach Grady would likely reason it, in the moment of my opponent's clumsy attack my muscles simply reacted as they'd been trained to react over the course of a few hundred freestyle practices when I'd been pressed to exploit the vulnerability of overemotional opponents who in the final minute of a losing match would often launch forward in frantic, spread-winged anger. Though I was never honestly convinced of this reasoning, I pretended to be convinced of it for the following afternoons of jobless seclusion, which were largely dedicated to bong hits and soap operas in Zach's bachelorized bedroom during his day shift up at Gordo's. (I have no idea what strain of cannabis Zach was smoking at the time, but it was potent and forcibly reminding of the antidrug counselor back in Davenport who'd warned us of the twelve-year-old marijuana addict whose testosterone turned to estrogen, causing his testicles to shrink and his mammary glands to swell until he'd grown a pair of little boy breasts.) More than once I discovered, halfway through one convoluted drama or another, that all the actors were speaking Spanish. I constantly peered through the basement windows for signs of Sigma Pi posses on patrol. Even more upsetting than my paranoia was the moment I came to the understanding—during a double feature of softly upsetting commercials for adult diapers and laser hair replacement—that a dear, intangible part of me had just broken away, setting sail for nonviolent adventures among moralistic peoples.

But I already decided to avoid the specifics of those first maddening weeks of grief, and have now clearly regressed. I scurry ahead to events more apropos to my relationship with the Schell family, beginning with my two unplanned encounters with Mr. Schell. The first of these occurred at the Seventy-third Street YMCA, which I began attending in an effort to restore a modicum of emotional and cognitive stability. (Colin Franzen, who worked at the front desk, offered me a membership discount usually reserved for stroke and car wreck victims in rehabilitation.) By then I'd more or less regained my appetite and was benching as much weight as ever, a feat no doubt motivated by the conceit that Katie Schell was my invisible spotter, urging me on for additional repetitions that in reality put me at risk of having to crawl out from under a two-hundred-twenty-pound bar pinning me to the bench. But the first hour or two after exercising were my most optimistic of the week, and the Saturday morning I encountered Mr. Schell was no exception.

That day I arrived to a shower room that was empty aside from the one old guy who was always there scalding himself in a cloud of steam. I chose a showerhead at the far end of the row and began lathering myself, taking pride in the noticeable swell returned to my shoulders and chest, the cable cord veins in my forearms. A minute later Mr. Schell showed up still dripping in a red Speedo and matching swimming cap. He looked so different from every other time I'd seen him that it took me a few seconds to recognize him. At that point I quickly turned into the spray so that it masked my face, hoping he hadn't seen me glance over as he walked in. I washed my hair, applying liberal amounts of shampoo in order to conceal my ebullient identity and occasional sidewise, stinging-eyed surveillance. I couldn't help wondering why he was slumming it at the YMCA when almost all of his neighbors attended the Timberline Club, where for three hundred dollars per month you could work out on plush aqua blue carpet and drink all the mineral water you could handle. He hung his swimsuit and cap neatly over the shower bar, then squeezed soap over his hand scrubber that fit like a glove. Despite his chicken legs and frowny-faced ass covered with stretch marks, I couldn't help but notice the surprising definition of Mr. Schell's upper back and shoulder muscles, which forced me to recall Katie's assertion that once upon a time he'd competed as a lightweight boxer.

After what seemed an hour considering how to take the first brave step toward reconciliation, I concluded that the shower room at the YMCA was neither the time nor place for a conversation about the exact truth of what happened out at Saylorville Lake. Certain that Mr. Schell had yet to recognize me, I took my opportunity to escape as soon as he went for the shampoo lever and started washing his hair. But he turned around at the exact moment of my flight, just as my manhood began bobbing side to side like a resolute pup on a happy sidewalk strut. His eyebrows furrowed and his shoulders lifted up. With his hair slicked back he appeared an eagle who'd caught in its radar a little mouse scurrying out from a hole hundreds of feet below. This reaction almost immediately gave way to an expression of doubt and depression, but by then I was already puffing my chest out and roughly scratching a few places that didn't itch. Mr. Schell peered into my eyes with such a pained and polite hesitation that I felt like a customer whose business he simply couldn't risk his respectability by accepting. I swaggered into the locker area, feeling hotheaded, spiteful, etc.

I took my time drying off to compile a list of similar adjectives I'd hardly have used to describe myself a few months before. Sitting on a wooden bench with my face in my hands, I summoned all the apologies and humble condolences I intended to offer Mr. Schell as soon as he entered the locker area. But I suspected my chance had passed and couldn't be recovered, that Mr. Schell had no intention of quitting his shower until he was certain I'd already left.

Twenty-six

Our second encounter occurred late one night after I'd been driving the same circles around town that I used to drive with Emily, only instead of deejaying and faking choking fits for the entertainment of our neighboring drivers, now I was poring over minor moral compromises such as the slow killing of my first buck after I'd tagged him in the hind, wobbling and almost felling him before his rack twisted and his hind legs kicked and he dashed away, bouncing off a tree trunk before switching directions and blending into the woods and becoming forever lost. After wasting over a quarter tank of gas I ended up cereal shopping at Hy-Vee, where I ran into former student council member Kip Nevins. Based on our conversation, apparently he thought he'd been voted into a lifetime position related to psychological guidance. "You should really *be* with people," he kept saying, after inviting me to join a group of classmates heading to a free concert of a band whose name he couldn't remember. On the drive home I noticed Mr. Schell's Beemer parked next to a cluster of lesser vehicles in a run-down strip mall off Hickman Road. I slammed on the brakes and made a two-hundred-seventy-degree turn, not knowing why I was doing it, but parking at the far end of the lot, which by night held an air of kinky secrecy that I blamed on the red band of neon along its wooden awning, and the dubiously unmarked offices smattered among Irish sweater, classic bicycle, and other such specialty shops on the first level. The Down Under Bar was located on the second level, up a flight of splintered stairs, and was the only establishment in the strip mall still open.

I sat for a while with the headlights dimmed, listening to the soft drone of AM radio while asking myself if the blame Mr. Schell had assigned me was inordinate, whether it represented a just response to my negligence, or rather an irrational parental instinct for scapegoatism. I imagined the conversations that might arise if I were able to join him for a few stiff drinks. While I had no intention of positioning myself as Mr. Schell's rival, after our shower room run-in I sensed I'd been drawn into an unspoken debate where all our arguments were waged by telepathic intuition. (I'd already transferred my YMCA membership to the Eleventh Street branch, feeling I'd lost the opening battle and ought to nobly concede the west side of the city.) But I harbored little bitterness for him and could hardly breathe when imagining the pain he was suffering living in a house suddenly void of the gonzo comedy of Katie Schell, with whom he spoke a father-daughter idiom that no one else understood. Since her diagnosis he'd done everything in his power to comfort her—often neglecting his business to remain at her side during her weeklong visits to the Mayo Clinic in Minnesota—and I had no doubt he'd lost more in Katie's death than any of us.

At some point during my musings a county cab pulled into the lot and parked by the stairway leading to the second level. Mr. Schell stepped outside, trailing a shorter man who was clearly drunk, clinging to the railing on his way downstairs. Both men were wearing business suits, though only the second man's tie was still tight, pinching his neck and exacerbating the fact of his big bulbous head. Given that Mr. Schell wasn't much of a drinker (he drank nonalcoholic beer well before it was in vogue, if that day ever came), I guessed he'd gotten stuck in a dinner meeting with a client who'd given Schell's Shirtworks enough business that he wasn't embarrassed getting plastered on a weeknight. Mr. Schell opened the taxi door. His associate hardly noticed and kept chattering on, every once in a while slapping Mr. Schell's shoulder in a way that made me think he had no clue that this man had just lost his younger daughter and was likely to collapse of sorrow the moment of their parting. Even I was relieved when the cab finally pulled onto Hickman and headed east. Mr. Schell rubbed his temples as he ambled across the parking lot to his car. He drove off in the opposite direction of the cab. I decided to follow him.

There was hardly another car on the road. I tailed Mr. Schell at a safe distance for about ten minutes, most of which was spent following his lead of fairly quick accelerations succeeded by bouts of reductive coasting. Eventually he turned onto Seventy-third Street and approached the stop light at University. There was no avoiding pulling up right behind him. It was dark, but I was certain Mr. Schell recognized me when he peered into the rearview mirror, his face lit by the blue glow of the driver's display. Even after the light turned green he sat there, glancing back and forth from the rearview mirror to his hands on the steering wheel. (The incident was queerly reminiscent of the pinnacle scene in *The Bridges of Madison County*, when Francesca had to decide if she'd leave her husband and jump into the truck with Robert Kincaid. Except in this version of the story it was only the two men, and they would either go for a drink and reason it out, or brawl right there in the street.) I sat waiting for Mr. Schell to decide, thinking it was better to set the record straight now than to suffer a lifetime of silent judgment. I considered my options, sounding out the decision with Smitty, my parents, anyone I trusted who I thought might still be awake and listening. I guessed Mr. Schell was doing the same, only talking to his wife instead of his best friend and parents. He made a right turn toward home, finally, like nothing at all had passed.

I turned left, disappointed that our standoff ended so quickly, even though I didn't know my purpose when I started following him in the first place. But then a few minutes later, while driving along Westin Parkway composing a belated funeral speech, my attention was drawn to the rearview mirror, where a black Beemer was fast approaching, flashing its high beams and yellow emergency lights. My first reaction was to ditch Mr. Schell, despite the absurdity of attempting to escape now that our roles were reversed. I pulled onto the shoulder and flipped the lights off. Mr. Schell did the same. We'd parked on the only dark block on the street, adjacent to a cut cornfield (owned by an infamously stubborn farmer who would eventually lose to the city's claim of imminent domain). There was no traffic whatsoever when Mr. Schell stepped out onto the pavement. I stepped out, too, wanting to face him, but trying to reduce the confrontational appearance of the movement by throwing my arm over the top of the open door the way a person might do if they expected to be asked directions to an all-night service station. Mr. Schell was wound up and skittish, appearing a righteous juror who'd set himself to the task of raw justice, if only as a midlife personal challenge. His tongue swam around in his left cheek. His right hand pumped up and down in his jacket pocket (thus marking my initial inkling that Mr. Schell would one day shoot me).

"I know you were waiting for me," he said, almost stuttering, shifting from one foot to the other and back again. "You left your parking lights on. You trying to scare me?"

"No, sir," I said, trying to sound as unthreatened as possible, but perhaps overdoing it and coming off aggressively unscared.

"How do you think it would look, George? How would it sound

if I called the police and told them you were following me around town?"

I let my eyes fall to the pavement. Eventually my sight line made its way toward the grass and cornfield. I hadn't planned to fight the guys on the golf course and I didn't want to fight Mr. Schell, either.

"I asked you a question," he said.

"I was only waiting outside the bar because I wanted to talk to you. But then when I saw you, I didn't know what to say."

"There's nothing to say. There's nothing at all to talk about. Emily's lost her little sister, and she's broken up enough without you calling all the time."

"I haven't been calling," I said. "I don't know what you mean."

"Ha," he said, giving me a little grin, like it was so pathetic of me to lie. "A customer of mine told me he was up at McGirk's the other night where your brother had an argument with an off-duty cop. Apparently your brother went out into the parking lot, smashed the guy's car windows, then went back inside and bought him a drink, like he'd just gone to the bathroom. Is that true, George?"

I knew what Mr. Schell was saying was true, though I thought Zach had gotten away scot-free. Farther down the road a sequence of traffic lights all changed from red to green.

"Is what I heard true?" he pressed.

"How do I know what you heard?" I said. Judging by Mr. Schell's smirk, it was exactly the sort of response he was fishing for. The dome light in his car turned off. His face went dark, allowing him to study me without revealing nearly as much of his own countenance. He shook his head, making me feel like some stupid kid whose own guilt would catch up to him worse than any punishment he could ever serve up.

"I'll admit, you had me fooled for a while, but it turns out you're just as big of a menace as that goofed-up brother of yours."

"I'm sorry, but my brother's got nothing to do with it."

"You have no idea. You don't know the meaning of *sorry*."

"But I *am* sorry. I know it's not good enough, but I'm as sorry as anyone's ever been. I shouldn't have left her alone like that."

"That's right," he said, throwing his hands in the air and turning to the cornfield. His bangs blew from one side of his head to the other. As he shouted, spittle sprayed the hood of his car. "*Sorry sorry sorry! Poor George Flynn! He's so sorry!*"

He turned back to me with his fists clenched. I was certain he'd charge me with one of his old boxing ring uppercuts. I felt my shoulders turning inward and my neck muscles tightening. My toes curled up in my shoes.

"Stop following me!" he shouted, desperately, like I'd been hounding him for years, day and night, driving him to the absolute edge. In the course of shouting this he stepped onto the road and halved the space between us. I practically fell into my car seat. I locked the door and fumbled for the gear shift. When I hit the gas I was too fearful to look back at whether Mr. Schell had jumped at me or hurried back to his car or pulled a handgun from his jacket pocket. I took the first possible turn and sped down one side street after another, staring into my mirrors, zigzagging my way home, praying Mr. Schell didn't know which house was mine.

Twenty-seven

The way I see it now, those of us who were close to Katie were like fallen leaves discarded to the wind, by no great coincidence swirling across the same streets, bound to find ourselves raked up in the same piles. My mind was never far from my next run-in with a member of the Schell family, though after that night I hoped it would be with Mrs. Schell, or one of Emily's aunts or uncles, if only for the sake of variety. (The recent advent of online movie rentals came as a major relief, knowing the regularity with which the Schells used to frequent Mr. Movies, whose vast selection of classroom and concert videos, over the past decade, was no small sacrifice.) Smitty did his best to keep me busy. We went to I-Cubs games and motocross races, even a few dive bars on the South Side for such un-Smitty-like activities as pocketball at happy hour. Smitty was there for me, as the saying goes, even if he seized the opportunity to convert me into an upstanding Catholic. For a short spell I was as devout as the most disenfranchised of troubled, truth-seeking souls, wandering various parishes throughout the city like a bohemian altar boy on tour. I studied my First Communion catechism and rehearsed Old Testament parables until I'd practically memorized them. I even prayed the rosary each night on my knees at the foot of the bed. I bartered a life of devotion in exchange for Emily's love and her parents' forgiveness, beginning with a holistic and filthy confession, my first since the St. Collette days when it was a school requirement and we used to subvert the whole process via brainstorm sessions where we'd come up with "safe sins," then argue over who would claim to have committed them. I needed to begin with a clean slate (which is not only possible for Roman Catholics, but one of the great bonuses, however underappreciated). It must've been my mom who informed me that Mr. Schell had begun attending the short Mass at Mercy Frederick, likely out of shame for his wife, who decided she'd sat through enough Sunday services for one lifetime, no matter the denomination.

Drawing to the point, on my fourth or fifth Sunday at Smitty's side, I spotted Emily parting her way through the exiting swarm of St. Anthony's parishioners who'd spent the majority of the previous hour practically on the edge of their seats anticipating the collapse of their octogenarian pastor. She was wearing a lemon sundress and cork sandals, a trendy combination much more to Ashley's taste than her own. I might not have noticed her if she hadn't been stopped by a pair of towering Sudanese men in marbled long-sleeved shirts. (I figured at least one of them was an actor, and it turned out I was right.) They took turns questioning her, piquing my curiosity when she abruptly cut them off and headed for the prayer niche on the far front left of the church. At the final notes of the choir's go-in-peace performance, Smitty patted my shoulder and made his exit, leaving me to decide on my own if I would approach her. For the moment I waited and watched, dropping down to the kneeler, partially hidden behind a wooden pillar, improving my inconspicuousness with an open copy of that week's hymnal. Emily slipped a folded dollar into the donation box, lit a candle, and knelt. Bowing beneath a gilt-framed icon of the

Virgin Mary, silhouetted in visible beams of sunlight through stained glass, she was the epitome of holy melancholic innocence. But instead of feeling blessed by the sight, I submitted to an old sex dream involving Emily as a nun, lifting her black habit to proudly show me that she was wearing nothing underneath. I slipped out the double doors to the vestibule, where I found Smitty looking lost among a hearty group of parishioners chatting and kissing cheeks.

"Looks like your prayers have been answered," he said. "And I thought you were just closing your eyes, trying to decide what to order at Perkins."

"I think I should go to confession again."

"Christ. What is it this time?"

I walked him to the parking lot. Smitty wished me luck and drove off. Ten minutes later I found myself wandering toward Emily's car, casually circling it, then checking her tires, then cupping my hands against the windows to search the seats and floors for hints of her life without me. It was all ordinary clutter: unmarked CDs, loose change, a faded beach towel, a balled-up B-Bop's sack.

"Planning to steal my stereo?" a voice shouted from a ways off. I looked up, blocking the sunlight as Emily slipped her sunglasses on and stepped from the curb. "I've heard of people stealing from cars in church parking lots, but I didn't think you were the type."

I held my hands in the air, hoping she'd assume I was expecting her at any minute, which by some lapse of consciousness I wasn't. The parking lot was mostly empty now. Soon Emily was standing in front of me, shining fresh freckles that caused me an abrupt and unbearable sadness, as though each one represented a bold new experience she might not be willing to share. I stood there sweating like a goon. All of my imagined scenarios of our reunion involved two people who'd already overcome the disaster. Emily stepped forward to inspect the thick stubble on my cheeks and beneath my chin. She scratched along the right side of my face. I didn't know what to do with my hands. I wanted to hug her, but I didn't.

"Saint Anthony's, huh?"

"Smitty said there'd be free doughnuts in the parish center."

"I come for the candles," she said. "They burn good and slow. More for your money. So what'd you do with Smitty?" She bent down to check under the car.

"He left. I asked him to go on without me."

"I see," she said, pulling suspiciously at her chin as she walked around the car. She stepped inside and closed the door. I leaned down by the driver's-side window to find her fanning herself with her tongue hanging out. The windows all rolled down. "You coming or what?" she asked.

"Where to?"

"You know me better than to ask questions like that."

I opened the door, immediately pressed by the trapped heat as I stepped inside. We set off east down Ingersoll Avenue, cruising along, mostly hitting green lights. I was still trying to come up with a conversation a few silent minutes later when a pager started beeping and vibrating in the cup holder. Emily clicked it off and tossed it in the backseat.

"Anything you want to tell me about your summer job?" I said, as though there weren't a film canister of pot in my front pocket. "I mean, should I be worried if we get pulled over?"

"That's just Maureen Schell probably wanting me to pick her up some lip balm or avocados, maybe a fresh deck of cards, just in case she feels like a game of solitaire. Last time it was a Lotto ticket. Can you believe that? Maureen Schell playing the Lotto?"

"Maybe it's a good sign," I said, relieved we'd finally found a topic. "Maybe she's raising money to take the old band on tour."

"What old band?"

"Whatever band she played in when she was rocking her acoustic guitar back in Bolivar."

"Right," she said, after pulling up next to a phone booth at the Kum & Go station. "I believe she was a member of the tabernacle choir. Wait a minute while I buy us some time."

She shifted into park, grabbed a few quarters from the dash, and hopped out. I flipped through her CDs, struck by an uneasy desire upon sighting the two or three albums I could only associate with our make-out sessions before school. I couldn't figure out if Emily was content to see me, or just playing it cool to avoid a conversation about why she hadn't called in so long. I played Bob Dylan's *Blood on the Tracks*. Emily stepped inside and turned the volume up. When we reached the river she followed the signs to I-235 and then I-80 heading back west. I had a feeling she'd already decided on our destination and was having a good time leaving me guessing. I didn't say anything, even when we were well west of the city, passing exits for Van Meter and Earlham. Again I found myself digging deep for a conversation, which seemed silly once I realized it was her birthday the next day.

"I suppose you've got a few checks coming your way, huh?"

"I suppose so," she said, flashing me a pleased little smirk. "But the real question is if you were planning on buying me a present or just letting it pass like any other day."

"You don't think I'd even get you a card?"

"Don't dodge the question," she said, letting off the gas and turning to me. "And don't look so scared. I'm not trying to trick you."

"I'm not scared. I'm just wondering why I haven't heard from you in so long. I was waiting for a call, and then after that I was planning on buying your present."

"So if I didn't call or happen to run into you, I wouldn't have gotten anything?"

"Not from me, anyway."

"Damn," she said. "And I suppose you never considered calling me? I mean, not to be insensitive about the trickiness of that sort of thing, but did you ever think about throwing your voice? You might've called and said you were Alfred Watson from the admissions office at Yale."

"Yeah, like your mom wouldn't be listening in on the other line, or nailing you with fifty questions the second you hung up."

"I would've told her it was some creepy student with a work-study job in the admissions office. I'd say he saw my photo and called to tell me how he'd *really* tried to convince the board of my qualifications, and even though it didn't work out, if I didn't have any plans over the summer, maybe I'd like to keep him company in that big empty dorm overlooking the quad."

"So you're going to Northwestern?"

"That's right."

"I always thought you'd be better off in Chicago."

"Me, too," she said, more optimistically than I knew how to interpret. We kept to ourselves for the next few miles. I tried to guess the cost of regular visits back and forth to Chicago. Emily cut the music off, mumbling something about folk singers being a bunch of sourpusses. When we finally exited we were halfway to Omaha in a town called Brayton, home of the "world famous Barrel City Barbecue & Brewery." It didn't take long to figure out what she'd gotten us into when we passed a tray stand loaded with enough meat to reconstruct an original carcass. A sign on the wall informed us that Barrel City was a family-style restaurant, and that it was our responsibility to make room for ourselves at whichever table we could. We ended up scooting in next to a family of five who were joyously forking at each other's neck, shoulder, and loin cuts, dripping the checkered tablecloth with every flavor of barbecue sauce in the house.

"Hog Heaven!" Emily shouted, perusing the menu and winning

the laughter of the youngster next to her. "I'll take the Pork Challenge Number Three. Five Alarm Sauce, if you don't mind."

"To drink?" the waitress asked.

"Homebrew," she said. "A pitcher. I'm turning twenty-two tomorrow."

"Got ID?" she said.

"Nope. My *husband's* driving. He's paying, too. When it comes to birthdays, I try to stretch it out for at least a week. At the *very* least."

The waitress patted me on the shoulder, as though to say, *Hang in there, pal, it'll all be over in another couple of days*. I ordered the pulled pork. Soon enough we were pouring beers for our fellow diners, taste testing each other's pilsners and lagers, and sharing in kettle-sized servings of coleslaw and potato salad.

"You all from Des Moines?" the wife asked. Her name was Sherri. She had marshmallowy arms and legs but a small, pointy face.

"*He's* from Des Moines," Emily said. "And he comes from money. Old blueblood money that's been stashed up for a century in one of those big mansions south of Grand."

Sherri's husband reeked of cigarette butts. He nudged my elbow and waved a rib bone in Emily's direction. "Looks like you've got yourself a real firecracker over here."

"Yes, sir," I said, raising my glass, feeling like some sort of minor celebrity. We drank. Soon enough Emily was telling them all about the fortune my family made bringing cable TV to Iowa. I added flourishes here and there, particularly in concern to our Vegas wedding that took place in a big ballroom with a few hundred other couples, some of whom had met their betrothed for the first time that very day. By the time I paid the bill we were more than buzzed. We shuffled into the parking lot holding our stomachs. Emily wiped my hands and face with half a dozen moist towelettes. (My last girlfriend discovered one of these while digging through a desk drawer for a pair of scissors, setting into motion a chain of events that ultimately placed me, at a dinner celebrating her dad's retirement, at the very same table where Emily and I had eaten.) We fell up against the car.

"Happy birthday," I said, stroking her hair and gently pinching her right earlobe. "I suppose you wouldn't have cleaned me up if you weren't looking for a kiss."

"We'd better find *something* to do to sober up."

We kissed. It was a long clumsy kiss, but we didn't care, even when it came to the disapproving glares of the exiting customers, whose sudden turns of attitude reminded me of I-Cubs fans after a botched save. Eventually Emily pulled the car around to the rear lot. She climbed into the backseat and I followed her and we continued making out. I kissed her neck and buried my head in her breasts. She pulled her sundress up around her stomach, then undid my zipper and began stroking me while she stroked herself at the same time. Her hand rattled between her legs. Her hips thrust out and her hair grew thorny and static as her head grinded against the upholstery. I had the feeling I wasn't the only one abusing myself over the previous few months, which made it seem even more essential that I pull her on top of me and seal the deal on our reunion, even if it meant losing my virginity in the back lot of a barbecue restaurant. But Emily was in too deep to be distracted. I held back, saving myself for a main act that was never to be. Emily moaned and stretching stiff-legged with her head pressed to the door. This proved too much and I came a few seconds later as she cried out and kicked the back of the seat. We crashed into each other, sweaty-faced and cotton-mouthed, suddenly bursting with laughter, like we'd just come to the screeching end of a roller coaster, and we hadn't died after all, and we were doing the right thing, and in fact if we raced back to Des Moines that very instant we'd find that nothing at all had changed since graduation, that in fact we were just a normal pair of decommissioned high schoolers chumming along from one year to the next.

awoke an hour later to the sound of Emily's pager vibrating across
the floor mat. Emily was just waking up. Her hair and sundress were
crumpled, her arms and legs gone languid in the hormone-drenched
humidity. She climbed barefoot to the driver's seat and turned the
pager off. We rolled the windows down and drove across the road
to gas up and buy drinks. Emily reached for my hand as we pulled
onto the highway heading west to Omaha. We'd been talking about
escapist road trips since the beginning of our friendship. In a sense
we'd been preparing ourselves for the better part of our junior and
senior years while listlessly circumnavigating the city. A series of
muscular pickup trucks roared past. We made small talk as we skirted
Omaha, randomly guessing at Nebraska's official state birds and flow-
ers and trees. There was intermittent rain and highway construction.
Horizons looped. Flood plains gave way to western Nebraskan wind
farms, more wheat fields, distant hills that I mistook for mountains. I
knew sooner or later we'd come around to the topic of Katie. It didn't
happen until well past dark, when I was starting to question the decision to flee.

"She was supposed to go to wilderness camp," Emily said. "One of the counselors called last week when she didn't show up. I know it's strange, but I kept imagining being the kid sleeping under the bunk with the name Katie Schell on it. You know, like the counselor pulling me aside to say, *Sorry dear, but Katie's not going to make it this year. She had some bad luck out at Saylorville Lake. Would you like to switch bunks?*"

"I doubt they would tell the kids what happened," I said, turning my attention to the mile markers glinting and shuttering past, projecting my prodigal son return onto dynamite-sculptured cliffs lining the eastern Colorado highway.

"She's got friends from all over the state that she only sees in the summers. A lot of them probably didn't hear anything. You think they'd play dumb? Tell the kids she moved to another state or something?"

I didn't say anything. I started packing an empty McDonald's sack with plastic Coke bottles, candy bar wrappers, and gas receipts. Emily looked over and shrugged, like she didn't know why I was bothering but wouldn't stop me if I was in the mood.

"Anyway, so the call from camp came on a Sunday. Then on Monday morning, my mom decides she's ready to start cleaning Katie's room. She's not sure she's going to move any furniture or anything, but she's already sniffed the pillows and bedsheets until there's nothing left to smell, so now she thinks she'll vacuum a little and dust, maybe take out the trash. She ends up spending the whole day in there, and eventually finds a load of trashy romance novels hidden in shoe boxes. Ever heard of Celeste Elston?"

"I've heard of her," I said, growing jealous thinking of Mrs. Schell already on the trail of Katie's time capsule.

"It's pretty smutty stuff. She also found a Wiccan *Book of Shadows*, which gives all sorts of practical advice in witchcraft."

"We should call your parents," I said, wanting to hear more but feeling sick, like this information wasn't meant for me and was tarnishing my relationship with Katie. "They probably think I kidnapped you at gunpoint. They've probably got the cops after us."

Emily found this hilarious. "We're adults," she chuckled. "And we didn't break any laws. The cops can't do a thing."

"That's not the point," I said, for the first time asking myself why I cared so much what her parents thought. But there was no avoiding that I did care, even with Emily at my side primed to run away with me. I couldn't believe she was as unconcerned as she was acting. I told myself that she'd adopted a pose of Katie Schell bravado that would eventually wear off.

"Pull over at the next exit," I said. "If you won't call them, I will."

Emily checked the rear- and side-view mirrors. She tugged idly at her seat-belt strap and continued driving, as though I hadn't said a thing. But a few exits later she flipped her turn signal and veered into the right lane. "If you absolutely *can't relax*," she said, not exactly thrilled, but deciding to be impressed that I was willing to make the call myself. "Just don't tell them where we are, okay?"

"*We* don't know where we are."

"Good point," she said, happily, which made me think she was only pulling over to call my bluff. We parked at one of the more impressive truck stops I've ever seen. There were dozens of shower rooms, pool tables, extra-wide phone booths with massage seats. Emily cruised the trinket aisles while I dialed her parents, having rehearsed my monologue enough to decide that the more I rehearsed, the less likely I was to make the call. Mrs. Schell answered like an eager attendant at a corporate calling center.

"Schell residence, may I ask who's speaking?" I gripped the mouthpiece with both hands, recognizing her doom and desperation that needn't be mocked by half-truths. I opened my mouth, but nothing came out. "Hello?" she said. "Is that you? Emily?" Her voice cracked on the word *Emily*. She took a long, controlled breath. "We're just sitting here. We're at the kitchen table, wondering where you've gone, and trying not to panic. No one's going anywhere, and we don't want you to go anywhere, either. You've got rehearsal tomorrow and we just want to know where you are. Please would you tell me where you are?"

I waited, feeling more trapped as I prepared my statement. It was too late to hang up and now Mrs. Schell was waiting, probably suspecting that the sound of her own voice was enough to drive Emily further on. "Everything will be all right," I thought, rehearsing again. "I promise. Everything's fine. Emily will be back in a few days, full of clean mountain air and hope and a whole new attitude. Just two or three days and Emily will be sitting right next to you, ready to talk about things you couldn't talk about in the past." But before I actually said any of those things, a series of derelict breaths huffed through the receiver, the kind that don't exist without tears. Mrs. Schell had been trying her hand at sensitivity, caution, carefully avoiding the shrill soprano of frightened, overbearing mothers. Being worn out from the road didn't help and I started crying, too. I covered my mouth, but a whimper escaped like a pup's first hungry moan. I coughed to cover myself. Within seconds Mrs. Schell had already hung up.

When I stopped crying I went to the bathroom and washed my face, careful to erase all traces of tears. For extra measure I perused the trinket aisles. I returned to the car to find Emily fingering a Colorado atlas and listening to a collection of heehaw country hits I'd seen advertised for three bucks on a rack by the register. She was angry I'd gone through with the call, but trying not to show it. "So?" she said, neatly folding her atlas. "How are *things*?"

I waited awhile, staring across the parking lot at a pink neon sign for FOOT-HIGH PIES. "She's trying. She was trying to be understanding."

Emily pulled her hair in a bun. She crossed one leg over her knee and starting flicking her fingers on the steering wheel. "I don't need to know what she said. I'll trust you if you tell me we have no choice but to turn around, but just don't tell me what she said. Was it so bad that we absolutely have to go back?"

I turned the stereo down and thought about it. I thought about my own parents and the decision I'd made hours ago not to betray our escape by calling them and reducing my individual risk. I considered whether the Schells would ever know how I'd placed their priorities over my own, and if we turned back whether Emily would bother seeing me again before she left for college. The call of love on the run was as electrifying and fear-provoking as a new, life-altering drug. In one moment I was ardent, in the next numb and hesitant. "Did you find anything on that atlas?" I asked.

"I found Rocky Mountain National Park." She opened the atlas to give it another glance. "If we keep on keeping on, we'll be there when the sun comes up."

"I've been meaning to tell you. Last week I was high most days by ten in the morning, which I think means I'm becoming a pothead."

Emily turned sideways to face me, waiting for her smirk to wear off enough that I'd receive her question sincerely. "Are you carrying pot on you right now?"

I pulled the film canister from my pocket and handed it to her. She opened it and took a deep whiff. "All right," she said, nodding and pursing her lips, like this revelation was unexpected and significant, but one of those things that happen that we simply have to handle the best we can. "I haven't been driving more than ten or so over the limit, which I can easily correct. We're not exactly in a hurry, right?"

"I don't think so."

"Okay. I've seen at least one of our highway neighbors passing a joint, and they looked like completely normal, responsible, nine-to-five kinds of people. Besides, maybe it will be nice for you to get high while I tell you about my dreams. They're epic these days. They go on and on for so long that I feel like I'm sleeping when I'm awake, and really living when I'm asleep. It's like my dreams are where the real action takes place. Is there anything else I should know about you?"

"I don't like being ignored for long periods of time when I'm upset, especially when I know that you're upset, too."

"Understood. I can't explain it, but I didn't like it, either."

"And if I take my shirt off, so I can feel the wind blowing on my chest, I don't want any trouble about it."

"I can handle that," she said. "Everyone gets a little jealous of hillbillies driving around with their shirts off."

"Davenport people aren't hillbillies. They're just regular people."

"*I know, George*. I didn't say that. But ten o'clock sounds a little early to get stoned, even for a hillbilly. Anyway, this subject relates perfectly to one of my dreams. About a week ago I dreamt I was singing *Jesus Christ Superstar* with a bunch of skinny hillbillies in tap shoes. I believe we were panhandling on a subway train. And everyone else on the train was wearing tuxedos and evening dresses. I've never been on a subway in my life."

"I don't have any interest in riding a subway. It's humiliating being forced underground like that."

"It's cowardly," she said, buckling up again and starting the engine. On the entrance ramp, when Emily reached for the stereo, I leaned over and kissed her lips. The tires hummed over gravel as we drifted onto the shoulder. "Thank you," she said, swerving back onto the road.

I packed the one-hitter I'd been sucking on like a pacifier all summer. It was a giddy and lackadaisical high with the windows down and Emily rattling on about dreams, then dreamlike directors like Bergman and Kieslowski and Lynch, which eventually led to a lesson on the sordid history of old Hollywood. My stomach hadn't completely settled since the phone call, but I was feeling better. I'd even convinced myself that our escape really would benefit Emily's parents, that it would wake them up to the reality of being on the verge of losing the one daughter they had left. Emily and I made bets on how many bridges we'd cross before reaching Rocky Mountain National Park. We mused on techniques for avalanche self-defense, the existence of carnivorous plants, the probability of simultaneous cougar and bear attacks. We stopped at more rest stops than we needed to and bought travel toothbrushes with toothpaste loaded in the handles. We took our time on the road to the lower Rocky Mountains, those squat sumo wrestlers with poker-faced peaks, the sunrise bright across their stone blue bellies.

Twenty-nine

Our summer vacation officially began in Glacier Basin, a chummy camping village of tents and cabins, a petite outdoor amphitheater, and the world's most expensive general store. After renting all the basic camping equipment, including a requisite bear-safe container shaped like a miniature keg, I attempted to persuade Emily of the good sense of a pre-hiking warm-up and stretching routine in the debauched privacy of our tent. This plan was spoiled by a pair of hyped-up Oregonians expounding the rules of backcountry camping, which stated that all campers must hike beyond the basin, which required covering at least seven or eight hours of trail. Recognizing the couple as a source of much-needed information, Emily was soon plying them with all sorts of practical questions, including the cause of the black smoke plumes wafting over the western ridges. (The Oregonians were more than happy to answer her, and even indulged her in a ten-minute lecture on "prescribed fires," a technique that involved clear-cutting, digging down to the mineral soil, and hiring helicopters to drop loads of fire suppressant.) Before I knew it we were scampering on our way, minus a map and a million other things,

attracting more than a few laughs over Emily's sundress and sandals
and the pretty-boy khakis I'd worn to church. The most avid hikers
were appalled, shaking their heads and clucking their tongues as we
cut back and forth across the mountain. It was a great relief when we
found a path of our own where we were free to be awed by marmots
and falcons, rocky groves of aspens chatty in the breeze.

"Not tired, are you?" she asked.

"Going strong," I said, for the first time realizing we hadn't slept
the night before.

"I feel like I just woke up from a coma. I don't know if I'll sleep
ever again. Maybe when I get to Chicago, I'll rent my bed out and
spend my nights smoking cigars at all-night jazz clubs."

"Why don't you sing at the all-night jazz clubs?"

"Even better. By the way, what do you know about your roommate up at Iowa?"

"You mean over in Davenport?"

"No kidding?" she said, slowing down for a few steps to catch her
breath. I could already feel my legs swelling and the muscles shifting
back and forth under my skin. My lungs were wide open, my tongue
detecting the faint ash in the breeze. "Sometime you'll have to show
me the house you grew up in. I've got this mental picture of your
old high school and your old neighborhood, but I'm probably very,
very off."

"To be honest, I don't think I'll ever go back there. All the good
people moved away and my dad said that the people who live in our
old house painted it lime green. I think they put up a fence. If they
hadn't insisted on moving in so soon, my family wouldn't have spent
our first night in Des Moines at the Holiday Inn."

"Oh, let's not think about that," she said. "I was talking about seeing your old house."

"It's not my house anymore."

"Fine, fine, fine," she said, taking the lead. Her ponytail swayed back and forth above her backpack. With each step her sundress bunched up under her waist strap, allowing a full view of her legs, barely covering her ass. When it became clear I was dogging it for the view, Emily pulled her dress down and motioned me ahead.

"Beautiful country," I said. "Makes you proud to be an American."

"I feel your pride burning two holes in my butt. You getting hungry yet?"

"I can wait a little longer."

"Can you?" she said, taunting me with a last little flip of her dress. We kissed for a while. After catching sight of the first hiker to pass in over an hour we trekked on, holding hands. At the peak of the next ridge we found ourselves looking down over Loch Vale and its dark blue lake, perfectly mysterious and still. We sat on a set of loveseat boulders and absorbed the rugged skyline of forest, bald peaks, and black burned-out hills, all mirrored in the lake. A spindly waterfall splashed through a crevasse on the opposite side, falling at least fifty feet to trickle from one pool to the next.

"I've got an ugly question to ask you," Emily said, running her hand flat along the rock, almost massaging it. "Do you ever wish you never moved to Des Moines? Please don't think I'm suggesting *I* wish you never came, I'm just wondering what you'd choose if you could turn back the clock."

"I try not to think about turning back the clock."

"But I'm asking you," she said, leaning back on her elbows, looking tired for the first time the whole trip. "Just this once I'd like to know."

"If it meant Katie would still be alive, I'd stay in Davenport. Who knows, maybe I would've fallen in love with some other girl and ended up miserable like my friend Kevin. He moved to Atlanta with some girl who's got him working the third shift at a frozen foods warehouse because it pays a dollar fifty more than the day shift. Who knows? Maybe if you never met me, you would've spent less time messing around after school, scored a few points higher on the SATs, and ended up at Yale just in time for some whacko who didn't get accepted to shoot up a few lecture halls."

"All right, George. I'm sorry."

"I'm not angry," I said, softening my voice and looking her in the eyes to convince her. The sound of Katie's name seemed to crank open the sky and pump up the heat. "If I could turn back the clock, instead of fishing, we'd have gone to a matinee, then snuck around from theater to theater all afternoon."

"And if the movie screen collapsed and killed all three of us?"

"We'd make the front page," I said, trying to sound as assured as an old monk who'd pondered such questions for decades. I could've been more honest. I could've shared my feeling that Katie's drowning was more than a random accident, that there was culpability to be shared. In the end my remarks were no more than a pale reflection of Emily's own advice on the pedestrian bridge over the highway, a submission to inevitability and fatalistic acceptance that absolved all three of us. We marched on into a thinning afternoon, saving our breath as we marveled at butterflies and hawks, towering spruces as perfectly straight as giant handcrafted spears.

It was late afternoon when we realized we hadn't bought nearly enough food or water, our muscles having clearly absorbed every calorie of our banana-sandwich-and-trail-mix lunch. The altitude was catching up with us, causing prickling hands and pulsing heads. We found our first argument at a crossroads beneath a signpost indicating two opposing trails to campsite #21, the first backwoods campsite outside Glacier Basin. When we couldn't agree on which was the shorter route, we decided to split up and bet two tanks of gas on who would arrive there first. This was without doubt the most foolish decision possible, even given our certainty that we were less than an hour from the site and that a healthy competition was just what we needed to raise our spirits. But there was no hiding the fact that our road trip had already evolved into some kind of knowledge quest, in the very least a search for a new and more natural perspective. Under these terms, the decision to trek alone and cover two paths instead of one wasn't as idiotic as it sounded. It seemed the most legitimate way to *feel* the mountains and glean a modicum of wisdom from them.

"Don't touch our rations," I said, as we back stepped in our own directions.

"Still glad you saved ten bucks on mosquito sauce?"

"They don't go for O negative."

"They sure as shit went for O negative on the Upper Iowa."

"And if you see a bear, stay calm and talk to it. Convince it not to eat you."

Emily stopped for a moment to search the skies, apparently for help in dealing with me. "No camping on the trail," she shouted as she started around the bend and out of sight.

I'd hardly turned my back before regretting our decision, not to mention feeling guilty about laughing off the possibility of a mountainside emergency. I couldn't forgive myself three hours later when I ran out of water. By then I was regularly fooling myself into thinking I'd reached the summit only to discover another ridge and the understanding that I was still several uphill miles away. I hadn't seen another hiker since I broke with Emily. I found my only company in a lone helicopter that occasionally circled overhead, seeming to defend the theory of life's randomness by offering the possibility of being firebombed on my summer vacation. Anxiety turned to rage and delirious panic, incremental with every step. The burning sun leaked carelessly into clouds, painting a watercolored sky. As darkness approached I prayed and chased butterflies, hoping if I caught them before the sun fell beneath the horizon that the campsite would suddenly appear and I'd find Emily happily sprawled across a pair of sleeping bags, which she'd already zipped together for warmth. At some point I imagined one of the forest service helicopters swooping down with Katie leaning out, holding on by one hand, her big-time mood cracking loud and clear through a megaphone.

"Would it help if you changed into your wrestling tights? Maybe you should ditch those sally boy boots for the final lap. Pain in the feet is the best kind. This will clean you right out."

"I'm hungry," I shouted back, not bothering to look up.

"Tell you what. If you keep going I'll meet you at the peak and give you a little hint about my time capsule. I'll sit with you by the fire and you can ask me anything you want. By the way, you still thinking about that life jacket?"

"It doesn't make sense," I said, marching faster, lifting my knees higher. "It'll never make sense to me. If you weren't strong enough to swim, why would you unbuckle yourself after you fell in?"

"I'll meet you there," she said. "With erotic campfire stories and all the answers."

I stopped to face her as the helicopter drifted upward. I imagined her sitting down now, strapped in with her bare legs dangling over the side. She held the megaphone out like a pistol, and closed one eye and aimed.

"See you at the peak, okay? That is, if you think I'm worth it."

She fired a few warning shots near my feet. Pebbles scattered inches from my heels. I marched into the darkness, fearing twisting an ankle or climbing that mountain for the rest of my life. My flashlight dimmed and I tripped and skinned my knees. I swallowed trail dust. When I felt my lips splintering like the scales of a dead fish, I reconsidered the acting ability of those crybaby lost boys from *Into the Night*. My flashlight was practically dead by the time I reached the final ridge. I made out the faint sparkle of a campfire at the end of a needled pathway through the thicket.

Thirty

After an all-too-brief motherly scolding and hands-on physical, Emily opened a surprise package of hot dogs and Wonder bread buns she'd covertly acquired while I was debating myself over an extravagant purchase of camping pillows. After dinner, more or less rejuvenated, we set up our tent and hid the bear box that now contained two hot dogs, three buns, an apple, and a handful of trail mix. Together we scavenged for more firewood, which was not so simple a task in spruce and fir environs with one working flashlight. The farther we wandered from the campsite, the more we concerned ourselves with the task of bear detecting, stopping every few feet to scrutinize all upcoming bushes, boulders, and even a few blank pockets of moonless night. Through the right eyes they all resembled black bears in sinister, shape-shifting poses. The most convincing of them crept onto the trail thirty feet behind us, then camouflaged himself low against the thicket to play an inchoate evergreen. He stared at us through sad, crescent-shaped eyes, his short sigh-breaths like a warm, bulky breeze.

"Let's spear him," Emily whispered. "We'll make bear hamburgers for breakfast."

"*Shhhh!*" I warned her, attempting to draw out the bear with a fist-sized stone. It thumped against the trunk and shook the branches. I laughed out to embolden myself.

"I told you it was nothing," she said. She moved onto a flat slab of rock to pick up a few midsize logs. After gathering a few of my own, and while reaching for what I assumed to be a long shadowy branch, my stomach suddenly dropped. A feeling of intense vertigo struck me as I realized that the black branch I'd been reaching for was the spectral night and nothing more. Emily screamed and dropped her logs, which clanked against the rock. She continued screaming on the ground, kicking backward, and I dropped down next to her, gripping the rock with my hands and knees, my elbows and feet, sensing the cliff moving in on all sides.

We turned the flashlight off and waited. When our eyes had adjusted to the darkness we crawled back to the campsite hunched over like frightened cavemen knuckling their way to safety. We assembled the tent and then lay silent on uneven ground, side by side, awaiting the next disaster. As my fears gave way to exhaustion I silently laughed at my recent attempts at religious faith and servitude, those mysterious creeds my parents and grandparents had clung to over the years. Already sliding toward the foot of the tent, I threw an arm over Emily and whispered good night. I placed my hand over her chest and felt her heart thumping. After I'd begun rubbing her breasts and she'd rolled onto her stomach, I tried to guess where we would've woken up after our near free fall in the cool black sky. Midway through the night I dreamt up the faint murmur of a phone ringing. I squirmed from the bottom of my sleeping bag and crawled from the tent, digging the phone out of a cubbyhole in the side of a boulder.

"This is George Flynn," I said.

"I know," the voice answered, low and throaty.

"Who am I talking to?"

"This is Special Agent Tikki Tavi of the FBI."

"Oh," I said, quickly coming to my senses. "Did you get him yet? Did you catch Nicholas Parsons?"

"Gotcha!" Katie yelled, cackling much longer than seemed fit. "Come on, George. *Rikki Tikki Tavi?* Are you even awake?"

"Barely. You didn't keep your promise, did you?"

"I'm keeping it now. I've never been to Colorado, except when I changed planes once in Denver. So if you care at all about my time capsule, you're pretty friggin' cold searching around up in the mountains. And one more thing. I miss you, George. I've got lonely lips over here."

suddenly feel I've wasted enough pages on our Rocky Mountain camping trip that in the end proved more unorganized and toiling than adventurous and romantic. I'll consequently forgo detailed descriptions of our mournful alpine descent and even more tragic return to Des Moines, which mostly involved Emily jerking from lane to lane, begging me to comment on her nerve-racked recklessness. Concluding the matter, I'll say that on witnessing Emily's bloody-footed reappearance, Mrs. Schell was far less sympathetic than my own parents, who were still adhering to the laissez-faire mind-set of the weeks following Katie's death. While Emily merely sketched the punishing new schedule she'd been assigned, the severity of her situation was well reflected in a stony new expression and pair of black aviator sunglasses that perfectly articulated her detachment from any emotion connected to sorrow, vulnerability, or pain. That said, she made no attempts to seclude herself, and engaged nearly every trick imaginable to arrange our furtive rendezvous. She was as enthusiastic as ever when it came to impersonating our inimical Perkins waitresses and psychoanalyzing foreign dictators and outwitting her mother, though her soldierly posture in more intimate situations hinted that she was not only a hardened babe with a history, but smarter than all the nitwits around her, including myself. (It should be noted that two weeks after our trip she was fired from the Public Playhouse performance of *Guess Who's Coming to Dinner* after taking up the cause of her Sudanese co-lead, a fellow cast member from *Othello* who confided grave fears of exploitation, typecasting, and alienation from his community of disapproving brothers.)

Only three days before my collegiate departure, I received a call from a Menard's pay phone where Emily was meant to gather materials for a laborious gardening project in her parent's backyard. She asked me to meet her at Saylorville Beach, which had recently expanded when the park board bought a load of sand from Saudi Arabia. This purchase turned their little pebble farm into a quarter-mile of Maui, only with an infestation of milfoil weed and much fewer coconuts or waves. While I can't explain why, I was certain Emily had chosen this venue to more dramatically present her plan for our bold new lives as urban Chicago cohabitators. Before hanging up I was already imagining massive bartending tips and hands-on business training programs.

It turned out that the only other beachgoers that day were a glaringly pale middle-aged couple fumbling with an unassembled volleyball set and two obese preteens trying to wade as far out as they could without getting their shorts wet. We laid our towels down at the edge of the woods, allowing ourselves to easily switch between the sun and the shade. After ten minutes of silence I was still convinced that Emily had some major news to impart, though I was certain it had nothing to do with us moving to Chicago together. She didn't make the slightest attempt at conversation and went about sunbathing as though I wasn't there. While I first interpreted her behavior as a statement about the peaceful quietude that average nincompoops always felt the need to fill, I soon gathered that the real cause of her silence was her anger over the fact that I hadn't brought a swimsuit.

In no time her body was glistening. She had one arm thrown languidly over her forehead, revealing the tiny black stubble of her armpit as her chest rose and fell, her breasts leaning slightly to the sides. I turned my attention to the ripples in the lake, fully tortured as beads of sweat trickled down my brow and cheeks, salting the edges of my mouth. I pictured Katie's body swaying stupidly in the weeds and I told myself that if I was a soldier and the solution lay on the other side of the battlefield, I'd cheerfully lead the charge. I'd go it alone if need be, facing down bullets and land mines if there were only a simple flag to capture, brightly colored, flapping high on a hill. But as it was I was still squatting in the foxhole, unsure how to engage the enemy, who the enemy was, what this war was all about. Emily's bikini breasts swelled before me as she rolled to her side and lowered her sunglasses.

"Not going to take your shirt off?"

"I will."

"If you want, you could probably get away with wearing your boxers. Those guys won't tell the difference from over there."

"I don't feel like swimming. That's why I didn't bring a suit."

"All right," she said, rolling onto her back again. "But I didn't say anything about swimming."

She pushed her sunglasses back into place, smirking a little and leaving me to wonder if she was serious about some sort of sexual exhibition. I made a point of loudly unzipping myself. Emily sat up and watched me remove my shorts and T-shirt. I guessed she was curious if I had an erection after staring at her for so long. I didn't know if I should be embarrassed at not having an erection or embarrassed if I did. I felt the situation could go either way depending on what she said next.

"Better?" she asked, taking a drink of bottled water and handing it to me.

"Uh-huh."

"Maybe you'd be even more comfortable without the boxers."

"You think so?" I said, understanding that she was testing me. The two girls were swimming now and having a splash war. Their bras were perfectly visible under their T-shirts. I lifted off the sand and peeled my boxers down, dismayed by the childlike fuzziness of the red plumage below. "Why don't we go into the shade?"

"Think that would be safer?"

"Sun damage," I said. "We're too young to let ourselves go."

Emily chuckled and gave my thigh a little pat. I wrapped my towel around my waist and crawled to a weedy stretch of shade at the edge of the woods, semi-obstructed by a crooked maple. It seemed unlikely we could get away with anything serious, but I decided I wouldn't let two blubbery kids or poison ivy stop us if Emily wanted to try. We lay side by side on our backs, staring up through the branches. Soon Emily's hand was searching between my legs and I found myself distracted and my resolution faltered. A cool breeze blew over us and I shivered, suddenly alone, again picturing Katie in a dark underwater cavern, her face numb like the victim of a half-assed lobotomy. For a few long seconds I could hardly breathe and felt claustrophobic in a way that I can only compare to the sensation of a superior wrestler locking you in a hold you can't get out of, but you still haven't been pinned. My penis was crawling inside itself.

The situation grew worse when I began to expect that at any moment Emily would take her sunglasses off and put into words all the questions I was already asking myself in a man-to-penis interrogation. As she continued stroking me I closed my eyes to indulge in all the Katie Schell fantasies that since her death I'd steadfastly denied. I pictured her staring into the bathroom mirror, lifting her nightshirt to massage her petite, conical breasts. I saw her nipples presented in full when she greeted me at the edge of the bed, requesting immediate attention to that overanxious seedling that in her Celeste Elston novels would "pop forth from the warm earth like a prized radish." For one night only she'd beg for experience in every pose and position, desperate that her future lovers never know a piece of flesh I had not already tasted. I placed my hand flat on the bikini triangle between Emily's legs. She parted her thighs in stages as my penis swelled, soon inviting me to slide my hand under her bikini and over a mat of moist hair. As she fondled me with her right hand, she placed her left hand on top of mine, directing it up and down in long pressing strokes. Her hips lifted off the towel. Her sex was wide awake, bursting open even as my penis outstretched in her hand. She stroked faster as I dipped my finger inside her.

"What do you think?" she asked, her voice like a siren's voice calling out from deep beneath the sand, all the way from Saudi Arabia. I'd often imagined us making love for first time on Saylorville Beach, hours after the park had closed. We'd park down the road and hike through the woods, mostly knowing what we were going to do and bringing the necessary precautions, but not speaking of it. We might have gone there every night to practice, keeping our lips locked the whole time and speaking simultaneous gibberish, not understanding a word, letting our awkward knees, elbows, and noses say the stupid things while our hips and thighs poeticized.

I reached for Emily's sunglasses. When I pulled them off I found her searching the edge of the woods. I turned toward the volleyball couple who'd now disappeared, possibly relocated to a hiding place from which to spy on us. I wiped the sand from Emily's legs and stomach. She pulled her bikini off, inviting me to stare for a while at her wet tawny wirework.

When she undid her top I slid over her and kissed all around her chest. In the sunlight slipping through the shadows her nipples were the same color as her lips. I wasn't sure if my erection was aimed correctly or if it was somewhere above or below or stuck in the sand. As she reached down I kissed her. She was deeply concentrating and still squirming when I felt her body suddenly surrounding me and clenching. Her neck bones protruded as her chin jutted out and her head stretched away.

"Slow," she said, whispering in a strained grunt, low and unpleasant. I started to pull back but she gripped my hips and held me. "Tell me how it feels."

"I love you," I said.

Emily closed her eyes. She directed my hips back and forth, pushing and pulling until I was moving fast, feeling an initial coming sensation burn its way from my testicles up through my entire body. I pressed into that feeling, praying it would lead to a moment of clarity that would solve our lives in one fast shot (despite my certainty that it wouldn't). I felt suddenly thrown into a weird translation of my own fantasy, mistimed to include fat girls, a middle-aged couple who might've gone for security, a ghost on the set. I kept diving in and out, changing knees, pressing for a new deal, wanting harmony but achieving only morsels. We were two bad actors and there was almost no pleasure involved, just the feeling of the first seconds when I thought nothing and only felt—that initial vaginal clench, her hands squeezing my upper back and sides, that tingling pendant of hope.

"I love you," I said, louder than the first time. Emily reached into the thicket, holding herself in place by grasping at roots sticking out of the mud. Her head bobbed about brainlessly. Her breasts thrashed round and round, losing their shape like lopsided bowls on a potter's wheel. It was all guilt and nothing good until she pressed her forehead against my neck and we stopped colliding and moved together. She kissed my lips and suddenly we were okay and nothing was broken between us and I thought I understood the answer to everything. But whatever knowledge I'd gained in this moment was lost the second I shoved backward and Emily's thighs slammed closed and I came into the weeds. She watched the milky mess ooze out of me onto the maple tree. When it was done she parted her legs and sat up, staring in disgust at the red traces of blood on her inner thighs and stomach.

"What did you say?" she shouted, picking up her broken aviator sunglasses.

"What?" I said, understanding what fools we all were and falling back against the maple tree and squeezing out the last drops. Emily snapped her bikini on. I stepped into my boxers. We cleaned off in the lake, then dripped our way back to the parking lot.

Thirty-two

In the aftermath of the episode just reported I recalled with humiliation my adolescent fantasy of colliding with the sort of tragic drama that spawned the careers of countless artists, typically drug-addicted and hypersexual. While I avoided mentioning it before, in the wake of Katie's death I wallowed in the hopeful conviction that I would soon find myself bowled over by a creative inclination that would allow me to rise each morning certain of my life's purpose and the meaning of its prerequisite misfortunes. But three months had passed and no such inspiration had revealed itself. Assuming it never would, I was resigned to thinking that at best I'd end up one of those silently scarred old men who fascinates us all, a lonely nutcase who'd rant against seat belts and bike helmets and nicotine patches, all the things that made us weak and disallowed the possibility of a true death at a young age when we could still respect ourselves because we hadn't compromised a single inch. While I refuse to believe that I've really become such a person, from time to time I lose myself and go silent for a few days, or curse more often than feels healthy, or consider buying a one-way ticket to Tonga without warning anyone of my plans or bothering to inform them afterward. Just last week I received a surprise visit from Zach's family that found me alone in my garage, grimacing over a model train set and snapping at my two kid nephews when they suggested I was setting the track too long and I'd run out of rails and there'd be no way of connecting the loop.

The summer after my senior year came to an official close with a Labor Day barbecue in my parents' backyard. Under the glow of a neon blue bug zapper, during a grown-up deliberation on the increasingly fine line between office heckling and harassment, I began perusing the possibility of quitting college before I'd bothered to start. My final decision in this direction came early the next morning, hours before I was set to leave for Davenport on the same highway that Emily would take to Northwestern. Since my parents had taken the day off work to help move me into the dorm, we found ourselves with more than enough time for a round table discussion on the nobility of confronting life's most spectacular challenges. In illustration of this point my mom detailed the difficulties of working forty-five hours a week for a cowardly dentist named Dr. Rudge, who hated all his patients and insisted she keep them at bay until the last possible minute, after she'd finished all the cleaning and scraping and there was nothing else to do but smile and nod at the X-rays. But when it became clear she was beginning to doubt the rewards of these daily struggles, my dad played the angle of mathematics, somehow summoning an impromptu set of statistics relating the relationship between "temporarily" delaying college and lifelong economic failure. At one point they even suggested I live at home for a semester and commute to Ames, even though my dad played for Iowa and we'd spent half our lives ragging on the Cyclones. In an attempt to prove my desperation, I ended up begging them to take their old jobs back so we could all move to Davenport together. To my adverse surprise, my mom reacted as though this were a reasonable option, which forced me to make an ugly blubbering mess of myself, claim a mental breakdown, and swear to pursue an ambitious independent education while battling my Des Moinesian demons.

Let me say that these declarations were not as fickle and insincere as they probably sound, especially in the absence of the more personally cogent argument I'd developed throughout the previous sleepless night. The full truth is that I harbored grave discomforts at dragging a less than healed version of myself back to the city of my childhood, thus poisoning a sanctuary of purified memories with all the anxieties that marked life after Katie's death. While I've vowed not to dwell on the nastier episodes of my grieving process (and already broken this vow in the long-winded account of my experience with Mr. Jaffe and Hu and the hole sixteen golfers), it is necessary to know that at various stages throughout the summer I'd experienced no less than cloak-and-dagger nightmares, birthmark distortion, the sprouting of one glaringly white arm hair three inches long, false awareness of leaking faucets, jealousy, constipation, denial, as well as suspicions of premature balding and total spiritual collapse. (Imagine such a specimen cruising the Davenport Children's Zoo entangled in wanton images of a five-year-old version of himself happily slapping a goat as it stuck its head through the fence to take a bite out of his Captain America T-shirt.)

In terms of reasons unrelated to physical health, I should mention that I had no enthusiasm for bunking in a concrete cell with a complete stranger, or pledging a fraternity, or making new friends. I'd also shunned all aspirations of studying journalism, largely a consequence of being slandered in more than one article in the *Des Moines Register* (which I still consider unworthy of its national repute). Earlier that morning I'd reexamined one such article, paying particular attention to the front-page photo of Katie dolled up in her confirmation dress, trying not to smile, but surrendering a last-second smirk reminiscent of a horny young bride on her wedding day. As I stared into her eyes I began developing threads of reasoning connecting Katie's crush to her death, a tentative theory that she'd staged the accident as a way of tempting me to dive from the tree and race out to save her by way of mouth-to-mouth resuscitation while treading water in the middle of the lake.

accepted my first full-time job a few days later at the urging of Frank Moretti, the husband of my mom's best workmate Barb, and my dad's singular substitution for his "good-time boys" from Davenport. The Morettis didn't have kids and were famous for bragging about Zach and me (they once drove to Red Oak to cheer me on in their hometown where all the locals booed and called them big-city traitors) and somehow Frank convinced me I was doing him a big favor. In the mid-nineties, when Frank's company was still called Moretti Construction and he wore a handlebar mustache and couldn't stop eating the fat off of everything, Frank had at least half a dozen crews working simultaneously around the city. This made it possible for him to transfer me from one demolition job to the next like an itinerant patient with a prescription for cathartic sledgehammering. Over the next few weeks I smashed outdated kitchens and bathrooms, condemned pool houses, old-time bingo parlors, and even a few bankrupted, fancily decorated dinner clubs on the South Side. (On one of my first days a ceiling fell in on me and a fellow worker while ripping up a basement left water-damaged since the Great Flood. Neither of us was badly hurt, but I passed out and dreamt I was the construction worker star of a soap commercial, scrubbing away the day's grit and grime while Emily waited with a towel outside the shower door.) I woke even earlier than I had to, doing a hundred push-ups before setting off on long morning runs like an Ironman triathlete who'd stepped it up from wrestling rednecks with cauliflower ears to battling mountains, deserts, and oceans. In the early evenings I got to know every librarian at the Urbandale library—more precisely, they got to know me—and I checked out stacks of novels, plays, and epic poems, mostly working with a group of Russians armed with ferocious reading lists of their own collected works. I teetotaled and went to bed at ten and charged my new friends (some had the gall to impose strict codes of daily conduct, puritanical mores, philosophy, etc.) with training me as a virtuous troublemaker, a dissident troubadour on the hunt. Classes that fall were bedroom dialogues with compassionate outcasts and intellects like Alek, Fyodor, Mikhail, Boris, and their lesser-known acquaintances whose moral sensibilities still crushed me down to size. I cross-examined them, underlined and vocalized them, lay for existential banter on the plush couches of their margins. (What the Schell girls would think if they could see me now! Swathed in the bandages of a mind-bending new idiom!)

In Emily's first month of college we spoke at least once a week, though she was generally vague about her social life and our conversations often ended with me pondering the sordid possibilities of her big-city, self-help regimen. The biggest news I can recall from this period was that her parents spent the whole week of orientation at a hotel downtown. Apparently Mrs. Schell took the campus tour three or four times and persistently showed up at the dorm to deliver soaps, monogrammed towels, and other cutesy items she'd bought at expensive boutiques around town. But as the length and quality of our calls decreased, my thoughts shifted to Katie—her brazen pleasure in shouting my name, her tall tales addled by overwrought vocabulary, the way her piercing eyes gathered every detail at once, in a glance, like Emily's but with the sly edge of the undercover. I relived every incident of her physical flounderings, including her crash to the Whitfield sidewalk and the spilled orange juice on the morning of her death. I even saw her in the moments I wasn't there (alone drafting comics, laughing at her own jokes) and that might never have happened (bossing a frightened boyfriend to the back row of a movie theater, taking the initiative for her first kiss). It was during this period of labor, literary enlightenment, and reverie that I became entangled with the subject of Katie's time capsule, soon convincing myself that it not only existed, but contained articles of profound insight into her life that would add layers of meaning to her obscenely premature death.

It must have been mid-October when I embarked on a short-lived search for the capsule, beginning with a dramatic visit to Bud Fuze Fords where I bought an eight-year-old pickup with new tires for less than the amount of my first Frank Moretti paycheck. I drove directly from the dealership to Whitfield Academy to casually interview a few of Katie's old classmates. After witnessing the lineup of mothers edging inch by inch around the circular drive, I parked along the outer road, then progressed onto the school grounds in the character of a confident young administrator with an avid interest in secular education. As classes had just ended for the day, I found the hallways crowded with uniformed students ferreting through lockers and chasing one another, seemingly still caught in the happy throes of a playtime reunion after the summer break. I started off consulting the freshman bulletin board in the hallway. According to the lists of students, Katie's former class consisted of three forms, each composed of approximately fifteen students. While I recognized few names on the lists, and none of the students at the lockers nearby, I happened on better luck when I entered a ninth-grade social science room covered with enormous maps of practically every region in the world. With the full realization that I had no idea what I was looking for, my curiosity led me to a series of blown-up satellite photos, one of which overlooked the Whitfield grounds and gave me the impression that, if caught rummaging around, I'd be prosecuted to the fullest extent of the law. Midway through a quickened tour of class photos and sign-up sheets, I found myself perusing a poster for an academic club called "Republic of the Debate." While the poster was dated for the current semester, the promotional photos were clearly taken the previous semester, when I had a good feeling Katie had been involved. Sure enough, on further review, I found her posed as the most serious member of a foursome that included a curly-haired kid trying to cozy up to her, back-to-back with his arms crossed as though to lend the impression that he and Katie were the cornerstone powers of the squad. According to the text below, this student was none other than Thomas Staniszewski.

Feeling that a return visit would raise undue suspicion, I quickly headed for the parking lot, where I asked a random sampling of students if they knew where I might find him. I received more than a few condescending laughs at my mispronunciation of his surname, but was eventually directed to the far end of campus where I found him sitting alone on a cement pyramid, absorbed in a banged-up copy of *Moby-Dick*. Thomas Staniszewski was a sturdy young guy with baby fat and soft freckles. I judged him an obvious outsider, but also a guy who exuded the sort of quirky confidence that would eventually attract what I considered the right kind of women.

"Thomas *Stanshefski*?" I asked, mumbling over his surname as I took a seat next to him.

"Stan-ih-*shevski*," he said, rolling his eyes. "The *w* is pronounced like a *v*."

I repeated after him, noting a moderate nervousness as he looked me over, trying to figure out what I was up to without asking. I can't say that I blamed him. While preparing for the role I was currently performing I'd not only worn a pair of ironed khakis and navy sports jacket, but shaved my facial scruff until all that remained was a thin auburn mustache, neatly groomed in the Cuban style. While a broad, toothy smile might have better accompanied such a cut, in reaction to Thomas's obvious unease I felt my voice drop an octave and my expression shrink into something confused and borderline grim. Rendered speechless, Thomas turned his attention back to his book.

"Pardon the interruption," I said. "I'm Rick Wilder, on special assignment from the National Board of Education. I just had a meeting with your principal concerning Katie Schell, who was one of the top contestants this year in our Odyssey of the Mind Competition. First off, let me say how sorry I am to hear about this summer's accident."

Thomas clapped his book shut and began packing his backpack with the notebooks next to him, obviously on his way to ditching me. I can only guess that his eventual decision against this course of action was based on my mention of his principal, which might have given him the impression that I wouldn't be so easy to avoid the next time around. Before he spoke his shoulders dropped and he nodded to himself, softening his defensive stance.

"I was her classmate even before this school. But I don't know anything about the Odyssey of the Mind. What is that?"

"It's a nationwide problem-solving competition for gifted students. The winner gets a scholarship to the college of his or her choice. Here's the thing: in our last correspondence, we asked Katie to provide us with additional materials about her improvements to current weather balloon designs. Well, despite the circumstances, without these materials we can't grant her family the reward. So, the reason I'm talking to you is—"

Thomas scrunched his face up and turned to me, planting a hand on his hip, rather effeminately. As for myself, I was performing much better than I'd expected, even if my Rick Wilder character was emitting more of a Bud Fuze vibe than I'd intended.

"What's the point in giving her the scholarship now?"

"The board decided to award it to Katie's sister."

"The National Board of Education?"

"That's right."

Thomas started zipping and unzipping his backpack, his mental gears obviously grinding. "What exactly are you looking for? Some blueprints or something?"

"You got it," I said, feeling the interview starting to get away from me. I cleared my throat in an attempt to regain some sense of authority. "It's a pretty complicated design, and Katie forgot to send us the blueprints for one of the more minor sections of the model."

At this point Thomas was thoroughly flustered. He wiped his glasses in his shirt, apparently to better scrutinize my face, during which time he kept nodding to himself and sighing. I couldn't guess where he might've seen me before, but my mind raced to come up with the fewest number of questions that would offer the greatest set of answers, feeling it was only a matter of time before he identified me.

"Katie's parents have searched everywhere and can't seem to come up with these blueprints. I was hoping you'd know what she might have done with them?"

"I told you I've never heard of the Odyssey of the Mind."

"But you might have a guess about where she collected her work, a secret hiding place or something like that. When you consider the potential value of the project, it's not so surprising that she would've done everything she could to protect her plans."

"I wouldn't know about that," Thomas said, shrugging in apparent disagreement. He shaded his face and searched the lineup of cars, taking his time to think it over. "I guess I'm not *surprised*, but I doubt she was worried about someone stealing her plans. She probably just didn't want her parents to find out. She wasn't supposed to enter any more contests until after the surgery. That's why she didn't take the national Spanish exam."

"Surgery?" I said, breaking character by way of an anxious tone unbefitting an academic contest facilitator with no relation to the contestant. I stared into the sun, trying to hide my astonishment in the glare. "I knew Katie had multiple sclerosis, but I wasn't aware of any multiple sclerosis surgery."

"There isn't any. At least not that's *proven*," he said, apparently drawn in by my concern. At that moment Thomas seemed suddenly much older than before, even given the youthful blaze in his cheeks and the occasional cracks in his voice. "She was supposed to join a *clinical trial* at the Mayo Clinic up in Minnesota. They were going to take some cells from her *ankle* to replace the damaged ones in her *brain* and *spine*." He stared into the illustrated cover of *Moby-Dick*, sighing deeply, apparently annoyed at himself for getting so worked up. "Anyway, it's complicated and Katie didn't talk about it, so I don't want to talk about it, either. I knew her since we were six years old."

I pulled at my mustache, glancing nonchalantly in the direction of a group of boys shouting and laughing as they tossed a tennis ball from one to the other, teasing a kid who'd been playing catch with it against the side of the school. Meanwhile Thomas turned to a lone cloud, likely considering his own questions that only Katie could answer. Soon enough he grabbed his backpack by the straps and stood up, looking like he regretted the conversation and was planning to walk off, even if his ride had yet to appear. But again he decided against it. (Perhaps talking about Katie made him feel she wasn't so far away, though I really don't know why he sat back down.)

"Her doctors told her that all these contests made her more stressed out and caused her symptoms to get worse. And if her symptoms got worse, she couldn't have the surgery. They said she'd be too weak to recover."

I nodded, like this information might somehow help me find what I was looking for. I wondered if Katie's other classmates knew about the surgery or if she'd only confided in Thomas. I wanted to believe that she hadn't confided in anyone, and the only reason Thomas knew was because Mrs. Schell had informed one of Katie's teachers who wasn't as discreet with the information as he or she should have been. When Thomas stood up for the last time, I rose with him and reached for his hand.

"Thanks for your time," I said. "It sounds like I talked to the right guy."

Thomas shrugged and stepped back. "I don't know anything about these blueprints. All I know is that I've seen you before and your name isn't Rick. Besides, there's no such thing as the National Board of Education. It's the Department of Education. Everybody knows that."

Thomas waited for a response with an expression akin to a father's pity and disappointment for his fledgling teenaged son. When he realized I had nothing to say he turned and walked away, dismissively cool, appearing much closer to his lady-killing years than I initially thought.

Thirty-four

While the additional facts I received that day have led me over the years to consider gross revisions to the notion that Katie's drowning resulted from a jinxed slip out of a mostly buckled life jacket, I have never shared this or any other alternative theory with anyone. That is not to say I never felt tempted or occasionally entitled to ask Emily about Katie's attitude regarding the experimental operation she was scheduled to undertake. Perhaps someday I'll change my mind, but that day has not yet come, and I hope it never will. In any case, according to my research in the days after my meeting with Thomas Staniszewski, the half dozen surgeries of the type Katie was supposed to receive all resulted in modest decreases of the debilitating symptoms afflicting her. Even in the two cases where patients experienced only the mildest improvements, no records exist to suggest that they suffered additional damages. According to my interviews with several eighth-floor nurses at Mercy Frederick Hospital, Thomas Staniszewski's story checked out. These are the facts. It is enough to conclude by saying that I regretted my visit to Whitfield Academy and wished I'd never considered, nor would continue to consider, the questions it raised.

Thirty-five

'm now recalling a snowy Sunday, staring out my window at a vision so blurred by white windswept veils that I felt a mirage of Tolstoy's tundra arising between the space of my bedroom and the now invisible, brightly shuttered house across the street. It was unlike Zach to bother answering the phone. I guessed it had been ringing all morning.* Zach handed me the phone and marched out of my room as fast as he'd marched in. Emily and I hadn't spoken since her family's decision to spend Thanksgiving in Tennessee, and were incommunicado for several weeks before that.

*Recently Smitty figured out how to coordinate his bimonthly phone calls with my fifth-period lunch break. His last call came from a GI bar in downtown Seoul, which he claimed had an impressive library of classic vinyl, a decent porterhouse, and Korean bartenders who not only performed flame-juggling cocktail shows, but would write your name on a bottle of booze and not pour it for anyone else. I advised him to go AWOL on the slow boat across the Pacific and through the Panama Canal, all the way to the Gulf of Mexico and up the Mississippi to Davenport, where I'd pick him up and drive him home. But after I said this the phone went silent and all I could hear was Willie Nelson crooning on one of those vinyl albums he'd mentioned. "I've never even been *tardy*," Smitty finally said. "And I'm never gonna *be* tardy, either." I only tell you this to point out the irony in the fact that every once in a while I still consider visiting the recruiting station and signing up.

"This is Emily Schell's study buddy informing you of her updated status as a collegiate dropout. That's right, she's failed, and the city of Chicago has requested that she kindly buzz off back to the farm. She will henceforth and hitherto begin her march of shame back to Des Moines, though she's considering taking a personal weekend on the way with the only redhead who ever really gave a crap about her."

"Did you get my electronic mail?" I asked, having deliberated for weeks if I'd inspired our latest bout of silence by a misdeeded adjective or adverb.

"Yes I got your *e-lec-tron-ic* mail. But Becky's waiting in the car as we speak and her dad owns several Hy-Vees and it seems she's in a serious rush."

"You're coming right now?"

"Didn't I say *henceforth* and *hitherto*? It's right here in my script. So do you think you'll have enough time to break up with your new girlfriend and erase all evidence of her existence?"

I looked out the window, suddenly convinced she was on a cell phone and sneaking up the driveway. "Are you still reading from the script?"

"I cut that line from the opening statement, the longer version. But I'm glad I got to use it."

"Oh, well, I don't have a girlfriend. Did someone tell you I have a girlfriend? Smitty's the one with the new girlfriend. What the fuck is wrong with people?"

"Sorry," she said, getting serious. "I guess that was a bad joke. No one told me anything about your girlfriend. But here's the deal. Becky's from a wonderful little place called Davenport, Iowa, which is three hours from here, and only two hours from Des Moines. So, what would you say about meeting me at the Davenport Super 8, then driving me the rest of the way in your big badass Ford?"

"I'd say I'll be waiting for you."

"You know your way to the Super 8?"

"Don't worry about me. Just make sure Becky doesn't make any sudden turns. There's a lot of black ice out there."

"We'll be careful," she said, affectionately flippant. "Thanks a million, George. I'm really glad it worked out this way. I'll see you in three hours, okay?"

"Three hours," I said, then hung up, immediately attending to the preparatory details of sallying forth in the middle of a storm. First thing I called Frank, who in typical fashion didn't ask a question and told me to take whatever time I needed. Next I wrote a note to my parents, showered and shaved, checked the pickup's fluid levels and tire pressure, packed the cab with a tow chain and security blankets, gassed up, bought condoms, and set off for the highway feeling that every action since hanging up with Emily was accomplished in one sinuous balletic sequence. But as soon as I entered traffic one of my windshield wipers defaulted and I passed a minivan bunked down in the ditch and soon found myself crawling at forty miles per hour, keeping much more than the recommended distance behind my fellow drivers, even though the roads were recently plowed and salted and everyone else was cruising along with little more caution than usual. I listened to the radio for weather updates, hoping my patience over the previous months had paid off, but trying not to think about whether we'd soon return to official coupledom.

When I reached Davenport the snowstorm was building up again, despite giving passage to a few bright rays of light. The office build-ings next to the Super 8 were curiously shorter than I remembered them, surrounded by parking lots covered in fresh white sheets, everything flatter, like a vast plain. After nervously pacing about my quiet motel room, I paged through a few magazines in the lobby, then stepped outside to wander the premises. Despite the fact that I was waiting for her, my first sighting of Emily caught me even more off guard than her phone call. She was strolling down the sidewalk with black bobbed hair and blunt bangs. I might not have recognized her if she hadn't stopped at the edge of the parking lot, dropping her gym bag and smiling, like that was it, she'd shown up after all, new and improved, full of raven-haired wisdom and intrigue. As always I was struck by the lovely intelligence of her smile, but even that reflected her adoption of a new persona that I could only compare to an unruly starlet of silent film. When we met in the middle of the lot, she kissed my cheek and ran her fingers through the hair on one side of my head. I didn't know what to do or say except to stare into the most familiar aspect of her visage: her hazel eyes, more forlorn than when I'd first studied them outside the St. Pius auditorium, but tempered by a customary measure of rapt wonderment. We held hands and smiled, then hugged for a while, making sure it was really us.

"Should we start off with a tour around town?" she asked, tugging at her navy peacoat and thick woolen scarf. "This is your town still, isn't it?"

"We get offended when you call it a town."

"If Chicago's *that toddlin' town*, then Davenport can be a town, too."

"I'll run it by the committee," I said, strolling around her to inspect her haircut. The new look would take a while to get used to, but it was mature and exotic, seemingly fit for a dauntless actor paving her own way. I pulled at my chin and nodded.

"It's okay?" she asked.

"It's more than okay."

"Then I'll keep it," she said, stomping a foot in the snow for effect. I took her gym bag and we started toward the entrance to the motel, wondering where Emily had come from, but assuming Becky lived nearby, that for our first encounter in three months Emily preferred we meet alone.

"Who gave you the new coat and scarf?"

"I did. I've given myself a lot of new things. I'm thinking about giving myself an honorary degree."

"While you're at it, might as well make up two of them."

"I will," she said, stopping and swiping a hand over the iron railing. A sparkling cloud of snow flittered to the pavement. "But first things first. I know you're going to play tough about visiting your old neighborhood, but you should at least show me the kennel where you and Zach let all the dogs loose."

"I wouldn't call it *my* neighborhood."

"Neither would I," she said, raising an impertinent eyebrow. "I'd call it your *old* neighborhood. It's really a beautiful drive into town, or the city, or whatever. It's a pretty nice place, George."

I took a peek inside her gym bag, which was hardly packed beyond a pair of jeans and a sweater. "So you're really quitting?" I asked.

"It's a done deal. I'm hoping it will soften the blow when my parents realize I'll be living at home for a while. My mom calls about ten times a week." She stretched her arms out, yawning and lifting onto her toes. I had a feeling she wasn't as sure as she sounded. "Maybe you should take me for a walk by the river. It's not that cold, really."

"All right, but I should warn you that I'm reading a lot of Russians. I'm much more serious now. In a few more months I'll be *thinking* in Russian."

"Sounds like we're headed for an intellectual weekend. Is there hot chocolate in the room?"

"It's free in the lobby. Coffee, too."

"What will we eat? I'm hungry and I doubt this place has a restaurant."

"No idea," I said, gripping the railing on each side of her. "You look amazing. I don't know why I'm so surprised, but you're really beautiful."

Emily covered her lips and smiled. We were staring at each other again, fully appreciating that we were now two postsecondary deadbeats on a romantic weekend at the Davenport Super 8. The clouds shifted, blocking whatever rays had broken through. Emily looked away, breaking from what was evolving into something like meditation.

"To be honest, George, I was starting to get the feeling we'd never talk again. I'm sort of shocked to even be here right now. I've been thinking a lot about the way I acted at the funeral home and on the bridge, even how I kept so distant from you on the drive back from Colorado. I didn't have to be so hard on you, and I started to worry that even if I hadn't completely pushed you away, you'd never be able to see me the same way as you did in the beginning. But now I think maybe you've seen the worst of me and it will never get that bad again. It's not so bad to think that the worst has already passed."

I turned toward the road, where an old couple was shuffling down the sidewalk. I hoped she was right. I tried to believe the old adage that it gets easier after the first year, but even then I realized that we were only halfway there.

"The second I started to feel like myself again, I decided to leave school and come to see you."

"Let's go to the room," I said.

Thirty-six

We spread out on the bed, listening to a silence episodically broken by branches tapping Morse code against the window. I tried to forget everything that had happened since the last time I'd seen her. Emily didn't have much of a plan beyond driving back to Chicago in a few weeks to gather the rest of her things. Maybe she'd start up at Drake in the spring. One of her professors from a summer workshop had asked her to audition for his new play, but Emily wasn't sure.

"I can't concentrate," she said, for the third or fourth time. "I'm all stuck where it counts the most. We do these silly exercises onstage, whooping and coughing and making all sorts of weird noises. It's the only time that I feel comfortable. After that we play word games and partner up. We practice talking over each other without losing our train of thought. You have to keep going even if the person standing next to you is throwing out every line they can remember from *Julius Caesar*. One time we had a homework assignment to come up with a story that would make everyone cry. It could be real or made up, we didn't even have to say afterward if it was true. I couldn't do it. I skipped class for three weeks to avoid it. After that, everything I did was phony."

"Sounds like torture for the sake of torture. I would've skipped, too."

"I hope you wouldn't have. I hope you would've just told the story as it happened. Played it perfectly straight. Everyone would've been bawling."

"I don't see the point," I said.

"The point is that it's a really hard thing to do and everyone knows you're trying to make them cry, which makes it that much harder. Don't you ever wish you were brave enough to do something like that?"

"I guess you could call it bravery. But to me it's not that different from meeting someone who tells you all their life's tragedies in the first five minutes. Maybe I should understand that they're only asking for help, but whatever happened to keeping your private life private? I'd think you'd agree with that more than anyone. People who spill their guts like that creep me out. But, okay, what was I saying?"

"Something about bravery."

"Right. I definitely wouldn't be brave enough for an exercise like that. I get stage fright every chance I get."

Emily thought about it for a few seconds, then sat up and slapped my chest with the back of her hand. "Man, did you freak out when you got crowned homecoming king. Ever tell your construction buddies about that?"

"I'm sure they'd be real impressed. You really think I don't know you stuffed the ballot box?"

"You don't know that."

"Yes I do. Tino told me. He said you and the other girls wrote my name on a bunch of ballots and threw out all the extra ones because Peyton's aunt worked in the office and she was going to make sure he won no matter what."

"You should've seen your face!" she said, cackling and rolling onto her back again. "When the DJ called your name, you were *so serious*. Like you really thought you'd won some official post. Like you'd be stuck spending all your free time hosting meetings for the PTA!"

"I was confused, that's all. We'd just had our picture together, and I was trying to figure out if that was the closest I'd ever get to you. I didn't even vote that week."

Emily squeezed the pillow to wipe her eyes. I brushed a few strands of hair off the side of her face as she released a final leftover chuckle. She picked a loose hair off the comforter.

"My stylist said that every once in a while I should wash it with beer. It's supposed to be really healthy. You pour it on your head in the shower and when you come out, it shines like the top of the Chrysler Building."

"I'll bet it's even healthier if you drink some of it."

"I couldn't argue with that," she said. I pushed quietly out of bed, stepping toward the bathtub just as tenderly as we'd been speaking, practically tiptoeing. I flipped the light on to discover the bathtub fitted with a safety bar and antislip strips. I leaned against the doorway, facing Emily as she curled up in the bed.

"I don't know how this sounds, but I figured out that when you're in a really hot shower and you've got a cold beer, you can feel it go all the way down your throat and slide into your stomach. It's one of the best feelings in the world. If you want to know what it feels like, I'll go get some beer and we can take showers and drink some of it. You can wash with it, too."

Emily sat up and tucked her hair behind her ears. I had no idea what she was thinking, but throughout the next twenty-four hours random confessions kept spurting forth, wedged between our regular bouts of nonsense on everything under the sun. It was like we were bobbing back and forth between two worlds, sometimes floating effortlessly and other times treading hard. In any case, we found a balance and managed to keep each other afloat. She looked up from the shaggy carpet and caught my eyes. "I'm sick of feeling bad," she said, her voice quivering. "I don't want to feel bad anymore."

I nodded, trying to indicate my resolve to work things out no matter how long it took. But I was hardly sure of myself and wondered if in the long run it would be easier to cope on our own. This was a painful question to consider and I was growing impatient with pain. I grabbed my coat and walked back to the bed, leaning over to sniff along her neck. "I'll go for the beer," I said, kissing the top of her head.

It was a blustery ten-minute walk to the liquor store. By the time I arrived I'd already indulged fears of spotting Emily on the way back, marching swiftly along the opposite sidewalk with her gym bag under one arm and her black hair whipping in the wind. But when I returned to our room she was still there, smoking at the window ledge. She grabbed two beers and headed into the bathroom, instructing me to relax on the bed until she called. I drank by myself as the showerhead moaned and spat. When it was clear she was planning to torture me as long as she could, I undressed and banged twice and barged in. The bathroom was thick with soapy steam. Through the space between the curtain and the wall I spied an empty beer can and the back of a wet leg. I parted the curtain and stepped inside.

Emily was bright red from head to toe. With her back facing me and her chin propped on her right shoulder and her hair flat against her head and her eyes like planets and her eyelashes thick like the arms of starfish, I felt a heavy veil had been lifted and I was finally seeing her angelic face in full. She turned step by step in the spray and her naked body said everything it needed to about her personality and experience: her ears perked up and dripping, her arms crossed over her chest, gripping her shoulders; her hips jutting in and out; her thigh muscles flexing and unflexing; her knees locking and unlocking; the triangular fluff between her legs shimmering with radiant water beads like chandeliered crystals. She let go of her shoulders to expose her serious plum breasts and proud nipples that I could never imagine fitting anyone else. After wholly seizing her in my gaze I grabbed the beer can from the soap rack and poured it slowly over her head. "Kiss me," she said, arching her back as the beer dripped onto her shoulders and streamed down the crevice of her spine. She wanted a kiss on the lips but I kissed her everywhere else, lowering myself up and down to reach her breasts and stomach, her inner thighs and shins and arms and cheeks. She finally stood me up by the ears, drawing me into a long, tough stare-down before snatching the beer can from me, reaching down to cup her hand beneath my testicles, and pouring. I shouted out and shivered and pressed against her. Emily laughed as she crouched down to plug the drain. It wasn't long before we were sitting in a warm and shallow pool, clinking cans and covering our heads from the hard, limitless downpour. We left the beer cans in the shower, dried off, and crawled back into bed. My skin was chalky and numb and we were light as ghosts.

"Why didn't you kiss me?" she whispered. "What are you waiting for?"

She didn't give me time to reply. And that's when I learned that the right girl can kiss a man as if he were a dying bear she'd nurtured all winter and made him strong again so that the forest would tremble in fear at his hungry rebirth. (My love for her was different then, and looking back I blame this change less on the new look than on her rambling stride, which I could still pick out a mile away. I'd already noticed it on our brief stroll across the parking lot, like a wandering promenade built for the velocity of her imagination. There was evidence of it even in her kiss.) We made love locked together in a hug still sweating from the bath. Emily wanted me to talk to her while we rocked back and forth, but I couldn't. She moaned in a series alternately subtle and guttural, and then in one long sigh when her cheeks gushed and her legs locked around my back, holding me motionless until her whole body went limp. I fell back and she fell back with me, collapsing on my chest. We lay tangled up flesh to flesh while I wondered how long such a serene feeling could last, whether we'd have to continue drinking in order to make it work that well every time. A few minutes later Emily was rubbing her chest against my stomach, then straddling one thigh and grinding against it. Soon enough we were at it again, but this time she was so worked up and writhing that I had to grip her by the back of the arms just to stop her from slipping away.

Thirty-seven

ate that afternoon we arrived at the Machine Shed Steakhouse with famished stomachs even greedier than our eyes. We wolfed down steaks, potato pancakes, heaping salad bar salads, then rounded out the meal with cheesecake and a twenty-minute conversation on nonconformity as a necessary fuel of democracy.* After paying the bill Emily decided we'd better walk a while before returning to the motel. We ditched the car and headed for the snowplows hustling up and down Third Avenue, beeping and flashing emergency lights. When Third Avenue dead-ended at a rural highway we kept on going, soon passing an abandoned gas station and a chicken farm. The setting sun reflected

---

*This past fall I was invited as a guest speaker for an extracurricular class called Modern Lifestyles, which is basically a euphemism for Home Economics, despite its greater emphasis on personal well-being in an age of increased options and changing gender roles. I was asked to present the students with a portrait of singlehood. But in the middle of extolling the benefits of unhindered self-exploration—citing my own discoveries in Portuguese and slam poetry, as well as my extensive tours of India and Brazil—I ended up losing my train of thought and silently indulging the possibilities of a marriage to all three Schell women: the enormous bed we would share, waking to rest my head on the buoyant buttocks of one, laying a gentle palm over the sleepy nipples of another, and kissing the third on her warm pink cheek moments before she crawled from bed with the wispy hairs at the small of her neck silhouetted in the light of dawn.

kaleidoscopic off the crystal frost in the trees, the last rays of light so bright I swore summer was creeping in through the sparkles in the snow. In the roadside ditch heaps of snow slumped next to sheets of rippling mud. We must've walked a couple of miles around the country, yakking on about electronic matchmaking, chatting, cyber dating, etc.

"Oh, the lovely Internet," Emily said, stomping through a fresh mound of snow. "Can't say that I mind the convenience, but I don't know how many nights my roommate kept me up till three in the morning designing a webpage with her whole life story in photos. She's got photos of babies in bathtubs, dogs in bathtubs, and profiles of pretty much everyone she's ever met. I don't even want to think what she's writing about her whacko roommate."

"I'm not gonna use the Internet. I can hardly type anyway."

Emily hooted and patted my back. "Good luck with that, George."

"Smitty's getting into it. Apparently he's making a website for some politician who's lost his last three races for governor."

"Can you call yourself a politician if you've never been elected?"

"Maybe not," I said.

"Don't they have some kind of three-strikes-and-you're-out policy? How can someone just keep going around losing like that? Does he even care about winning, or is he just in it to argue with some bigwigs on TV?"

"I don't know, but I kind of like the guy, even if he is the most famous loser in the state. He's an advocate for pesticide-free farming, which pisses everyone off, and apparently he wants to run the Iowa caucus out of the state until the federal government dumps the electoral college."

"Interesting idea," Emily said, seemingly impressed by my venture in politics. "Here's another one. Let's invite more politicians to the caucus and pesticide the whole bunch."

"Even Slick Willie?"

"Slick Willie's not *just* a politician. He's an artist. An actor. A pretty good one, too."

We held hands and took turns kicking a plastic bottle down the road. I thought about Clinton's first love, what she looked like and where she ended up in life. "I hope after he leaves the White House, he finds a girl with a little more spark. It's hard to believe he couldn't do better than Hillary. Jesus, is she harsh."

"Maybe *now* she's harsh. She's got to be, George. She's living in the lion's den. Don't you know that any woman with an ounce of ambition has got to turn herself into a man, a trash-talking slimeball of a man, if she's ever going to win any respect? Her tenderness, her natural aversion to violence, her willingness to talk things out—all her best womanly qualities gotta go right out the window."

Emily was walking faster now, taking long strides, shaking her head and waving her hands. She booted our plastic bottle into the ditch. "It's like that girl wrestler from Winterset. She had to turn into a complete jerk just so the guys wouldn't forfeit, so they'd at least take her seriously and walk onto the mat and give her a chance. But men, well, they have all sorts of options. They just typically choose to be hypocrite slimeballs. On the road to success, that's the fastest, easiest way."

I stopped, caught by a cramp that forced me to bend over and clutch my stomach. "This hypocrite slimeball's got half a T-Bone working itself into a cramp."

Emily bent over just the same. The way she held her side let me know she'd had a cramp, too, but wasn't planning to mention it. "You were saying?" I asked.

"Nothing. I've been reading too many newspapers recently. I should stop. This world can sure put me in a foul mood."

A truck zoomed down the road, kicking up gravel that scattered over the ice. We decided to turn back. On the way Emily informed me more gently about the latest international happenings: Kofi Annan, the new UN secretary-general, protease inhibitors for AIDS patients, even details of the Hutu refugees returning to Rwanda. I could see the new Emily Schell arriving confidently at Hollywood's doorstep, armed with all the political and karmic righteousness she'd need to pound her way in. We stopped near a frozen pond to watch the sun winking over the horizon.

"That girl wrestler," she said. "She was pretty good, right?"

"She didn't get a lot of matches, but yeah, she was tough. She beat one of Valley's best guys four or five times. Never pinned him though. They always went at it the full six minutes."

"Did they become friends or anything like that?"

"I don't know. There were all sorts of jokes about them, but I don't think they ever saw each other anywhere except the tournaments."

Emily nodded, looking impressed, like she wished she'd been a wrestler in high school. She gave the setting sun a wave goodbye. I threw my arm over her shoulder and we kept on.

"You know, George, if you were running for office, I might even vote. But only if you grew a curlicue mustache."

I thought about my Cuban mustache, which reminded me of Thomas Staniszewski and the question of whether it was right to ask Emily about her sister's operation. Emily sensed I'd moved onto more serious thoughts and kept turning to me, waiting for me to spit it out. "I think you should vote for Smitty's guy," I finally said. "Martin O'Toole. Maybe he'll bring just the change we're looking for."

Emily smirked, knowing I'd evaded whatever other question I'd been considering. "Just to clarify, George. If you ran for office, I said I'd vote, but I didn't say I'd vote for *you*."

"I wouldn't vote for me, either."

Thirty-eight

That night a local cable channel was showing Alfred Hitchcock's *Notorious* with Cary Grant and Ingrid Bergman and enough melodramatic one-liners to keep Emily pumping her fists like a child conquering level after level of a new video game designed just for her. She was so mesmerized by the opening sequence that she lowered the TV to the floor and lay in front of it, propping up on her elbows with her long piano fingers fanned out over her cheeks so that the black-and-white images flickered scene by scene across her face. She cheered and hissed, mimicking the grotesque expressions of the Nazi scientists as they crept their way nose to nose with the lens and the audience. We agreed that the plot didn't entirely make sense, but that didn't matter; it was enough to appreciate Grant's hard paralytic kisses with Bergman (the most convincing Hollywood beauty of all time, against whom today's leading ladies frump and slouch and melt like the Wicked Witch). The snow was beginning to pile up again as we crawled into bed and fell asleep.

At some point in the night we woke and made love without a word. When we finally spoke our voices were slow and extraneous, like we'd floated above ourselves to untangle a mystical web, beginning with the branch still tapping at the window, issuing messages from the far side of consciousness.

"Can I ask you a question about Katie?" I said, kicking up a static spark as my knee jerked under the sheets. Emily's eyes widened and she nodded, like it was in the interest of safety to say yes. "How much did she know about us?" I asked.

"She obviously knew something," she said, pulling the covers over her bare chest. "But she didn't know we were meeting up before school. I never told her about the night of the movie premiere or our mornings before school."

"Because she would've been jealous, or because you just didn't?"

"I don't know. I wasn't trying to deliberately keep it from her, but everyone at school was asking me so many questions, like it was their automatic right to know all the details. Whenever I could avoid talking about it, I kept it to myself."

"What about your parents?"

"My mom knew something, but I'm sure my dad didn't know. He always thought we were just pals. I mean, when you think about it, for most of the time he was right. But as far as Katie goes, well, I have to admit that I wasn't really looking forward to sharing all the details."

I scratched the back of my neck, my telltale sign of nervousness that only Emily recognized and commented on. But she didn't say anything this time and only smirked and pushed out of bed to crack the window open. On returning she sat up and lit a cigarette, changing the subject for a moment to explain that since ninety percent of the theater department smoked, she'd been inhaling a pack a day anyway. We passed the cigarette. I never asked whether her parents had made gestures toward forgiving me, but she sensed my anxiety and ended up finding her own way to the subject.

"The important thing is that you were always good to my sister. Even my mom can't deny that. Everybody tiptoed around Katie because she was sick, but you treated her like a regular kid. I mean, Jesus, it wasn't a big mystery why she talked about you morning, noon, and night."

At this point in the smoky dark Katie grew closer and more real than ever. I swore I felt her wind-up laughter echoing through the mattress, flattering me in the same sonorous way that she always had, so effortlessly and matchlessly that for months I'd forced myself to forget it. I started sobbing, caught in such an overwhelming storm that attempting to stop it would've only rendered it louder and more ludicrous, as absurd as the twisted faces of the cinematized Nazis. Emily wrapped her knees around my waist and her arms around my neck as her cigarette smoked in the ashtray. It took a long time to breathe normally. I tried to explain myself but my voice wasn't ready and instantly filled with all the emotions that feed on themselves and force you backward.

"I don't understand," I finally said, steadying myself, but still sucking air. "I just want to know exactly what happened."

"Come on, George. She unbuckled it while you were swimming to shore. She put the rod down, unbuckled the life vest, and we didn't notice. Why would we?"

"Even if it fell off, she could've grabbed it and stayed afloat."

Emily put her cigarette out and moved the ashtray to the bed stand. She waved a hand though the lingering smoke. "She was weak that day. You might not have noticed, but I did. She was always trying to look strong around you, but every step she was struggling. She knew she was weak and she panicked. You can't panic like that. That's what really did it. Panic."

"How do you know?"

"Trust me. However much you've cried about it, turned it over in your head, I've cried twice as much. And my parents, they've never stopped crying."

"They don't even know the truth," I said. "They still think she wasn't even wearing a life jacket."

"No one knows the *truth*, George, and knowing that she was wearing the jacket wouldn't make it easier. Just please do me a favor and don't let me fall asleep for the rest of the night. I've gotta go home tomorrow, so let's just keep practicing what we've been practicing and not sleep at all. Are you tired?"

"No."

"Good. Now give me a hug."

I pulled her close, squeezing her as she dried my face with the back of her hand. In some ways I felt my breathing never returned to normal the whole night, even at three a.m. when she promised to try every position we could come up with if I pledged not to fall asleep, no matter what. She didn't seem to understand my repugnance at the idea of sneaking around our whole lives, my need for her parents to realize the true limits of my negligence. But I didn't explain this. I didn't want to appear selfish and make an even bigger fool of myself than I already had. I needed Emily to understand this point on her own.

"I thought you were gone for good," I said.

"I guess that's just not how the story goes."

"Any idea how it ends?"

"No sé, mi amor. No sé."

A minute later Emily brought her Spanish textbook to bed. I kissed her everywhere, snooping around her ankles and knees while she sat back in bed with her book propped up on her chest so I couldn't see her face. She taught me adverbs that meant "slowly" and "softly" and verbs that meant "to ignore" and "to behave." By dawn she was standing with a blanket draped over her shoulders, studying herself in the mirror while leaning against the closet, her hair thrown over to one side like a juvenile delinquent, the work of my combing hands after our last round. I was there, too, in the reflection, sitting on the bed in the lower right corner, the morning light casting long vertical shadows through the blinds. Emily was stronger than before, sturdier, and when she stood on her tiptoes her stomach flexed and her hips swelled with courage. She looked at herself and then at my reflection as I scratched my chest. The heater cranked and hissed. It was snowing again and the branch commenced its tapping routine against the window. She came back to bed. We guided ourselves in pleasure and hope all morning and into the afternoon, and each time I clasped her feet at the dire peak.

Thirty-nine

As I noted when first introducing him, my father served in the Vietnam War, an experience that most of its veterans either speak unreservedly about or never speak about, and my dad is one of the latter. I mention this now because over the course of the year in question he seemed to have adopted the burden of my stress to such an extent that we all noticed him transgress in his ability to separate himself from the memories of his losses, which included, in the most tangible terms, his older brother. Though Zach and I knew few details of his tour beyond what we gleaned from offhand remarks every few years (like when he told us, during a reality show competition in sleep deprivation, how easy it was to stay awake those three days he'd spent trapped on a mountainside as Victor Charlie tunneled in and fired from every unseen angle his delirious mind could fathom), after Katie's death I had the impression that he felt closer to me, as though I understood something of his experience that my mom and brother never could.

While we never had a conversation about the deaths he'd presumably caused or witnessed, that December he set up an artificial

Christmas tree he'd won in an office raffle, then woke the next morning with the decision to stop shaving for the first time since his service days, when in a short-lived exhibition of solidarity his platoon gave up the razor to become the only band of bearded warriors in the war. He told me all about it during halftime of a Bears–Packers game after I'd noticed him anxiously eyeballing the tree's shiny plastic branches, many of which twisted under the weight of ornaments into sideways angles not found in nature. Over time this glare became so filled with contempt that I swore he was expecting an assault rifle to peep through the branches for a quick round of jungle-loving potshots. But while splitting a six-pack of Old Milwaukee, he ended up describing the Christmas he spent in Da Nang, which was highlighted by a surprise visit from the most famous actor to ever play Tarzan at the unfortunate moment when half the soldiers in his tent were sitting on the edge of their cots, crouched over their knees, sniffling along to an Andy Williams Christmas album. Even more significant than their visit with Tarzan was the following day's encounter with an elderly Vietnamese with a thin white beard and a trained elephant. As a Christmas present the man offered each soldier in my dad's platoon a free elephant ride, promising it would ensure their protection from evil wherever they may roam—which of course ended with their decision to superstitiously quit shaving. A while later, after our conversation had already veered off course and my dad was beginning to relax, he even went so far as to tell me that he fell in love with my mom when he was eighteen, one year before he shipped out, and was perfectly content that she was the first and last lover he would ever know.

This father-son heart-to-heart wasn't the only surprise that Christmas. A few days later we ended up hosting a dinner in honor of Zach's new girlfriend (now his wife, for whom at the time he'd sworn off all relations with Gordo's waitresses that he typically banged for a few weeks while doing his best to avoid being spotted with them in public).

Zach originally met Rachel two years previously on a secluded retreat called "Teens Encounter Christ," where he and a group of fellow seniors from around the state sat Indian style around candles crying and hugging and spiritually bonding over their most incestuous secrets. Who knows what lies Zach spun about his catastrophic childhood or the psychological ill effects of the Holiday Inn murder, but apparently he'd made enough of an impression on Rachel that out of nowhere two years later she called to inform him that she was now living in Des Moines, doing an internship at Wells Fargo while attending part-time classes at Grand View College. When she showed up for dinner with a homemade cake in the shape of a shamrock, topped with a frosted leprechaunesque Santa Claus, my mom nearly burst into tears.

Rachel was bubbly and crystal-eyed with an innocent, if somewhat annoyingly shrill, voice, so kind and confidently affectionate that she even inspired my mom to share a story about the first time she met my dad (unrelated to my dad's amorous revelation; she told this story all the time) back when she was a grocery store cashier and he saved her from a lewd drunk who followed her into the parking lot and sprawled over the hood of her car begging for a kiss. But what was most surprising about Rachel's visit was Zach's reaction to her. Not only did he display a previously unknown amount of manners and genteel formality—despite attempting to cancel the event earlier that afternoon on the grounds that they were still unestablished—but over the course of the meal abandoned his fixation on hiding all evidence of interpersonal affection. For most of the dinner he simply observed her, awestruck by the skill with which she charmed the pants off us. Even as she shared the cutesy details of their time together at T.E.C., and the nervousness she felt calling him after two years out of contact, Zach only beamed brighter and prouder, as though he wished the night would never end. Perhaps in my reverie I go too far, but at the point I caught my brother and Rachel slicing their braised chicken, noticing the parallel synchronicity of each other's movements, and glancing up and smirking before taking their simultaneous bites, I felt a part of an extraordinarily rare episode when one has the opportunity to witness a man and woman fall instantaneously and determinedly in love.

Meanwhile Emily and I continued operating in the realm of the underground. The next morning I received a phone alert informing me that her parents had just left for the company Christmas party and planned to be out the entire day. I raced over, parked at the West End Club, then walked the remaining five or six blocks, as instructed. But my enthusiasm significantly diminished after meandering through a set of festive subdivision streets marbled with melted snow only to confront the Schell home, whose minimalist decor was wholly dependent on a blinking string of white bulbs in the bushes next to the garage. Before I'd even reached the driveway Emily was at the door hurrying me inside.

"Feliz Navidad," she said, snapping the door shut behind us and kissing me and pointing at my boots to let me know I'd better get them off pronto. Then she grabbed my hand and dragged me upstairs to her bedroom, immediately drawing the shades closed to avoid being scoped by her neighbors across the street. She sat me down at her desk, then sprung from one side of the room to the other to retrieve a shoe box–sized gift wrapped in the Sunday comics.

"I didn't know we were exchanging presents," I said, having special-ordered a sleep therapy sound machine that had yet to arrive. Emily plopped into my lap and handed it to me.

"We're not. I'm giving *us* a present."

I ripped it open. It was a set of two-way radios from Radio Shack. "They work like magic," she said. "Up to ten miles. Go ahead and try."

I opened the box and loaded the batteries. It was a much better present than I'd bought for her, despite remembering a time when we used to make fun of the uninspired majority for shopping at places like Brookstone and Radio Shack. But I also recognized the rationale behind her present given the amount of time I wasted waiting for her to call me, or being forced to communicate in codes that most of the time I didn't understand. Emily wandered downstairs to initiate a game of hide-and-seek. While waiting the fixed five minutes before beginning my search I perused Emily's bookshelf and media rack, which was now slumping with the weight of bizarre foreign film collections and CDs of obscure bands I'd never heard of. On examining the photographic collage over her desk, I noticed an obvious reworking of images in favor of her new friends from Northwestern, most of whom appeared carefree and self-assured, if obnoxiously clean-cut. I identified myself in only one photo, a shot from our senior skip day where I stood half hunched over in laughter, pointing excitedly off camera. I must've been staring at myself for several minutes, trying to remember what I was laughing about, when Emily's voice crackled through the radio.

"Are you coming or what?" she whispered. "You'll never find me. Over."

"Look out, look out," I said, heading to the middle floor and checking the front hall closet at the bottom of the steps. After noticing several parkas and raincoats Emily had worn over the past few years, I flipped the light on, knowing she intended to give me a good challenge and making sure she hadn't concealed herself behind the suitcases on the top shelf. There was nowhere else to hide in the front hallway, so I moved to the dining room, already raising the radio to my mouth in search of a hint.

"I thought you were a big fan of the Schell's Shirtworks Christmas party. What happened? Over."

When she didn't answer right away I checked behind the thick curtains and strolled around the table, soon regretting the decision on noticing the tracks I'd left in the pristine carpet.

"I *was* a fan," she finally said. "Back when Santa came and there were presents for all the kids. This year it's adults only. Over."

"What time did the party start?" I asked as I approached the living room. Emily waited even longer to answer than the first time, which made me think she was hiding nearby, under one of the couches or behind the antique filing cabinet in the corner. All the furniture had been rearranged and now faced the cedar trees in the backyard. The TV was gone, likely moved to the basement, which I remembered Mr. Schell had planned to redesign as his entertainment headquarters. As usual the house was spotless, everything in its proper place, including ornate candles with fresh wicks over the mantel and a Versailles photo book on the coffee table casually opened to invite a view of its symmetric gardens.

Gathering no evidence of Emily, I progressed along to the kitchen. On opening the door to the pantry I discovered its cereal and snack boxes lined up by height, its hundred or more canned goods grouped by category, all facing forward. (There was probably enough food to wait out the next five floods.) The radio sparked up.

"Where the heck are you? Over."

"I'm helping myself to a few snacks," I said.

"Clear out of there. It's not real food, just part of the set design."

The only detectable trace of Emily's voice was through the radio. Otherwise the house was completely silent, except for the occasional sound of the automatic heating vents. I thoroughly searched the rest of the kitchen and laundry room, then moved on to the basement, which was entirely remodeled. There was a pool table and a bar, a leather couch facing an in-home theater, a mounted antique pistol with a silver-plated grip—all the props of a man's quarters with none of the feeling. The bar was decorated with drink coasters in a little rack next to magazines fanned in a semicircle. In a closet near the half bathroom I found a shelf stacked with Emily and Katie's old children's books and sing-along records. Below it were two shelves dedicated to every board game ever produced by Milton Bradley, all as neatly arranged as the cans in the kitchen pantry. Next I checked the storage room, which turned up nothing more than a row of metal shelving half stacked with Schell's Shirtworks boxes. As a matter of course I peeked into the biggest boxes, most of which were filled with sleeping bags, old blankets, and bedding. The exception was the box nearest the doorway, which contained four variegated stacks of T-shirts, one of them displaying the image of an elementary-school-aged Emily in a tuxedo tailcoat and tall black hat on a mock playbill for a show called *Me and My Shadow*. I continued to the shirt on the stack next to it, lifting it by the collar until it fell open to display a photo of Katie as a toddler crying on a neighborhood curb while Emily patted her back, advising by way of a comic strip balloon, "It's tough being a kid."

Knowing I didn't have enough time or skill to refold the shirts correctly, I still continued to work my way through the box, soon discovering an entire family history in stenciled T-shirts, many accentuated by clichéd captions like I'M WITH STUPID, which I discovered beneath a vacation photo of Katie staring dismayed at the camera while in the background Emily—along with her saddle—was sliding halfway off a yawning horse. The most interesting shirts were those printed with collegiate photos of Mrs. Schell sporting long hair and blue eye shadow, displaying such a broad, healthful smile that for the first time she reminded me of Emily. I eventually came upon a series of sexy leg T-shirts that made me more depressed than anything else, imagining Mr. Schell after hours in the back room of Schell's Shirtworks, slung over an industrial fabric printer next to a box of family photos he'd likely been ordered to ship out of the house. There stood Mrs. Schell performing her own barelegged version of *A Chorus Line* atop a dorm room windowsill during a campus snowstorm. There again with her legs dangling out the passenger window of a 1971 Dodge

Challenger on a shirt labeled in hot pink lettering: MY SOUTHERN SWEETIE! I didn't notice a single photo of Mr. Schell until I reached the bottom of the box, where I found a black long-sleeved shirt depicting a young skin-and-bones Richie in the center of a boxing ring, flexing bare chested with his hair greased back and his taunting fists raised in battle. In the bold type of a newspaper headline the caption read WORLD CHAMPION DAD.

Expecting at any moment to be caught, I quickly stuffed the T-shirts back in the box, saving my folding efforts for those at the top of each stack. I nimbly loped to the top floor, knowing it was unlikely that Emily would hide in Katie's room, but inspired by my last discovery and struck by a perverse curiosity to know what Mrs. Schell had done with the space. I stepped as lightly as possible along the upstairs hallway—figuring now that Emily was hiding in the kids' bathroom and might be on to me, but deciding to check Katie's room anyway—expecting to find it converted into either an office or a small exercise studio. But on turning the door handle and gently pushing my way inside, I found it looking exactly as it did when Katie was still alive. It was as though someone had come in to dust and empty the trash, but hadn't touched anything else. There were movie and animal posters still covering the walls, a bottle of water half full on the nightstand, a desk cluttered with little notebooks decorated with stickers, CD jewel cases, and a fancy coin bank with a combination lock. Even the bed was still unmade.

Without pausing to think about it, I launched into an immediate hunt for her diary, for common snooping purposes, but also bowing to a resurgent compulsion toward uncovering a hint of the location of her time capsule. I searched drawer after drawer, scanning through notebooks and sketchbooks, pausing on cartoon drawings of Columbus and Magellan, a few indecipherable margin notes, several half-finished haikus. The only real clue I came up with was a telephone book–sized edition of *America's Best Colleges* whose underlined sentences served to illuminate the subtle hues of Katie's future plans, her markings highlighting her interest in such campus offerings as "a proud history of political influence," "tremendous rates of food service satisfaction," and "options for triple majors." I was flat on my stomach poking around under the bed when Emily's voice broke through and I quickly turned the volume down to avoid giving up my position.

"You aren't in Katie's room, are you?"

"None of your business," I whispered.

"I'm not in Katie's room, okay? Over."

I crawled out from under the bed and exited as carefully as I'd entered, twisting the handle to mute the sound of the lock clicking against the plate. Next I checked the linen closet, then the bathroom, where I braced myself for a shock if Emily decided to jump out from behind the shower curtain. But she didn't, so I proceeded down the hallway to her parents' bedroom, cupping my hand over the receiver and whispering, hoping for a tip-off before my next intrusion.

"I'm on your trail," I said. I could tell by Emily's voice that she was cupping the receiver just the same as me.

"How long are you planning on taking to find me?"

"I planned to find you ten minutes ago."

"I have a feeling you're really cold, George."

The Schells' bedroom looked like a fake set for a furniture catalog. There was a smooth, king-sized canopy bed, a perfectly polished armoire, his and hers reading lamps, and chairs at each window. The whole sense of the room oozed suspicions that someone had just wiped it clean of blood and fingerprints. I started off searching the closet, a long walk-in with cedar panels, rows of suits and oxford cloth shirts along one side, plastic-covered dresses and blouses along the other, all those shoulders swaying lifelike as I reached between them to cover every possible hiding space. Next I crossed over to the bathroom, where I burst through the door fast and brave, immediately switching on the lights to find myself confronted with a dozen reflections in three mirrors, each version of myself assuming the role of the creep in a commercial for burglar alarms. Certain that Emily was somewhere else, but feeling the game ought to last a while longer, I turned back into the bedroom to peruse the armoire, its swinging double doors revealing a wide variety of compartments seemingly designed for distinct secreting purposes. In little time I discovered a treasure trove of items in a drawer that on the surface provided housing for nothing more than baby blue boxer shorts and thin black socks with gold toes (an undergarment that ever since I've considered creepily effeminate). With some courage I felt my way beneath the pile, where I soon removed an official Major League baseball encased in a hard plastic cube signed TO MY PAL RICH, BEST WISHES FROM WILLIE MAYS. Other items included a gold watch with a cracked face, a yellowed leaflet missal from midnight Mass at the Vatican Basilica dated December 25, 1943, a laminated wallet-sized copy of the Serenity Prayer, and a battered paperback edition of *Shane* by Jack Schaefer. I replaced the items as I found them, then crept my way from the room, returning ever so quietly to the basement where I immediately spotted Emily's bare legs dangling over the edge of the leather couch. I stepped around it with one hand out like a pistol, only to find Emily shaking her head, looking bored in a Santa Claus hat, a Jake the Chili King T-shirt, and plain white panties.

"Not sure how I missed you the first time," I said.

"You weren't looking close enough. What were you doing up there? Trying on my mom's dinner dresses?"

"Just the black one with the sequins. It didn't fit me."

"I'm surprised," she said. "You've got such dainty hips. By the way, did you shower this morning? Your hair is looking pretty scruffy and I think I like it."

"Thanks for noticing. I didn't shower yesterday, either. Did I see a set of double showerheads in your parents' bathroom? Do they really shower together?"

"They didn't *choose* the double showerheads. This was a model home," she said, pinning one foot over the other, curling her toes together. "They don't even sleep together. My dad's on the floor now. He says it's better for his back. Anyway, are you gonna help me inaugurate this new leather couch or what?"

"You sure we have enough time?" I asked, sitting down next to her and running a hand along each leg. She was already peeling my shirt off.

"The party doesn't even start for another hour. They're probably still out running errands."

I leaned over to kiss her, still trying to figure out where she'd hidden herself. I doubt another minute passed before we were watching ourselves having sex in the reflection of the big-screen TV. Emily kept laughing whenever I'd suddenly pop my head over the couch, thinking I'd heard footsteps. These fears distracted me enough that on our first round I lasted fifteen or twenty minutes. Each time after that Emily orgasmed well before me. I didn't let up, taking her on the carpet, over the pool table, propped up on the cool marble counter where we could watch ourselves in the mirrors over the bar. Between couplings I chased, tickled, and pinned her down, every once in a while slapping my chest and growling as though gearing up for a back alley brawl. As afternoon passed into evening I remember feeling so purely concentrated that there was no question I'd fully sated myself, that one more touch would only prove my greed and intent at personal sabotage. But Emily kept insisting I stay another five or ten minutes. The whole downstairs reeked of sex by the time we finally got dressed and headed upstairs, ducking under all the windows on our way to the kitchen. We were eating an oven pizza on the floor with the lights off when Emily started talking about buying a rope ladder so I could sneak though her window in the middle of the night whenever I wanted. In the clearheaded aftermath of our binge I recognized all we were putting at risk, and wasn't nearly as enthralled by the idea as Emily.

"Maybe we shouldn't test them so much," I said, imagining Mrs. Schell asking Emily how she'd eaten a whole pizza by herself. I couldn't figure out why I hadn't already left.

"They're playing their games, and we're playing ours," she said, like she'd thought it all out. "You know, George, the only reason they didn't toss me in the car and drive me straight back to Chicago was because I caught them in a lie. I never called them to say I was coming home because I was convinced that if I gave them more time to think about it, somehow the news would hit them much worse. I wanted to show up and tell them I couldn't take it anymore, to just cry and act like a baby, then go to bed and worry about everything else later. But when I showed up, it was obvious they'd been living in complete ignorance of each other ever since I left. I know that's the reason why we went to Tennessee at the last minute for Thanksgiving. They didn't have the energy to fix up the house so that it might appear a married couple was actually living there. The whole house was divided up, almost as bad as the idiots down the hall from me who actually taped a line across the room and vowed never to cross it. You should've seen the downstairs. A little sleeping bag spread out on a cot, half of the couch covered in all my dad's favorite books and magazines. Even his socks and underwear were stacked up along the bar. He was *living* down there! He gave her the whole rest of the house!"

"All right," I said, hoping a piece of intelligent advice would miraculously follow. But I only sat there staring at the kitchen tiles, guessing at the appropriate steps for a couple working their way back from such a devastating fall. While I was convinced that Mr. Schell was still in love with Mrs. Schell, I questioned if she was still in love with him. Then, in the face of Emily's swift bitterness that seemed to erase whatever victory we'd just accomplished, I wondered if the question of love even made a difference. (The threat of divorce was so thickly insinuated that I half expected Emily to hand me a letter from James Dickerson Divorce containing the details of her parents' "one-two-three and you're free" separation.)

"Now it's just the silent treatment," she said. "Neither of them likes to raise their voice, so instead of fighting, she just goes her way, and he goes his. Personally, I think they'd be better off punching each other's lights out than moping around all week like deaf-mutes."

"The holidays are supposed to be the hardest. Maybe they just need more time."

Emily patted my arm, clearly finding my advice as platitudinal and worthless as I did. She picked up another piece of pizza, even though she hadn't eaten much of her first piece. She waved it around as she spoke. "You know, the more I look back, the more I think this sort of thing has been going on behind the scenes for years. I can't remember the last time they took a vacation alone together, and now it suddenly seems very curious the way my dad spent so much time out at Stacy Setnicker's after her house got flooded. I mean, he had other employees dealing with the same situation."

"The girl who runs the front of the shop?"

"She's a manager. She's the first person he ever trusted to run the place besides himself."

"Are you serious about this?" I asked, smirking, but quickly adjusting the expression to reflect discomfort and shock. "Your dad doesn't seem like the tomcat type to me. Besides, I doubt your mom would stick around with someone who was cheating on her."

"How do you figure that, George? Where would she go? She doesn't have a college degree, you know." She tossed the unbitten pizza slice back onto the plate. "All I'm saying is it would explain a few things."

I shrugged. Instinct told me that she was jumping to conclusions, but I knew very little of her parents' relationship and couldn't make an assured argument either way. We sat for a while listening to the soft hum of the refrigerator.

"How would you feel about a double date with Zach and Rachel?" I asked, standing up to clean my plate, considering if I should take the pizza box and remains along with me. A pair of headlights panned across the living room windows and I dropped to the floor.

"Go!" Emily shouted, with a hint of glee. She lifted onto one knee, chopping her right arm in the direction of the front hallway. *"Go go go go go!"*

I ducked down and raced to the front door. Emily chased after me, clipping the radio onto my belt as I bent over for my boots. "Your coat!" she shouted, laughing now ("We're invincible!") as she dashed up the stairs. I didn't wait. At the sound of the garage door cranking up I escaped onto the porch, shoving into my boots and sprinting for the neighbor's backyard, jumping their wrought-iron fence, nearly stumbling into their empty pool and trying not to think about my tracks in the snow as I made my frantic way out of sight.

Forty

On Christmas Eve in the middle of the night I woke with a start as the radio sparked into sound under the covers next to me. Before going to bed I'd been reading Fyodor Sologub's *Petty Demon* and first interpreted the strange voice calling out to me as the demon berserker himself, hissing assurances that we'd all fallen foolishly victim to a classic disappearing act, which Katie Schell had obviously mastered with the help of her Wiccan *Book of Shadows*.

"Still awake?" Emily whispered. "Over."

"I'm here."

"Do you see Rudolph's red nose flying through the sky yet?"

"Not yet. What did you ask for this year? Over."

"Nothing. I told them not to give me anything. I insisted. How about you?"

"An electric razor. Over."

"Well, it's late, so I'll keep this short, but I'm sitting in my back-yard now with a lighter and a bag of Doritos."

"I'm listening," I said. "What are you doing?"

"I just remembered Katie telling me about the easy way to make a campfire. Apparently her camp used to have a contest about which group could get their campfire going the fastest, without any newspaper or lighter fluid or anything like that. Katie said she always won because she figured out that Doritos are flammable. So, my question to you is, do you think she was telling the truth? Do you think you could start a campfire with Doritos? Over."

"Sounds like a tall tale to me," I said. "How could you sell flammable snacks? Over."

"Guess we'll see. But you'll have to wait a minute, 'cause I need both hands. I'm going to put the lighter to the chip right now. So wait, okay? Over."

I sat up on the edge of the bed, my shoulders sinking and turning inward at the thought of Emily out in the cold on Christmas Eve. I pictured Mrs. Schell alone under a king-sized canopy, Mr. Schell on his basement couch watching *It's a Wonderful Life*. I was scratching at the frost on the window when the radio cut in again.

"You wouldn't believe it!" she said. "I've got a Dorito fire going and the flames are green and blue! It's burning perfectly from one chip to the next, right on top of the snow! How the hell did she figure that out?"

"She's Katie Schell," I said. "Over."

"She was right, George!"

"I wish I could see it. I wish I was there with you right now."

"Me, too. It's really pretty amazing. Okay, well, Merry Christmas, George. Good night. Over and out."

"Merry Christmas," I said.

Forty-one

Our decision not to attend Nat Fry's New Year's Eve party mostly resulted from a mutual wariness of rumors that Emily had blamed me for what happened to Katie, and sworn never to speak with me again, and even sought a restraining order against me, just in case. But after luring us into their cars, our old gang conspired against us, admitting our true destination along with the excuse that we couldn't possibly skip a party hosted by the richest kid in our class and one of the richest families in Des Moines. It was guys in one car and girls in another as we cruised down Grand Avenue, strangely delighted when we arrived to the sight of a squad car parked in front of the Fry mansion, which led us to assume that a minor had already alcohol-poisoned herself and there'd be a big public lawsuit against Nat's parents. It was somewhat anticlimactic to find out that Mrs. Fry had hired a security guard to ensure that all Nat's guests returned home with a sober driver. (I should mention that Hads was now shockingly wattle-jowled and unwieldy, while Tino was still wagging his head with each sentence and throwing his shoulders back so that he appeared to be strutting even when he was standing still.) We parked and then trudged up the long, arching driveway to the front door, where Mrs. Fry was greeting a fiftyish couple in a tuxedo and long satin gown. She gave us the same warm smile as she did her more formal guests, then instructed us to follow the brick path to join our classmates in the tent around back.

Ashley started complaining before Mrs. Fry had even shut the door. "It's *fifteen degrees*, lady. Perhaps we'll join the *inside* guests."

"Maybe they've got a pool house with a heated pool," Hads said.

"Did you bring swimsuits?" Smitty asked, suddenly worried.

"If they have a heated pool," Tino said, "I don't see why they wouldn't provide us swimsuits and our own personal Swedish lifeguards to swim alongside us."

"That makes *a ton* of sense," Lauren said, as we turned the corner to find ourselves confronted with an enormous white tent with plastic windows and multiple canopy peaks. As soon as we stepped inside, we were welcomed by patches of applause, goofy smiles, and waves. The tent was packed with former classmates and various acquaintances of Nat's older brother, almost all of them dressed up and lounging around white table-clothed tables under the orange glow of heat lamps. As Emily hung her coat up she was swarmed by all the gal pals she hadn't seen since the summer, each one of them flipping out in sequence over her radiant noir hairstyle and low-cut blouse and expertly managed cleavage, the sight of which forced me to question if she'd been as duped about our destination as I had. They kissed cheeks and complimented one another. I turned to face the crowd, immediately realizing I wasn't the only one clocking Emily's every move.

While I tried my best to enjoy the free booze and the company of my old gang, almost immediately they were all were mingling in separate groups, jabbering away like it was their last night on earth. It didn't take long to spot Peyton Chambeau all gelled up and spiky, haranguing a group of former teammates on Iowa State's most lucrative majors. It was mostly similar conversations all around—comparisons on the wildest fraternities, hippest underground bands, coolest campus radio stations, etc. At one point I ended up a chance spectator in a mature debate on "problem" refugees from Sudan, where I learned that upon deeper academic inspection our natural redneck assumptions about blacks, Mexicans, and Jews ruining everything were proved to be well founded. It was a relief to receive a few minutes of weight room advice from Marcus Panozzo, who'd traded his baby fat for a square jaw and shirt-stretching muscle, as well as a visit from purple-toothed Heidi Sneed, our former class slut, who told me: "Everyone says you sell pot." I ended up nursing my beer, suspecting at any moment the lights would dim and the DJ would call my name, igniting the crowd before urging me to take the microphone and share my version of what happened out at Saylorville Lake.

Before I knew it everyone was blurry-faced and shouting, none more than Tino who started blowing kisses to everyone before each drink. "Who shrunk Jodie's titties?" he yelled, referring to her breast surgery that was now common knowledge. "We'll lynch the biological bastard!" I ended up slumping at a quiet table near the entrance, mostly watching Nat's older brother make his moves on Emily. When she finally caught sight of me she marched directly across the tent, enflaming my covert pride as she reminded everyone that she was the hottest girl in the room and she was coming and going with me. We hadn't discussed the matter of how we'd compose ourselves in public, but she stepped up close and lorded over me, putting one hand on her hip and wincing in a way that let me know I was in the good kind of trouble. I felt more than a few pairs of eyes on us as I gripped her by the waist as though measuring whether we'd make a proper match.

"Have you see Tino in a while?" she asked. "Ashley said she caught him removing the ham and roast beef from all the little sandwiches."

"That's what they get for buying the expensive stuff. Bread sandwich leftovers."

"I think you'd better give me a kiss and put an end to all this curiosity."

"Shouldn't we wait until midnight?"

"In terms of building the drama, I would normally say yes. I might even suggest we wait until *after* midnight. But your hands are already on my waist and your eyes are on my breasts and I'm just standing here letting it happen."

"Practically dangling yourself in front of me."

"Practically," she said, directing me to my feet with an upward nod.

We kissed. We heard a few whistles and catcalls but didn't bother looking up. The kiss ended at the sound of firework explosions from the backyard. Nat raced helter-skelter for the exit, drawing half the tent springing behind him. Emily and I took the chance to refill our beers, stepping outside just as one of the older guests lit a string of about five hundred jumping jacks that bounced willy-nilly across the snow, whirling balls of red, orange, and blue.

A minute later Peyton swaggered over from the other side of the lawn. First thing he gave Emily a little shoulder massage, as nonchalant as ever, like we were all adults now and wouldn't it be silly to consider that he was still sore about her dumping him in high school way back when. He even slapped my back and shoved a cigar in my mouth like some kind of backroom Depression-era cardsharp.

"Good to be back in the old DMZ," he said, nodding in general approval of the whole scene laid out before us, as though Ames were hundreds of miles away. "Not too shabby spending New Year's with the cream of the crop."

I lit my cigar, hoping that Emily would deal with the situation, perhaps by way of a comical inquiry into Peyton's status as big man on campus. But she only turned her back, peering toward the edge of the tent where Lauren was teaching Hads a snowy Irish jig.

"You should see some of the girls up in Ames," Peyton went on,

swearing a few times and slapping my back again. "It's just fucking ridiculous. And they're dedicated fans, let me tell you." He kept
nodding and smiling, like he really knew what he was talking about.
"So what's up with all these girls with boyfriends in *South Dakota*
and *Canada*? Shouldn't they be able to have a little fun at midnight? I
mean, it only comes once a year, right?"

I nodded along, trying to appear joyously distracted. After a brief
exchange about the exact start time for the breakfast buffet, I thanked
him for the cigar before turning my attention to back to Emily. She
was flicking a lighter, smoking, and doing her best to look completely
bored. But Peyton wasn't finished yet and stepped around me to continue the conversation.

"How's *Chi-town*," he said, smiling all gangly and glassy-eyed.
"Getting any acting gigs? I mean, it's a pretty good city for all
that, right?"

"Nothing to report just yet," she said.

Peyton kept nodding, like that was nothing to be discouraged
about. "It'll come. Those folks out in L.A. struggle for years. Then
one day . . . WHAM! They're on Letterman telling the whole world
about their sex lives!" He threw his arm over my shoulder, laughing
like it was his best wisecrack in years.

"Sorry, what was that?" Emily said, shaking her head as though
reviving her lost concentration.

"You heard me," he said. "And when it happens, don't forget who
tried to help you out when you were still small potatoes."

For the first time he won Emily's attention. She turned to him with
such a sharpened gaze and smirk of coded distain that I wondered if
she and Peyton hadn't mixed words earlier in the evening.

"You have some connections in the theater business?" I asked.

"Nothing like that," Peyton said, waving his comment off as hardly
worth explaining. "Over the summer my dad wanted to put Emily in

one of his commercials, but she wouldn't have it. He was gonna pay her two hundred bucks, but she blew him off, told him *TV wasn't her thing.*"

Emily covered her face, shaking her head like she regretted her decision now more than ever. "Some opportunities only come around once," she said, laughing now as she took the cigar from my mouth and tossed it in the snow. "Care to dance, George?"

"I only know the tango and cha-cha and mambo," I said, giving Peyton a good-night nod as we headed back inside. Whatever mood of analysis I might have attached to the conversation was washed away with a fast shot of wine and a kiss. I directed Emily toward Smitty and his barefooted dance partner, Mandy Anderson (whose wild braids and braless chest had pushed us all at least once to thoughts of nude grassland barbarism). Near midnight small portions of champagne were poured and passed around. By this time several tables of former classmates and even some of the elder Frys' more professional associates were flipping quarters into mixtures of red and white wine, forcing one another to slam them down in one gulp. A few caterers grew fed up and rude, employing liberal elbows as they pushed through the crowd. I caught Smitty and Mandy making out behind the tent well before the countdown. Despite judging them as overanxious cheaters, I was making gestures to follow their lead when I received an authorial two-finger tap on my right shoulder. By the look of blank confusion suddenly crossing Emily's face I might have guessed to duck—I'd already thought it possible that Peyton was left unsatisfied by our exchange and might attempt to prove the macho superiority of basketball players to wrestlers, a challenge he was smart enough to realize I would have welcomed—but I didn't and simply rotated around as anyone would at a New Year's Eve party in a lavish tent filled with reunited classmates. I only hazily recognized the piggish figure winding up to punch me, and was even less sure about the meaning of his swinging spitfire insult.

"HOWDY, ORLANDO!" he shouted, a split second before his fat fist audibly flattened my nose, driving me backward into the breakfast buffet. I collapsed against a metal tray of scrambled eggs and its reciprocal hot water pan that banged to the floor, inspiring a series of sobering shrieks from the drunken splashed. But even more startling than my mystery opponent's punch was the speed with which the breathalyzing security guard hulked onto the scene, plucking my assailant from his feet with all the ease and skill of a Kodiak dragging a goggle-eyed doe by the pelt of its upper back so that its limp hooves swept the path of its own fatal departure. From the mere profile of this guard, in particular his hardworking neck and hands, I immediately recognized him as the man I'd spoken to in the bathroom at the Cohen funeral parlor.

It was only a few minutes after midnight when Mrs. Fry bustled her way onto the deejay stand, putting a fast stop to the music before taking the microphone to cite juvenile roughhousing, illegal fireworks, and the mounting damage afflicted upon the tent and other rental equipment as reasons enough to pull the plug on the festivities. Without a moment's hesitation the caterers removed all remaining sources of alcohol, returned the buffet trays to the catering truck, then dismantled the event chair by chair and table by table. My nose was smashed and my shirt was splattered with blood. Emily took me by the arm and led me away, uttering curses at Marcus Panozzo, who was doing all he could to identify our enemies and exploit the unruly mood for an all-out brawl.

By the time we arrived around front my security guard had already locked his suspect in the backseat. I wanted to thank him, but he was now facing a line of about thirty designated drivers, half of whom were certain not to pass his test. I wanted to ask what else he remembered from that day at Casey's General Store.

Smitty handed me a stack of cocktail napkins. By now everyone knew that my attacker was a guest of Nat's brother and had moved on to the question of his motive, part of which involved interpreting his cryptic insult in the seconds before his assault. I pressed the napkins to my nose, denying any clue of who he was or what he'd meant. With an air of Christmastime generosity I suggested the matter be dropped, that I'd simply fallen victim to a case of misidentification. "Besides," I told them, pretending to be drunk, "a man isn't really a man who hasn't had his nose broken at least once." But of course I knew with one hundred percent certainty that the young man now slumped in the back of the squad car was the person I've previously described as the most pacifistic member of the collegiate foursome with whom I'd altercated on the Urbandale golf course. I also recognized his "Howdy, Orlando!" battle cry as a reference to the Saturday-morning documentary program *Fishing with Orlando*, which he'd clearly intended as a below-the-belt crack at my conscience.

After Smitty dropped me off that night I went directly to the front hall bathroom to clean the congealed blood from my cheeks and attempt to reset my nose in the fashion of beat-up boxers hoping to convince judges and opponents they're less damaged than they really are. I straightened it as best as I could, but no amount of adjusting was able to fix the pronounced mid-bridge hump.

After showering the swelling worsened. I lay in bed with my eyes open for at least an hour in expectation of one of Emily's late radio calls, which over the previous week had become part of the regular routine. But the call didn't come until four or five a.m., when I was caught in a deep REM cycle. (Over the years I've come to question if I ever truly awoke from this sleep, despite my perfect memory of the conversation; the slurring voice on the other end was eerily reminiscent of my grandfather's after his second stroke, in the weeks before he died.) My initial reaction to this call was to assume that Emily's radio had been picked up by a drunk at whichever bar the girls hit on the way home, or that

I'd fallen victim to the demented mumblings of a radio pirate who'd invaded my signal. In the following days I was able to eliminate the former option as a possibility.

"Habby," the voice said. "Habby New Year. How about a drinkie-tinkie! Over!"

"Happy New Year," I said. "Is this your radio? Over."

"Sonva gun!" the man said. I guessed his finger kept slipping off the TALK button because his voice kept flashing in and out. "—and I think I'M having the party, but HE'S having the REAL party! Oh yeaaaaah!" The man laughed hysterically. "Right here in River City! Right under MY NOSE! Over!"

"Who *is* this?" I asked, speaking as calmly and clearly as possible, hoping to inspire similar such articulation on the other end. But apparently the caller hadn't finished his previous point.

"—twenty-four hours a day since nineteen eighty-one! You believe me what I tell you BOIY!"

"I believe you," I said. "Can I meet you tomorrow to pick up my radio? Over."

"Ever doggone day . . . I tell you it NEVER goes AWAY!"

Part

Three

Forty-two

A week into the New Year, Frank Moretti called to let me know he'd just won a big contract for a piece of the action in the state fairgrounds restoration project. "If you feel like making some real money," he said, "you'd better get to work out in the cold like my father used to back when only the old-timers took winters off and being a construction man actually meant something." I accepted the offer, if not for the much-needed income than for the distraction from the lies I'd been passing to my increasingly anxious mom in connection with my crooked nose and the inkwells beneath my eyes that grew more colorful and unsightly day by healing day. After hanging up with Frank—in the spirit of planning for a dynamic and nourishing New Year—I called Grand View to sign up for night classes in Oriental Philosophy and Literature of the Civil War, then radioed Emily to invite her to an afternoon of movie hopping at the new Mega Screen theater in West Des Moines. It turned out she couldn't meet me until later that evening. I headed downstairs and flipped on the TV, just in time for a newscast on the four Waukee students who'd torched the most famous and beloved of the Madison County bridges.

The report focused mostly on an interview with a Madison County fire chief who detailed the evidence linking the culprits to the crime, thus prompting the same investigative aspect of my personality that led me to Thomas Staniszewski to again rear itself and set to work. During the ensuing Bears–Vikings game, while watching our replacement quarterback spend the first half running scared, scrambling backward and zigzagging in circles, I began to consider the event of Katie's death: such peculiarities as the well-timed disappearance of the Eagle Scout from the rental hut, his false testimony about the numerous life jackets he spotted by the shore, the lone canoe turned over in the muck, the collaboration of the police and the *Des Moines Register* in the official mistelling of the account (they even bumbled such details as the day's wind conditions and the class of algal infestation that had caused the frogmen so much hassle in discovering her body), Katie's closed casket, the revelation of her experimental brain and spine surgery, her claims of having planted a time capsule, not to mention the broader environmental factors such as her parents' serially mute relationship and the still unknown whereabouts of the strangler Nicholas Parsons.

But as the reader well knows, this is a realistic story told in a realistic fashion, which means it would be inappropriate to detail the various conspiracies or other metaphysical trickeries I might have been tempted to attribute to the incongruity of Katie drowning while wearing a life jacket. Katie slipped out of her life jacket and died, either because she unbuckled it without my noticing, or because the life jacket was defective. These are the only conclusions I have faith enough to pass along. That said, by the time the clock ran out on the Vikings (after a harebrained quarterback tuck-and-run that ended in a touchdown after his miraculous emergence from an opaque mob of purple and gold), I'd already decided to drive out to Saylorville Lake in order to preserve a piece of evidence that I knew over time would dissolve and allow an even greater shroud of mystery to befall the incident in question.

That afternoon I trudged the same path from the parking lot to the lake that I'd marched on the morning of Katie's death. Starting from the canoe racks, I made a hard half circle around the lake through heavy, frosted weeds to the hunched willow that once ensnared my favorite lure. Of course it was unlikely that anyone would have noticed the lure or taken the time to retrieve it, but on finding it perched in such a remarkably observant and lifelike pose I burst into astonished laughter, ignoring the fact of its inherent artificiality in order to marvel at the sight of a frog that had not only adapted to the winter freeze, but also taught itself to climb trees. Despite my bulky boots and gloves, I mounted the willow's icy spine just as I had the first time, undistracted now as I worked my way from one bare branch to the next, noticing the places where eight months before I'd snapped off a sprig or two in order to more easily reach my target. This time I did reach it, and carefully plucked the barbs loose with both hands in order to prevent myself from dropping it onto the frozen lake below. I didn't leave right away, but instead lay like a snoozing cat across the trunk, admiring my lure—its leopard spots, cool white belly, and phosphorescent eyes—every once in a while looking up to peer dreamily over the snow-covered lake. I didn't climb back down until I'd come to a clear decision about what I had to do.

Forty-three

A week later I found myself bundled up in as many flexible layers as possible, already waiting at the curb at five a.m. when Frank picked me up to head to the fairgrounds in East Des Moines. He was pumped about the big contract, already singing along to Stevie Wonder and grinning ear to ear, popping open the glove compartment to retrieve a photo book of the restoration models on display at the Historical Society downtown. On the whole, he and a dozen other contractors were embarking on a $30 million initiative aimed at restoring the original fairgrounds of 1842. This mission involved the complicated task of reviving the original ecosystem, including all the underground water channels that once served the Grand Basin, the original symbol of the fair. Frank's enthusiasm had a way of spreading and soon I was grinning alongside him while paging through original photos of ancient Ferris wheels, young girls in bonnets smiling out of covered wagons, a group of roughnecks posing next to a snarling cougar in an iron cage. Even our small contribution to the project was massive: we were to dig up seventy acres of frozen ground, much of which had been employed as a landfill from the fifties to the seventies.

I didn't see how it was possible to complete the restoration before the fair kicked off in August, but I never mentioned my doubts, knowing Frank wouldn't have heard them anyway.

"Wait till you see the equipment you're gonna to be working with," he told me as we started over the river. "The state's providing most of the heavy artillery, including skid loaders with ripper buckets that'll tear us right through to China. After we haul out the lot, we're gonna thaw the ground beneath it with a Thawzall system they use up in Minnesota and Canada. We'll thaw a foot a day until the weather warms up."

It was strange driving onto the fairgrounds in the middle of winter. First thing I changed into padded overalls and a Carhartt work jacket Frank gave me. Most of the crew members were already waiting in their trucks with the windows cracked, smoking and exchanging hearty laughs about how fat they'd gotten collecting welfare over the previous two months. But they were eager to work and it didn't take long before we were all moving fast and talking fast and downing enough coffee to motor ourselves clear through the afternoon the following Friday.

The first task on the list was to rip up a parking lot that another company was rebuilding on the other side of the park. We'd all seen the blueprints, but before we went to work busting up the concrete Frank gave an inspirational speech to help us better picture the whole gorgeous plan. This involved him strolling back and forth along the edge of the woods, twirling an imaginary umbrella and swinging his hips side to side to let us feel the romance of the arching footbridge over the basin, just like it was back in 1842 when the grounds were crawling with homesteaders twenty years ahead of the western migration. By the heroic fury in his voice I had a feeling that within a few weeks he'd be adding to the effect of his handlebar mustache by greasing his hair back and parting it down the middle like the pioneers in the original fairground photos. "These was the wild days!" he shouted, seeming to snatch the cold right out of the air. "We're gonna be digging up the graves of pistol-whip frontiersmen and their horse-jumpin' girlies! Now mount them steel bulls, boys! We're making history here!"

We laughed and tightened our bootstraps and went to work, still hooting and hollering when that first rockwheel went spinning into the pavement. That first day was about as brutal and bitterly cold as anyone could have imagined, especially for those few of us out in the naked wind, jackhammering old cracked-up sidewalks in all the wooded areas too tight for the skid loaders. When it was finally over I couldn't have felt more healthfully exhausted, though that wasn't my only reward for a hard day's work. Minutes after Frank dropped me off I received a radio transmission from Emily informing me that she'd booked a room at the West Des Moines Days Inn (a particularly welcome gift considering the previous week's semipublic sexual mishaps while parked between eighteen-wheelers in the overnight lot near the airport). Thus began a weekly routine, soon moved to Fridays, which was Emily's day off from rehearsals for her upcoming production.

"It's called *Tinker*," she later explained, while dabbing the sweat from her chest with a hotel hand towel. She pulled a T-shirt over her head and kicked her legs onto the desk. "We've got a month of hard-core rehearsal, then it's three weeks of shows at the Garage Theater, which in my opinion puts the Playhouse to shame. The script is pretty wacky, but Tony's really going for it. He's definitely going for something. It could be great."

I laid a bath towel under the door while Emily packed a glass pipe. When she lit it and sucked in, her eyes constricted and her lips sealed tight. There was a slow jazzy movement in the smoke. I held my first hit in as long as I could and when I stepped up to the window to exhale, barely any smoke escaped and I was already high. In the parking lot below, the stores were all closing, the cars clearing out. Judging by the largely unlit windows at the Holiday Inn (sulking curbside along University like a forlorn bully), I guessed they were still struggling to overcome the negative publicity that for the last two and a half years they'd yet to live down.

"I checked my e-mail down in the lobby," Emily said, coughing out the last words. "Looks like Schell's Shirtworks is going national, so my dad's in Arizona. He sent me a pretty deep letter, telling me what a rock I've been over the last year, how glad he was that I was back living at home, even if he still didn't recognize me from a distance. It was nice and everything, but still, *e-mail* from your dad? It's so quick and easy. *I love you* and boom, express delivered."

Emily handed me the pipe. I leaned down to kiss her shoulder. She reached for her cigarettes and turned to the blank TV, clearly occupied by other thoughts.

"Who taught him how to use e-mail anyway? I sure didn't. Only a few months ago he was spending half his weekends sitting in front of the DVD player, pressing every button on all five remote controls, hoping to luck out on the right sequence to get the stupid thing going."

"At least he's trying," I said. "Not too many parents out there riding the electronic wave."

"Hummm," Emily said, lighting up.

I took another hit, then paged through a misfolded newspaper on the desk. Emily had no doubt read every article, including the censuring op-ed column on the rising belligerence of the city's youth. The piece included a photo of Hogback Bridge as it appeared on the cover of *The Bridges of Madison County*, juxtaposed against a charred and skeletal after-photo. "What do you think about those kids on trial?" I asked.

"The pyros from Waukee?"

"Yeah. It says their friends ratted them out for the reward."

"Some friends," she said, exhaling. "If I was those guys, I'd beg for a long stint in the pokey. Pretty soon people are gonna find out where they live, and they're gonna get lynched by every man, woman, and child in Madison County."

"It sounds like it might've been an accident," I said, moving on to the sports pages. Emily grabbed the op-ed section, looking over it again and chuckling to herself.

"How do you accidentally burn a bridge to ashes? Of course they said it was an accident. They just meant to singe a few names off the panels and accidentally torched the whole turkey. Never mind that they were drunk and it was two in the morning."

I shrugged and sprawled out on the bed, wondering what my chauvinistic Civil War professor (who in our first class had insisted that Iowegians had saved the country from irreversible ruin at least a dozen times) would view as proper punishment for such a crime.

"You know, George," Emily said, quickly rapping the heating vent as though reviving a thought she'd nearly lost. She slid her legs off the desk and leaned forward. "After I read that article I got this really great idea for a short film. Something to send out to all the Hollywood casting agencies. You know, as a résumé film for potential agents."

"Is that how it works?" I asked, distracted by the sight of her legs crossing at the knees. (I remind you that she was wearing no under-wear, if this point wasn't well enough implied.)

"I think that's one of the ways. Anyhow, the idea involves starting a few more fires down in Madison County. The movie would begin with a damsel-in-distress situation, like a bunch of gangsters inter-rogating a girl about a big drug shipment that they think's gonna wipe out their business. When she refuses to talk they pour gas all around her, then leave her in the middle of the bridge as they continue pouring gas and block both sides. Of course they offer her one last chance, but she just gives them the finger, real scared, but real cool, you know? So the gangsters on both sides of the bridge count down from ten, matches in hand. Only problem is that when one of them strikes his match, immediately the fumes alight and he ends up running around in a ball of fire. But the trail of gas still ends up catching, so none of this really helps our damsel, who's now got flames zooming at her from both sides. At that point we cut to the only exterior shot of the film as she takes a leap from the bridge down into the creek. And that's it. For the rest of the film we just watch the bridge blazing and crackling and falling apart. *The end.*"

"How does she jump into the crick from a covered bridge?"

"The what? Did you say *crick?*"

"Whatever. Creek."

"Haven't figured that out yet," she said, taking a puff from the cigarette she'd left burning in the ashtray. When she couldn't get any smoke from it, she opened her pack and lit another one.

"Does the girl die or what? How deep is the water?"

"It's deep enough that she's completely submerged, but the audience doesn't know if she survives or not. Maybe there should be one more shot where the leftover gangster stares down into the creek, wondering."

"So she *doesn't* die."

"Probably not," she said, shining me a big smile and rocking one leg over the other. "Better to keep her alive for the sequel."

"Onto the next covered bridge, huh?"

"Pretty crazy, huh?" she said, then started whistling the chorus to "Light My Fire." I sat up and leaned against the headboard, looking at the time and sighing. Emily eventually quit whistling. She uncrossed her legs and shook her head at the ceiling before waving forth my criticism.

"I used to imagine having sex with you on those bridges," I said. "One right after the other. And as I was driving to pick you up on the night of the premiere, all I could think about was how I'd get you to go skinny-dipping with me in the crick below Hogback."

"The *creek*?" she asked, making a face that involved halving the height of her forehead and allowing one side of her mouth to stretch open as though being reeled in by a fisherman standing directly behind her.*

"Okay, the creek," I said, shoving off the headboard and onto my back to close my eyes. According to the auditory cues that followed, Emily shoved her chair against the wall, dragged her feet to the bathroom, turned a squeaking knob, dipped her head under the faucet, turned the knob back, then slapped the toilet seat down and plopped herself on top of it. Then she stood up again and stopped dragging her feet and for several minutes I lost track of her. By the time I marked her again, she was already standing over me with her hands on her hips at the edge of the bed, staring inverted into my eyes.

"I want to know the truth, George. Do you have a *plan* for us?"

"A *plan*? What kind of plan?"

"A *plan*. A *map*. A *design* for the future."

"What's *your* plan?" I asked.

"My plan is obvious. Breast surgery, as soon as I save enough money. Then maybe a few ski bunny movies. But we're talking about *your* plan, George. I'm having a hard time seeing *your* plan and I'm starting to get the feeling that you'd go along with just about any idea I presented you, as long as it didn't involve starting any fires. Tell me the truth, if I said I was going to get breast implants and then move to Canada to make direct-to-video movies, would you follow me?"

"I'm just not a fan of torching the bridges for a bunch of short films. That's all I was saying."

---

*Emily Schell was never one to make faces. Katie was the face maker, despite a grave countereffort not to be. "Congenitally screwed," she once told me. "And all Emily's got is a birthmark shaped like a friggin' three-leaf clover."

"Or maybe you *do* have a plan, and you're just waiting for the right moment to spring it on me. Maybe I've got a future waiting for me in a small town in the Ukraine, which you probably consider part of *your Russia*, and any small town as *your* small town."

"What if I told you I was saving up for a Claddagh ring?"

"I've *got* a Claddagh ring," she said. "It goes nicely with my dad's little pistol."

"What's that supposed to mean?"

"What do you mean, *What's that supposed to mean?* His little pistol on the bar downstairs. You haven't seen it? It really shoots, you know?"

"I doubt that," I said. "Though it might explain a few things if it did." (Though I wasn't exactly sure what I meant by this comment, it was certainly received with every ounce of its incestuous implication, particularly when considering the delicate subject of our original abstinence.)

"I was *joking*!" she shouted, waving her fists so angrily that I was certain they'd slam against something before coming undone. "You think I'd really get work with a film like that! You don't recognize a joke when you hear one!"

"I knew you were joking," I said, still lying on my back, breathing in long, slow breaths, watching the moment play out from some other place.

"Jesus Christ, George."

Forty-four

A few hours later, after what amounted to a long, touchless nap, I ended up squatting down in the bathtub to absorb myself in a reading assignment on the division of Iowegians who fought on the first day of the battle of Shiloh, nicknamed the Hornet's Nest for the deafening whiz of bullets through the sapling and peach trees. I imagined the battle from a dozen angles, reliving six hours of onslaught along that sunken Tennessee road, when the Unionists never broke, even when the Confederate artillery lined up sixty-two cannon at point-blank range, the most ever used at that time in a war effort. All but wiped out, the Iowa boys held them off long enough for General Grant's reinforcements to arrive by steamboat. Under a heavy rain and snowing peach blossoms, surrounded by more than twenty thousand American dead, Grant's army pushed the Rebels back where they came from and changed the course of the war. The writing was battle ready and emotional. I guess you could say it worked on me because I hopped out of the bathtub full of pride, embracing the attitude that if I left our petty skirmish to brood unattended, it would only spread and threaten to destroy everything we'd so recently regained.

But when I marched into the room, prepared to serenade Emily with all the poetic whispers of a quixotic knight-errant, I was immediately derailed by my wake-up call that sounded in four or five rings like furious cowbells that sent Emily's knees and elbows leaping skyward as though yanked into action by a crude marionette puppeteer. She covered her ears and pinned her face into the mattress, her bloodless right hand soon slapping the empty side of the bed, in rhythm with the rings—a tin drummer rapping out a seismographic beat meant to probe the mattress, and the Days Inn motel, and the earth holding us up for proof of their immeasurable stupidity.

Forty-five

February brought record low temperatures and a sense of frozen time, intensified by such a layering of motion-restrictive clothing and the sudden lack of shame in the sporting of thermal face masks that I hardly recognized my fellow crew members except by the shouts of their profane invitations to the unforeseeable spring. Emily returned to the theater full force, pouring all her energies into the creative invention of a dramatic other, in this case an Irish gypsy who'd never known a moment's rest from society's glaring sidewise judgments. (I felt I was doing the same, molding myself to the character of spineless sap with infinite patience for guilt trips and stoned motel room digressions in nihilism, then absurdism; I would have lost her if I didn't.) As for her parents, her dad continued traveling to meet with potential business partners and scout new store locations, while her mom joined a support group for parents of deceased children, then broke with her doubles partner in exchange for a punishing season of singles in a more competitive and younger division. Under other circumstances these actions might have been considered healthy, but that was never my impression, particularly in the case of Emily, who'd taken to such radical shifts of behavior that I was forced to interpret many of her unwelcomed commentaries as those of a character playing an actor, as opposed to the other way around. (Perhaps this was also the case in earlier moments of effrontery tracing as far back as our junior year on the day she summoned me from class in the spirit of a strict secretary, after presenting a notably less dominant personage when I first met her a few days before.)

At any rate, we continued meeting every Friday at the Days Inn, where one night I arrived key in hand to find her parading about naked while rearranging the furniture to enable more preposterous positions and deeper penetration. While testing such a position—which might have been more easily enjoyed minus the nightstand turned on its side and the desk chair stacked on the love seat—Emily ended up role-playing an enraged and poverty-stricken publisher, designating me the hermetic author of a science-fiction manuscript that for personal reasons I had refused to release.

"I *made* you!" she screamed. "You recluse! Prick tease! You hack!"

"You're a leech! You're all leeches!"

"Tell me the story!"

"No!"

"Tell me the title!"

"No!"

"Gimme the first page, you flaming, pissant, cocksucking *hobbit*!"

"On the first page *YOU GET FUCKED!*"

And so it went back and forth as I cranked her legs over my shoulders and she pounded the wall. Next she played a mail-order bride with rape fantasies, then a Christian missionary undergoing her own conversion in a Bible-thumping gang bang. Emily was still inventing new characters and asking me to help her prop one end of the bed up on the desk when I complained that I couldn't keep up with the dialogues, admitting that anyway I'd squirted myself dry. We ended up smoking a bowl on the windowsill, where Emily told me all about the propaganda films she was studying.

"The best thing about them is that they're all epics. You've got to see *Pulgasari*, which is this absurd Godzilla rip-off they made in North Korea. I mean, everything about it's ludicrous, including the fact that the director was kidnapped from South Korea after he got fired from his studio. After watching it, I had this amazing dream where I was a cute little Asian girl who was actually a badass spy. Do you ever have dreams like that? Where you end up a character in the movie you just watched?"

"We've got pay-per-view right here," I said, standing up to push the desk back against the wall. But Emily caught my arm and shook her head, knowing I'd sit right back down. "For all the movies you watch, we haven't ordered a single one since we started coming here."

"Next time," she said, strumming her fingernails along the heating vent. "I promise. Anyway, my *Pulgasari* dream was so real, I remember thinking that being a spy is basically the same as being an actor, except without the audience. It's perfect in so many ways. But anyway, there I was in North Korea, mingling with the enemy. So one day over tea my friend keeps staring at me, giving off a major impression that she's figured out I'm not who I say I am. *You work for the Americans,* she finally tells me. *But I'm still not afraid because I know we can never be defeated. Under Kim Jong-il's leadership, our resolve will never be silenced. You think you've learned our secrets, but you haven't learned anything. We can even breathe underwater.*"

Emily laughed a heinous little laugh. I threw my arm over her shoulder and closed my eyes, like I'd had too long a day to stay awake another minute. But Emily pulled a hair from the top of my head, accusing me of professionally offending her by falling asleep during her performance. She lit a cigarette and shoved it in my mouth. I sat up again and leaned my cheek against the cold window, staring out over a thin stretch of woods toward the blinking lights on University.

"So is this friend a government official or something?"

"She's just a regular old cadre," Emily said. "But her husband works in a secret nuclear facility. He's the real target."

"All right," I said. "So what happens next?"

"I decide to act like I'm actually a government agent hunting counterrevolutionaries, not telling her as much, but hinting that I'm proud of her and that I hope she continues saying everything she's supposed to say to pass my test. *Come on,* I tell her. *Nobody can breathe underwater.* But she just smiles and drinks her tea, like every time I open my mouth I'm just convincing her even more that I'm a spy. *We can,* she says. *It's a routine element of our training. Since everyone does military service, everyone can do it.* I end up laughing, realizing that I'm trapped because I trust this woman, she's my best friend actually, and now I really want to know how she learned to breathe underwater. So I play it like no one in my home village has ever heard of such training, which makes sense because we're mountain people and we train differently. But my friend only gets angry, telling me she's sick of my lies. She knocks her cup of tea onto the floor. *You're too cocky, little sister. Think about it. H_2O. That's two oxygen molecules for every one hydrogen. That's enough to keep breathing.*"

Emily paused for a moment, smirking as she flashed one finger, then two, then one finger, then two. "Go on," I said.

"You're thinking about it, right?"

"I'm thinking what you would look like in sandals and one of those rice-paddy hats."

"Good," she said. "That's the next scene. My friend insists on showing me how she can breathe underwater, which is great, except now I'm starting to realize that this is probably just a trick to take me down to the rice paddy and kill me. But of course I follow her anyway.

I watch her wade into the knee-deep water. I do everything she asks me to do, even though I have no idea how this will turn out. *It's all a matter of willpower, belief, mental toughness,* she says. She lies on her back so that only the tips of her feet are above water, completely submerging herself and gripping the rice stalks to keep from floating back up. Twenty seconds pass, then forty, a minute, a minute and a half. When her legs stop moving I get scared and grab her shirt, but as soon as I pull her up she kicks and slaps my arm away. Actually, that's not what happened. She didn't just slap my arm. She gave me a big okay sign, which I guess was a joke, since giving an okay is such an American thing to do. Anyway, a couple more minutes go by. The routine continues. I get worried again and try to pull her out, but she flashes me another okay and stays under. After about ten minutes she finally stands up. She's covered in mud, which she wipes from her forehead and cheeks, but she's not at all out of breath. *Are you ready to join us yet?* she asks me. *Are you ready to believe?*"

I laughed Emily's heinous little laugh, which I thought would tidily wrap up the story. But Emily repeated her "Are you ready to believe?" line; this time her Asian accent dropped off and her voice rose just enough to let me know that she wasn't acting anymore, that she was herself again and she was asking me a direct question. She took my cigarette and stole the last puff.

"It's a good story," I said, yawning. "Let's go to bed, okay?"

"Do you think it would work? Do you think if I filled the bathtub that you could breathe underwater?"

"How could I even try without knowing the secret? Your friend never actually revealed *how* she breathed underwater."

"I didn't tell you the end of the dream," she said. "I could tell you the secret if you feel like testing it?"

I pushed off the windowsill, walking around the disarrayed room, trying to decide where to start first. "Maybe it's time for a new film series," I said, throwing the comforter back on the bed. "I think all that propaganda is starting to work."

"Of course it is. Propaganda works like magic. It's probably the reason why I rented a room at the Days Inn instead of Best Western. Advertising and propaganda are basically the same thing. You can think you're smarter than both of them, but once they get their jingles into your brain, repeating over and over, there's not much you can do."

I nodded along, deciding that the best way to get her to bed would be to limit my answers to nods and head shakes, to remain as quiet as possible while moving the furniture back. But as I was searching for my wallet, I was struck by the exact sort of jingle she was talking about and couldn't hold back from singing it out. *"Don't baste your barbecue, don't baste your barbecue . . . it's what you do when you barbecue . . . you gotta Maull it!"*

"Exactly," she said, returning the telephone to the nightstand, then switching it with the lamp on the other side. "Maull's Barbecue Sauce. I wouldn't baste my barbecue if my life depended on it. I Maull that shit every time."

"You *gotta* Maull it," I repeated, still considering her challenge to breathe underwater in the bathtub. I placed my hands over the heater, noticing all the lit billboards across the horizon with their familiar advertisements for gas station convenient stores, the latest fast-food inventions, winter clearances at malls and sporting goods stores.

"So Peyton's dad wanted you in his shoe commercial, huh?" I watched Emily's reflection in the window as she pushed a chair back under the desk. "Did you run into him at the mall or something? You never said anything about seeing him over the summer."

"Oh *that*," she said, sighing like I'd just ruined an interesting conversation. She pulled the chair out again and plopped down in it. "I can't believe it took you this long to ask. I didn't tell you about seeing him because I didn't want to hurt your feelings. Has anyone ever told you that you're sensitive, George? You're really touchy sometimes."

"You still haven't told me," I said, turning around. "What happened?"

"Nothing happened the way *you're* probably imagining it, even if we did go on a date. I mean, I'd rather not call it that, but I guess that's what it was. A few weeks after the funeral we went to a movie. Immediately afterward I made him take me home."

I turned back to the window, struck by the same instinct to flee I'd felt earlier in the night when she kept shouting and biting as we screwed. (I'd spent half the session staring at the little red light on the phone in anticipation of a call from the motel manager.) It didn't help that I was still stoned and that Emily was broaching the subject as though it didn't mean a thing.

"What happened?" I asked, inadvertently revealing all the jealousy and distrust she'd preemptively accused me of.

"I told you what happened. I don't know what I was thinking, but I was lonely and thought he was the sort of person I could go out with who wouldn't try to give me any genius advice. I just couldn't take any more advice, and I was tired of being alone."

"*You* called *him?*" I asked, already tormenting myself with Peyton's double-dealing condolences, Emily's desperate grief, their violent kisses in the back of his car.

"I needed to get out of the house," she said, wrapping the phone cord around her arm. "You can't imagine what it was like eating dinner with my parents, having my mom hug me good night and thinking, *She's faking it. She doesn't love me at all. She thinks I lied to them, and she doesn't even love me anymore.*"

"She knows you're angry with her," I said, crouching down next to her. "She probably just doesn't know how to act while she and your dad are still sorting things out."

"I don't know," she said.

"I don't know either, but I think you made the right decision coming home. Even if they're not talking much, it would be much worse if you weren't there."

Emily unwrapped the cord from around her arm and hung up the receiver. She started paging through a motel brochure she must've paged through fifty times before. I stepped into the bathroom, fully aware of her difficulty in meeting my eyes. "If you don't want to talk about your date with Peyton," I said, squeezing toothpaste onto my brush, "it's all right. I'll just forget it and trust that nothing happened."

Emily slapped the desk and laughed. Her laugh said everything it needed to about my insecurities. The lighter sparked as she lit another cigarette. I was brushing my teeth, expecting another long, silent night, when she started delving into the details, more apologetically than I expected.

"He brought up the commercial idea after the movie. By then I already knew I'd made a mistake in going out with him. I knew I'd made a mistake before the movie even started. But when I told him to take me home, he kept fighting me about it. He kept talking about some college party on the South Side and trying to hook up with me. Eventually he gave up, but for a few weeks after that he kept calling the house late at night, usually drunk. He'd hang up whenever my parents answered."

I spit and watched the toothpaste swirl down the drain, asking myself for the first time if I believed her. I stared into the bathroom mirror, questioning whether she'd dreamt that story about being a spy or simply made it up just to tease me. I wiped my mouth and stepped back into the doorway. Emily was leaning over the desk with her hands flat on the glass top, silhouetted in the low-wattage lamp, her head low and heavy like an old bull.

"I suppose your parents think it was me calling, huh? After my call from Colorado, it only makes sense."

"I told them it wasn't you," she said, slowly turning her head so that her hair fell in and out of the lamplight. "But like I said, they don't trust me. And to tell you the truth, I don't even blame them anymore. I wouldn't trust me, either."

"So I shouldn't trust you, either, I guess?"

"Whatever, George. I'm sick of arguing. Think whatever you want to think."

"I wish I could," I said, grabbing my T-shirt and pants from the back of the door handle. "Your parents must think I'm a real prankster."

"Go ahead and go. I know you're already sick of this place. I'm sorry I even called."

I pulled my pants and shirt on as fast as I could, grabbing my shoes and preparing to storm out, still swinging my belt and kicking the walls. (I considered breaking the full-length mirror, but didn't when I realized the action would prove far less poignant than it did in the Mexican drama I was recalling, involving a two-faced maid and her matron's heirloom.) But I couldn't find my socks and ended up scrambling on all fours, searching around the desk and nightstands, lying on the carpet reaching under the bed with my head pinned to the floor. Ten minutes later when I still couldn't find them, I stepped into the bathroom and unthinkingly opened the faucet to fill the tub. Emily told me it was all her fault. I told her it was all mine.

Forty-six

I f my account of these bleak months feels hurried and disrespectful of its odd moments of tenderness and teary affection, it is only because my stomach still bears the thorns of our sharp-tongued exchanges (which often burrow deeper during the brief, so-called power naps that I've now forbidden myself). While the majority of our disturbances contained obvious links to the unfortunate chain of events that began at Saylorville Lake, Emily and I also found ourselves wading through a host of unrelated anxieties, as though Katie's death had opened the floodgates for all our private horrors—past, present, and future— which our foolish bodies attempted to purge in one fell swoop. Instead of assuaging our respective fears we poked and prodded them, soon arriving at a bitter acknowledgment that there were simply no effective words to speed their course. It seemed our whole lives had been whittled down to our Days Inn motel room, where more than once Emily articulated her dreary future of anonymous back-alley auditions with seedy, second-rate agents whose nineteen-year-old product was already damaged goods. When she wasn't practicing her lines in the bathroom mirror (or speechifying in an actor's warm-up gibberish that I could never decode), she racked up pay-per-view charges for movies she barely watched, usually after ordering Italian and Greek restaurant deliveries for meals she hardly touched. At least once a week we'd accuse each other of being clueless or hopeless or insane, which might've easily been construed as true, especially considering the subjects of our quality-time debates, not the least of which involved wagering on when her mom would finally open one of her credit card bills and uncover our secret. But I played along with our little scam, typically encouraging Emily to order us the most expensive items on the delivery menus, pretending not to notice that she could hardly swallow two bites of a Caesar salad, that oftentimes we weren't even kissing or using protection, that in sex she was like a rude dog with its ass in the air, jaw clamped shut and eyes clenched, masturbating herself while I gripped her hips and ankles like handlebars, pumping madly and all the while feeling like a snake oil salesman in a two-timing affair with the only girl I ever wanted to love. For better or worse we stuck together, likely as a result of the exchanges relegated to the hours of our separation when we'd lie in our childhood beds with the lights out, whispering by radio with such tenderness and understanding that I was able to set out each morning optimistically indulgent in hope—that cruel crutch known as much for its trickery and ravage as its splendor.

received my first speeding ticket on the night of the *Tinker* premiere—knocked down from the insurance-raising eighty-five miles per hour to seventy-five, which I accepted as a upbeat omen— while racing home from the fairgrounds in order to shower and shave, then sprint back east to the historic Sherman Hills district in my new pair of wool pants and herringbone blazer, forgoing the customary tie because I'd worn my only decent one to Katie's funeral. The Garage Theater turned out to be housed in a converted mansion, which I entered by way of a long set of creaking wooden stairs ending at the front door, followed by an elegantly dusty foyer manned by a col- lege student in a black turtleneck sitting at a card table with one hand limp over the cash lockbox like he was swearing himself in. (While he harbored obvious ambitions for the theater, any noticeable talent was supplanted by his priggish attitude in securing my eight dollars before allowing me to peruse the playbill.) In an area of the house where one would normally expect to enter a kitchen or living room, I parted my way through a velvet curtain to discover a long and narrow theater space with an unexpectedly high ceiling, though dark to the point of nearly total obscurity. While imagining that each patch of unseen audience represented a formal faction of the metropolitan arts community, I felt my way along the side aisle, choosing a folding chair in one of the mid-front rows in order to avoid unnerving Emily by sitting too close. My eyes adjusted to the darkness as a pair of Drake track runners still in their warm-ups sat down in the row behind me, swapping impersonations of faggoty theater types. A group of camera-toting family members crowded in next to me, the grandmother giving me the willies when she covered my right leg in the shawl she was wrapping over her cold knees and ankles.

About five minutes before the play began, when the theater was only a third full and the ticket prig was ordering us all closer to the front, somewhere in the lurching darkness I spied a familiar voice arguing the threat posed by such hazardously poor lighting. (When it came to family and friends, Emily always pushed for their attendance at mid-run performances, particularly in the case of her mother, who was also her harshest critic; apparently Mrs. Schell couldn't wait.) I turned my attention to the details of the set design, dominated by a canvas backdrop of a crummy city comprised of pointy tenements overshadowed by a Gothic church. The stage was extremely tight with much evidence of fire safety irregularity, highlighted by cheap yellow bulbs poking through the canvas, posing as lampposts, and nests of electrical wires at each end of the stage feeding stage lights with unprotected bulbs. I tried not to care if Mrs. Schell noticed me or not.

The lights went up and Emily was the first actor to appear, though it took me a few seconds to recognize her. While I'd imagined her gypsy character bold and vivacious, costumed in variegated skirts and scarves that would launch her forth from the set like a Technicolor Dorothy after ages of black-and-white, instead the costume designers had obscured her with a tangle-haired wig, filthy sneakers, and a bra that slung one breast high and the other low. She wandered to the center of the stage, then plopped down cross-legged to hawk change on an imaginary street corner, her eyes twitching in hungry suffering as formally dressed pedestrians crossed left and right, unnoticing of the tinker, who was apparently meant to blend chameleon-like into the sooty set. (These "pedestrians" made no more than eight to ten strides before being forced to stop and portend window-gazing reflection while waiting for their fellow extras coming *up* the steps.) Emily's accent was like nothing we'd ever heard.

"Born na more then tree kicks from this carb," she called out to the audience. "Come oot backward, spaykin' Frinch."

Hearty laughter sounded throughout the space. A few gypsy sentences later it stopped. A morose confusion spread the theater as we all realized the accent wasn't meant as a parody. A mother and daughter next to me started squabbling over their differing translations. I could barely understand a word and couldn't relax until the following sequence, which was mostly silent and allowed gesture to do the majority of the telling. A canvas representing a rail-yard slum scrolled down as the tinker returned to her boxcar home, laying to rest her sprightly gypsy daughter.

The play gathered some momentum in the second panhandling scene when the tinker reaped the attention of a gangly police officer who for the previous few minutes had been looking lost on the other side of the stage. He stepped wide-legged in front of her and wagged his nightstick. Framed neatly between his knees, the tinker peered hopelessly into the darkness of the theater.

"Now I've warned yeh, tinker garl," he said. "Warned yeh fer the last time."

The tinker was inured to the routine. Her pale gaze panned the audience, shifting from one audience member to another until it stopped at me. As Emily stared directly into my eyes I stared back, smiling without moving my mouth, encouraging her by way of a wink and a slight emotive nod that she pretended not to notice. The scene ended with the tinker walking off with the policeman. He threw his arm over her shoulder, promising to protect her from the dank street and the night before suddenly stopping, turning both of them toward the audience for his ten-minute soliloquy on the subject of Great (*great* inflected to mean *shit*) Britain's historic use of Irish debtors' prisons, which often doubled as insane asylums and quarantines for drunks and gypsies. The audience groaned, in unison, practically on cue. Scene by scene the plot grew more fandangled, the tinker more inebriate and incomprehensible. As far as the rest of the audience was concerned, the only saving grace seemed to come from the tinker's daughter, a curly-headed girl with oval glasses who looked much less a street urchin than a lackadaisical magician. The second act was mostly melodrama of the following sort:

DAUGHTER: Mum, is Daddy a tinker?

TINKER: No, me luve, eh's a gent'amin.

DAUGHTER: You won't marry the chief. Promise?

TINKER: I'm ownly the yeast in eh's mouldy bread.

Where the narrative began as a young woman's struggle to forge a better condition for her daughter, it evolved into a political drama in which the prime minister of Ireland, played by a nasal and self-aware blonde, was discovered to be the underground leader of an anti-British terrorist organization. This revelation inspired a litany of squawking seat backs: the track runners walked out, the families of the actors started speaking in plain barroom voices about their desire for an intermission (that would never be granted), a sarcastic older man in a group of professors a few rows back (I'd previously overheard them dubbing the venue the "Garbage Theater") offered his interpretation of the tinker as an "antifeminist twat." While I hadn't exactly forgotten about Mrs. Schell, my concerns about her attendance disrupting my suspension of disbelief were so overwhelmed by a sudden urge to drink and smoke as to render her presence a moot point.

The third act gave start with a bawdy love scene between the tinker and the police chief, who shoved his face in Emily's cleavage and grabbed two good handfuls of her quaking ass as he kissed her lips and face and neck. By this time it was evident that the tinker's greatest motive in the story was to see her daughter, now suffering an unknown illness with symptoms of dizzy spells and ringing ears, admitted to Belfast's elite academy for girls. She begged the chief, "You'll see to er wearin' the skarts wit tha leither shoes ind tassles?"

While the actors all knew that their bold experiment had realized itself as a complete disaster, to their credit they all kept on just as bravely as they started. The only exception was Emily. Not only did she quit her gypsy brogue, but started employing the mocking accent of a begrudged pirate. "Yuze never teakin' a warm hand to me," she once shouted. "Nor a glance o forchin' on me *garrrrl!*" But this was nothing compared to her aside a few minutes later, when she yanked her theatrical daughter by her wrist to the front of the stage and cried out with all the vehemence of the dying betrayed:

"*I-may Od-gay, I-may Od-gay, I-way ave-hay oo-yay orsaken-fay e-may!*"

While the chief and his housemaid did their best to pick up the pieces of a suddenly impromptu and multilingual narrative, they only grew more visibly confused and botched their lines and ended up stomping around in exhibition of pseudo-dramatic, incongruous affectation. These actions provided Emily enough glee and inspiration that she snapped back into character for a few scenes, after which time she grew bored again and turned her back to everyone onstage, leaving them no option other than to speak their lines directly to the audience. It was sabotage, plain and simple. In what I guessed to be the play's original climax, when the tinker was to finally break free of the chief, Emily shoved the guy so hard that he stumbled backward halfway across the stage, knocking over a pitcher of water as he tried to steady himself against the table. The pitcher banged to the floor, startling the audience in the front row (one of whom awoke looking content and peacefully rested until he realized the play hadn't actually ended). When Emily stormed off the stage, I didn't know if she was abandoning her daughter or the entire cast, crew, and script.

The play ended a few minutes later in a strange roundup scene where each character received his or her personal denouement. This sequence was highlighted by the chief's housemaid, who stopped referring to gypsies as "tinkers"; the chief, who started smoking a pipe; the prime minister, who exchanged her weapons for a much-desired British diplomat and lover; the tinker's daughter, who stopped punching rich girls in the stomach during field hockey games; and finally the tinker, who returned to the stage with her long hair brushed, all spruced up in a tweed skirt and Aran sweater. After it was revealed that she'd been hired as a comedic radio personality for an audience who thought they were listening to an impersonation, the lights shut off and the actors made their shuffle-footed retreat.

When the lights came up again, the actors returned to the stage like bumbling squirrels at the dead end of a laboratory maze, all except the prime minister, who bowed much longer than the others, apparently sensing her performance had risen above the script. Emily was the only actor who'd already changed out of costume. She bowed proudly at the end of the row in jeans and a red T-shirt, shimmering with pleasure. Despite her makeup, which was designed to suggest the suffering pallor of the underprivileged, she now appeared a sneaky charlatan heiress. Most of the audience clapped as though it was their most embarrassing chore, already bundling up for the exit and giving the actors such a poor reception that at one point the chief burst into liberating laughter that spread like dominoes across the stage. Emily laughed along with them, even louder than the others. I could still hear her cackling when I turned around to catch Mrs. Schell ducking into the foyer, wearing the pin-striped suit jacket I'd seen hanging under transparent plastic near the back of her closet.

Forty-eight

The premiere after-party was held downtown at the Blackhawk Hotel, a soulful if somewhat decrepit old place with a lobby of elaborate arches, brass handrails, and pinkish red carpet. After passing a pair of arguing bellhops in woolen red coats, I tucked Emily's roses under my arm and made my way to the pub, where to my surprise I found the event uncanceled (though I should note the atmosphere of denial; the main actors had even driven en masse in order to appraise their performances while the mood remained unbroken). The cast was gathered around their weirdly frisky director, a dangerously thin man with tall fluffy hair and facial skin like cracked granite. I joined a group of significant others seated at the end of the bar, most of whom were perusing the pub's concave ceiling with its views of dancing gilt reindeer and buglers in fading lederhosen. The only patrons besides the *Tinker* assembly were a pair of young businessmen who kept mocking the director's coy smirks and demonstrative hand gestures, every once in a while glancing over their shoulders to study up again before chuckling and carrying on. At this point he was praising the cast's youngest actor, joking that she was certain for stardom, even if it came in the boxing ring. Emily rocked side to side on a stool at the outer edge of the circle, sucking her gin and tonic through a straw.

"In all seriousness, I'm proud of you all. While I'm aware that Broadway may not be ready for such a bold production, I hope the critic from the *Register* will recognize that what we've got here at the Garage Theater can't be found in New York or London or Belfast!" He laughed and raised his Guinness—the only full glass in the room. "To a brilliant review!" he shouted. The actors politely clapped, then shoved up to the bar for rounds of raspberry kamikazes.

After Emily had taken her first group shot, I made my semi-studious approach. She turned and stroked her chin, surveying my new getup and nodding in apparent approval. I presented her the roses. She kissed me and pressed her nose into one of the blooms. Her cheeks were already flushed and she seemed much calmer than I expected, raising the question of how many drinks she'd slurped down during her director's speech.

"So do you think anyone recognized you from *The Bridges of Madison County*?"

"Hilarious," she said. "Do you want a cocktail? It's free, you know. Might as well get *something* out of the night. Whiskey?"

I nodded. She ordered a double on the rocks and another gin and tonic, casual to the point of boredom, like she'd been hanging out in dark hotel lounges all her life and had long grown tired of the routine. Soon the chief was hovering at my side, swinging his arm around the waist of his somber girlfriend who looked like Anne Frank and seemed reluctant to be introduced around. When it was clear that Emily wasn't planning to facilitate an introduction, I smiled awkwardly and offered my hand. I even fed him one of his own lines: "Quit yer dancin' in the mucky muck!" But as soon as the bartender finished pouring our drinks, Emily took my hand, making no effort to excuse herself before leading me to a small table by the windows. She propped the roses up on the third chair and sat for a while admiring them.

"After *Othello* you gave me a pineapple," she finally said, somewhat giggly. "And after *Our Town*, correct me if I'm wrong, you handed me a watermelon. Were they out of pumpkins or something? Or are you just getting formal in your old age?"

"I waited outside your changing room. I waited for hours . . . days even, but you never came out."

"You mean the bathroom, right?" she said, laughing and taking a sip sans straw. (She still puffed her cheeks out when she drank alcohol, which in my opinion made it that much harder to stomach.) She glanced away as she swallowed, wincing, but trying not to show it. "I suppose I could've painted my name on the door. Maybe that's a good idea."

I smiled and took a generous drink, feeling an immediate sting that warmed my throat and stomach, practically singing out to me as it coursed through my veins. Emily bobbed her head to a piano jazz album, eyeing me up and down again, looking impressed. I knew I'd end up giving her my harshest review to date, but I hadn't decided on an appropriate tone and was more than worried how far the path of truth would eventually take us.

"Well, out with it," she said. "I can handle it. Maybe you can start by talking about some of the confusing parts of the plot. Unless you want to ease our way into it? Care to talk about the news for a minute or two? There's plenty of *that* to talk about."

"All right," I said, appreciating the extra time to consider my approach. "What's the latest?"

Emily sighed, like she didn't know where to start. When she caught my eye again, her eyebrows folded into a V and she leaned forward. "You're joking, right?"

"If I'm joking, I don't know what I'm joking about."

"Jesus," she said, leaning back and covering her forehead. "You really don't know? The latest on Nicholas Parsons?"

"They caught him!" I shouted, much louder and more gleeful than I'd intended. Almost everyone in the bar turned our way. It took Emily a few seconds to wipe the smirk off her face, at which point she leaned in and lowered her voice.

"He showed up at Missy Patterson's house. In the middle of the night her dad heard some banging around in the garage and ended up finding Nicky crouched down in the corner fixing up her old bike. He'd already put new tires on it and oiled the chain. He was almost finished fitting it with professional pedals."

"Was he armed?"

"Mr. Patterson or Nicky Parsons?"

I took another drink, leaning back to eye her up and down the same way she'd eyed me. "You'd better not be making this up," I said. Emily laughed a slow, breathy snigger ("How funny it is how little you know me!"). I didn't apologize. We'd done enough of that, and anyway my apology was all over my broken-glass face. "So what happened?"

"First I want your review," she said, crossing her arms over her chest. "You haven't said a word yet, and I'm starting to think you'd rather avoid it all together."

"I'm not avoiding it. But now that we're talking about Nicholas Parsons, I want to know how it ended."

"First my review."

"I knew you'd do this," I said, taking another drink, recognizing the uselessness in attempting to change her mind. Maybe it was better this way, I thought, just to spit it out all at once. But the second I opened my mouth I grew suddenly nervous about how my review would affect the outcome of the Nicholas Parsons story, as though it were a movable narrative with grand implications for our future. "For the first act I believed you. You were sad and nervous, and I liked how your eyes never strayed too far from your daughter. I liked that a lot. You also never looked like you were trying too hard, unlike the prime minister, who kept flapping her arms every other line like she was trying out for a modeling contract. Like she was deathly afraid the scouts might not notice her."

Emily covered her mouth, suppressing a laugh. But so far she was nodding along, enjoying my review much more than I'd intended. "So you didn't get jealous?" she asked. "All that funny business with the chief?"

"Maybe I did get jealous a few times, but by the end of the second act I was just disappointed. Your accent fell apart, and you didn't look like you were even trying."

"The accent wasn't working anyway."

"Maybe it wasn't, but you were mocking them. You were mocking your own character. Shit, whenever you came upon a word with an *r* in it, you'd growl like Captain Hook."

"*Garrrrrrrrl,*" she whispered, covering her mouth and laughing again. "Did it get any better in the third act? Before you answer, let me tell you that all along he encouraged us to *absorb the script*, which sometimes results in line adjustments in the middle of the performance."

"You did some serious absorbing."

"I'm a serious actor, George."

"You used to *love* the theater," I said, taking a drink and turning toward the bar. The chief was starting to get playful, shadowboxing and slapping people's backs. Emily drummed her drink on the table and I turned back to her.

"Don't let me stop you now," she said, arguably indifferent. "You're not a fan of *improvisation*? A little freestyle *realism*?"

"The first time I saw you act you had a bunch of assholes for an audience, but it didn't matter, because you weren't afraid to let them know that you *loved* the theater, that you were going to perform in spite of them, even if it killed you. I'm still amazed how you kept your concentration. I watched you for ten minutes and already knew you were *meant to act*. But tonight . . . tonight I didn't even recognize you up there. You weren't even an actor. Tonight *you* were the fucking asshole."

Emily nodded and took a calm drink, this time forgetting to hide how nasty it tasted. She turned to the thick velvet curtains, parting them and staring out over the empty downtown streets. I swear all the slow dizziness that struck me in the next minute revealed itself on her dark and falling cheeks. In the slashing yellow light of an old-style streetlamp she suddenly appeared so sick that I expected at any moment for her to lean down between her chair and the curtains to vomit. I shoved my drink to the center of the table, not wanting any more, wondering what the hell I was doing drinking double whiskeys before heading out on icy roads. Emily turned back to me and the curtains fell closed.

"I agree with your whole critique," she said, meeting my eyes. "Seriously. On the ride over here Tony basically said the same thing. I'm not the lead anymore. Tomorrow night Cathy will be the tinker. I'm the new prime minister, or the new terrorist, or whatever. By the time my parents show up, I'll probably be playing the field hockey coach."

I stared into my melted drink, trying to recall everything I'd just said and only coming up with the decision that whatever it was would come back at me in spades. Emily obviously didn't know that her mother had been there, and I didn't see the point in telling her. "It doesn't make sense," I finally said, backing off my criticism, just as I knew I would. "Does Cathy even know the lines?"

"A lot of times we rehearse in other roles. It's usually Cathy and me switching characters. She'll do fine."

"You had a bad night, that's all."

"No I didn't. I knew what I was doing, and whatever came of it is all my fault. But it really doesn't matter. I guess this will only disappoint you even more, but I'm thinking about going back to Chicago. I'm still working out the details, but I told my adviser why I left and she said she'd help me. They might let me come back in a few weeks."

"I thought you hated it there," I said (coughing? falling out of my chair? bursting with panic-stricken flatulence?), again raising my voice.

"I didn't hate it. I thought I had to come home is all. I've been home, so now I can go back."

"In the middle of the semester?"

"Oh come on, George. What are we gonna do, spend our whole lives hiding?"

"We can do whatever we want," I said, almost believing it. "We just have to want it and then do something about it."

"Did we want everything that happened to us at Saylorville? Can we really do something about all that?"

"How about a martini?" I said.

"What are you talking about? You really think these cocktails are free, don't you? We're not even supposed to be drinking in this place."

"Let's have martinis," I said, knowing how ridiculous I sounded but unable to stop myself. "I've never had a martini. We'll be like old actors from the fifties getting drunk in a hotel. We'll drink the place dry and then get a room upstairs."

Emily set her glass down, letting it slip at the last second so that it dropped and rattled and spilled. The green carpet soaked her drink in seconds, leaving only the ice cubes like emerald lozenges. "Wake up, George. Don't you ever consider that we should've just stayed friends? Maybe none of this would've ever happened if we'd just stayed friends."

"I'm not asking you to get married," I said, contradicting my intention to let her know I was prepared to stick it out to the end, to weather the storm however long it took to build ourselves back up to the sturdy young people we once were. "Let's get a room upstairs. A suite. I just got paid."

"This isn't my kind of place."

"All right. Forget it. But how can you go back to Chicago in the middle of the semester?"

"I don't know," she said, setting her empty glass back on the table. I grabbed both glasses and pushed my chair back like I was going for refills. Emily held her hand out, stopping me and reaching for her roses. "I'm sorry, George."

"Just a few more minutes. You didn't tell me what happened with Nicholas Parsons? At least you could stay that long." Emily set the roses across the table. She closed her eyes for a minute, trying to calm herself enough to remember where she'd left off. "Nicky was in the garage. He was on the ground, putting new pedals on Missy's bike."

"Mr. Patterson was shocked," she said, more or less pulling herself together. "Especially when he saw the blood on Nicky's hands. He screamed or something. Obviously I don't know the details, but I guess he screamed, and then shut the door and locked it and called the cops. They showed up a few minutes later, but all they found was an empty garage with a bunch of bloody fingerprints. The report said that Nicholas had just come from the Drake Diner where he'd shot up the place." Her voice cracked and she started to cry, though she didn't stop or even slow down. "He killed a waitress who sort of looked like Missy. He shot her six or seven times."

By now the cast were all staring at us, whispering about her fallen drink, my fancy clothes, our past, etc. I wanted to pull the velvet curtains around us. I wanted to hug Emily, even knowing she didn't want to be hugged.

"You shouldn't have performed tonight. Tony should've postponed the premiere."

"He should've replaced me a long time ago," she said, wiping her face on her sleeve and standing up.

"You look dizzy," I said.

"I feel dizzy."

"Let me take you somewhere. Let me take you home."

"No thank you," she answered, politely, without another thought, and started across the room. I shot to my feet, but didn't move beyond that. Under the paralyzing glare of the entire cast panning back and forth between us I didn't say a word or move an inch as Emily inspected bar stools draped with coats, attempting ease and balance but causing half a dozen coats to slide to the floor amid the search for her own. She wrested her hands into her leather gloves and threw her woolen scarf around her neck so that it swung low on one side and barely clung to her neck on the other. I sat down again, picking up one of the long-stemmed roses and twirling it. I stared hypnotic into the bloom as my stomach filled with heat, roiling with the thought of never again knowing Emily's fierce loving gaze, the sharp rupture of her blushing orgasm. When I looked up she was already gone. A bulb of blood appeared on the tip of my thumb and broke. I pulled the curtains back just in time to catch her cross the street and turn the corner, which is when I understood there was no sight more beautiful or crushing than Emily Schell walking away.

Forty-nine

If you want to know the entire truth of the evening, several hours later I found myself soaking in a steaming bath with the lights off and shower curtain pulled, designing various suicide plans that would fool family, friends, and enemies into believing that I'd parted this world in a selfless act of gut-wrenching heroism. I came up with a number of plausible death scenarios as the bath cooled, during which time my weak stomach for damning and culturally uncouth endeavors was steadied by the hurtful understanding that at that particular moment (and numerous other moments I intentionally neglected to mention) I viewed Katie's death and her parents' grief as nothing more than insults toward my happy future with Emily. My amoral resolve waned within the hour when my testicles sank lower than perhaps they ever had, lending the impression of their shame and hinting at an exploratory underwater search for a more courageous host. With chattering teeth I dripped my way down the hallway to my bedroom above the garage, soon weeping wet-headed under the covers, incubating myself in sheets and blankets in a way that triggered memories of all those early-morning swimming lessons with the Guppy Group at the YMCA back in Davenport. One memory led to the other and soon I was reliving several boyhood episodes that made me crack up under the covers and feel I had not entirely lost myself, that deep down I was still the same kid who'd made his mother laugh like a fool on mundane trips to the grocery store and dry cleaners, who'd put his life on the line defending the weaklings from Dan Burns, the school bus sadist, who'd even been bucked from a lunatic horse at wilderness camp and landed flat on his feet, arms in the air like an Olympic champ. I remembered all those first dives into the freezing-cold pool at the Davenport YMCA, when I spent every water-treading minute waiting for the moment when our instructor would blow the whistle and I'd scurry up the ladder, tear across the slick deck despite the signs and shouts to where my mom was waiting with her turquoise half-hoop earrings and gigantic diamond-patterned purse that always slipped off her shoulder and down her arm as she kneeled to wrap me up in a big towel hug and take me home. Later that night I sat by the window for a while and prayed, then removed the batteries from my two-way radio and tried to go to sleep.

Fifty

When I set out on the final night of the *Tinker* run at the Garage Theater, I had a good idea where I'd end up, though I didn't exactly plan it. I started off driving west on Hickman, eventually cruising past the water tower in Clive and crossing into Jordan, flipping through radio stations while rehearsing arguments from both sides, trying to decide where exactly the story started and ended, all the while unconsciously making turns in one direction or another as I curved my way around the semirural outskirts of the city. I had no idea what route I'd taken when I pulled into the Schells' neighborhood, despite my strange suspicion that it had been tracked by radar monitor in their kitchen. The house was dark but for the candelabra fixture over the bare dining room table in the front window.

Soon after ringing the doorbell, I heard the approaching thumps of bare heels on hardwood floor. Mr. Schell opened the door in suit pants and gold-toed business socks. His face was slightly darkened by a five o'clock shadow and there were yellow pit stains in his under-shirt. Appearing more worn out than surprised, he cranked his shoulders back and widened his stance, offering nothing more than a lame gaze that related a feeling that I'd been bugging him all week and had better have a damn good reason this time. He wiped his face, waiting for me to say something. I had no energy for being brave.

"Can I come inside?" I asked, my graveled vocals doing the work of acknowledging my audacity.

"Emily's not home," he said, staring me down and wiping his face some more. It was obvious that our Days Inn rendezvous since Christmas weren't much of a secret.

"I was hoping to talk to you for a minute. You and Mrs. Schell."

Mr. Schell leaned to one side, eyeballing my truck parked at the curb. (Something about Mr. Schell's small sparkling eyes made me feel I wasn't talking to the real Mr. Schell, but his doppelgänger stand-in. This intuition forced me to consider that I wasn't myself, either, which added up to a set of circumstances that might have proved beneficial to the negotiations that lay ahead.) He took a long time answering. "Does Emily know you're here?"

I shook my head.

"Do you mind speaking up when I'm talking to you?"

"She would have no way of knowing," I said.

Mr. Schell nodded, seeming to understand the full implication of the remark. To his credit, he didn't wallow in the satisfaction that Emily and I were no longer on speaking terms. "Your nose is crooked," he said.

"It's broken."

"Somebody clocked you?"

"That's right. On New Year's Eve. He got arrested."

"Did you fight back?"

I shook my head, remembering a second too late Mr. Schell's warning against nonverbal responses. He noticed my slipup, but didn't call me on it. I had a feeling this was the only freebie I would receive, and that he'd only given it to me because we were still warming up.

"Turned the other cheek, huh?"

"Security broke it up," I said.

Mr. Schell nodded, acting like he preferred whatever version he'd come up with for the story. "Can I come in?" I asked.

"Suppose I say yes and then my wife says no?"

"Then I'll go," I said, matching my irritated expression to his, trying to apologize for showing up without throwing myself off the porch at the same time. After a while he turned sideways and flung his arm in a sweeping motion, ushering me inside. I stepped into the front hallway and bent down to take my shoes off.

"I don't think I'd bother," he said, upsetting whatever expectations I had for a thorough tête-à-tête. He led me through the living room to the kitchen, flipping the lights on and turning around to check the floor for tracks. After pointing to the nearest chair, he disappeared upstairs. I sat down, noticing the countertop littered with plates and glasses, an empty calzone box and a plastic container with soggy left-over salad. There were only three chairs at the table now, the fourth chair piled high with newspapers, moved to the corner next to a tower of Schell's Shirtworks boxes. Out the back window a pair of crows roosted on opposite fence posts. Faint whispers like scampering cats seeped down from the upstairs balcony. When the Schells finally made their entrance, Mrs. Schell started off by lowering the drapes above the sink, then loading the dishwasher. Mr. Schell sat down across from me, following his wife's movements over my right shoulder. His chin was jutting out now and his head seemed a thousand-pound weight on his neck and shoulders. I imagined he'd been on the road all week, and just pulled into the garage a few minutes before I showed up.

When Mrs. Schell finally sat down, she folded her hands on the table and glanced up at me with the physical disposition of a public lawyer forced to defend some sicko she knew was guilty as sin. She'd clearly just gathered her hair in a bun; it was tightly combed and

pressed to her scalp, not a strand out of place. But she was also wearing an old Lake Okoboji T-shirt and short bedtime shorts, showing
off more of her humble unmade self than ever.

"I saw you at Emily's performance, sitting by yourself," she said,
turning to Mr. Schell and raising an eyebrow, like I'd been up to something funny in my private seat all alone. She probably thought my visit
was no more than a cheap trick to win Emily back.

"I saw you, too," I said, wanting to add that she, too, was alone,
but deciding instead to *act* like I'd said it. Mrs. Schell smirked and
scratched her nose, like that's all I represented to her, a little nose itch
easy enough to scratch away. Mr. Schell was struggling to sit still,
uninterested now in whatever small talk he'd tested me with at the
front door. His deliberate tone let me know it wouldn't take much for
him to change his mind and throw me out.

"You said you wanted to talk," he said. "So why don't you say
something?"

"I thought you might have some questions for me," I said, my conviction less apparent than I'd intended. "About the day we all went
fishing. I thought you might have some questions that I could answer.
Emily only remembers that day in bits and pieces. But I remember it
all. I remember it perfectly."

Neither of them answered right away. It was so quiet for a while
that I eventually found myself focused on the most timorous of ding-
ing sounds that I ended up tracing to a deluxe barbecue pit out back: a
metal spatula swinging back and forth in the breeze, tapping against
its leg. I already regretted my approach, feeling I'd inadvertently
taunted them with the fact that I knew what happened and they didn't.
In the end it was Mrs. Schell who nodded for me to continue. "Go
ahead and tell us," she said, clearing her throat against what might
have emerged as a vocal quiver. I also cleared my throat, then adopted
the bearing of an unaffected cop. (I accepted Mrs. Schell's view of the

situation as similar to an attorney's jailhouse conference, but was still mindful enough to recast myself as someone other than the accused.) I had no intention of breaking down at any point during the forthcoming narrative that would for the most part have the Schells on the edge of their seats, clinging to every word, even if they did their best to appear skeptical and unimpressed.

"I'll start with the mosquitoes," I said, already sighing and fixing my gaze, attempting to establish patience and accuracy as the central tones. "They were all over the place. We got mauled on the path to the lake, and Emily and Katie were pretty annoyed by the time we found our canoe, which ended up being the one canoe lying facedown in the mud." (I passed over my failure to insist that the girls buy fishing licenses, an omission in the service of a streamlined story more than an avoidance of personal misdeed.) "When Emily saw it all mucked up with crickets and spiderwebs, she decided right away she'd be fishing from the shore. That's why Katie and I set off on our own. Of course the guy at the rental hut gave us three life jackets, but when Katie and I set off she was the only one wearing hers. Emily left hers on the shore, and I tossed mine in the bottom of the canoe, where Katie ended up grabbing it to use as a seating pad. Anyway, since Katie wasn't much for casting and kept getting her lure tangled, we spent most of the first hour paddling around"—a slight exaggeration, given that I did *all* the paddling; I considered it a gimme after such an unflinching clarification in concern to Katie's life jacket—"to different coves where she could just drop her line and wait for a bite. But it was hot that day and we started late. The fishing wasn't looking very good. We tried top-water lures, divers, jigs, but none of us got even a nibble.

"Eventually Katie decided she wanted to move from the middle of the lake and try our luck along the shoreline. I'm talking about the shoreline almost directly opposite the beach. For the first couple of casts it was more of the same; she kept plopping the lure down right next to the boat. But when she finally let one go, she really let it go and it ended up sailing into the trees. The situation went even further downhill when she snapped the line trying to yank it out. That's when I jumped out and swam to the shore, to get the lure back—"

Mr. Schell stopped me. He waved his index finger and rapped his foot against the stem at the bottom center of the table. "So *you* tipped it," he said, his voice cracking high and windy, as though it had whistled through a gorge. "What did you think would happen jumping out like that?"

"I didn't tip it," I said, flatly, like it wasn't as simple as that and the story was far from over. "I was careful, and the canoe hardly rocked. It's not such a hard thing to do. And if you want to talk about the lure, well, everyone I know would've gone after a lure hanging in the trees like that, one way or another. The bigger mistake was the anchor. I shouldn't have jumped out without dropping the anchor."

Mrs. Schell stared down at Mr. Schell's leg until he stopped shaking it. She didn't care about the life jacket or the anchor. She wanted the rest of the story (which I'd only related twice before: once to the police and once to my parents, in fewer details at that; the only other person I've trusted with this account since then was a young Mexican divorcée I ended up dating for a few weeks following an award dinner for "Iowa Teachers of the Year"). Mr. Schell leaned back and crossed his arms. I craved a cigarette and for the first time considered myself an addict, increasingly dependent on muscle tension and aggravation to continue where I'd left off.

"I climbed the tree," I said. "I was in the middle of reaching for the lure when Katie ended up hooking a brown trout. She was using my fishing rod, which had a different reel that she didn't know how to use. But she cast it perfectly and when she hooked her fish I actually saw it swallow the lure and take off, in the water right below me.

Katie started shouting and cheering for herself, even though she didn't really know what to do next."

"Did she land it?" Mr. Schell blurted.

"She almost did. The canoe tipped as she was taking the hook out."

"So she took her jacket off while you were out in the middle."

"She undid the top buckle, but she didn't take it off. Maybe I should've said something, but it wasn't like the whole life jacket was loose. Not at all. She was still wearing it when she hooked that trout."

Mr. Schell laughed. His laughter wasn't nearly as precise as Emily's, and until his ears turned bright burning red I didn't know exactly how to interpret it. He regained his previous composure while fixing his gaze on the leaning T-shirt boxes. It wasn't easy. He didn't want to break down in front of me, either.

"How big was it?" Mrs. Schell asked, pretending her question was forensically relevant and nothing more. I held my hands out the width of my shoulders. She turned to Mr. Schell only long enough to roll her eyes. "You're exaggerating. We've got trout streams in Tennessee, you know."

"Then you know that trout usually get bigger in streams than in lakes, and either way a five-pound brownie is an absolute hog. When it came splashing out of the lake, I practically fell out of the tree."

Mrs. Schell turned to the windows and smiled, really smiling, like she'd seen her fair share of brown trout take to the air and there was no greater thrill. When she turned back and nodded for me to continue, her smile hadn't entirely left her. "She fought it for a long time," I said. "I don't know exactly, but almost ten minutes, I think. I was giving her instructions and Emily was cheering her on. Katie kept cursing the fish, calling him names. She couldn't figure out why he kept hiding under the canoe."

"What names did she call it?" Mrs. Schell asked.

"Little bugger. Little bastard."

Mrs. Schell covered her mouth and turned away again, chuckling this time. Mr. Schell couldn't believe it. He stared at her as he might've stared at an exotic bird let loose in his kitchen, flapping wildly. She laughed herself to a few eye-swelling tears, then leaned on her elbows and wiped her cheeks. She didn't look up again until she'd composed herself, when I started to get the feeling she'd been training herself to ignore me, and simply focus on the story.

"It was a long fight," I went on. "Part of the reason it took so long was because at one point Katie accidentally opened the reel. I could see it spinning backward, which meant her fish was running away with the line. But she'd hooked him good, and I thought she'd still catch him if she could get the line taut again."

Mrs. Schell leaned forward, only slightly, but enough to let me know she wanted the story to continue forever, like the story was keeping Katie alive. But I couldn't stretch it out because Mr. Schell was losing his patience. He knew the ending and was acting wary of the possibility that I'd change it, that I was inventing as I went along. His chin jutted out again and he tilted his head down so that his pupils were aimed up in preemptive warning. I kept going, just the same as before.

"By then Emily had made her way around the shore and was standing next to me. We kept telling Katie to sit down and hold the pole up high. That's when her fish broke the surface, wiggling in the air and trying to throw the hook out. After he splashed back down Katie put a hand on the spool to stop it from letting out more line. She started reeling in again, as fast as she could. When we saw a bunch of splashes on the far side of the canoe, we knew she had it close. She leaned over to pull it in by the line."

Mrs. Schell raised her hands, frantically interrupting. "You didn't have a net?" she shouted.

"I didn't think we'd need it."

"Why not?"

"I don't know," I said, raising my voice. "I just didn't." Which is when I realized it wasn't just the anchor that was the big mistake, it was the net. Mrs. Schell saw that I recognized her point and nodded for me to continue. "So like I said, there were a few splashes, then at some point Katie let go of the line and jumped back. Maybe she thought the fish would bite her or something, but as soon as she jumped back the canoe tipped one way and then the other way. That's when she fell in."

Mr. Schell turned toward the backyard and his barbecue pit, looking like he wanted to crawl inside it and close the lid so he wouldn't have to hear any more. Mrs. Schell held herself perfectly still, except for her quivering chin. When she lost it a few seconds later, Mr. Schell started searching the ceiling and mumbling under his breath, likely advising himself to hold it together for a few more minutes, *then* let go. Mrs. Schell covered her face with two flat hands. Her shoulders bowed inward and heaved. I didn't know how to adjust my tone without crying so I just kept on with the confidence of a journalist who'd already told the story a thousand times.

"Emily dove in with her shoes on and everything. The canoe had drifted a ways, so it took us a couple of minutes to get out there. Maybe two minutes. I don't know if Emily ever saw her underwater, but I didn't."

"When did she take it off?" Mr. Schell demanded. "When did she toss the life jacket?"

"I told the police it must've happened after she fell in. But they didn't believe me and kept insisting she'd taken it off sometime before that. I didn't know what else to tell them. I still don't understand it. All I could figure was that her fish took off with the pole, and maybe she unbuckled herself to go after it. That was only a guess. We couldn't see her from the shore, and when we swam out to the canoe, the first thing I noticed was *two* life jackets floating away."

Mr. Schell tilted his head back again and gnashed his teeth and flared his nostrils. (It seemed he'd become an expert at these ill-tempered gestures, recasting himself as impulsive and unpredictable, qualities that I consider a greater threat than size and muscle.) I swore he was using every ounce of restraint not to upend the table and charge. "Emily told us!" he shouted. "None of you wore your life jackets because of the heat! You ditched them from the start!"

It was the worst time to lose my nerve, but while caught between summoning a response and attempting to understand Emily's lies I ended up shoving backward in my chair, banging against the countertop and yelping in surprise. Mr. Schell jumped to his feet, slamming his knuckles down on the table and leaning forward so the hanging candle lamp shone white on his face.

"You actually believe your own bullshit, don't you? She was never wearing a life jacket. You thought you were such a hotshot with a canoe she wouldn't need one. ARE YOU LISTENING TO ME, *BOIY?!* WHEN WILL YOU BE READY FOR THE TRUTH?!"

"I was ready for the truth when I rang the doorbell," I said, tapping a source of previously unknown equanimity. "Either the jacket was defective, or Katie unbuckled it after she fell in. But I've already explained everything I came to explain."

Mr. Schell smiled big and toothy, refusing such an ending, tempting me to stand up and meet him eye to eye. Mrs. Schell covered her splotchy cheeks and forehead, every once in a while shaking her hands out as though begging for something she couldn't put into words. And that's when I closed my eyes and my lips fell open and my chest expanded and my whole body rose. In the next couple of seconds I summoned such a colossal pillar of breath that I felt it sucking in from a collective sigh at the center of the room, as if I were breathing not only for myself but for all of us, all the Schell family and all of mine, our ancestors, too. When I opened my eyes again—in all likelihood I'd only blinked—Mrs. Schell was reaching for her husband's clenched fist, pressing her head to his knuckles and wetting them with her tears. His boyish eyes were still bulging, deliberating between courageous revenge and confused retreat as I rose to my feet, moving with such deliberate gentility that there was no doubt I was only standing up to leave. I pushed my chair back under the table and turned around, half expecting Mr. Schell to now draw his antique pistol and shoot me in the back. But he didn't, and soon I was past the hallway and out the front door, crossing over a moonlit lawn glistening with melted snow.

After I stepped into my truck and started the engine, I surprised myself by pausing before driving away. I looked up at the Schell house and thought about all the times I'd waited like a chimp on the front porch. I thought about Katie's schoolbooks in her closet that had already lost a good deal of their value and might never get resold. I thought about all those corny stenciled T-shirts in the storage room downstairs. After a while I realized I was mostly staring at my own reflection in the dining room windows, absorbed in a brief meditation that might've been broken with the filmic sight of Mr. Schell stepping into the window frame and aiming and firing. Of course that didn't happen, but I imagined it would and had to laugh at myself as I drove away, knowing perfectly well that Mr. Schell was sitting at the kitchen table huddled around his wife.

realize now that in the course of my mission to accurately record the final act of my first romantic relationship, I've neglected several significant coinciding events, such as the surprise I received one frozen February morning when I woke to find Zach at the kitchen table, already several cups of coffee ahead of me, slopping through a bowl of oatmeal as he described the incredible new sickness he felt blowing all his bartending money the same night he made it, especially since his dear Rachel wasn't the type to wait at the end of the bar for the last hour of his shift like a common-law, good-for-nothing tramp. Of course Frank had been more than happy to loan him a few pairs of padded overalls, "so long as he gave them a good workout," which it turned out he did. Even during the most trying weeks of our endless winter, Zach took an enthusiastic interest in learning all the tricks of the Moretti trade, which included becoming fluent in veteran jargon, and never complaining, and lending a hand wherever he could. (This is not to suggest he didn't find his place as the joker on the crew, only now he considered his sophomoric high jinks as essential to our esprit de corps, usually presenting them in combination with the ritual one-hitters he passed around before our rush-hour ride home.)

After only a few months, everyone agreed that Zach had found his calling, especially in view of his intense pride in his ability to operate every piece of machinery on the site, including breakers, crawlers, excavators, dozers, augers with big ripper buckets, and skid loaders with hydraulic tiltrotators. He even gained such a reputation for innovative time-saving suggestions that Frank decided to introduce him to the political nuances of the process by requiring his attendance at all meetings with the state overseers. By the end of April we'd already finished most of the preliminary work to reconnect two lagoons, thus restoring the original free-flowing water system and putting to rest a great deal of concern over the timetable for our part of the project; at one point we made more progress in ten days than Frank thought we could in three weeks. As for myself, I passed most of those days in the former landfill, rocking around in a caged tractor, trying to convince myself I was digging up a glorious past when in fact I was only taking out the trash.

But none of this really matters. This story is almost over* and my whole purpose of describing the work we did that spring is to share the fact that at some point over the course of working together and sharing lengthy commutes beginning at five a.m. (in Zach's stealthy new Ford F-Series; my truck blew a head gasket and more or less bit the dust), I realized that Zach and I had quit conversing like pipsqueak adversaries and become friends. For the first time since childhood I became aware of the deep security I felt having Zach as my brother, going so far as to think that all his efforts for Frank Moretti were

---

*One of my initial hopes in composing a book-length work was to prove to my students that their composition teacher could actually write something. As luck would have it, I'm now hoping none of them will ever hear about it, and certainly never read it. The same goes for the Schells, my parents, their friends, Zach, and basically everyone I know except Emily.

somehow part of an endeavor to win the brotherly respect he felt he'd failed to earn in all the years before.

That said, I'll now relate a particular conversation in early May that found us gazing over an almost surreal landscape of men and machines in fluid motion, crisscrossing one another under the watch of wind turbines whirling in distant fields. Zach and I were sitting at a picnic table near the trailer, shoveling down nearly expired emergency meals left over from the flood.

"A lot of people are taking notice of this project," Zach said, shouting over metallic cranks and roars (the remedial sound effects of progress, as we saw it then). "Shit. Frank says they're planning a big conference in a few months with city planners from St. Louis, Cincinnati, Dallas, New York. If things work out here, we'll be a model for parks around the country."

"You think you could keep this up for thirty years?" I asked, half choking on the steam.

"Hell yeah. I'm feeling stronger than ever. We should think about starting our own company. I'm serious. I like this business and we could be good at it. You're a natural-born salesman. You could manage the business end while I take charge of the crews."

I nodded along, acting like it was an interesting idea, but that I wasn't sure if it would really work out. Zach played his hand the best he could, changing the topic when he realized I wasn't in the mood for a hard sell. "I was thinking," he said. "If you've got the time, I know this kid from Iowa City who's living practically for free in his grandpa's cabin out in Montana. He's got it pretty good out there, and it's just him until October—" Zach paused and looked up. He skipped whatever he was planning to say and took another bite.

"What is it?" I asked.

"Well, I was gonna say I could bring Rachel and you could bring Emily, but I guess you two broke up for good, huh?"

I nodded.

"What happened?"

"I don't know," I said, reaching for the napkins before the whole stack blew away. Zach balled up his disposable meal tray and dumped it into the metal can next to him.

"Shit, man. You've had a pretty rough go this last year."

"I know," I said.

"I liked Emily."

"Me, too."

For a while Zach just sat there shaking his head. He probably wanted to say something nasty about Emily but he didn't. In the end he just kept staring at me and smirking. "What?" I asked.

"He ain't heavy, mister. He's my brother."

"Is that from *Boys Town?*"

"Probably," he said, still smirking as he nodded at the stack of emergency lasagnas. "Let's split another one, okay?"

"Okay," I said, even though he was already opening the box. He poured the water pouch over the chemical pack and shoved it back inside. A minute later there was steam pouring out the corners of the box. Zach gave me a look like perhaps we should talk a little more about my troubles. "I'm gonna be all right."

"I know," he said, shaking his plastic fork at me, like he wasn't so sure, but he'd let it go if that's what I wanted. "What you need to do is to sign up for some business classes. You think you could work on site all day and manage a few business classes at night?"

"I doubt it."

"Hell yeah you could—" But then he cut himself off, realizing that my attention had drifted and I wasn't really listening. "Are you really all right?"

"Yeah," I said, tossing a pebble at the portable toilets near the woods. "I was just thinking about that girl from the Holiday Inn. Do you ever think about that?"

"I try not to, but I think about it. What's got you thinking about that now?"

"I don't know. I have to think about something. I always wonder why we didn't hear anything. She must've screamed at least once, but no one heard a thing?"

"I guess she should've screamed louder. They say you should yell fire when you're being raped, 'cause if you yell rape, people run away. These days you try to help someone out, you end up getting sued. It's a liability helping people."

"So is screaming," I said, tossing another pebble at the toilets. "Did you know Nicholas and Missy were both devout Catholics? Did you know he never slept with her, or raped her, or anything like that? He strangled her without even kissing her."

"That's fucking beautiful, George."

"At least he had *some* principles," I said. "At least he believed in *something*."

Zach blew off the comment with a backhanded flick of the wrist, shaking his head like he didn't understand and he didn't want to understand. "I just can't believe they haven't caught him. Little bastard's probably in Mexico by now, living the life. We should become bounty hunters. We could live the life, too."

"Maybe," I said, thinking that maybe I'd fall out of love or maybe I wouldn't. Maybe I'd meet another girl and fall as hard for her as I did for Emily. Or maybe I'd never know such desire ever again and I'd be better for it.

Ten minutes later we were back to our tractors, digging up what would eventually become the Grand Basin. It was a slow and tedious process. Here and there among the rusty tin cans and glass bottles we'd stumble upon small treasures: an iron sculpture of mating frogs, a perfectly shaped Superman lunch box filled with quarter-sized slugs likely once engaged to cheat 1950s slot machines. Later that day one of our diggers uncovered a pair of decorative shell ear spools and an ancient hoe. As required by law, Frank called the Iowa Archeological Society, whose experts uncovered several additional artifacts, mostly whittled from bison bones (that they eventually traced to the Mill Creek culture, which thrived in Iowa about a thousand years ago, before they migrated upriver and all but vanished).

Caught in the excitement of the discovery, over the next month I spent more than one lunch break strolling the park perimeters with an eye out for evidence of disturbed ground, still clinging to the notion that at some point I'd begin a secret and meticulous excavation of Katie's time capsule. By then I viewed the fairgrounds as the most ideal burial site, particularly in terms of the childlike wonder it exuded on all who openheartedly entered its premises. Perhaps this wonder and consequentially innocent way of seeing deserves more credit than anything else for my detecting one day, while trekking through the woods not far from the main park entrance, a noticeably irregular and leafless sapling sprouting through the dirt near the base of a walnut tree. On further inspection my hunch was verified; the twiggy youth was actually a steel wire sticking out of the ground, offering no apparent purpose, and fully resistant to being yanked out of place.

While I didn't expect anything to come of this finding, I nonetheless went through the motions of a minor investigation. This began with having Zach check the utilities survey in Frank's trailer, which resulted in his assurance that the steel wire in question couldn't possibly have marked an electrical cable or telephone cable because there were no cables of any kind buried in the fairground woods. Of course this information proved nothing, but it still offered me enough motivation to continue my little quest by returning the next day with a set of excavation tools. During my initial bout of digging I tried to imagine where the steel wire might lead, if not to Katie's time capsule. But I couldn't think of anything else I might find, and ended up only advancing my expectations by deciding that I was the only living person Katie had warned of the time capsule's existence. This allowed me to suppose that whatever letter she'd included in the capsule would somehow connect to me, which in fact it did:

> *To the Finder of This Registered and Legally Protected Time Capsule:*
>
> *First off, I know that you are not George Curtis Flynn who was born in Davenport, Iowa, on May 30, 1978. While I cannot expect you to refrain from reading this highly personalized communication, it is my duty to inform you that you have already broken the law. You opened mail that was not addressed to you. That said, I will forgive you if you fulfill your moral obligation to submit this package to the nearest authorities, to be forwarded to George Flynn or his living relatives, a group of people that depending on the velocity of fortune's breath might now be considered my own relatives.*
>
> *Dear George,*
>
> *I love you. This is the sum of what I have to say, a statement whose genuineness I am so certain of that everything that follows can be considered mere babble. I am only continuing to write because there is so much I wish I could say to you right now that I simply can't. While I know you have an inkling about my feelings for you, and perhaps even feel the same way, it is my opinion that by saying these words right now, to your face, would only cause damage to the only person in the world whose love and high regard I could not bear to live without. I am talking about my sister Emily, obviously. It is possible that this letter will find the two of you married with children,*

in which case I will wish I'd never written it. Chances are by that time I'll have adapted myself to the strict and affectless demeanor of the mature capitalist, which will entail hiding my feelings under multiple layers of professional and profit-driven sophistication. If this is the situation, then you will have no choice other than to assume the juvenile crush you all suspected me of has long passed, without a remaining speckle of the romantic silliness so common of teenaged sisters rivaling each other for attention. I assure you now that silliness has nothing to do with it. I love you. This is the only sure thing in my largely uncertain life that is currently posed with such questions of common adequacy as the capacity to walk under the power of my own muscles, or even more frighteningly, my future ability to see.

The idea for this time capsule comes at a particular moment of fear. I have an upcoming surgery scheduled for August 5, 1995, in Rochester, Minnesota, that will supposedly shorten my relapses and lengthen the periods between them. If I should die during this surgery, or somehow lose the ability to think clearly, I'll likely never have the opportunity to say the words that I believe everyone should be given the chance to say, with the greatest amount of selfless indulgence and romantic sincerity, at least once.

I have one gift for you. No matter what happens, I will never attempt to publish the following comic series, the original first edition of which I've included in this time capsule, taking every preventative measure to ensure that it remains intact, and choosing this location so that my capsule will be found before the contents would unavoidably yield to dust. As you will see, "The Red Menace" details the life and adventures of a scrappy former wrestler turned lovable schizophrenic superhero. His existence results from a botched CIA experiment involving the implantation of the preserved left brain of J. Edgar Hoover, as well as mass injections of gorilla testosterone, in the hopes of creating a police servant with enough balls to single-handedly

hog-tie every deadbeat, rapscallion, and otherwise weak link in the
nation's all-encompassing army of one. A kiss from me to you.
  Love,
  Katie [signed]

We can all correctly assume that my discovery of this letter was met with cathartic doses of tears and laughter. For a moment while hovering over my ditch in the woods I felt our baffling world had been whittled down to its most affirmative, life-giving functions. But despite Katie's sparkling prose, handwritten on parchment as perfectly preserved as she'd intended, it turns out that the airtight, leak-proof package in which her letter was housed was buried too deeply to be recovered within the span of a workingman's lunch hour. This required that I continue my dig the following day, when I found myself marching from one end of the forest to the other still smirking at every word of Katie's ghostly confessional that lay buried in rich Iowegian earth near the base of a walnut tree at the end of a long steel wire that I was destined to stumble upon once and then never again.

Fifty-two

As I feel myself yielding to a habit of resurrecting every glossy-lipped memory that gives a man the false impression that the lips in question remain forever as willing and pliant, prompting him every few years to write courageous love letters that he will never mail, to addresses unknown, I will only say that this account has failed in its primary purpose: to once and for all rid the author of his pull toward a past that in a mere decade has rendered its real-life characters no more than ghosts, fictions of a mind that would rather believe what could have been than in what was. I leave the reader with a brief and ultimate exchange with Emily Schell. The location was the Iowa State Fairgrounds, the time the 155th anniversary, a mere matter of weeks after our crew had gathered at the mouth of the Grand Basin to witness the gentle unifying flow of red clay waters pouring in from the lagoons and streams that linked our new lake to the Des Moines River, knowing from there we'd tapped into the Mighty Mississippi and the Gulf of Mexico and all the great oceans across the globe.

While Zach had joined our crew for another lake-digging assignment in a residential development out in Clive, Frank gave me two weeks off so I could volunteer at the fair and enjoy the crowd's response to the fruit of our labors. By lottery during the first training day I scored one of the prized jobs at the highly popular state fair beer garden. As expected, a record-setting crowd turned up for the opening day, when it was hard to find a single man without a wife, girlfriend, or child stacked on his shoulders. With an up-close view of the whole scene I swore the heart of the American Midwest was pounding more crudely for those ten blazing days than ever before. Everyone raved that it was the best state fair in memory, with much improved fireworks and music performances, and even an impressive competitive pickle eater from Red Oak who stole the show by bringing a world record to Iowa. But the biggest news of the week related to the freshly established tradition of couples kissing the moment their paddleboats drifted beneath the footbridge over the Grand Basin. While there was little consensus over the exact brand of fortune this act was supposed to bring, soon there was a line a mile long to rent paddleboats, and more than enough TV crews and cheering crowds for the moment one of the mariachis, propped up on the footbridge railing in an attempt to romance the kissing couples beneath him, tumbled head over heels into the basin.

Serving Oktoberfest mugs in the beer garden was a high-profile position. I ran into all sorts of people I hadn't seen in years, including Tommy Wick from the old neighborhood in Davenport, Coach Grady and his hermetic shifty-eyed wife who no one had ever seen before, and Jessie Walters, the girl wrestler from Winterset who was now engaged to her high school rival, Dave Friberg from Valley. I even ended up being approached by Floyd Truman, the big man from the funeral parlor who practically shook my hand off my wrist, introducing me to his date as his "old pal George" before bragging about his luck shooting thirty-seven ducks in a row.

On the final night of the fair, before Emily even crossed the threshold of the beer garden tent, I spotted her rambling along the midway arm in arm with Lauren and Ashley, attempting to drag them into a soothsayer's booth called "Fiona's Fortunes." Her hair was still dyed jet-black, though it was nearly the same length and style as when I first met her in the hallway outside the St. Pius auditorium. As soon as they stepped into the tent, Ashley and Lauren whistled and shouted my name, beaming like the Fourth of July until Emily snagged the backs of their shirts, thus halting their forward progress. After a brief, secretive exchange, Ashley and Lauren planted themselves at a table facing the grandstand, freeing Emily to make her solemn honor-guard approach. On reaching the counter she draped herself over a prop wooden barrel of ale, then leaned on her elbows to survey the boister-ous scene. I continued dunking mugs in the tub, pouring a few pitch-ers until she turned my way and sighed, gazing all around me like she was searching for something she might have left behind the bar.

"Can I help you?" I asked.

"Just looking."

"How about a beer?"

"I'll be taking the night off, thank you. All right if I stand here a minute?"

"All right by me," I said.

She tipped her invisible hat, apparently content to catch her breath, mostly fixing her people-watching gaze on a stage barker across the midway playing Guess Your Weight. In the chaos of pop music and drunken sing-alongs, we were almost anonymous enough to feel alone.

"You staying for the fireworks?" I asked.

"Of course. Any word on who'll be playing the grandstand tonight?"

"That's top secret."

"Didn't tell you, did they?"

"I can't even tell you whether or not they told me. That's the biggest secret in the state."

Emily nodded, playing less than pleased with my snobbery. I had the feeling that unless I did something about it, our conversation would continue just as flirty and aloof as it started. (Perhaps that would've been for the best, though I still haven't decided.) The song changed to an album of screaming country rock. I knew our time was almost up, that soon Emily would tell me what an expert I was at pouring beer, and maybe wink, then return to her table and that would be the end of it. When I felt certain she was ready to go, I spoke up and told her exactly what I was thinking. I told the truth, more for myself than anything.

"You know, when I think about Katie now, I don't think about the girl with the crutches and the ponytail."

Emily turned around, pushing a few empty glasses along the bar just as casually as if I'd asked how her semester had ended. "So what's she like now?"

"She's changed a lot since then. She's more mature now and she's not dead at all. She's alive and I sort of feel about her the same that she felt about me. Like an immature crush, something that will probably never work out. I know that's strange, but I hope you don't take it the wrong way. It's just that she's become this beautiful and wise little girl and I can't help trusting her with all my biggest decisions. I see her all the time, but it doesn't make me feel sad. Seeing her doesn't bother me at all."

Ashley and the others started waving their glasses in the air, calling the both of us over to join them. Emily leaned on the bar, not seeing them, or anyone else. "You sound like a person in love. You sound like you're in love with her."

"I don't know. Maybe I am. What's not to love? She's perfect. She always says exactly what I need to hear. And she doesn't judge me, no matter what mistakes I make. She's just there to tell me she believes in me and she wants to help out."

Emily moved a few glasses around, almost like a dealer in Liar's Dice. She got lost for a few seconds, trying to understand. "What does she do? Like, what is she doing when you see her?"

"Usually I find her standing in some hidden area of wherever I am, just looking at me and waiting for me to notice that she's there. Once I was walking across the Hy-Vee parking lot when it was raining. I saw her standing under a black umbrella behind the place where they line up all the grocery carts. I was thinking about everything that happened with us, and how I don't feel like going to college but I'll probably have to. How I have no idea what I'm going to do with my life. You know, worrying about everything at once. Katie skipped on over to me and put her arm around my shoulder and said, *You can cry, George. Nobody's watching. Let it all out.*"

Emily looked away, pursing her lips until they lost their color, turning suddenly sad and silent. A waitress shouted an order and I poured a few more pitchers. The beer garden wasn't the place for such a scene. I regretted making more of the conversation than necessary. I suddenly felt that I'd gone too far.

"You said she skipped over to you?" she asked.

"Yeah, she's usually skipping, like she's in remission and feeling strong. Like she might even be cured."

Emily thought about it, squinting as she pondered the possibilities, like they were all there swimming in my eyes. "You know, the worst is when people ask me how many brothers or sisters I have. I never know what to say. It's hard when you *used to* be someone's older sister."

She paused, waiting for a response. But I didn't say anything. I had no idea how that must have felt. Emily pushed off the counter, taking another deep breath and smiling. "Good to see you, George. I think I'll go sit down now."

I gave her one last smile as she turned and walked away. While I thought I'd made progress in closing my heart to her, at that moment I knew I'd failed. I cursed the fact that there was never enough time, that I still loved her in a way that felt impossible to repeat. She was halfway across the tent when I caught up to her and tapped her on the shoulder. I couldn't let her go without asking. When she turned around, her hair swung in front of her face and she tucked it behind her ear.

"If someone asked you who was your first love, would you tell them it was a redhead from Davenport?"

"No one's ever asked me."

"But if they did."

"What do you think?" she said, taking a half step back. "What do you think I would say?"

"I don't know."

Emily's gaze sharpened over the swarming crowd. A summer shiver briefly raised her. She replied in one blushing word, deep and stretched and falling.

"George."